Advance praise for T[

"Gritty and gripping, I couldn't put it down!"
—*New York Times* bestselling author Lisa Childs

"I'm a sucker for thrillers involving twin sisters, and this one did not disappoint. *The Other Sister* is a fun, twisty read that had me quickly turning the pages. The twist was well-done and satisfying, and, bonus, I did not guess it! I enjoyed every moment of this book and highly recommend it!"
—Amber Garza, author of *When I Was You*

"*The Other Sister* is a masterful blend of suspense and shocking revelations. A must-read for anyone who loves a dark and thrilling tale of family, secrets and the fight to survive."
—Lynette Eason, bestselling, award-winning author of the Lake City Heroes series

"Jessica Patch can always be counted on for nail-biting suspense. *The Other Sister* is no exception. One warning—don't start reading too late in the day. You'll be up all night turning the pages until you reach the satisfying conclusion!"
—Nancy Mehl, author of the Erin Delaney Mysteries

"Not a romance—and not for the squeamish—but filled with so many intriguing twists and turns it should come with a whiplash warning."
—Irene Hannon, bestselling author of the Undaunted Courage series

"Disturbing, twisted, and absolutely addicting, *The Other Sister* delivers all of the spine-tingling chills and thrills."
—Natalie Walters, award-winning and bestselling author of *Living Lies* and The SNAP Agency series

"*The Other Sister* is an amazing story I didn't want to end! Jessica Patch's writing chops are really on display in this tightly spun tale."
—Carrie Stuart Parks, multiple Christy Award–winning author

"If you're after a heart-pounding psychological thriller full of dark secrets and jaw-dropping twists, this one will keep you hooked until the very last page."
—Lisa Harris, *USA TODAY*, ECPA and CBA bestselling author

"No one writes psychological thrillers like Jessica R. Patch. She takes them to a whole other level and leaves you on the edge of your seat."
—Sharee Stover, *Publishers Weekly* bestselling author

THE OTHER SISTER

JESSICA R. PATCH

LOVE INSPIRED

Stories to uplift and inspire

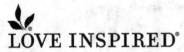

LOVE INSPIRED®

Stories to uplift and inspire

ISBN-13: 978-1-335-99412-7

The Other Sister

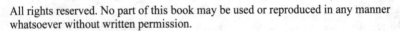

Love Inspired
22 Adelaide St. West, 41st Floor
Toronto, Ontario M5H 4E3, Canada
www.LoveInspired.com

Printed in U.S.A.

For my sister by blood and my sisters by choice.
Thank you for being just the right amount of psycho.
Forgive me that I'm not. And to the Sweet Valley High Wakefield twins—
who gave me my first love of a devious twin sister.

Then

Her eyes are vacant orbs that pierce my soul and chill my bones. The kind of chill that can only be warmed by immersion in scalding water. The kind that leaves a paralyzed shiver in its wake.

I stand with one clammy hand on the railing and the other pressed on the pain that constricts my chest. Am I having a heart attack? This must be what a heart attack feels like. Tight and heavy with shocks that ripple like electricity along my left arm, leaving me stunned and my pulse out of rhythm.

My hand slides along the cool wrought iron, my knees languid. One push is all it would take to send me to my death.

I know she's thinking about it.

Her calculated gaze swings from me to my hand to the stairs and then to the cold marble flooring below.

"Whatever you think you saw—you didn't," she says with a narrowed glint. "You shouldn't even be awake. Have you taken your pills? The doctor said you can't skip them. If you do, you could hallucinate."

"I—I didn't hallucinate what I witnessed just now." But I haven't taken my pills tonight, and I can't remember if I took them last night. My days have run together lately. However, my eyes didn't conjure up the atrocity I walked into five minutes ago.

She creeps into my personal space, predatory like a lioness. She's hungry to pounce, but she's careful, strategic. I am her prey, and I don't understand how we've gotten here.

That's a lie.

I do know.

I know exactly how we've gotten here.

"You're sick," she says in a gentle but mocking tone. "You've been sick a long time. You know this." Her lips turn down as if she feels sorry for me. She doesn't. She has no pity or compassion because she feels nothing. Her heart is a black abyss.

"Let me help you back to bed. Give you your meds and some water. You'll feel better in the morning."

I don't want to take my pills. I'm fine without them. I've been having more good days than bad. Besides, they make me tired and foggy. She eyes me, holding my gaze. She's not going to back down.

But I know what I saw.

The horror was real, and the terror that races cold through my blood proves I saw it with my own two eyes.

And I have no idea what to do but allow her to gently but firmly guide me to my bedroom like a naive child. I've tried a million different things. Interruptions. Distractions. I thought distance would solve it.

It didn't. Things actually grew worse.

"Okay. You're right. I—I'm not thinking clearly. What would I do without you?" I fake a smile, and she returns it in an equally saccharine measure as she helps me into bed. After I slide into the soft sheets, she picks up the brown pill bottle and empties two trazodone into her palm, then holds them out to me.

I willingly accept them, and she hands me the water, the glass cool against my fingers. I drink and swallow.

"Good." She pats my head like I'm a petulant child. "You'll feel much better now. You'll see more clearly in the morning."

No, I won't.

"Good night, Mother."

"Good night," I murmur. After she leaves the room, I spit out the pills. I'm seeing more clearly now than I ever did on these things. I've been on and off meds, switched meds, new meds, old meds for decades. I'm over it.

And I know what I saw.

I slip my diary out from between the mattress and box springs and grab my pen from the nightstand. I've been chronicling her behavior for years. No one has believed me. According to her, it's nothing but a diatribe from a broken woman.

But I know the truth.

I fear this will be my last entry. But I fear every entry might be my last.

She's tried to kill me before.

Chapter One

Chicago

It's early, but my body is on an internal clock that screams "up and at 'em" at six o' clock. Covering my face with a flat pillow that's left a crick in my neck, I attempt to drown out the news filtering through the thin apartment walls.

Mrs. Donlea has clearly lost her hearing aids again, and I expect a knock on my door to help her find them any moment.

And I will.

Not because I'm sick to death of hearing daytime TV or the news, which I am, but because Mrs. Donlea can't help that she has dementia, and I like the woman. Maybe I can down a hot cup of Folgers's finest before she arrives in a panic. She can't remember where she left them, but she remembers that she has them. How does that work?

I scoop heaping grounds into the filter and add water to the tank, then hit the button. I tell myself I should buy a Keurig, but they're expensive, and I don't have a job at the moment, which is why I had the two hours to help her find them yesterday. Then I stayed for a cup of tea and chitchat about how she knew Elvis because in the summers she worked at the Arcade diner he frequented in Memphis. I don't know if it's true or not, but it feels true. She uses such great detail, and I looked it up—the Arcade is a real place, and they even have a booth dedicated to him because he sat there most mornings.

However, her dementia is progressing, and the family she moved here to Chicago to be closer to rarely if ever visits or looks after her. At some point, she'll end up in a home where people are paid to take care of her but not necessarily like her. I know because I cycled through those kinds of homes until I turned eighteen. Just me, foster care homes, group homes and my meager belongings.

I peek out the window and peer up at the early May sunshine and think about my own mother. I did try with her for as long as I could. Tried to keep her clean and sober and in her right mind. Contacted local services to bring her meals.

Those acts were more than she deserved.

The coffeepot gurgles and huffs as dark brown brew drips into the carafe next to my favorite mug with a stick person family and a pink heart encircling them. At the bottom it reads, *I love my family.* Sometimes, I pretend I have a big family. That Tillie and Tommy are my siblings, not childhood friends from a few foster homes we were in together at one point. Mrs. Donlea is our aging grandmother. Our parents love us, but they travel extensively since we've flown the coop and gone out on our own. My apartment doesn't overlook the dumpster in a back alley, and I don't have to sip my first cup of coffee to the sound of the homeless man relieving himself on a pile of garbage.

No, I'm in a penthouse in the best part of the city, watching the skyline and the world come to life. I have a fireplace in my bedroom and plush carpet that wraps around my feet, and the floor tacking doesn't stick out and impale my tender toes.

My walls are lined with my own art, and I have a little gallery in the Arts District where I do very well. Some of the wealthiest people have purchased a Charlotte Kane original, and it makes me happy that I've brought a sliver of joy into their days. A piece of me lives in their homes even if I do not.

The coffeepot beeps, bringing me back to reality. I pour a cup, adding a hefty splash of milk because heavy cream is pricey. I add a spoonful of sugar and stir, then head to my bedroom and my laptop to search for a new job. I've had a myriad of jobs. *Myriad* was my word of the day yesterday, which hits my inbox every morning. I try to use the new words in my day-to-day conversations. I might have dropped out at sixteen and got my GED—I might even be uneducated in some ways—but I am not stupid, and I do enjoy learning new things about new places and people.

I sip my coffee, set it on my night table and open up a job search page. I worked for an antiques shop, Sobo's, for six months but was fired for stealing. Janice Sobolewski had it out for me from the first day because her father, Sobo, liked me better than her. She couldn't care less about vintage pieces. After my first two weeks, I knew more about them than her, and she'd spent all her days there.

In the end, I didn't fight it. I learned very early on in life never to burn a bridge even if someone else lights the match. Never strike the first match.

Once, when I was cycling through foster homes, I stayed with a single woman named Candace Matherly. She had two cats and loved yellow. Upon arrival, I told her that too many shades of yellow made her home look like a big house of cheese. And it smelled like cheese too.

I stayed with her three whole days and learned a valuable lesson at seven. Never speak negatively to a person's face. You love the mushy spaghetti. Hunks of crunchy onions in the chili *are* delicious. Broccoli is your *favorite*, and the sheets don't reek of mothballs. They're Downy fresh.

Flattery would take you places honesty never could. Keep you in a warm bed longer—even if it did smell like an attic. Keep you fed, even if it tasted like trash, and sometimes it even ensured your safety.

Sometimes.

Pangs of old rejection turn the acidy coffee in my stomach, but that doesn't stop me from pouring more into the cup to reheat it and hit me with caffeine that I don't need but want. A soothing herbal tea would suit my mood best.

The news silences through the wall. Showtime. I go ahead and pad to my door as her knock comes. I open it. Mrs. Donlea is on the other side, her shoulders stooped and her shock of white hair erect. She wears a thin floral blouse that's buttoned wrong and revealing a portion of a worn tan bra underneath. Her polyester pants have a brown stain on the thigh. Maybe tea or coffee.

But she's in a strand of pearls, and her pink lipstick is perfect, not even a swipe on her teeth.

"Good morning, Mrs. Donlea."

Her smile is as crooked as her coffee-and-age-stained teeth, but her watery eyes are sea glass blue and bright. "I seem to have lost my hearing aids. Would you be a dear and help me search for them?"

I put my coffee on the table by the front door and grab my keys. I don't trust anyone not to slip inside while I'm gone and rob me of half a box of chocolate puffs and a quarter pot of coffee. "Yes, ma'am," I offer and follow her into the hall. I lock the door behind me.

"Anything important on the news this morning?" I ask as we enter her apartment.

"A scandal has broken out," she says in her sweet Southern accent, which I happen to love and mimic when I'm with her. "Why, it's shocking and appalling. They're calling it Watergate."

I tsk President Nixon and join Mrs. Donlea in the past. "Why, honey," I drawl as a Southern belle surely would. "That is an absolute travesty." I clutch my own chest, and she nods with enthusiasm.

"It is. I tell you it is. Is no one out there good and honest anymore?" She holds her pearls and shakes her head.

"All that's good is our daddies and sweet tea," I say, holding out the syllables. But I have no idea who fathered me.

She laughs at this. "You really are whistling Dixie, darlin'."

Unsure of the phrase, I agree anyway and lift a couch cushion. Mrs. Donlea has the cleanest couch. Not a single crumb under here, or even a penny or quarter. I used to find loose change under the couch cushions in foster homes. I'd squirrel them away with the dream of saving enough to run away or buy a real art set. I still don't have top-of-the-line supplies, but that doesn't stop me from painting when I have time.

Under the third couch cushion, I find her hearing aids and glance up. Mrs. Donlea is in the kitchen with a pound of bacon in a frying pan and a carton of eggs on the counter. She meets my eyes and is startled, then brightens. "Charlotte, dear, I didn't know you were coming by. I'm about to make breakfast. Are you hungry?"

Without her hearing aids, she won't hear me, so I don't speak and instead nod an enthusiastic yes. I'm not the kind of girl to turn down bacon or an old lady who's confused and needs a friend. Really, she needs a nurse and a nanny. I hold up her hearing aids, and she puts down the spatula and claps. "I was looking for those," she exclaims and shuffles toward me with outstretched arms. Once she's plugged her ears, she can hear again. "You hungry, Charlotte, dear? I'm making breakfast."

"I am. Can I help you?" She won't let me. I've tried before.

"Oh, no. You rest yourself. I know how hard you work. Those unruly children won't teach themselves." She thinks I'm an elementary school teacher like she was for over thirty years. "You know, I taught fifth grade for thirty-five years."

"Yes, ma'am, I do." *Ma'ams* are a big thing in the South, and she likes it when I use my manners. I study her soft gestures and sweet Tennessee accent. I imagine her loving and nurturing every single child in her classroom.

"Brats, the lot of them. Snot-nosed, whiny brats," she mutters and returns to the kitchen, an open window separating us. She pokes at the sizzling bacon. The scent is now permeating the room and watering my mouth. "Just utter little monsters," she hisses as her bright eyes darken.

And I remember I'm not the only one in the world who can pretend to be someone they're not.

As I leave Mrs. Donlea's apartment after breakfast, I step into the hall to see Glenda, my old social worker. She still checks in on me from time to time, but it's been a long time since last we saw one another. Sleek in her tan pantsuit, she tosses me a wave. Over the years, lines have formed like fissures around the corners of her eyes, and her once blond hair is now gray and cut in a chin-length bob.

"Are you checking up on me?"

"Call it an old habit."

Glenda wasn't family, but she was *much* better than the woman who incubated me.

"How long has it been since you saw Marilyn?" she asks.

Speaking of the woman who birthed me... "Not long enough."

"Can I come in for a few minutes?"

My stomach lurches. "Is Tommy in trouble again?" I love Tommy; he's me and Tillie's brother by choice, but he's forever impulsive and has a gambling habit but no real money.

"He's thirty-two, Charlotte. Not my problem if he is."

I'm not her problem either, but here she is, checking in on me at thirty. I invite her in and offer to make a fresh pot of coffee, but she declines. Instead she sits on my cracked pleather sofa and scans my apartment. "How long you been here?"

"Three months? I was staying with Tillie before."

"Good. It's nice to see you settled. Job?"

I'm not a ward of the state anymore and don't have to answer her questions. "Why don't you cut to the chase?"

She graces me with a curt nod and pulls a piece of paper from her worn red leather purse. "I think Marilyn aspired to be a good mom. She just couldn't break free from her habits and mental troubles."

Where is this going?

"When you went into the system the first time, she tried to pull it together and did for a while. It didn't go the way she wanted."

The way *she* wanted?

"In case you forgot her address." She hands me the paper, which feels like lead in my palm.

"I understand the whole forgive-one-another thing. I sound more bitter than I am." Maybe. "But I will not go see her, Glenda. She's toxic, and I can't keep doing that to myself. I tried to help her. I gave her money when I didn't have it to spare. She repaid me by stealing from my purse." That had been my mistake for leaving it alone for her grubby paws to sift through. "And that's not even the worst thing she's ever done or allowed to be done to me. I've made peace concerning her."

Glenda blows a dead-dog-tired breath from her lips. "She died of an overdose two weeks ago. They found her last night."

Sadly, the only surprise here is that it took this long for her to do it. My chest constricts and aches, but I have no tears left for Marilyn Kane.

"Officer Jordan—you know him—called me this morning. He knew how invested I am in you and in trying to help Marilyn." Glenda eyes me and cocks her head. "She might have something of interest to you."

I snort. "Sorry, I'm not in the market for a crack pipe."

"I'm not talking about paraphernalia, Charlotte. What would it hurt to take a peek? You never know what you might find." Apology and regret simmer behind her gray eyes. "You only have a few days before they haul off her meager belongings to the trash dump, if they haven't already. Decide." She stands. "I'm here…if you need me. And, Charlotte, remember that sometimes my job forces me to remain silent about things. Things I wish I could share. Go to your mom's apartment. Okay?"

I'm pretty good at reading people, and this feels like Glenda apologizing and making amends all in one cryptic spiel. What has she done? Or allowed to be done? "I'll think about it. Thanks for stopping by."

What is in Marilyn Kane's apartment?

Chapter Two

Now, knowing Marilyn is dead has unlocked and pushed memories into the open. No longer sealed in the tomb I created for them.

I've discovered that if you suppress traumatic memories hard and long enough while telling yourself a new story in place of the truth, they stay locked down. Can't say it's approved by health professionals, but it helps me survive without a mental breakdown even if I'm consistently teetering on the edge—that hazy place that threatens to unleash every single morsel of misery I've spent years pretending didn't exist.

Now, thanks to Glenda, I'm back on the precipice of my past. My interest is piqued by the earlier cryptic conversation.

Glenda has never steered or done me wrong. In a slew of many people who have, that's saying a lot. If she insists I go, there must be something crucial for me to witness or discover.

Grabbing my purse, I head to the bus stop and then to Marilyn's rathole in West Humboldt Park. I keep pepper spray and a knife in my purse. Around here, you have to be armed and ready.

"Where you goin', baby girl?" a man on the stairwell asks. I'm unoffended by the pungent scent of weed. His eyes are inky like night and track over my body. He's blocking my ascent and knows it.

I have seconds to read him. Seconds to pull my act together so this doesn't escalate. Coming here was a mistake.

Stumbling, I reach out for air, and he chuckles, entertained by my wobbling. We're now equals. I'm on his level. My eyes droop, and I move like a cat around him. "You know where I'm goin', and you know why," I purr. He's not the only dealer in this building, but probably the only skunk dealer. He wears a red bandanna, and gang tats litter his face and neck. The fact he's alone means he's about to sell or he's waiting for other members, and I don't want to be outnumbered.

He leans back on the stairs. "You want something to chill you out, you come on back to me. Hear?"

"Bet." I squeeze his shoulder as I pass, ignoring his hand squeezing my backside as I climb above him, but that's as far as it goes. He thinks I'm expected elsewhere for a harder score, and holding me up with whatever he had in mind would get him in trouble. And that's how I move past him unscathed.

Apartments similar to mine line the worn carpeted hallway. A whiff of burning metal and cigarette smoke clings to my hair and skin. Marilyn's apartment door is ajar, and using my foot, I toe it open. When I'm certain it's not invaded by squatters, junkies or sex workers, I enter the studio that's smaller than a Kardashian's linen closet.

The place reeks of death and decay.

Carpet the color of mud is littered with crumbs and trash. I maneuver around grease-spotted food bags with edges chewed and waxy wrappers. It's hard to believe that I called places like this home as a child, except for once.

Once I lived in a large, upscale home and I thought it was

going to be like Cinderella. I'd finally become a princess, and my life would be a fairy tale. I even had a brother.

But that did not work out.

From then on, every apartment or run-down house with Marilyn was the same. A revolving door of junkies and floors filled with filth. I can't count how many of these wrappers I licked old crusty cheese from to put something in my starving belly because Marilyn forgot to feed me.

I slowly inspect the place. Nothing that would require Glenda's subtext. Then I spot the closet. I've looked at everything else.

Using my jacket sleeve over my hand as a glove, I open the accordion doors. Marilyn never had a washer and dryer, and in place of the appliances is a rectangular-shaped spot that's clean compared to the rest of the peeling linoleum.

The apartment door opens. I pull my knife from my pocket and spin around, but instantly recognize the landlord. He's sketchy, but he won't harm me. He carries a box about the same shape as the spot on the closet floor.

"Oh, hey, Charlotte. I heard someone was in here. Hoping it was you. Saves me the trouble of hunting you down. Your mama left this in the closet, and I thought you might want it. I sees you do." He lowers the filthy, tattered cardboard box back on the closet floor. "Sorry 'bout your mama."

"Thanks," I mumble and stare at the box. "That all?"

"Dat's it." He quietly leaves, and the door clicks shut behind him.

I flip open the lid with my foot and find mouse droppings and old papers inside. Unsure if a beady-eyed creature resides underneath, I kick over the box.

Photos peek out from beneath a frayed, ratty garment. Upon closer inspection, I discover it's a pink baby blanket. No. Two small swatches of faded pink material.

At this moment, I wish for fingernails. The long, manicured kind with white tips. I don't want to touch the photos, but... I stoop and pick them up, shaking them free of any leftover "gifts" from the mice. They've already munched around the edges.

One photo is Marilyn, around eighteen or nineteen. She's healthy and lean with long, thick, honey-blond hair and bright sage eyes brimming with hope. I never realized how much I resemble her, down to the dimple in our left cheeks. Most of my life, she was gaunt and pale and missing teeth.

In a few photos, she's with an attractive older man with a Tom Selleck mustache, and they appear happy. Might be my father. I have no idea who he is and always suspected Marilyn was as clueless, but now I can't say for sure.

Another photo reveals Marilyn a little older, but still young, with glazed eyes and scraggly hair, holding a bundle with a cap of cotton-white hair tucked into a pink blanket. A cigarette hangs from Marilyn's mouth, the smoke pluming above the child.

Above *me.*

My heart leaps into my throat. I've never seen baby pictures of myself before. Never seen this box prior to today, but she's kept it all these years, and Glenda has seen it or she wouldn't have encouraged me to search the place. But my baby photo isn't what hits me like a 747.

She's not holding only me.

She's holding two identical babies in pink blankets.

I have a sister?

Paying no attention to the biohazard, I sort through the filthy papers.

What happened to the other baby? Is she dead? Is this why I feel an overwhelming sense of emptiness and loss? They say that twins have a bond like no other, and when separated, they feel the slice.

A stained envelope has stuck to the bottom of the box. Gently I remove it, but some of the paper rips. Inside the envelope is a letter written on lavender stationery with a gold *B* embossed at the top middle.

Miss Kane,
Again, we can't thank you enough for what you've done. I wanted you to know that baby Acelynn (that's what we named her) is doing well. She's finally eating better and her colic cleared up, though at times she's still fussy. Her room is done in pretty pink horses. I think she likes it. I can't believe she'll be a year old soon. We're planning a birthday bash with a pretty pink cake. I thought you might want to know how she's faring.
Sincerely,
Lucille Benedict

My hands tremble as I read it two more times. I have a sister. Somewhere in the big wide world. A twin.

Acelynn Benedict.

Thoughts race, disconnecting and dropping off before a new thought begins. Why didn't the Benedict family take me? Why was I left behind? Whose decision had that been? I frantically dig through the box for further answers, but nothing is left but receipts, bills Marilyn never paid, decor magazines—of all things. As if Marilyn could make a ratty hole a home. She never had a penny to her name, not even when we lived with *him*.

The men cycling in and out of the house paid for her habit.

And I've paid for her habit. Involuntarily.

I could have been Acelynn Benedict. With a room full of pretty pink ponies and a family who loved me, provided for me and protected me.

Why not me?

A tear escapes the inner corner of my eye, and I swipe it away with the back of my now filthy hand.

I could have had the life I always dreamed about. I have to know more. I won't be able to sleep or move forward until I do. Do the Benedicts know about me? Does Acelynn?

Then

The instant I embraced her, I was beyond captivated. A wave of elation washed over me. She had a perfect little ruby-red mouth that formed a perfect little O. A thick cap of fine blond hair and long, delicate fingers. I brushed the tip of my index finger along her cheek. Her skin was velvety like a rose petal.

"Petal. That's what I'll call you." I hadn't even picked out a formal name at this point. I had initially planned to name her Eloise after my grandmother and call her Elle. But when I laid eyes on her, I knew she wasn't an Eloise or an Elle. She was definitely a Petal.

A mother dreams about her child long before conception. I dreamed of a house full of children when I was playing babies on the porch at only six years old. I had named each doll with consideration and cared for them with such tender devotion to prepare for my own little tykes.

After marriage, I was eager to start a family, but we agreed it wasn't the right time. Six years later, it was one of our right times, and so we began trying for a baby. Each month when my period came was another month of agony, disappointment and frustration. Another month to wonder why I was defective.

Then the most wonderful event happened. I finally received the answer to my pleas and prayers.

A baby girl.

Waiting is hard. Waiting for life to give you a shot. Waiting for help. Waiting for hope. Waiting for the next thing and the next. But waiting is worth it. In every way.

I'm not sure what I expected. I'd read books about rearing a child, but the adjustment was far more difficult than I'd anticipated.

After the first night of sweet bliss, things changed. Petal cried all night most nights. She cried most of the days too. A mom should be able to soothe her child and attend to her needs. Recognize her needs, but Petal was needy in a way I never fathomed an infant could or should be. Bottles didn't soothe her. Burping her didn't. Changing her diapers didn't do the trick. Swaddling her might as well have been like suffocating her. She hated it. She'd push her little angry fists from the blanket and squirm to be free. Independent.

In control.

I shouldn't have felt frustrated that the little pink blanket I purchased was going to waste, but my frayed nerves and spinning, foggy mind got the better of me.

She cried and shrieked.

I felt like an utter failure and couldn't tell a soul. I'd begged for this child, even when I finally realized my husband, who hadn't wanted a child, still didn't. He had been little help, and I couldn't call my own mother for her to rub yet another failure in my face.

Nothing soothed Petal.

Nothing made her happy or calm. My carpet had a path worn from the endless pacing. Mothers in nursery groups gave me advice from whiskey on her gums to specialized harnesses I could wear to make her feel safe.

Shouldn't my arms be enough?

Shouldn't an infant take comfort in the bosom of her mother?

Dare I admit I sometimes regret this decision? My daughter is inconsolable and my marriage is on ice.

Late at night, when I'm bouncing her and singing through tears trying to soothe her, I think about things a mother never should. Things like placing a pillow over her face to muffle the wails. Or walking out of the house and never returning.

But I take my pills and refuse to let intrusive thoughts rule me.

Nothing soothes her.

Nothing soothes me.

It's colic. Bellyaches. Everything from *A* to *Z*, say my family and friends and books. I'm not sure it's any of those ailments, and the doctors insist she's healthy.

Yet something feels wrong, and guilt gnaws at me for letting it cross my mind. That my sweet little rose petal is broken and I cannot fix her with diaper changes, cereal in her formula, rocking, or swaddling with that sweet pink blanket.

I can't share my dark thoughts with anyone, so I share them in a new journal I purchased. To force them out of my head, where they do not belong, and onto the pages I keep hidden.

These thoughts terrify me, but so does my child, and I am all alone.

Chapter Three

Somewhere out there is my sister. No, not somewhere out there. This isn't *An American Tail*—a movie I was forced to repeatedly watch in my third foster home. I was eight. No, seven. But it feels like it a little, I guess. Like I've been separated from my family, and I'm alone in that glass bottle drifting across the sea of life, trying to find her.

After leaving Marilyn's apartment with the photos, letter and baby blanket, I open up my laptop and do a Google search on Acelynn Benedict in Georgia, and find her in Savannah. A beautiful city full of charm and grace. With large live oaks dripping with Spanish moss, wisteria climbing up trellises, and rich history.

My twin. My identical twin.

She's an actual public figure. Important. Classy. Sophisticated. I bet she has a rich Southern drawl. She could be considered a Southern belle, though I'm not sure that's PC anymore. Women don't really want to be synonymous with hoop skirts and fragile constitutions, and she appears to be a real power-house, anyway.

Her blond hair is the same length as mine but luscious and shiny with a few blonder highlights and layers. In most of her photos it's pulled into a chic low bun at the nape of her slender neck. She contours like a dream, and her nails are sport-length with a muted pink color in almost all of the photos.

Acelynn Benedict is a socialite and has multiple social media accounts, which she uses to showcase her interior designs with her tagline: *If you want a beautiful home, you need an Ace in your pocket.* Clever. I remember the decor magazines in Marilyn's apartment. Did we inherit our creative genes from her?

Acelynn's Instagram is flooded with short videos with decorating tips, and as I play one, I hear I was right. Her voice holds Southern charm. Longer drawn-out vowels but not hillbilly, and a little more refined than Mrs. Donlea's. My sister is incredibly talented, and my heart swells with pride and joy, even if it's tinted in green.

I don't understand why the Benedicts didn't take both of us. This could be my life. I scroll through dozens of photos of her with friends and a tall, good-looking man, mid- to late thirties. He's tagged in one of them.

Philip Beaumont.

Sounds like old money. Acelynn's on his arm at a swanky event where she's dressed like she's up for an Oscar. As I continue to scroll, they're on the river in a fancy boat, and she's wearing big sunglasses and a wide-brimmed hat. He's handsome, but his bright blue eyes hold a sense of entitlement and arrogance.

I google him, and my mouth drops open. He's the chief assistant district attorney.

Wow.

I open a bag of Doritos and shove one in my mouth. Bet Acelynn doesn't eat junk. Me? I can't help myself. I'm twenty-five tabs open and a family-sized bag of Doritos in the wind when banging on my door sends me jumping from my chair. I glance at my phone. I've missed six texts and three calls from my best friend, Tillie. She's going to kill me. I've broken a rule by not answering.

"Charlotte! It's me. You in there? You okay?" She bangs again, and I know if I don't sprint to the door and open it, police will be at the threshold for a wellness check. The last people I want to see are cops.

"I'm fine," I holler and lick the cheesy film from my fingers, then open the door to see Tillie hunched like a human battering ram, her fist in the air, about to beat in my door. Her typically rosy cheeks are pale, and her wide blue eyes are anxiety-filled.

"What's going on?" I ask. "Is it Tommy?" It's usually Tommy. I rub my left wrist. When she notices, I stop and shove my hand in my jeans pocket.

"No, it's not Tommy," she snaps. Now that she sees I'm okay, she's angry. "I texted you half a dozen times and tried to call you. You know the rule."

The three of us made a pact a decade ago, because of me, and I haven't strayed. Not until today. I was so engrossed in my research, I didn't hear text notifications or the phone ringing.

"I'm sorry." I motion her inside. She storms into the living room, which is open to the dining area and small galley kitchen, where the fluorescent light flickers. "I didn't hear it."

"Were you in the shower? You have to take the phone in there with you. You scared me half to death, Char. I thought..." Her eyes fill with moisture, and I sigh.

"I know what you thought. Let me make you some tea. Have a seat." I swiftly move to the kitchen. Seeing Tillie this upset hurts my heart. She depends on me as much as I depend on her. Tommy? He's less dependable but there in a crunch. When he's off in a casino with poor cell service, her nerves fray like old jeans. He's constantly wearing our hearts out with his impulsivity and gambling issues.

Tillie has a better job than we do. She's book smart and never fell through the cracks in school. She knows sophisticated words without a word of the day dropping in her inbox or perusing dictionaries and the online thesaurus like I do. A lot of her money has been flushed down Tommy's gambling toilet.

I put on a kettle of water and drop two chamomile tea bags into two white mugs I purchased from Goodwill along with my other kitchen appliances and dishes. And I have a few things I took from Sobo's. A mixer, several wooden bowls and spoons. A couple of vintage pieces I left at Tillie's.

When I glance up, she's hovering over my laptop, investigating my latest searches. Wide eyes stare at the screen, and her thick, pouty lips are pursed. "What is this, Char?" Her long, dark hair that hangs in loose waves swings as she directs her attention to me. "What...what have you done?" She's beautiful and doesn't even know it.

Tillie was a dream to foster dads with dark fantasies.

I kept her safe as much as I could, no matter the cost, and I think it's why she's as loyal to me as a rescue dog. I don't take advantage of that, but Tommy does. He knows how she feels about him. Since she was fifteen, Tillie has been in love with Tommy DeMario. At twenty-nine—our birthdays are almost a year to the day apart—she still has no clue, or she simply hasn't voiced her feelings. I try to be a buffer and spare her bank account. She can't tell him no. My shoulder should be out of joint from carrying the brunt.

"Marilyn died."

"You told me," she says. "That doesn't explain this." She points to the screen.

"I didn't do anything. I found out I have a twin sister. You're looking at her." After my trip to the apartment, I needed time to process. I'm still processing. But I had every intention of informing Tillie.

Till shakes her head as she stares at the screen. "I don't understand."

"How twins work?" I ask as the kettle whistles.

"Ha ha. Charlotte, now is not the time for your snarky comebacks. This is serious. Explain."

As I pour boiling water over the tea bags, a sweet fragrance fills the kitchen, and I share the shocking news.

She sits quietly with her thoughts, then points to the laptop. "Why are eight of these tabs about Philip Beaumont? Is he related too?"

"Boyfriend. Hers, not mine." I shrug and use a spoon to move the steeping process along faster. "I was curious." I don't have to meet Tillie's gaze to know it's drilling into me. My cheeks flush, and I try to put her at ease. "That's all. Curiosity. Wouldn't you want to know everything you could about a twin you never knew you had? And her life? The people in it? It's perfectly normal behavior." I toss the tea bags and add sugar to each cup, then set hers on the table.

"Curiosity is normal in other people. You're not other people," she says slowly, like she's attempting to avoid hurting my feelings. She's failed.

"Well, you haven't seen me fly to Savannah to knock on her door, and it's been over twenty-four hours, so…" My words are a sharp prick to her heart, and she flinches.

"No, but things always start innocently, and then—"

"This is different, Till. This is my sister. We're identical. I—I want to know her. Is that wrong?" I sip the tea, but it doesn't settle my bloated stomach thanks to the family-sized bag of Doritos. I eat my feelings in crunchy, salty snacks. It is what it is. "Is that wrong?" I repeat.

Tillie rubs her brow like she's trying to erase an ink stain. Her skin is turning red. "Wanting to know her isn't wrong,

Charlotte. You have questions. I do too. But I called you no less than half a dozen times, and you didn't hear it. Don't lie to me either and use the excuse the phone was in another room by accident. You could hear your phone ring if it was next door at Mrs. Donlea's. Thin walls. Small units. That…that concerns me, hon. It's only been six months, Charlotte. Six."

Like I need reminding. "You have nothing to be afraid of." I slam my mug onto the counter harder than intended, and Tillie shrinks back. Loud noises and jumpy movements have always sent her into skitters. But it's me, and she has no reason to be afraid of me.

"I'm not literally afraid."

Her face says otherwise.

"Do you think she knows about you?" Tillie asks, changing the subject to a safer topic.

That was the million-dollar question.

"I'm going to find out."

Chapter Four

Tillie's gone and has left me with a piercing reprimand to let it go. She thinks it's a bad idea to reach out. If Acelynn doesn't know about me, it's because her parents didn't want her to know or they didn't tell her she was adopted at all, and they had their reasons. I should respect their privacy.

But what if Acelynn is hit by a car and needs a kidney? Is that the way she should discover she's been adopted? During a traumatic crisis when her life is on the line? No.

I put the laptop on my dresser, standing in front of it as I study Acelynn's next-to-newest YouTube video. "Pops of color are everything when it comes to your personality," she says.

I throw my hands to the sides and widen my eyes like hers. "Pops of color are everything when it comes to your personality," I mimic. It's too twangy. I back it up and give it another go. Then another until I nail it, which only takes four tries. I'm good at accents. For the entire three months I was a barista, everyone thought I was British. No one ever guessed I wasn't.

"Your home should reflect not only your style but the mood

you want to be in when you're there." I hold out the vowels a touch longer than necessary and raise my eyebrows as she does with the inflection on the pronouns.

New content uploaded last night, but I'm one behind. Now that I've seen it, I start the latest tutorial she's doing. She has over one hundred thousand followers. I have zero followers because I don't have social media. I have Till and Tommy.

But people want to see and hear Acelynn. She has clout and influence, which goes to show that your upbringing, on some level, matters.

My life would have been different had I stayed in my favorite family's home—the Thompsons. Upon arrival that Saturday morning, I was enthralled but not hopeful. I had learned hope could easily be dashed. The place was classic but homey and smelled of cinnamon toast and pancakes. They enjoyed Saturday morning breakfasts after a trip to the farmers' market, which included their golden retriever, Roxie—who I was deathly allergic to, but I hid it. I didn't want to leave the Thompsons' and definitely not over pet dander.

Sundays were reserved for church, and Mrs. Thompson had purchased me a gorgeous pink jumper, new white dress shoes and a little gold cross necklace, similar to the one Acelynn wears in all her videos and photos.

I'm not sure what happened to my necklace; maybe I lost it or misplaced it at some point. But the fact that I had one like my twin sister somehow bonds me even more to her.

People at church, that first Sunday with the Thompsons, doted on me and oohed and aahed over how pretty I was, like people surely dote on my twin now. They told me they were excited I was a part of the Thompson family. I don't think I'd ever felt more loved by so many people in my ten years of life.

Ten was a great year.

That was the year I knew I was going to become Charlotte Thompson. No longer Charlotte Kane. I would have a brother and sister and dog—that made me want to scoop my eyes out with a spoon from the dreadful itching. I was going to carry a little white Bible to church on Sundays and have picnics in the park and maybe take ballet lessons like Phoebe, who was two years older than me.

Phoebe wasn't happy about my presence in the house. She didn't like the attention I received from her parents, her older brother, Andrew, or the dog. She definitely didn't like the rallying around me at their church.

She'd stood in the hall by the water fountain with steely gray eyes, and my heart had sunk to my feet. In that moment, I knew my stay with the Thompsons was about to be short-lived if I didn't try to head it off at the pass, and it worked for a while. Then one afternoon, Mrs. Thompson sweetly asked if I'd seen Mr. Thompson's leather wallet with the letter *C* for *Chris* burned into the center. He always kept it on the table by the front door with his keys.

I hadn't, of course.

Funny thing, though—it turned up inside my pillowcase when she was doing laundry. Saturday was always bed linen day, and I loved the scent of spring meadows. Loved crawling into fresh sheets after my nighttime bath as the scents of roast being prepared for Sunday lunch wafted upstairs and into my room. My safe, secure room no one creeped into at night.

I wasn't scolded for the wallet, but I wasn't so stupid to believe Mrs. Thompson thought I was innocent. Disappointment had flooded her kind eyes at my refusal to accept responsibility. She had a little chat with me about honesty and the importance of building trust. Trust was like building a bridge one plank at a time. Each person had to lay one down until they met in the middle, creating one long solid foundation for two people to be close. When a lie was told, a plank was broken. With each act of dishonesty, another one would be ripped up, until it caused a great divide.

Trust could be rebuilt, but it would take time.

"Do you understand, Charlotte, sweetheart? You're in a safe place now, and you can be honest. Honesty—even if you do something wrong—won't make us not love you or send you back."

I had understood. She wanted me to confess my sin. Except I hadn't sinned. Phoebe had. Phoebe had sinned and was in her room getting away with it. If I wanted to stay and build that bridge to stick around, then I had to do what needed to be done to lay down a plank.

I confessed.

Wallets meant money, and money meant I could eat and not go hungry. I was sorry for taking Mr. Thompson's wallet. Mrs. Thompson had tucked me in, prayed for me and kissed my forehead with promises I would never go hungry in their home. "Doesn't that feel good, Charlotte? The truth will set you free."

I didn't want to be set free. I wanted to stay. And the only way to beat Phoebe at her own game was to join her in the lies.

I don't want to lie and pretend I don't have a sister now. If the tables were turned, I would hope my sister would contact me. So I open my email and type, then hesitate. I'm not ready... No, I am.

Acelynn,

This may come as a surprise to you, but I am your identical twin sister. A few days ago, I found a photo of us after we'd recently been born, and a letter from your adoptive mom, Lucille. You were almost one, and it was to fill our biological mother in on your pretty pink horsey nursery and upcoming party. I was shocked, to say the least, as I have never known about you. But sadly, our biological mother has passed from an illness. I would like to know you, if that's something you'd be interested in. I know it's a lot to process.

I don't mean to turn your world upside down, especially if this news is the first you've heard about the adoption. I apologize for causing you any distress or pain. If you'd like to connect, please reply. I live in Chicago, where I've lived all my life. Unfortunately, I don't know much more about the adoption than I've already noted, but I'm willing to try and find out, if possible.

I look forward to hearing from you.

Charlotte Thompson

Staring at the screen, I take another drink of my now luke-warm coffee. Do I send it? What's the worst that could happen? Crickets? Before I have time to talk myself out of it, I hit Send and listen to the whoosh as it leaves my outbox.

The tiniest fleck of guilt pricks my chest at fudging my last name. But I think of all the googling and research I've done on Acelynn. She'll do the same to me.

And I can't afford for her to set me free before she ever begins to know me.

I want to stay.

Then

"Petal, stay put and don't lie to me."

She stands before me in the playroom, her wide eyes blinking in innocence, but behind them resides a sinister twinkle. Four-year-olds aren't supposed to know evil or wickedness. But Petal exudes darkness. She expels it from the windows of her soul, revealing the malevolence within her empty, black heart.

My inner dialogue brings me grief and fear. If I were ever to voice my deepest thoughts, I'd be locked up.

Again.

"I'm not lying. Brother broke it." She casts her sights on Bubba, who is sitting in a corner with his knees drawn up and his lips buttoned tight. Even at two, he knows never to contradict or call out Petal.

When he was only three months old, I was rocking him in the nursery. My presence soothed him, unlike Petal, who could never be soothed. And no, it was not colic. Or gas. Milk had pooled in the corners of his mouth, and his little cheek muscles twitched, forming a sleepy smirk. My sweet boy. My precious boy, who had been born gentle and soft and truly innocent—and a precious surprise to us all. I kissed his soft baby brow, inhaled the powdery scent of a freshly bathed babe.

Petal toddled into Bubba's nursery, which was decorated in a myriad of soft blues and earth tones and filled with plush teddy bears, reminding me of him—cuddly.

Mother had put her to bed twenty minutes ago, while I had taken a long bath and anticipated my time with Bubs. A time of peace and tranquility and zero anxiety. He was a bundle of light and joy, and I craved bath and bedtime with him. Putting my index finger to my lips, I'd breathed out a quiet "Shh."

Petal, with her long curls and pink footie pajamas, had sidled up beside us. "Kiss, Bubba," she'd said in a sweet singsong voice. I think Petal loves her brother, but I'm not sure that's the right word. *Obsession* fits more aptly. In the hospital, when she'd first visited us, she'd been eased onto the bed, where she'd cradled his head and leaned in and kissed him. In that brief moment, I believed she might have something in her besides the darkness. Maybe a sweet brother would be her salvation. She'd rubbed his cap of blond hair and gently kissed him again.

But I was wrong.

Bubs wasn't her salvation; he's mine, though. That tiny bundle wrapped in a blue blanket with teddy bears came to rescue me.

A tiny hiccup of anxiety had run through my veins and sped up my heart. "Brother is going night-night."

"Night-night," Petal had whispered, running her hand along his velvety cheek. She'd bent down to kiss him, and I was elated.

But it didn't last a millisecond. Bubba had wailed, piercing my ears, and when Petal had peered up, her teeth were stained red. My mouth had dropped open, and I gawked in utter shock, then glanced down at my sweet boy.

A perfect circle had formed along his cheek with teeny indentations. From those indentations, pinpricks of blood rose to the surface of his skin.

Petal had bitten my baby boy, her baby brother.

Her wide eyes had met mine, feigning innocence, but she had known what she'd done even at two years and three months.

Just like she stares up at me now in the playroom while Bubba cowers in the corner. The same age she was when she'd taken what was sweet and sunk her evil teeth into it, disrupting peace with pain.

All Petal causes is pain.

"Brother would never have taken this vase from the table and done this. Tell the truth, Petal. We do not lie in this house. We do not lie at all. Lying is wrong." Bubba couldn't have carried this vase in here. It's as big as he is, and he couldn't even reach it on the table in the foyer. Not to mention it's crystal and heavy.

Glass lies shattered on the nursery floor, and water streams down the walls. A four-year-old girl might not be able to have thrown it with enough force to shatter against a wall, but some days I think Petal isn't even human—or that something otherworldly resides within her, empowering her with superhuman strength. How else can I explain it?

Footsteps click along the hall. Petal grasps my hand, and I feel a pinch. "I didn't do it, Mama. I told Brother not to take it. He should be punished."

Anger bubbles to the surface. It's been at a simmer since Petal was born. Now it's reaching the boiling point. "*You* should be punished."

Already she's been in trouble at preschool. Biting—no shocker there. Throwing tantrums when reprimanded. Stealing a blanket from a child and cutting it up—though I blame the teacher for that one. How does one leave a pair of scissors out, or not see that Petal had them? To be fair, Petal is sneaky and slick. We've had four incidents in the past month, and one more is going to land us out of the best preschool in the city.

No one takes that into account when I voice my calm concerns about Petal. I'm the bad guy. I'm seeing things that aren't there. I'm the unstable one.

I know who's coming down the hall. I have my own private nanny, and I bite back the bitter thoughts. My own husband and mother have conspired against me and decided that it was best for Mother to move in with us. To help with the babies. I need sleep and rest. Without it, I can become...*fragile*. That was the word they'd used. As if I'm this vase. Appearing strong, but in actuality, delicate and easily broken.

A broken woman can be glued back together. Even if there are scars proving she'd once been torn apart.

A shattered woman can't be repaired. Too many slivers and shards. Too much work and time necessary.

Once Mother took residence in my downstairs guest room, I began keeping my thoughts to myself, but they grew and expanded, consuming every crack and crevice until I couldn't think of anything else but Petal and her nefarious presence in my life. I needed an outlet. A way to spill the dark thoughts and make room for light, so I use the journal I purchased after Petal was born.

That's all it took for me to realize something was wrong.

By two I knew it; she was also broken.

And now at four, I'm convinced she was born shattered. And there's nothing that can repair or restore that kind of natural-born damage. Not even I. Yet what can be done? There has to be something to protect me and Bubba, other children she's tormented and pained.

I've considered the unthinkable. Imagined it. Slipping quietly into her room while she sleeps. Even her slumber is fitful as she thrashes in the sheets and growls like a rabid animal. No peace is at home within her. All I'd have to do is take the fluffy pink pillow and bring it gently down on her perfectly adorable face and hold it there, applying a bit more force until she no longer breathes. No longer lives. No longer can fulfill her dark destiny.

Because I know that's what she's headed for. If I can't stop her, no one can. She'll continue to spread her disease and sickness throughout our home and lives and then onto the world. Consuming it with her evil ways.

God will have to forgive me for what I consider to be mercy. Surely He would find her death merciful. He couldn't possibly want this out in the world.

The door opens, ripping me from these thoughts. Thoughts a mother should never have for her children. I'm not crazy. I know it sounds insane.

"Oh my!" she calls through a shaky breath and presses her hand to the hollow in her throat, her big, fat diamond glittering. "What have you done, darling?"

I look at my hand and stare in confusion. Holding it out, I inspect it and notice a small cut along the palm. I'm...bleeding.

Mother gapes at the wall, the water running like clear blood and a shattered vase in pieces scattered across the floor. Fresh flowers I'd carefully arranged this morning lie in a withered heap. Bubba cries in the corner, and Petal stands over him, alligator tears streaking her cheeks.

Mother gasps and races to her, taking her hands and checking them. Not a single cut.

"What have you done?" Mother asks me.

"Nothing! I've done nothing." I stare at the remains of the vase and then at my own bleeding palm. "I didn't do this." Why would I?

"I heard you yelling at the children." She shields them as if I'm the wolf in sheep's clothing. They huddle in a unified trio. Are they all against me? Has Petal's darkness touched even Bubba? My one bright spot.

"Petal did this."

My mother's mouth turns grim, then softens in pity. "She's

four. You think she picked up a vase, threw it against the wall with enough force to shatter it? Think clearly now," she says as if I'm a small child. It's me at Petal's age, and I'm in my bedroom with Mother standing over me. "You did this."

Think, darling. How would your kitty have gotten into the cupboard, stolen the cookies and brought them all the way upstairs to your room? Admit you're not telling the truth. Lies are for naughty children and wicked grown-ups. Who really took the cookies?

I clung to the lie.

I'm not lying now.

The pinch I felt when Petal took my hand. I should have known it wasn't in tender affection. Petal shows no affection, nor does she enjoy human contact—flinching from hugs. But now she allows Mother to cradle her against her bosom as if she's taking comfort.

Lies.

Petal slowly stretches her mouth into a ghoulish grin, and in between her teeth is a small, jagged piece of glass, her teeth again stained red like when she sank them into Bubba.

And I know what she's done.

Staring at my cut. The pinch. I know.

If she can do this at four, what will she do at ten…sixteen… twenty-one?

My thoughts return to the fluffy pink pillow.

Chapter Five

Two days have passed since I emailed Acelynn, and it's been crickets, as I feared. The email might have landed in her spam folder. Should I send another one? Wouldn't it land there again? I'm going a little mad with my thoughts, but I haven't admitted that to Tillie.

She'd worry I was slipping into obsession, which I am not. I think I'd know if that was the case, but then…maybe I wouldn't. Either way, I'm fine.

I check the clock on my cell phone, and it's almost lunchtime. I've thrown together some taco meat, shells and a can of refried beans. The chips and salsa are on the table, and Tillie should be here any minute. We do this almost every Saturday, and today Tommy is joining us.

But I'm nervous to see Tillie. I splurged some, which was a bad idea since I'm jobless, but I had a little nest egg saved up, and it's not like I'm hurting anyone. I was curious.

Tillie won't see it that way.

At straight-up noon, a knock sounds, and I know it's Tillie.

She's punctual like the sun. My stomach folds in on itself, but I smooth my hair and mask my anxiety as I open the door. "I can always count on you to be on time."

Tillie stands in the hallway, her boho bag in hand. She's wearing a flowy red skirt and a shirt that hangs off one shoulder. Her walnut-colored locks are up in a messy bun. Slowly she removes her oversized sunglasses we found at a Goodwill that make her look like Audrey Hepburn. She even has the graceful long neck.

"What have you done?" She reaches out and handles my hair.

Called it. "What? I needed a fresh start before I go to interviews. Have to look my best, right?"

She frowns and enters my apartment, which now smells like tomatoes, onions, cilantro and spicy ground beef.

"Do you even like it?" I had a few highlights added and some layers around my face, then splurged a step further with a mani-pedi. My nails are now a sweet bubble-gum pink, and my ring fingers are dusted in gold as an accent.

Tillie hangs her purse on the back of the dining chair and folds her arms over her small chest. "You look like her."

I laugh. "We're twins."

She doesn't find my joke funny. "Your DNA can't be helped or altered. The pink nails with gold flecks. Same shape and same highlights. Same cut. And don't think I don't notice the change in makeup too—smokier eyes. Why? You're in a good place."

I bite my tongue. How can she call this apartment and my circumstances *a good place*?

"What did you spend on this 'fresh start'? You don't have a job yet. It's taking longer this time. I've noticed that too." She stomps toward my bedroom on the hunt for incriminating evidence.

"There's no reason to go into my room. It's a disaster." But I know my protests will fall on deaf ears.

"No, it's not," she says and throws open my door and gasps.

She's right. I hate clutter like some people hate nails on a chalkboard. But it is cluttered at the moment. I need more hangers.

She whirls around. "Tell me you didn't sink everything you saved as a cushion until you found a job on all of this!"

My hackles rise at her acute judgment. "Last time I checked, it was my money, my bank account and my life." I hate that I'm biting at her. My cheeks flush, and I hope she doesn't start ticking off all my other fresh starts and how they ended, the last one in particular.

Tillie snags my laptop from the bed and clicks on the various open tabs. She holds up the shimmery gold top beside her and points to the screen. Then another piece of clothing and another. Each one correlating with an open tab. "I don't like where this is headed, Charlotte Jean Kane."

"It's not heading anywhere." I simply wanted to step into Acelynn's shoes for five seconds. Feel close to her. She may never respond to my email. All I may ever have is her reflection in the mirror. Tillie can't possibly understand. She's not a twin. I sigh. "I'm sorry. You don't need to worry about me. Really. I know what I'm doing."

"You're fixating."

"I am not."

She snorts. Then her eyes soften. "I *am* worried, though."

"It's in your nature to fret." Which is why I have always protected her. "But you have nothing to worry about. Let's eat. Fill ourselves with tacos and binge *Botched*. If I had the money, I'd have Dr. Nassif fix this little indentation on the end of my nose. I hate it. I wonder if Acelynn hates hers. She has it too. I guess we inherited it from our dad. Whoever he was."

Tillie exits the tabs and shuts down the computer. "You said you weren't going to reach out to her. You haven't, have you?"

"No, *you* said I shouldn't, but I never said that."

Fear bursts in Tillie's eyes. "Please tell me you didn't contact her."

"I didn't contact her." I'm not lying. I'm simply repeating what she asked me to say. Tillie worries too much. I know I've given her some cause in the past, but this isn't what she suspects it is. I have family, and I want to know my sister. Tillie can't begin to fathom this.

She eyes me with a degree of skepticism, but lets it go and makes her way to the kitchen, where she fills her soft shells with heaping mounds of taco meat and the fixings, then spoons on a hefty side of beans and crashes on the couch. For a few minutes, neither of us talks. We simply feast on the meal, and I turn on *Botched*. None of these people are happy or satisfied with their bodies, and some of them have done serious damage trying to upgrade themselves for a cheap price. But Dubrow and Nassif undo what lesser surgeons have messed up.

I touch my nose and imagine what it would feel like without the little dip at the end. It's a wee bit bulbous. I could stand for it to be smaller.

"I'm not sure I can watch all this cutting while I'm eating salsa, Char. Gross. I will never understand pain on purpose. Age gracefully already." She runs a piece of tortilla through her beans. "I hope by the time I'm major wrinkled, I have a big, happy family and lots of grandkids. I want to be called Grandma. No shying away from that. But I'll need at least a date to start that dream. And it's not like I can meet a nice guy at work. We defend criminals."

I shove a bite of beans in my mouth. "Not until proven guilty."

"Fair enough." She dots the air with her fork and is no longer worried about my mental health or the improvements I've made to my body and wardrobe. I'm my own Dr. Dubrow and Dr. Nassif. A discounted cosmetic surgeon, but not so low as the ones in Mexico. Half these botched surgeries came from there.

These patients are taking a gamble even Tommy wouldn't, and as if I've summoned him by my thoughts, his heavy signature knock raps on my door.

"I got it," Tillie says and is already sprinting. The real reason Tillie hasn't met anyone is that she's already met the man she wants to marry. And it'll be the man she divorces or keeps on retainer at her law firm. But she rarely brings up my faults, so I remain silent too. Love covers a multitude of sins.

Tommy looms in the doorway, his blond hair in need of a good haircut and his big brown eyes full of mischief. Tommy always looks like he's up to something, because nine times out of ten, he is. He greets Till with a big kiss on the mouth, and I grimace. It only fuels her infatuation. And he knows it.

He looks at me and the grin fades, because Tommy knows I know. We hold an unspoken conversation where I call him out on his junk and he apologizes and then begs me not to mention anything to Tillie. I roll my eyes. "Go make tacos. We're bingeing *Botched*."

Rashad down the hall lets me sign in to his Netflix account and use it for free.

But we all know nothing's free, and at some point, he's going to want a favor that I'm not willing to return. But I'll cross that bridge when I get there—without burning it, if possible. Never be a bridge burner.

"What's *Botched*?"

"Plastic surgery gone wrong," Tillie offers and follows him to the kitchen. I tuck my feet under my thighs, and I've started on my third taco when my phone dings with an email notification.

My heart lurches into my throat, and I almost drop my plate.

Acelynn Benedict has responded.

Chapter Six

This is it. The moment I've anticipated and dreaded, and Ace-lynn's answer will determine which. Glancing into the kitchen, I see that Tommy has loaded four tacos and a hefty helping of beans onto his plate as he and Tillie discuss what he's been up to. Too afraid to open the email, I study Tommy as he tells Tillie he's been helping a friend rebuild a carburetor on a motorcycle.

He's lying.

Besides the fact that his nails are squeaky-clean—no hint of grease or oil—he refuses to make eye contact with Tillie, and his answers to her direct questions are vague.

My guess? He's been to secret poker games and is too ashamed to confide or simply wants to avoid Till's reprimands.

I can't keep ignoring this email. It's now or never, but I don't want to do it in front of them. Leaving my plate on the coffee table, I head for my bedroom. "I'll be right back," I mumble, but neither of them pays attention to me, for which I'm grateful.

After closing my bedroom door, I ease onto my bed and hover my finger over the email. Worst-case scenario, she tells me to pound sand. I've been rejected enough times. I can delete the email and move on. Or I'll want to. Sometimes my heart stutters when my mind sprints. The clash between the two puts me in hard places. But this is my twin. She can't refuse me. She won't.

I hope—but not too much hope. Finally, I click the email and read.

Dear Charlotte,

She went with *dear*. I should have too. It was my initial thought.

I apologize for not promptly responding, but I had no idea I'd been adopted and I needed some time to process that fact before I could come to grips with the amazing news that I have a sister—and not only flesh and blood but an identical twin. Thank you for sending that photo of you and your best friend to prove to me it was real.

I knew it! She had no idea she'd been adopted, and this is why she never tried to find me, considering she has the resources and easily could have tracked me down—if her parents had given her Marilyn's name and location.

My heart soars, and the heavy tension that has built in my neck and shoulders finally releases. My tight lungs expand, allowing me to inhale a full breath.

Acelynn is happy about me. Happy that she has a twin. She wants me in her life.

I would love the opportunity to meet you and, if it's okay with you, would like to fly out next Saturday and spend a couple of nights. Would that be something you're interested in? I have so many questions, as I'm sure you do as well. I probably don't have as many answers as you will concerning our past and biological mother. I am sorry to hear about her passing. Please call or text me. We have so much to catch up on.

Acelynn Benedict wants to come to Chicago and meet me. I'm over the moon and suddenly nervous. Dread balls in my gut. My sister has the whole world at her fingertips. What will we have in common besides our DNA? Will she be interested in me, knowing I'm not interesting?

Sorry about Marilyn's passing? Well, to be fair, I never told her our mother was a mentally unstable addict, which is commonly called a disease, so saying *illness* wasn't a lie. The last day I laid eyes on her, she was ranting about some kind of evil presence in her house and then fingered me for it. Accusing me of making her see things that weren't there. I tried to explain calmly and rationally that she was delusional and hallucinating due to the drugs influencing her.

As early as six—before being taken away from her again—I had to parent Marilyn. Talk her off shaky mental ledges. No, I hadn't come into her room and taken her needles. No, I hadn't set her bed on fire. The drugs drove her mad, knocked her out for days or put her in a trance where she moved and talked and acted, but never remembered any of it. When I told her *she* had lit her bed on fire—that was the crowning moment of being taken away and yet given back two years later—she called me a liar and forced me to strip down and prove I hadn't stashed a lighter or matches on my person.

How does one tell a normal human being like Acelynn that this was the kind of life I'd lived and that, unfortunately, this same DNA coursed through her veins too? I'm fully aware that I have an addictive personality, which is why I am careful not to do things in excess, for the most part.

But no one is perfect, and I've stumbled a few times. My actions are mine, though, and I've never attempted to lay blame for them on Marilyn. I do blame her for her DNA making me weak. Though I doubt it's all her fault. Someone passed down some DNA to her too. Maybe we're all inherently evil, with tendencies to fixate or obsess on things or people. Perhaps some of us fight it harder.

I've zoned out again and return my focus to the email.

If this is acceptable and convenient, please let me know. I want to know you, Charlotte. I can't believe this is real. While I'm utterly shocked and confused, I'm ecstatic to have a sister! I've always wanted a sister. It's weird and it's not, if that makes sense. LOL

I laugh out loud too as tears fill my eyes, blurring the screen. I have family. Real blood family, and she wants me. I can't even begin to describe how this makes me feel—to be wanted, accepted, chosen and maybe even loved.

Finally.

Do I want to meet her? Absolutely. Am I terrified? Absolutely.

I understand if you need a few days to consider it, but I eagerly wait to hear from you.
With love,
Ace

Ace. A nickname, a personal one for friends—for sisters. Below her name is her number. This is a personal invitation to reach out to her. To text or call my sister.

Knocking startles me.

"What are you doing in there?" Tommy booms. "I haven't seen you in days, and you lock yourself up. You're not in one of your moods again, are you?" he asks, and it annoys me.

Quickly I press the number link and save it, then make Acelynn a contact in my phone under Sister. "My stomach is in knots. I'll be out in a minute." All true.

"Beans'll do that, Char. Hurry up, though. I can't stay long."

Dog track calling him? I hold back the biting remark and manage a weak *okay* before texting my sister.

I do want to meet.

And yes, this upcoming long weekend will be perfect.

I have all week to make it so.

Chapter Seven

Acelynn has touched down in Chicago, and my nerves are like jagged edges of glass poking at my skin while simultaneously riding a wildly fun roller coaster.

I'm going to meet her in the Ritz-Carlton hotel lobby. I've never been inside. I barely have money for the Motel 6.

She asked if she should come to my place, but until she gets to know me, I'd prefer her first impression not be soured. And a cracker box apartment with worn carpet the management won't replace plus the stellar view from my living room window of the alley and dumpsters isn't the vibe I want her to walk into.

Best foot forward, as Glenda always told me before I entered another foster home with my black garbage bag. Which is why I only buy white ones now. I want pure and white and clean, which is ironic since it holds garbage, but it feels like truth— nice and tidy on the outside, yet inside full of rot and decay that needs to be tossed out before it stinks up a place. Like Marilyn when she duped the system into returning me to her. I smelled the rot, and no amount of perfume or clean hair and clothes could mask that stench. Yet no one else seemed to catch a whiff.

Speaking of whiff, I spritz my new perfume, which set me back a pretty penny, but Jimmy Choo's I Want Choo makes me feel special and pretty and not poor.

Acelynn and I have been texting daily. It's been superficial so far, but I still feel like we've known each other forever. Her whole lovely life is on display throughout a myriad of social media accounts. She's transparent, and I appreciate that. Like when she talked about not creating the tranquil environment a client had hoped for. It had been a great disappointment to her, and at first, she was offended. But then she gave advice on how to listen to what a person is saying, even if they're not stating it clearly and directly. She listened to what the woman didn't say and used that to come back and redo it all for free— she guarantees client satisfaction or a redo is free. I find that selfless. All that extra time and attention and purchases on her own dime. Though she has the dimes to make it happen. Still.

I finish blow-drying my hair, which takes almost thirty minutes for someone with the amount of hair I have. I'm not complaining. In my opinion, it's my best feature, and since I've had it layered and highlighted like Ace's, it's now a shining crown of glory on my head. The last thing I want is for her to think I'm a copycat, so I style it differently than she normally does— a strategically messy bun at her neck with a few shorter bangs framing her sharp cheekbones. She styles herself as perfectly as her clients' homes.

I'm going for a cool side fishbone that will hang over my shoulder, and I'm going to wear a shimmery gold dress that I've had for ages. It was packed in a tub I'd left at Tillie's. Still trendy and smart and expensive.

By the time I reach the Ritz-Carlton, with a stunning view of Lake Michigan even at night, I'm a bundle of nerves. Acelynn wants to see the city and do fun things, and expects me to take her to incredible places. My bank account wasn't exactly fat to begin with, but it's gone from skinny to malnourished in the past week. Still, I want her to have an epic time while she's in town for the long weekend.

Simple touristy things will never do for someone as sophisticated and cultured as Acelynn, but you can't come to Chicago and not visit the Navy Pier and eat Chicago pizza. That would be a travesty.

She's already texted to meet her at the rooftop bar for mimosas before we venture out. A little small talk. Makes sense. Smoothing my Zara-brand dress, I wait for the elevator. My shoes are knockoffs but look expensive.

The elevator opens, and a couple in their early forties huddle inside as the scent of power and wealth wafts on the stuffy elevator air. I square my shoulders and step inside. "Rooftop." The man, who looks like he belongs at a PGA tournament, blocks me from the buttons and grins.

His wife, judging by the rock on her left ring finger, beams. "That's where we're going. Brunch."

Sizing her up, I return a friendly comment. "A good reason to day drink."

The woman winks and points at me. She thinks we're on equal ground, and it reminds me of the clean white garbage bag, rubbish inside. Illusions. "That's what I told Robert. Especially since we're spending the rest of the afternoon on the lake with his parents."

"Be sure to throw in a Bloody Mary with the mimosa, then," I tease. "Fabulous day for the lake—or tennis, which is where I've been this morning, so I've earned the calories."

"Amen," she says and nods approvingly. "I've been getting into pickleball. You play?"

"No, but I've been meaning to. Hard to find the time for both, you know?"

"I do. What do you do that keeps you busy?" she asks.

"I'm an artist." Actually, I'm a storyteller painting a picture for their merriment.

Her dark eyes, curtained with faux mink lashes, widen with utter delight. "How lovely."

How is my story any more fake than her lashes? Why is it okay to wear fake jewelry and knockoff brands and faux lashes, but it's not okay to fudge your occupation or pretend to play tennis? Aren't both a lie at the root?

"I love those earrings. Diamonds really are a girl's best friend, aren't they?" She wiggles her right ring finger, and a large sapphire with diamonds encircling it twinkles and shines. Her husband rolls his eyes, but it's with affection.

I touch my earlobes. "Nobody keeps a secret like jewelry. They were a gift."

"I feel a story there. Did you land him?"

I chuckle. Marilyn had landed him. "Father" had purchased all sorts of expensive trinkets for her, including pills. He pumped her full of white pills, yellow pills, blue ones. When it came to an end, I made sure to pocket a parting gift.

Each round solitaire a full carat and a half set in fourteen-karat gold.

Father owed me them.

Chapter Eight

My gold strappy sandals with spike heels click against the floor as I enter the rooftop bar, full of jitters and excitement. The bar is eclectic and classy and everything representing my sister, who will not be wearing knockoff brands of any kind.

I scan the crowded bar and spot her. She's not facing me, but I'd know that signature hairstyle anywhere. The slender neck and bare arms. My slender neck and arms. I swallow hard and release a pent-up breath.

Showtime.

Gliding into her presence, I paint a cordial simper on my face. Nothing too eager. I don't want her to think I'm clingy or desperate.

"Acelynn," I murmur, and she peers up, holding a mimosa, the golden drink glimmering. Her eyes, which are more green than hazel in her sleeveless green satiny dress with a high ruffled collar, meet mine, and her lips part before breaking into a shining and approving grin that could power the city.

"I can't believe it. It's like looking in a mirror." She puts down her glass, then stands and immediately embraces me. "I simply can't believe this! Also, you smell luscious. What are you wearing? I have to have it."

I'm not sure how she can tell the fragrances apart, now that she's left a layer of her own perfume on my skin, but I reveal the brand and slide into the chair across from her. "I don't know where to start."

"Girl, let's start with this city. I love it." She gestures animatedly. "I can't wait to see it all, and with you. My sister," she whispers and chokes up, eyes shimmering with moisture. "I just… It's all so overwhelming, in the best of ways," she says with Southern charm. I adore her accent. "What are you drinking?"

"I'll have the same."

Acelynn signals the bartender. "Rafe, another mimosa, if you have a minute."

"Rafe?" I ask.

"My mama has this phrase she uses about me. 'She doesn't meet a stranger.' And I suppose that's true. I love people. Love their stories. People are fascinating. Don't you think?" She eyes me with dark mischief, and it unsettles me.

What, if anything, might she know? I shake out of the paranoia and keep my fidgeting hands balled in my lap. "I'd rather spend my time with nature. It's more dazzling. More honest."

"Interesting. I never thought of creation as honest. Harsh, sometimes seductive, but never honest. I like that view, though." She leans back and folds her arms as she studies me with appreciation. "I want to see all the touristy things and eat at Uno's pizza. Buy popcorn. Pretend calories don't count when you're with your sister."

I agree. Calories shouldn't count. Ever.

Rafe brings my drink, then swaggers back to the bar, and she sighs. "He's a complete con artist, but he's dreamy. But aren't most men?"

"Dreamy or con artists?" I joke.

"Con artists. Always pretending in order to roll you into bed. As if we don't know this." She tsks and shakes her head. "But hey, if we know it, we can use it to our advantage, am I right? Play them at their own game." She winks, and I notice we share the same laugh.

"You have a good flight?" I redirect and sip the orange juice and champagne tonic. The citrus is bright, and the bubbles pop against my tongue.

"Girl, I sat next to this old broad who rambled on for the entire flight about the good old days and how aging sucks. It took her thirty minutes just to tell me every bone that pops and joint that aches." She rolls her eyes. "Me? I'm gonna die young, if that's the case. I thought I was gonna die having to listen to her." She laughs again, and I join in, but it's forced. "Old people are a waste of space."

I hold in my shock, thinking of Mrs. Donlea and how my sister probably would not have come to her rescue to find missing hearing aids, but some people aren't good with the elderly—no patience. I won't hold it against her. I'm not good with animals. Not that I don't like them. They're just not my jam, and I'm allergic.

Acelynn's phone buzzes. She glances at it, frowns and ignores it. My heart flutters. She's putting everything on hold for me. I'm the object of her affection at the moment, and I can't remember ever being someone's sole priority.

Pushing my drink aside, I lean in. "So, uh, last we texted, you hadn't told your family that you knew you were adopted. Do they know where you are now? And why?"

Acelynn runs her finger along the rim of her champagne flute. "Can I be real? Of course I can. We're sisters." She leans in too. "I haven't told them. I should and I will, but I don't want to do it while I'm angry, and I have been. They owed me the truth. I mean, what if I'd needed a kidney?"

"That's what I said! My friend Tillie didn't think it was a

good idea to contact you due to the possibility of messing up a family. I get that, but I'd have wanted to know."

"Exactly." She sips her drink. "I'm sure Daddy had his reasons. Protective. He's always hovering and reminding me to 'pay attention in parking lots, Acie. Stay off the phone. Carry a Taser.' I'm his little girl, and to him, I'm not adopted. As far as Mama, I think she believes I'm hers and no one else's, so it doesn't matter that I knew—though I disagree. What's our mom like? You never talk about you. We always talk about me."

She's far more fascinating than I am, but she's right. We always talk about her. Because I keep the conversation geared toward her. Now I have to share some things. "Marilyn had some mental health issues and a drug problem she battled most of her adult life. Which is what killed her in the end. An overdose." Addiction is an illness, like I stated in the email, so I wasn't lying.

She gasps. "Honey, I'm so sorry. Maybe that's why my mom never told me. To spare me that."

"Perhaps." No one spared me. I lived through it to the end. But my past is not on the table. It will never be on the table. At least, not the tawdry parts. "It was arduous at best." That was today's word of the day. Perfect place to insert it.

"But look at you. How you've overcome everything. You're my hero, Charlotte." She takes my hand and with the other raises her glass. "Let's toast."

I hold up my crystal flute.

"To a new today and bright tomorrow. May our sisterhood grow and nothing and no one keep us apart from here on out."

"Hear! Hear!"

We clink our glasses and sip our drinks.

"I see we have many of the same tastes," she says and points to my light pink nails and then my highlights. "Not surprising since we share DNA. Tell me you love true crime docs."

"But of course." Who doesn't love a good murder mystery? Though recently I haven't watched much TV except *Botched*.

"I knew it. Are you dating anyone?" she asks and finishes off her drink, then signals for another one. I've only taken a few sips. Most often, I steer clear of alcohol thanks to Marilyn's genes; I don't want to end up like her, which means I won't even take pain meds.

Rafe brings Acelynn another mimosa.

Dates. Zero dating. "No, not in the past few years. I've been focused on my art."

"Yes," she says and gulps her drink like a lush. "Tell me about that."

"I'm freelancing right now. I'm hoping to end up in a gallery soon. My work's being reviewed."

Her eyes light up. "That is amazing. I decorate and paint walls, but portraits and actual paintings—no can do. But my brother is an artist. Funny how y'all have that in common, and you don't share DNA."

"Theo, right?" We've briefly talked about him. A real estate agent, I think.

"I call him Teddy. He's like a teddy bear. So our friend group adopted it. Ha! Adopt."

I grin, but it wasn't that funny. "What's his focus?"

"Portraits mostly, but he can do anything. He's amazing. So smart. Like Daddy. Daddy wanted him to attend med school like him and his father before him, but the art bug bit Teddy. He's a creative—not a logical or analytical mind like the great Conrad Benedict. At least now I see why I didn't inherit that gene."

"I think our biological mom was a creative back before she succumbed to drugs and the disease ate away at her. I found decorating magazines in an old box where I found that letter your mom sent to let Marilyn know how you were doing. I think you might have been a fussy baby at first."

Acelynn's eyebrow rises, something mine won't do. Finally, a difference between us—in addition to the fact I'm good with elderly people and she is not. "Mama can be dramatic. If I cried once, I bet she called it colic. A sniffle from pollen might be influenza or pneumonia, but that was sweet of her. Do you think Marilyn told my mom there were two of us?"

Same question I've pondered for a week. "I don't know." Marilyn was unpredictable and impulsive. No way to gauge what she'd been thinking or how she met a couple from Georgia. Nothing was in the letter I read.

She finishes off her second glass. "I don't think my parents knew. No way they'd pass up twins. I can't see Mama separating identical babies. Two babies to adorn in pink." She grinned. "Probably why I love pink so much. Rose-gold is my fave."

"Me too—that I love pink."

"No doubt about it. We're the same."

I notice her gold cross necklace hanging in the hollow of her throat, glimmering like a diamond. Must be a declaration of her faith, and reminds me of the one I lost or misplaced or had stolen from me.

"I would love to see some of your paintings while I'm in town, and I must buy one to take back with me."

"Definitely, but to be honest, I haven't painted anything that I haven't already sold. I might have an old painting, though." I hope we never circle back to this conversation. I'm already juggling a million spiked balls. Any moment they'll fall and crash down around me, ending it all.

We continue making more small talk, and I listen as she rambles on and on about her babies—two Bolognese dogs named Tallulah and Rue. She takes them everywhere she possibly can, including shopping, clients' homes and even out with friends. Another difference between us. I refrain from sharing that I'm not that into animals.

Acelynn signals Rafe and mouths *check*. He nods, then disappears.

"I'm itching for nightlife since I rarely have time to break free. Do you go out much?"

I shrug. "Your sister is quite boring, I'm afraid. I'm an introverted painter who rarely goes wild on the dance floor. But in my early twenties, I hit some clubs with Tillie and Tommy."

"I want to meet them. They sound amazing. Tommy's in finance, you say?"

Yep. Gambling. "Yes, though I don't math, so don't ask."

"And Tillie works for an attorney?"

"Yes."

Her phone buzzes again. After glancing at it, she clears her throat and scans the room. "Why is it you can't escape the server until you ask for the check, and then they disappear into some vortex? You know what? Let's go." She harrumphs, takes my hand and pulls me to my feet.

My heart jumps in my throat. What if we're caught? I can't. "Um...you want to dine and dash?" I whisper.

"Charlotte, some people need a life lesson. This will teach a server to be prompt and to pay attention to patrons. Now, are you with me or not?" She gives me the same stern look Mrs. Kruek gave me in fourth grade when I couldn't figure out a math problem.

Not. A million times not. I can't get caught doing something like this, but I lick my lips and say, "Go! Go!"

With a spray of giggles and her hand still in mine, she leads me from the rooftop to the elevator. We laugh all the way down, but mine is fake. "I can't believe you'd do that."

A grin the Cheshire cat could be proud of spreads across her face, and her eyes hold a glint. "I can't believe *you'd* do that."

Irritation scratches inside my chest. I'm not tracking, and that's unusual.

"I didn't dine and dash," she says and shakes me playfully

as we step off the elevator and into the lobby. "They have my room number, silly. He'll charge it to my room." She slips her arm in mine and nestles against me as we walk into the spring air. "But *you* didn't know that."

Words won't form. She's right. Somehow, I feel played.

And I am *never* played.

My body stiffens, and my blood heats.

"Oh, Charlotte." She tsks. "Don't worry. Your secret—all your secrets—are safe with me."

Future or past secrets? What does she know?

Chapter Nine

The day has been perfection. After pushing away the paranoia, I was able to sink into the present and enjoy showing Acelynn around the city. We bought new tennis shoes. I was down with that because it meant not having to go to my place.

She insisted on treating me. Our tennis shoes with our cutesy dresses worked, plus we matched. After the purchase, we went to the Museum of Science and Industry, to the Field Museum and then to Navy Pier. Naturally we had to ride the Ferris wheel and eat Garrett's popcorn.

Now we're sitting inside Pizzeria Uno, which is where she's wanted to eat dinner all day. Me? I prefer Lou Malnati's, but it's her day and her fun, so I acquiesce to her wishes. We sit across from each other near the window and people-watch. Acelynn orders a craft beer, and I ask for a club soda. She doesn't berate me for it now that she knows the truth about our mother. I'm starving, and the Italian spices fill my senses with bursts of garlic, onion, basil, tomatoes and total anticipation for future yeasty bliss.

"Have you ever been to New York?" Acelynn asks and thanks the server for the beer. "I love New York pizza."

"No. I'd like to, though. Someday." I sip my club soda and watch through the window as a mom drags her two children toward a bench. She's exasperated, and they're crying and rubbing their eyes. "You ever think of being a mom? Do you and Philip talk about kids?"

She almost chokes on her drink. After coughing and tapping her chest, she laughs. "No. Philip is ambitious and has his eye on bigger aspirations. He won't even consider children until then. Me? I'd have a whole brood as soon as I could. There's nothing sweeter than motherhood. I hope to raise babies with my friends so they can grow up to be fast friends too."

I toy with the straw paper and feel a pang of jealousy. It's hard to make friends when you move from school to school and home to home. "Tell me about your girlfriends." She's already shared a few things through texts, but texting isn't quite the place to be long-winded.

For the next fifteen minutes, she tells me about MacKenzie Newsom, Drucilla Hilton, Bianca Lambert and the brothers who are more like afterthoughts or blankets they drag along behind them. Except Dru. Dru doesn't have a brother. She's an only child, and according to Acelynn, it shows. Finally, forty-five minutes later, our deep-dish pizza arrives, and as I pick up a piece, the cheese strings from the spatula to my plate in ooey-gooey goodness.

"I'm mostly vegan," she says. "But I do miss cheese. Don't tell."

I wipe my mouth. "Your secrets are safe with me." After repeating her earlier words, I study her for some kind of tell, but she holds my gaze innocently, even appreciatively, before breaking eye contact first.

After our meal, we head back to the Ritz. It's been a long day, and we're planning to rest, then go out for a night on the town.

"Oh, I need to run in the convenience store real quick, if that's okay."

I nod and we enter, perusing the makeup section. "What do you need?"

"I forgot toothpaste, of all things." She waves a hand at her mistake and picks up a tube of twelve-dollar lip balm with a pink sheen. "Would you mind grabbing me some? Tom's brand."

Okaaay. "Sure." Why can't she grab her own? I'm not her maidservant. As I round an endcap to the hygiene section, my gut signals me to pause. Peeping out from behind the section, I watch Acelynn as she nonchalantly drops the lip balm in her Prada handbag and moves down the aisle to the nail care section, where she drops two polishes in her purse. A berry pink and a rose-gold shade.

I duck back behind the endcap and scurry to the toothpaste aisle, where I grab Tom's toothpaste and return to find her holding a terry cloth hair band. "I forgot this too."

I hand her the toothpaste, fully expecting her to deposit it and the new terry cloth hair band into her handbag, but she promptly heads to the counter, where she adds cinnamon Mentos to the mix and pays the cashier while making small talk about Chicago and the pizza we just ate.

Outside, she opens the roll of chewy mints and takes one, then offers one to me. "Sisters share everything." I don't know why, but I feel like accepting this mint means something far deeper and darker than it should. But then, it might be the paranoia. I live in a world where one favor requires a favor in exchange.

"Charlotte, they won't bite." She nudges me with the mints. "Anything that's mine is yours."

I think she means it. So I take the mint even if it feels like I've signed my voice over to the sea witch.

Back at the Ritz, I try to hold in my mesmerized gaze. This

place is the epitome of luxury…and that bathtub. Oh, what I would give for a soak. Acelynn stands at the threshold in the bathroom. "I know what you're thinking, sis. Do it. Why not? I always say if it feels good, don't stop." She waggles her eyebrows and caresses her cross necklace, a habit I've noticed. Probably a nervous tic.

"Where'd you get that?" I ask.

"My maternal grandmother gave it to me. She was at our home a lot growing up, helping out. She spotted a unique gift in me from an early age, and she kindled it with encouragement. She always wore this necklace. Believed every good Southern girl should go to church and love the Lord. God rest her soul. I inherited this when she died and only take it off for showers or swimming. I like to think she's looking down on me with love from heaven."

She doesn't mention her own faith, though.

"That's nice."

"Now, about that little dippity-do in the tub. Go at it. Soak and enjoy. I have a little work to do anyway. We'll paint the town later. I'm not even sure what that phrase means."

I turn the knob. Hot water pours into the tub, steam quickly rising like fog over a lake. "I don't know either. But I'm sure we'll figure it out."

"Right? 'Kay, enjoy." She closes the door, and I finish letting the water fill the tub before slipping into it and turning on the jets. My whole body relaxes, and my sore feet are massaged. I hear her talking on the phone, but I can't decipher the conversation. It's not heated, but she's piqued my curiosity—again. I turn off the jets and cock my ear.

"Okay. You promise?" she asks, and her voice is sultry and flirty. She laughs. "Perfect. Trust me… You'll love it… Love you, babe."

I hear her rifling through something. Probably her stolen treasure trove. What was that all about? Is she some weird thrill-seeker? I mean, I'm not judging. I have no room. It's… it's unexpected.

Thirty minutes later, I'm back in my dress and heels, and it's almost eight. When I leave the bathroom, she's on the bed with her laptop open and her phone beside her. "How was your soak?"

"Amazing."

She closes her laptop. "So, I've done some research."

My stomach dips, and then a lump starts to form in my throat. "Oh, yeah?"

"Yeah." One of her slender eyebrows rises. "And I know exactly where I want to spend part of our evening."

My shoulders relax. "And where is that?"

"ROOF on theWit."

I can handle that. "Best cocktails ever." Not that I've ever had one, but once Tillie's boss, LB, took her there, and she gave me the lowdown. "Let's Uber."

As we leave the hotel room, I notice the polish she swiped from the convenience store is now in my bag.

Then

"It's pretty bad," she says as I enter the principal's office. It's not the first time I've been called into an office to discuss Petal. I know it won't be the last either. My stomach is in a perpetual knot. All I know is a little girl claimed Petal stole the pocket-sized doll she was given for her birthday and then, after the girl confronted her, pushed the girl off the top of the slide.

My daughter, of course, denies her involvement, and I'm now called in to help figure it out. As if I can figure out anything regarding Petal. She's six years old and the most diabolical child I've ever known minus the child in *The Omen*. Is Petal Damien? When I come within five feet of her, I feel the waves of wickedness rolling off her back and dripping from her tongue.

I enter the elementary school office. Petal sits in a plastic chair in the lobby, her feet leisurely swinging back and forth. She's the picture-perfect child with long blond braids and a happy expression and bright eyes, but it's a gloss of deception. It sounds crazy. A six-year-old child who is riddled with deceit, but I know what I know.

My legs are wobbly. The meds I despise taking haven't worn off, and a fog hovers over my brain and muscles. They'll see the dark half-moons under my eyes, but I hardly sleep at all, and when I do, it's medicated sleep and fitful. I worry over Petal and Bubba. Mother refuses to let me put locks on their doors to keep them in their rooms at night. She called it monstrous and told me I was overreacting and that the children were perfectly fine and there was nothing to worry about. She's wrong.

They're all wrong. Petal has them fooled.

But she doesn't fool me. I see what crawls beneath her skin. If she shed it, the world would see. The school secretary beams at her, and I notice she's given her a sucker.

Ah, the charm and grace of a monster that lurks in the soul of a beautiful child.

Petal spots me, and as a dark flash streaks through her eyes, I swear they change shape. Like a lizard. Then they brighten, and she jumps from the chair, her Mary Janes scuffing along the floor as she thrusts herself against me and hugs my waist.

I should hug her back. Do the motherly thing.

Except I feel nothing but revulsion. I want to peel her corrupt little fingers from my body and beg them to lock her up. Instead, I gently remove myself from her and squat at her eye level, shuddering internally.

"Did you take Hannah's doll, Petal?" A lie is coming. I already know it.

"No, Mommy. Stealing is bad. But Hannah says I took it."

"And did you push her when she accused you?"

She shakes her head. "Hannah fell on her own." Crocodile tears drip down her delicate cheeks. "Mrs. Krumm says I did it. Because Hannah said I did. You believe me, don't you, Mommy?"

Not on her life.

"Hannah's leg is broken. Principal Riley says she had to go to the hospital and have surgery."

She blinks; not a single drop of emotion or empathy shows. I've been reading up on sociopaths and psychopaths. At the library. I can't afford for Mother to see it or she'll run with it in a dramatic, over-the-top fashion, calling in medical professionals to put me in a straitjacket.

The door opens. Petal's teacher enters with another little girl who is sobbing and insisting she didn't take Hannah's pocket doll. Mrs. Krumm holds it in her hand. She sees me and sighs. "I am terribly sorry." She turns to Petal. "And I am so sorry, dear. Jayla Ann had the doll tucked in her supply box—at the bottom. Nice and hidden under the markers. She was also on the slide with the other girls. Hannah must have been mistaken about who pushed her in the chaos."

"I didn't take it! I didn't do it, Mrs. Krumm." Jayla Ann cries again, but it's Petal who draws my attention. She shoves her hand in her dress pocket, more amused than upset. Not vindicated but triumphant. Jayla Ann is directed to the chair Petal had been sitting in. Petal is still snaked around my leg, pretending to be shy and afraid and needing protection.

It's us who need protection from her.

Mrs. Krumm instructs the secretary to call Jayla Ann's mother and again apologizes to me and Petal, then reaches for Petal's hand. "Let's go back to class."

Petal lets go of my leg and skips to the teacher with a toothy grin, the kind that eats glass. "It's okay, Mrs. Krumm. I'm not mad at you." But that dark streak flashes again. Mrs. Krumm's in for it. Not today and maybe not even this month, but before this year ends, Petal is going to destroy her.

As she reaches out for Mrs. Krumm's hand, I see purple marker stains on the tips of her fingers. The same purple that stains the pocket doll's cheeks.

Chapter Ten

The club is packed wall to wall, and the live DJ is encouraging everyone to get on the floor. Acelynn's eyes are like flames of silver as she grins and pulls me next to two guys in their mid- to late thirties. They do a double take, then smile.

"Twins," they say with lascivious tones.

Yeah. Not happening. But Acelynn eats it up. "Ever been with twins?"

"No, but we do like trying new things." The man with darker hair and even darker eyes thirsts for her and moves up against her while the blond eyes me with equal desire. These are dangerous men. Former frat boys who know their way around roofies and naive freshmen girls, with no fear of being caught because they smell like money and power. They have fathers who are sharks in the ocean of law and would have them free and clear in a phone call.

I don't draw these kinds of men.

To be fair, they didn't spot us first. Acelynn gravitated to them. She approached them on the floor. I pull her aside. "Hey, these guys are cute but real trouble, Ace. No good vibes going."

She slaps at the air. "Nah. We'll be fine."

"What about Philip?"

She frowns. "What about him? I'm not cheating. I'm not going home with either of them. Regardless of what they think. Lighten up, sis. I got this. I'll keep you safe. Trust me."

I want to. But my gut is rarely if ever wrong. "Don't drink around them or let them bring you a drink. They're GHB boys. I'm telling you. I know my drugs."

She softens her expression, leans in and kisses my cheek. "I love you looking out for us, and we'll be careful. No drinks. Just dancing. Good old-fashioned fun. How can we say no?"

Well, with GHB in our systems, we won't have to. I bite down on the snark. This is what she wants. And I want her to love me. So, I fake excitement and sidle up to Blondie, not caring about his name, and purr into his ear. "Show me a good time on the dance floor?"

Acelynn nods her approval before grinding with tall, dark and trouble. Not sure what constitutes cheating in her and Philip's eyes, but in my mind, this is it. Maybe this trip is her Vegas and what happens here stays here.

I know I won't tell.

Closing my eyes, I sail to another place where I'm not being groped and ground on and lewd sentiments do not flow into my ears. I hate every second of this. But sometimes you have to do things you don't like to be accepted by the people you want to love you most.

More than anything, I want Acelynn to love me.

I want to be a part of her life. Fully and completely in it. Maybe after tonight, she'll tell her family she knows about me and invite me in. A big old welcome mat rolled out for the long-lost sister. Her overprotective father will adopt me, so to speak, and warn me about dangerous men and staying out too late and carrying a rape whistle. Her mom will open her maternal arms and call me "precious" and say she didn't even know about me. Or she hoped Marilyn would let me be adopted too, but in her stupid selfishness, Marilyn was saving me for a rainy day when she was broke and needed a fix.

Marilyn didn't adopt me out, but she definitely sold me out.

Who knows? Maybe me and Teddy will paint together. Swap art techniques. I might be able to talk Tillie into moving to Savannah. We could rent a cool place—if Acelynn doesn't invite me to live with her. Which I would. We could go into business together. I clearly have an eye for color matches and blending as an artist. We could be like the Property Brothers. Design Sisters. I'm heady with the possibilities. Blondie mistakes my bliss about the future for what's happening on the dance floor. I ignore his body against mine as we move to the seductive beat.

I want a life in Savannah with my sister and her family. And it scares me how much. So much I don't think there's anything I wouldn't do to make that happen.

"Isn't this awesome?" Acelynn says as she leans into me, dancing before me and turning me into the cream filling of this dance cookie sandwich. "Philip never wants to go out like this. Reputation is everything to him. Therefore, it's everything to me. Thank you," she hollers, and her eyes fill with moisture. "For giving me this taste of freedom. Not that I feel trapped, but sometimes a woman needs a night to be whatever she wants to be. Whoever she wants to be."

Now it all makes sense. She's testing waters Philip wouldn't approve of. She's not a klepto. She's sliding into a new persona while she's in a new place. It's a rush, and she's feeling it. Her cheeks are flushed pink, and her eyes are drunk with excitement. Maybe me and my twin are more alike than I originally believed.

"Be whoever you want to be, Acelynn." I'll keep her safe,

watch out for her while she does wild things she'd never do in Savannah.

"Sometimes I wish I could. Some days I'd trade my life with you. But not forever." She grins. "I can't imagine forever without my family and Philip. Only…a little while."

The music fades to a slow dance, and my phone buzzes. I check it and see six missed calls from Tommy. I've broken the cardinal rule by not answering my phone. In my defense, it's loud in here. "I have to take this. Don't leave here, and don't buy or accept a drink. Nothing."

"I promise."

I push away from Blondie and hold up my phone. He's disappointed I'm walking away. I couldn't care less. He could probably stand to suffer a little disappointment. Outside isn't much quieter, but it'll do. Tommy knows I'm meeting my sister, and if it's dire, he can always call Tillie, which means he's gotten in a jam she can't fix or he's so drunk he's forgotten I'm with my sister.

A text comes through.

911

That's no joke. My heart lodges in my throat. What if the 911 is Tillie? I call him, and he answers on the first ring.

"Char, I'm in trouble. It's bad. Real bad this time."

Chapter Eleven

My heart races as I return to our table at the rooftop club where Acelynn is sandwiched between the men dancing. Her bun has come loose, and a few stray hairs stick to her damp neck. I hate to kill the vibe. But I can't bring her with me, and she can't stay alone. Acelynn thinks she's having some harmless weekend fun, but these men are predators. If she stays, I'll have two crises to deal with.

Tommy has really stepped in it now. Frank Marchetti's men? I'm thankful he called me and not Tillie. The last thing she needs is to tangle with Marchetti. Not that I want to, but someone has to help Tommy out of this debacle. I might be infuriated, but I love him, and I would never let anything happen to him. Which is why, less than ten hours into meeting my sister, I'm going to leave her to save his bacon.

"Everything okay?" she asks as I approach.

"Actually, no. I have a friend who's in trouble, and I need to bail him out."

"Of jail?" Her eyes widen. She dates a prosecutor, so someone who rubs elbows with criminals is probably unsavory to her. But that's my life.

"No. A jam, but it's on the serious side, and I have to leave."

Dark-haired guy is practically salivating. "She can hang with us. We'll see she gets home okay."

"Scout's honor." Blondie crosses his heart as if that's the Scout sign.

"Yeah, I'll be all right, sis."

She has so much to learn about the world. "Can you get me a bottle of water for my trip, please?"

She pauses, bats her gaze between the men and me, but agrees and strides to the bar. I dip my hand into my purse and ease close to the dark-haired man. He's calling the shots. "I want you to both walk away before she returns. She's not staying."

"She's a big girl."

My insides are growing dark, and rage builds in my chest. "Big girls should be able to say yes or no, then, shouldn't they? I know what you are."

He hurls an insult at me and becomes downright nasty and lewd. He thinks I'm weak and gullible. This man has no idea what I'm capable of and grabs my arm. His short nails bite into my flesh.

I don't flinch, but hold his gaze until recognition dawns. He knows what's behind my eyes. It's behind his too.

"You have two seconds to release me."

One...

Two...

Still within his grasp.

He lets out a small cry and looks down to see my blade has poked a small hole in his shirt and is now tingeing it the faintest red—a superficial mark, but enough to snag his attention and make him aware that he can't take advantage of me. Therefore, he can't take advantage of my sister.

"Okay. We're out of here. Crazy—" They slip through the

crowd, and I discreetly replace my weapon. You never know when you'll need to defend yourself.

Acelynn returns with my water. "Where did they go?"

"Gone. Sorry to kill your buzz. Come on. I'll secure an Uber for you, and we can meet in the morning for breakfast and plan our day." I steer her outside and to the street, and we wait for her Uber.

She eyes my purse and me, and I'm not sure if she saw what transpired. I was careful. "What about you?" she asks.

"Don't worry about me."

Acelynn shoots another glance at my purse. "I think we both know you can handle yourself. I guess that's the good thing that came out of foster care, isn't it?" She now eyes me with pity.

No. It's a tragic by-product.

"If I could change things, Charlotte, I would. I wish you'd always been in my life. I've gone to bed these past few days thinking of all the things we could have done. Switched out on our dates and confused teachers. Lain in bed at night and shared secrets and dreams."

"We can do that now. Minus the dates."

She laughed. "Oh, how I'd get a kick out of messing with Philip. Even the Pinks."

"The Pinks?"

"Our name for each other. Bianca, MacKenzie and Dru would be so freaked out, and we could pull a fun stunt."

Her Uber parks at the curb, and I can't push her inside fast enough. Tommy needs me, and I fear I may be too late. Marchetti isn't one to be played.

She grabs my hand before I can close the back door. "I've gotten my own brother out of a few scrapes myself. We must share that gene. Be careful, Charlotte, but even more so...be smart." She squeezes before letting go. "Text me when you're home so I know you're safe."

"I will."

"Charlotte...I love you. Already, I do."

I want to cry, but I can't. "I feel the same way." I close the door, and she's off to her hotel.

Marchetti is like the new Capone of Chicago. Tommy should have known not to tangle with him for loans. He's in too deep for my pockets, but he thinks if he offers Marchetti two grand tonight, he'll cut him loose to pay the rest with a massive amount of interest. I'm not so sure. And even if he does, Tommy can't pay this money. He's a dead man walking. His only hope is to flee town and never return. Tillie is going to lose her mind. But I can't think of the fallout. I have to deal with one thing at a time. Right now it's hoping the eighteen hundred dollars I have left to my name will appease Frank Marchetti. But I only have some of it with me. The rest is taped behind the fridge at my apartment, and I have no time to go there to secure it all.

I hop the bus because I can't afford an Uber now with Tommy's problem.

The bus drops me at the corner. It's after ten, but the Laundromat is open, and the scent of spring meadows rides the soapy air.

Everyone knows Marchetti launders his money through Laundromats in a proverbial flipping of the bird to the very few cops who aren't in his deep pockets. I wish I could back the Blue, but they've never done anything for me except send me back into dismal circumstances or misunderstand my intentions.

I slink inside. Used dryer sheets litter the floor, and a few baskets full of unclaimed clothing are pushed into various corners of the room. Two vending machines hum as a light flickers overhead.

In the small alcove, two bathrooms flank a water fountain, and to the right is a hallway that leads to offices, where I hear muffled voices. Pushing my back flush against the wall, I scoot along to the cracked door and listen to a raspy voice.

"Thomas, we've been down this road. I've warned you what would happen if you couldn't pay. I think you're yankin' my chain."

I immediately think back to when he showed up at my apartment, bloodied and bruised with claims he'd been in a bar fight. I never bought it. Not with the fingers broken on both hands. But we all keep secrets, I suppose, and I let him think he had his.

"I'm not, Frank. I mean, Mr. Marchetti. I can get you about two grand tonight and then the rest by Monday. I swear." Tommy's voice is pitchy, and my heart goes out to him. Do I waltz up in there? If so, I'm directly involved, and I do not want to be in Marchetti's eyesight. Not even a peripheral view.

"See, I don't think so. I think you wanna give me enough money to let you go so you can skip town. Then I have to come hunt you down like the dog you are."

"No way. I'd never do that." Tommy's scared. So am I. Because that's exactly my plan, and Marchetti's guessed it.

Maybe I can give this money to him for now and talk to Acelynn about a loan to pay it all later tonight. I don't want her to think I've manipulated her into coming for a large sum of money, but I'm desperate. Frozen in place, I will myself to move. Get in there. Make a deal. Whatever I have to in order to pay off Tommy's debt. Even if I have to make a deal that turns my stomach. I'll do it.

But I have to go in there. Now. Right now.

I finally step in front of the door and reach for the knob to push it open all the way as Marchetti fires.

Tommy's head thrusts backward and I jerk away from the handle and cover my mouth.

Shock shoots through my system, and the world tilts in slo-mo. Tommy's been shot. Killed. I wasn't quick enough. But I better be quick now.

"Clean the mess up, boys," Marchetti demands. I turn and race down the hall, but as I round the corner, I smack into a rolling cart. It rams into the washers with a clang.

"What is that?" Marchetti hollers, and feet shuffle from the office.

I glance back. Frank Marchetti stands with murder in his eyes. No staying in the shadows and out of his sight now. He clearly sees me, like he's memorized my face.

"Get her!"

His men, bigger than the Rock, rush me, but I'm spry. Perk of being petite and experienced in running from predators. If you're quick, you can't be caught.

I blast out the door, my heart thundering, and aim toward the shopping area that's well lit but vacant.

They're gaining.

I'm not making it out of this one.

As I near a store on the end of the shopping strip, I see a potted plant in a heavy concrete planter resting by the door. Without hesitating, I lift it and heave it against the glass door, shattering it into a million fragments and setting off the security alarm, which peals at ear-piercing levels.

Already, sirens blare in accompaniment to the alarm system wailing. I keep running, my lungs constricting and blood whooshing inside my head, as I fly down a narrow alley. I can't tell if they're still on my heels or not, so I cast a glance behind me. Nothing but shadows.

Crouching behind trash containers, I catch my breath, steal a peek and see nothing but blue lights. I've halted Marchetti's men.

For now.

I've witnessed a murder, and Frank Marchetti knows it. It's only a matter of time before he discovers who I am and where I live. My mind races, and it hits me. I have to tell Tillie that Tommy is dead. And it's my fault for hesitating, although I'm certain he was dead either way, and if I had walked inside that office, I might be too.

I can't stay here and be found by Marchetti or the police. I cut down the alley and run until I reach the bus stop. The bus is pulling up, and I could shout and dance at the perfect timing. Hunching in the seat, I try to become invisible until it's my stop, and then I sprint to my apartment.

How much time do I have before Marchetti connects Tommy to me, then discovers my address? Not enough when he has cops in his pocket. After securing all my locks, I shove a chair in front of the door and close my plastic blinds before pacing the floor. Snagging my phone from the table, I go to Favorites and press Tillie's name.

It's almost midnight, but she answers on the first ring. She never breaks the rule.

"I was waiting to hear from you. How did things go with your sister? Is she cool? Did you get along?" Her voice is alert, proving she's been waiting up for my call or at the very least a text, but her questions are rapid-fire, and I can't concentrate.

"Tillie, I have to tell you something. I need you to sit down." How do I do this? Do I simply rip off the Band-Aid or ease her into the reality? How does one tell another person this kind of news?

"Did she rob you? Has she known all along? I bet she's a bad tipper. Rich people are the worst tippers."

"No, it's not about Acelynn. All was fine. It's Tommy."

A groan filters through the line, and she heaves a breath. "What's he done now? Do we need to bail him out of jail? I know you hate police precincts. And jail in particular."

Yeah. But this isn't about me right now. "He got himself in too deep, Till. With Frank Marchetti."

Her gasp says it all. "What do we need to do?" I hear her car keys jingle as she's readying to come pick me up and ride to his aid.

"Till. I left drinks with Acelynn to take him all the money I had on me, but when I made it to the Laundromat..." Tears burn my eyes. "Marchetti shot him, Till. I saw it happen, and they saw me and chased me, but I got away." I tell her how and then wipe my eyes but force my voice to remain calm and smooth for her sake. Inside, I'm going hot, then cold, on repeat. I might vomit.

Her sobs erupt. I can't understand her garbled words, but instead of asking her to repeat herself, I wait quietly for her to calm down, if she can.

"Are you sure?" she finally asks.

No time to give her the gruesome details. "I'm sure, Till."

"We have to go to the police." Tillie's voice is shaky, but her demand is taut and unyielding.

"You know we can't." Of all people, Tillie knows that cops have never helped either of us. "We can't be certain how many of them are on Marchetti's payroll or could be bribed if confronted by him. I don't have a death wish. Do you?" Tillie needs to think. Be rational. "And let's be honest. They won't believe me. They'll think I did it or had something to do with it. You know this is true."

She sniffs and blows her nose. "But they're going to get away with it. That's wrong. Tommy's going to be thrown into Lake Michigan or buried in concrete, and that's no way to rest in peace."

I'm not sure where or if he's resting at all. I don't believe you live and die and only turn into worm food. I think once you die, your soul lives on while your body decays. "Tillie, he's not there anymore. Just his shell."

"I know, but it's terrible. I tried so hard—"

"Till, you cannot change someone. They have to want to. And Tommy didn't want to. Or he couldn't find the strength to lay off the gambling. Maybe a bit of both. But the past isn't the issue. The present is."

"What?"

"Marchetti and his men *saw* me." Fear races through me, causing my heart to speed at dangerous beats. "It's only a matter of time before he connects me to Tommy and finds me. Which means you and I have to keep our distance from each other for a while. At least until I figure out how to keep us both safe."

Acelynn could help. I would have to swallow my pride, but I'm willing to do it to protect Tillie.

"Charlotte! I don't want to do that."

"Neither do I, but they're going to find me. If they see us together, they might think I've told you what happened, and you'll become collateral damage. I've spent my whole life making sure you were safe. I'm not going to stop now." Tillie is too fragile and weak to go toe-to-toe with Marchetti. Not that I'm some powerhouse, but I've been known to be scrappy. Till doesn't have a scrappy bone in her body.

"Sit tight. Stay away from me. Until I can come up with a plan." I have eighteen hundred dollars and nowhere to go. But I can't remain in Chicago.

"I don't want to be alone," she murmurs.

"You're never alone. Even if we can't be in the same room. I'm always with you, Till. But I need to do some figuring. Don't leave the apartment. Don't come over here. I have no idea how long it will take them to find me. They have so many connections, and Marchetti won't waste time." That terrifies me most. I'm fighting a powerful enemy that wants me dead. Their mission is to steal, kill and destroy, and now they've set their sights on me. How do you fight something so massive, all-encompassing and practically invincible?

After a few more words of consolation, I end the call with Tillie.

It's time to call my sister and see if she really meant that sisters share everything or if it's just mints.

Chapter Twelve

At 1:00 a.m., my sister knocks on my door. I've been watching for her. No time to be ashamed of my meager apartment or luxuries I don't own. My life, and possibly Tillie's, is on the line. I'm on the brink of panicking, but panicking only brings disaster and chaos. My only option is to breathe.

Slow and steady. Calm and collected. Read the situation. The people.

After a deep inhalation, I open the door. Acelynn stands on the other side, mirroring me, except she isn't looking as calm and collected as I am. Her eyes are shifty, and she's clearly shaken. She's still wearing her green high-collared dress, and her cross-body purse is hanging over her chest.

"What is going on?" She enters my apartment and does a quick sweep, but she's too preoccupied with my cryptic call to come quickly to notice anything, or at least to comment.

"Have a seat. I need a favor."

She cocks her head, but she doesn't stiffen or flinch, which means she's open to whatever is coming next. I'm relieved. "You can tell me anything, Charlotte. You can trust me."

A heavy weight lifts from my shoulders, and I sit across from her in the worn overstuffed chair. "It's about my friend Tommy. From earlier."

"Your foster brother. I remember." She leans forward. I have her ear, and I'm so thankful that the timing couldn't be more perfect. That I have found her now in my deepest time of need. That can't possibly be chance, can it?

"Things went bad tonight. I know you have a certain lifestyle and probably only read about bad things in the news or when Philip tells you about a case, but my life is a little different than that, Acelynn. I planned to tell you everything, but I wanted us to know each other better." I'm not sure if I'm telling the whole truth, but it doesn't matter what my intentions are or would have been. "Tommy's dead." I tell her everything about his gambling and why he called, what I saw and who Frank Marchetti is. I explain that his reach is far and wide and deep.

Acelynn listens to every word, her hand wrapped around her gold cross. Then she blows out a heavy breath but remains silent, so I continue.

"They'll find me. I might as well already be dead. I have to run and put distance between me and Tillie. I'd do anything to protect her, and if they see her with me, they'll hurt her or worse." Maybe it's in Tillie's best interest to come with me, leave town as well, but I know she won't. Her saving grace is Marchetti's never seen her with Tommy before.

Not the case for me. If they go through footage from the racetrack, they'll find me on it with Tommy. I thought I could help him control his bets, but I saw pretty fast I couldn't.

"What is it you want me to do? Give you money to go somewhere? Buy you a ticket overseas?"

"Do you think I could come back to Savannah with you? I know you haven't broken the news to your parents. I know how to be invisible, to stay out of the way. It would only be for a short time until I can figure out—"

She stands and puts her hand out to halt me from speaking further. "Say no more. Of course you can. I wasn't sure you would want to travel to Savannah since we just met, and I may have been a little off the rails in the club and given you a bad impression of me…"

She thinks I would think badly of her? My heart slows, relieved she wants me after all. "Of course not. I understand wanting to be someone else for a while. That was nothing—as you can see."

Acelynn hugs me. "Whatever you need. We'll help you. Philip and me. He can look into Marchetti, and I assure you he can't be bought. You'll stay with me."

"I don't want to bring danger to you."

"No one knows I exist in your world. They won't be looking for you in Savannah. And you're right about Tillie. Should she come with us?"

"She won't come. And she's not connected to Tommy that they know."

"But she's connected to you. If they figure out who you are, would they find her to find you?"

"I don't know." That's my biggest fear, but I'm not sure it's realistic.

Acelynn rubs her delicate chin. "If you go without her and this fast, Marchetti is likely to believe you vacated Chicago immediately and told no one. The fact she works for a criminal defense attorney—" her nose turns up at this for a brief second, but then, she's a prosecutor's girlfriend and biased "—will work in her favor. There's a code among them, even the office personnel. They don't snitch. Bringing her means she's in the know. My counsel is to leave her behind and let her be eyes and ears while you come with me. Also, I suggest burner phones in case they have people who can hack cell phones. If what you say is true and he's got the police and other professionals in his pocket, anything is possible, including retrieving texts and track-ing your phone. You and Tillie need burners to communicate."

I hadn't even thought of that. "You're right. I'll tell her. An-other thing…" I need her to know that this will have to be on her dime. I don't have the money she might assume I have. But looking around should be evidence enough. My face floods with heat as I swallow my pride. "I'm a starving artist here, so I can't… I don't—"

"Have funds?" she finishes for me. "Don't worry about it. Besides, you shouldn't use your bank accounts or credit cards anyway. He'll have people who can track you that way. You have to go completely off-grid. As if you, Charlotte Thomp-son, never existed. No paper or money trail. You just…vanish. Does anyone but Tillie know about me?"

Charlotte Thompson doesn't exist. And Acelynn has no clue. I've never mentioned Marilyn's last name. "No."

"We need to leave a fake breadcrumb trail. I'll book you a flight to Tahiti in your name, and we'll charter a private plane to take us home to Savannah—harder to trace, and he won't be-lieve you have the money to do that. Do you have a passport?"

I do, but Charlotte Thompson doesn't. If she sees my pass-port, she'll question me, and all this will burn to ash. "I do ac-tually, but I don't know where it is. I've never used it. It was one of those things where you believe a dream and work to make it happen. Envision it until it's a reality." But that doesn't actually work. I can obtain a passport and speak to myself about going places, but unless I make the money and book the flight, I'm going nowhere. But I was willing to try anything.

She stares at me as if she knows I'm fudging, but then bats her hand as if it's not a problem. "You don't actually need it since you won't be on the flight. You just need to have one to make it appear believable if necessary. That way, if they dig deep, they'll see you've left the country, and that alone will help keep your friend Tillie safe. We need to throw them off in every way. You need to drain your bank account."

"Done. I was taking all I had left except twenty dollars to help Tommy."

Acelynn cradles my face in her hands. "You are my sister. Whatever it takes to keep you safe. Like I said, what's mine is yours."

"Same. Though I don't have much." I hug her and try not to cry. This is the kindest thing anyone has ever done for me.

"It's going to all work out." Acelynn is pacing now as she thinks. I do the same thing. She glances down at my laptop. Another wave of heat fills my face, and I pray she doesn't notice all the tabs open, revealing my research on her and her life. It's one thing to be curious and another to cross into obsession. Or at least, that's what Tillie says. I'm not obsessed with Acelynn or her life. I'm thorough about things. "I'm going back to the hotel to pack. I think the sooner we leave, the better."

"Agreed."

"I saw a corner pharmacy. They'll have burner phones. While I'm out, I'll pick up two of them. We can leave one at an airport locker for Tillie." She notices the laptop again, but quickly looks away. "Once I have our flight secured, I'll pick you up. Don't leave on your own. I'll text you on my way. Be watching and ready to go."

I nod. My stomach feels bruised and battered, and my nerves are frayed. My adrenaline keeps me jittery, but my mind is clear. I've forced it to be. "Anything else?"

She hugs me again and smells of expensive perfume that is sweet and powdery. "Be safe. I won't be too long." On that note, she requests another Uber, then leaves my apartment in the middle of the night. I head to the bedroom to pack a bag, filling it with all my new clothes and hair products I've purchased since learning about Acelynn.

This is not the way in which I wanted to be involved in my

sister's life or to visit Savannah. But nothing has ever turned out the way I envisioned. Not that it's all been bad. Tillie is in my life, and she's been the one constant good thing. She's a reminder that there is good in the world. That when life kicks you and beats you down and stains you crimson, you can be washed clean. Walk in innocence even if it's been stolen from you. I cling to that now.

After packing a large rolling suitcase and a smaller carry-on bag, I make sure my passport is in my purse and scribble a note to the landlord that I've had an emergency crop up and I'll be back soon. I'm never returning. But they can't know that in case someone asks around about me.

Now I wait as Acelynn instructed. She's quick-thinking like me. Did we inherit that too?

I'm wearing the carpet even thinner with all the pacing. How long does it take to pack? How much luggage did Acelynn bring to Chicago? It's late, and it's not the safest neighborhood. Hopefully she didn't enter too seedy of a convenience store to buy burner phones.

Everything is ready to go. I have nothing to do but be alone with my thoughts, and they return to Tommy and the image of him falling to the floor with a thud. The sound of the gun, the metallic smell and the blood. It turns my stomach, and tears burn the backs of my eyes.

Tommy is gone.

And I'm leaving Tillie behind.

Thinking about that is too agonizing, so I pad to the fridge and pour out the remaining milk so it doesn't spoil, then toss out leftovers and anything else that might go bad.

Maybe I can settle into Savannah and create a new life. In time, convince Tillie to fly out. Her boss might have connections with other firms in the area, and she can transfer. I did my homework, and I know that Tybee Island isn't far. Tillie loves the water. I'm not a fan of dipping my toes into the ocean.

I don't like murky water. You can't see what's coming at you from below. I'm not a feet-out-of-the-bed sleeper either. Foster home number three's son used to sneak under my bed and wait for me to turn out the lights only to terrify me.

Third time was the last time before I returned the favor.

The following day I was sent back into the system for defending myself, even if I'd chosen to take the offensive angle to do it. No one believed he'd been terrorizing me first. I learned the only way to defend yourself was to do it secretly and subtly. Without evidence I'd been there at all.

Lights shine in the distance and Acelynn texts she's arriving.

My stomach bubbles and twists. I exhale a shaky breath, grab the trash I've collected along with my bags and leave the apartment.

As I walk into the breezy night air, I inhale the rot from the dumpster. Acelynn exits the Uber and waves. Then the driver leaves. How are we getting to the airport?

"Don't want him to see me, then you. I'll use another car service to pick me up, and then once I'm gone, I'll have you picked up. We can meet at the airport," she says as if reading my mind. It's the twin thing. I knew we had it, and it'll only develop over time.

She's thought of everything so we won't be seen together. "I'm going to toss the trash." I walk to the dumpster, toss in the trash and take a few minutes to gather my bearings. By the time I've pulled it together, I hear Acelynn's ride approach.

It's a sleek black or dark blue car, and my gut signals a warning as goose bumps break out over my skin. I open my mouth to holler for Acelynn to back away. Something isn't right. Something is off.

A quiet pop and hiss sound, and I stand frozen in between two dumpsters as my sister crumples in a heap onto the pavement.

Chapter Thirteen

My hands tremble, and my heart is in my throat. This is a nightmare. This can't be happening. I crouch as a man steps out of the car. He's dressed head to toe in black. A big guy. Like the big guys chasing me earlier tonight.

Marchetti has found me.

Except it's not me lying entirely too still on the dirty concrete. It's my sister. My twin sister. The man holds a gun in his hand and squats, puts a finger to her throat and then shoves the gun in his waistband.

No need for another bullet.

The one he's fired has already done the trick. But the shot was pretty quiet, and I realize he's a professional and has used a suppressor or something. He reaches out his hand, and the trunk pops open. No, he can't take her. I almost scream but stop just in time. I'll only get myself killed too.

It's dark and silent except for the sounds of traffic in the distance.

The hulk of a man lifts her like a limp rag doll. Her purse

falls from the crook of her arm, but he doesn't seem to notice. He drops her like she's nothing into the trunk of the car, and then he quietly closes it and scans the area. I crouch even lower, panicked and unsure what to do. He finally returns to the car and slowly drives away. I can't stop trembling.

My sister is dead. All because she tried to help me.

"I'm so sorry," I whisper. And I am. This was not how it was supposed to be. What will her family think? They don't even know she's here. She hasn't shared that she knows she's adopted. When she doesn't return home, they'll send out a search party. Their family will be broken and empty, and it is my fault. Tillie was right. Contacting Acelynn was a bad idea.

My only sliver of relief is that Tillie will now be safe. They think they eliminated the eyewitness. I'm no longer a threat. But then it hits me.

If I stay and they see me, they'll know I'm not dead.

I'm dead in their eyes. In everyone's eyes.

Staying is still not an option, but where do I go? And with what money? I'm broke.

A thought enters my mind. It's intrusive and disturbing and wrong in every way. And yet it lingers and forms more thoughts. No. No, I could never.

But I'm a survivor, and I have to survive and protect Tillie, even though I have everything to lose if this goes south. I quickly do the unthinkable as my pulse races, and I slink toward her purse, taking it, slipping in the dark, wet blood on the pavement. I notice her cross necklace has been broken and is lying nearby. Grabbing it, her purse and her bags, I toss my own luggage, remove my cash from my wallet, then chuck my purse in the dumpster too. I won't need them anymore.

My only option is to go to Savannah and lie low and think about how to fix this. Acelynn would want me to be safe. And I want Tillie to remain safe. I race with Acelynn's bags down to the corner, then two blocks over, before I use her phone to snag an Uber. As I wait for the driver, who is about six minutes away, I let myself freak out. How could this be happening?

Should I call the police? Why? There's no body. I don't trust them not to be in Marchetti's pocket, and they will not believe me if they aren't crooked; that's a fact. Besides, I am not going to cough up my name for Marchetti to discover he got the wrong sister. If not for self-preservation, then for Tillie's preservation. But Acelynn deserved better than this. I climb inside the Uber.

I'll call Tillie once I arrive at the airport and tell her what's happened and that I'm going to Savannah for at least a day, maybe two. No one will be expecting Acelynn home until Monday. Her house will give me a safe haven and a quiet place to think this thing through. Because I can't *stay* in Savannah. This is just a pit stop to somewhere else. That's it.

My blood pressure is probably skyrocketing. I might stroke out before it comes to boarding a plane for Savannah, Georgia.

I arrive at the airport and check my bags—Acelynn's bags— and roll inside with her purse and carry-on, where I find a semi-quiet spot. The terminal isn't as crowded this time of night. Day. Whatever. Hesitation holds my finger above the number buttons on the burner phone I found in Acelynn's purse. This is insane. Tillie's going to remind me of everything that's happened before. Use phrases like *track record* and *think things through*. Will Tillie believe me? A new fear bubbles in my gut. What if she doesn't? Why should she? No. She knows me. Deep down. She'll believe me.

I call her, and she doesn't pick up immediately, but then I remember she doesn't know this number and that it's me.

On the fourth ring she picks up. "Hello?"

"It's me."

She sighs with relief. "What's taking so long?"

My bottom lip quivers, but I hold it together for Tillie's sake and tell her what else has happened tonight.

A long silence filters through the phone. "They killed her?"

"Yes."

"And now you have all her belongings?"

What does that matter? "Yes."

"Did you call the police?" she asks, her voice squawky and heavy with fear.

"And tell them what? I saw a woman get murdered and thrown into the trunk of a car? That I slipped in her blood and had a meltdown in the alley? She's probably already at the bottom of Lake Michigan or under cement—God rest her soul. I can't tell them who I am. You know this."

I squeeze my eyes closed. Here it comes.

"What are you planning to do, exactly?" she asks warily.

I have to tell her the plan. "It's the only way. I can't be seen in Chicago, and I have nowhere else to go. It'll probably only be a few days max lying low in her home until I can figure out what's next." Or it might be longer. I might have to play her part even if I don't want to. "If word spreads she's missing and it goes national, which it will—she's high-society from a super-rich family, and her boyfriend is a prosecutor—rewards will be astronomical. Marchetti will catch wind. Then he'll know he got the wrong person and hunt me down. He might connect us, and then you'd be a fugitive with me. We can't trust the police. They won't believe me. That I had nothing to do with this. Not to mention we don't know which ones are in Marchetti's back pocket, and if we do find an honest cop, word will travel through the precinct. I can't risk it for my own safety."

"Uh-huh."

"Tillie, you don't think I had anything to do with this, do you? Do you?" I'm about to lose my sanity and go absolutely wild. "You know I would never *kill* someone." However, we both know I'm capable.

"Charlotte, calm down. You're getting flustered and angry, and we don't want that. I never said you killed your sister. You're paranoid."

She's not wrong.

She lets out a long breath through the line. "I don't think you should do this. If you're caught, you know how bad it's going to be."

Nobody knows better, but I don't see any light at the end of the tunnel. "If they find out she's missing and track her here and to me, what do you think is gonna happen? Same bad thing. Either way, I'm doomed. But this way, you're safe."

"Don't make this about me."

My jaw tightens, but I let it pass. She thinks I'm doing this for my own agenda. I'm hurt but not surprised. "I'm leaving a burner phone in a locker for you at the airport." I give the locker number.

"I don't like any of this. I'm afraid... I don't want you to—"

I know what she's going to say and what she means. "This isn't the same thing. I promise. Just keep an ear cocked and go about your business like you never knew me."

"This isn't like pulling the wool over some random joe's eyes. These people are rich. They're privileged and entitled, and they don't play games like you do."

I wouldn't call what I've done games per se. But I let the remark pass because Tillie's upset. "I probably won't even see one of them before I'm gone. I just need a place to think. To be safe. And money. She was going to help us when she was alive. I know she wants to help us in death too. I love you."

"I love you."

I end the call.

My brain is like a ball of rubber bands, the kind all knotted up on Mrs. Donlea's coffee table. Where does she even find that many rubber bands? Now another streak of anxiety rips through me. Who is going to take care of Mrs. Donlea and help her find her hearing aids? Pinching the bridge of my nose, I breathe deep. This isn't that different from other times when

I've had to do things I didn't want to do. When I had to make myself go away for a while and become someone else.

Play a part.

Accept the role.

How many times have I morphed into someone new? Too many to count. This time it's entirely different.

My sister is dead.

I'm now dead to the world. And no one but Tillie even cares. I'm nobody. I'm as invisible now as I've ever been.

A tear threatens to spill out, but I hold it back. Push it in.

I smell coffee and bleach as I head for the women's bathroom. Once I enter, I'm alone. The mirror reflects a tired, worn-down, fearful woman. After unzipping Acelynn's carry-on, I pull out her makeup palette and freshen up, ending with a smear of light pink gloss over my lips.

I use her brush to part my hair perfectly down the middle and pull it back into a tight ball with a few purposeful strays at the base of my neck, then slip into a stall and change into a pair of Acelynn's trendy jeans and a tunic.

Lastly, I slip on her dainty gold cross necklace, which isn't broken after all but had come undone, and return to the mirror.

"I am Acelynn Benedict." No. "I'm Acelynn Benedict," I say with more Southern drawl but not too much. Too much is butchering it. Too much is trying. "I am Acelynn Benedict."

I say it repeatedly until it flows naturally from the words to the dialect, then mimic Acelynn's close-lipped smile.

One beat. Two. My heart rate slows. I take each painful incident, tragedy and fear and tuck them away into tiny little honeycombs.

Tommy's death.

My pain. Tillie's pain.

Acelynn's death.

Marchetti's men.

My fear. Anxiety. Confusion.

The hive I carry in my heart could house dozens of colonies of bees. I'd feel their numbing sting every day. Never receiving sweet honey but the sour taste of experience and heartache.

Now I leave the hive as I have so many times before. I leave the pieces of me and stings of my life behind only to hear a faint buzzing. I look into the mirror once more.

I am no longer Charlotte Kane.

I am Acelynn Benedict.

Then

I lie on my bed, exhausted. The new meds I'm on at my spine-less husband's insistence and Mother's agreement have made my brain foggy, and nightmares keep me up. I've had to take sedatives to keep them at bay, and I'm like a walking zombie. But I need to drown out the terrors in my mind because I'm already dealing with horrors in the daylight hours. Whoever said spooks only come out at night never met my daughter.

The past nine years have taken a toll on me mentally; I will admit that. I'm not the young twenty-year-old socialite flitting from gathering to gala, hunting the right man for my life. I thought I found him. Our pedigrees matched, and we had the whole world as our oyster, or so the cliché goes. I have no idea what that even means. Is the oyster my world because within nestles a pearl? I have a string of those in my jewelry box, and I can assure anyone who asks that they mean absolutely nothing.

Darling Dearest has not met my expectations except in looks. He's a coward and cold. His parental involvement extends to their education and athletics. But neither child brings him joy.

Bubba on occasion puts a twinkle in his eye. A right chip off the old block. Petal is something different. I wonder if deep down he's afraid of her as well.

She knows he has no affection for her, and some days when he's home, she makes strides for his attention, which annoys him. I know his annoyance in the slight tic of his cheek. She's too young to notice the tells, but then I second-guess myself on that. She reads a person in a way a child shouldn't be able to. Maybe Petal is rattling him for her own good pleasure.

Mother picked the children up from school today, and I haven't seen either of them yet. Bubba is in second grade now and never an ounce of trouble. His teachers tell me he's quiet, attentive and a good student.

But wherever Petal goes, trouble always follows.

I focus on my boy. He brings me such joy. Such peace. He never leaves the house or climbs from the car without telling me he loves me or kissing my cheek. He's bright and kind and the absolute light in this dark, empty home.

It's almost four in the afternoon. I've been in and out all day. My eyelids feel like iron, and my mouth is cotton-dry. My limbs cling to the sheets, which are damp with sweat. I want a shower and a meal and to be light on my feet again, but Mother is a dictator when it comes to the pills and making sure I take them.

You're a danger to yourself if you don't.

I'm not the danger in this house. And these stupid pills make me slow and weak as if I'm molasses being poured out of a jelly jar. The door cracks open, and the sunlight from the windows in the hallway blinds my eyes. All I see is a petite shadow entering my room. I thought I'd locked the door, even though Mother scolds me for it.

A bright face with a tight-lipped smile greets me, slamming a barrage of chills through my blood. "Pee-t-t-tal…" I can barely force her name from my lips. My words might be lacking, but my fear is not. My heart isn't missing beats like my syllables. It's galloping as she approaches in her pink top and big-girl jeans. She always thinks she's older than she is. In deviant years, I suppose that's true.

Her hair is pulled back in a ponytail low on her neck, and a few strands around her face are strategically placed. All Petal does is strategic, even down to having my mom fix her hair perfectly so.

"Hi, Mommy," she whispers as if happy to see me. "Nana said you were sleeping, but I wanted to check myself." She never believes a word from anyone's lips. Probably because she's a liar herself.

"Hello, Petal." It's clear in my head, but I hear the heavy slur. "How was school?"

She props her little elbows on the edge of my bed, her chin resting on her hands. "Fine. Stella tripped in the lunch line and broke her tooth." She licks her top tooth. "She cried. Crying is for babies." Sighing as if the subject bores her, she scooches up closer to me, and I glance away. When she's up in my face, I see what hides behind her eyes. It's dark and menacing. Like she wants me to see it.

Only me.

"And Brother did something bad."

My chest tightens. "What do...what do you mean?" I try to rise up on my pillows, but my head might as well be thousands of pounds of cement.

She blinks repeatedly, and a ghoulish smirk plays across her lips. "You don't want to know. It's better you don't, Mommy. You're sick. You rest."

But my heart has climbed into my throat, and it's tight and sore. She slithers onto the bed, and I can't move fast enough. Her little body, with its bony edges, crawls onto my lap. I feel her warm breath that smells of peanut butter and a hint of grape jam.

She raises her hand, and I flinch. I have no strength to defend myself. What mother should even consider the need to defend herself from a child? But she doesn't strike me physically.

Instead, Petal smooths my hair back once, twice, with growing force. I feel the hair pulling tight at my temples and forehead. "Pretty, Mommy. Sick people die," she whispers. "Then people bury them in dirt, and worms eat them." She leans in, and my insides quake. "Worms are going to eat *you*, Mommy." She slurps the air, and her abrasive, tinkling laugh sends a shudder through me.

I have no words.

"Night-night. I'll go take care of Brother. He's been very, very bad." Petal hops off the bed and slips through the door but pivots, her eyes peeping through the crack. "I'll punish him for you." The door closes with a quiet click. I push my feet over the edge of the bed and slip into my satin slippers, then snatch my robe and fumble into it. I'm so tired. So weighed down, and my movements are disjointed, but Bubs is in danger, and I am the only one who knows it. She wanted me to know it. Why?

I stumble from my room and keep my hands along the cool wall. Bubba howls from downstairs, and my breath leaves my body. What is she doing to my baby boy? Where is Mother? "Bubby!" *It's okay, baby. Mommy is coming. I won't let Petal harm you.*

Rushing and holding on to the railing, I descend the stairs, but halfway down, I step on something hard. My ankle twists. I lose my balance and cry out as I flail and fumble, but I'm in no shape to regain my balance.

I fall.

My shoulder and hip hit the wooden stairs, and the acute pain steals my breath as I tumble. A pop fills the air, and a white-hot pain bursts in my ankle, searing to my brain. It's a raging fire. Nausea springs in my gut, and my mouth instantly fills with saliva.

I hit the bottom of the stairs and land on my wrist. The crack and splintering send another wave of searing pain through my body, and I cry out. Black spots dance around the edges of my vision, but I see the living room. The custom-made couch is covered in grape jam and peanut butter. I blink and see Bubba huddled in a corner, his little lips trembling, and then Petal eases into my view. She kneels beside me and cocks her head, dark amusement sparkling in her dead eyes.

I need an ambulance. I need help.

But Petal says nothing, and Bubba is crying and rocking against the wall. She turns to him. "Hush now," she says with such a caustic tone, he instantly dries his tears.

She leans down and licks a blob of grape jam from her index finger. That's when I notice she's only wearing one shoe.

The other is lying halfway up the stairs where I fell.

Chapter Fourteen

The sun is now up, and I haven't slept in almost a full twenty-four hours, but I'm still running on adrenaline and know the wall is coming. I'm going to crash.

Acelynn had a friend drop her at the airport, so I know her car won't be in the parking garage. I take an Uber to her address and pay the hefty fee, feeling guilty about using Acelynn's debit card, but I have no choice.

Now I stand in front of her house in the historic district. A park is directly across the street with pretty redbrick walkways and a large fountain.

Her house is a massive three stories and far bigger than one person needs; it's set back from the road and flanked by a four-foot black wrought-iron fence with little spiky arrows on the tips. It's something out of a movie. Acelynn talks about her historic home near Taylor Square often in her YouTubes, as she's still renovating and redecorating.

A three-tiered curved staircase leads to the large black front door, which pops against the peachy tones of the house. Large side porches grace the second and third floors, giving picturesque views to the incredibly lush courtyard and fountains. Perfect place for entertaining.

I open Acelynn's purse and take out her keys as I move to the side door, which feels more personal than going up the stairs to the front, and I imagine this is the way she entered her house.

This is it. No going back. I'm going to lie low a few days, figure out the next move and then make that move. According to Acelynn's original plans, she's not even due back until tomorrow, so I have a day where no one should be stopping by, and if I don't answer a text, no one will be surprised or suspicious.

Jasmine wafts through the air as I walk into the remodeled kitchen. Stainless steel, farmhouse sink and black-and-white-tiled floor. Butcher block counters and pristine white cabinets. It's a kitchen that doesn't seem well used. It's too clean, a real showpiece, but it looks unlived in.

Part of me feels like I'm invading her space, crossing a line, but she already invited me and wanted me here. It's the fact that I'm supposed to be here with her. She should give me the grand tour and show me to one of the six bedrooms. Right now, it's just me, and I'm in complete limbo.

I leave the kitchen, noticing dog bowls. Acelynn has the two Bolognese. Tallulah and Rue, which reminds me of Rue McClanahan. I love old reruns of *The Golden Girls*.

Acelynn's home is styled with quite a few antiques, not knockoffs—Sobo taught me how to spot the real deal, and these definitely are. Perhaps family heirlooms. Her home is authentic like her.

Me? I'm the impostor in this story.

The main living space is done in pastels, and a gorgeous rug on original hardwoods ties it all together. The massive fireplace, which has been restored to its original luster but converted to gas, catches my eye. Glistening chandeliers—crystal, not plastic—hang in almost every room, but they're not original to the home.

The front double doors open to a winding staircase. As I take each step, I admire the paintings on the walls. Mostly watercolors and replicas, nothing original.

On the second floor, I find an exercise room, a library with contemporary books. Romance. Mystery. Thrillers.

Her spacious home office is organized and tidy. Swatches of fabric drape racks on one wall. Samples of tile, wood and hardware and dozens of framed before-and-after photos grace another wall tastefully. Her desk sits in the center and is an antique, but her chair is modern. I ease into it. Cushy. I place her laptop I brought with me on the desk and leave it closed, then exit her office and enter the primary bedroom. This is where Acelynn will truly be revealed.

The bedroom is the intimate part of a person. Where her public and private life fade and the secret life remains. Where she is at most herself. The walls are a buttery cream, and the original crown molding is painted stark white.

Elegant and charming. Peaceful. The room is equally as tidy. I open the closet and find it as organized as the rest of the house. Acelynn had a place for everything, and everything had a place. Like her.

Unlike me.

Her walk-in closet rivals Paris Hilton's. Not that I've been in Paris Hilton's closet, but I saw a documentary on the people who broke in and stole money from her purses repeatedly and she didn't even know it. I'd notice if a dollar slipped my pocket. I pinch every penny and always have.

I browse through Acelynn's dresses. Suits. Jeans. Purses. Shoes. Blazers.

She wants for nothing.

I flip on her TV for background noise; it's on the news channel. Acelynn would keep up with what's going on in Savannah, what with having a prosecutor boyfriend. As the newscaster talks about a new murder in a townhome nearby, I drift into the bathroom.

Wow. An entire wall is nothing but shelves of nail polish. It's like I've walked into a high-end nail salon. I think of the two shades she stole and put into my handbag. Did she steal all of these? Are these little trophies on display, or am I running wild and loose with my imagination? I peruse the colors in matching shade palettes.

The claw-foot tub beckons me. I'm a sucker for a bath after only having showers. Before I think twice, I plug the drain and run hot water, the steam rising. Then I pour in her vanilla spice bubble bath, and the room fills with Acelynn's signature scent.

My bones ache, and my mind is muddled. I need to relax. Unwind. And think about what moving forward means. I slip into the hot water, and it tingles against my cold feet. Sinking down in the suds, I feel my muscles immediately loosen, and I lie back and close my eyes.

But happy thoughts and relaxation don't come.

A flood of the past few hours hits like a tidal wave.

One bullet blew my life to kingdom come, and another stole my future with my sister. The news reporter's voice reaches my ears.

"An elementary school teacher's body was found at four a.m. this morning by her roommate after returning home for the weekend. She too was left with a valentine on her chest. This makes the fourth victim in six months to die at the hand of Cupid. The FBI's Strange Crimes Unit is in Savannah consulting with local law enforcement."

A serial killer in Savannah? Well, that's great timing on my part. Acelynn never mentioned anything about this, and if she's a news junkie and true crime aficionado, she would have known. But then, I didn't mention a lot of what was happening in my city. And it got her killed. Here's to hoping that favor isn't returned.

"Now, talking with us is Special Agent in Charge Asa Kodiak out of Memphis, Tennessee."

A man's deep and raspy voice takes over. His drawl is deeper than Acelynn's but not quite as stretched as Mrs. Donlea's, who is from Memphis, which tells me he's likely from a different area of the South originally. "First of all, we don't want the citizens of Savannah to panic. Your local law enforcement is working diligently and tirelessly to find this killer, and we're working up a profile presently. We can't yet confirm it's a religiously motivated crime. Do be more cautious of your surroundings. Keep your doors and windows locked, even during the day. Don't put yourself in jeopardy over a nice early summer breeze."

He rattles off more safety guidelines, all of which are common sense and things women should be doing anyway, even if it's not fair we can't walk alone at night or sometimes even in the daylight. I'm not one to shove my feminism in a killer's face to prove I should have a freedom that I don't. Not worth ending up dead or victimized.

Instead, I tune out the voice but then wonder what he actually looks like. However, I'm not ready to leave the tub, so he'll forever be a mystery to me, or I'll look him and this SCU team up online later if I'm still wondering.

I need to try and sleep. Thinking clearly comes so much easier if I can relax. I close my eyes, and a clunking on hardwood piques my attention. But the only sounds are bubbles popping in the water and the steady whir of the air-conditioning. I must be hearing things.

A door shuts.

Nope. I'm hearing loud and clear.

Someone's in the house.

Chapter Fifteen

Another door opens and closes as if someone is moving from room to room. I hurry from the tub, slipping on the tile and biting down a shriek. The water splashes, and I pray no one has heard it. I thought I locked the back door when I entered the house.

All that blares in my mind is a serial killer is loose in Savannah and a special FBI unit is on the scene because clearly the local officials are inept. They can play nice on camera, but you don't call in special agents for tickles and giggles.

I snatch a fluffy white towel and wrap it around my body. Water dots the tile floor, and I'm not sure if I should hide, lock the door or what. No one can know I'm here. I'm lying low and leaving soon. At some point.

Who is in this house?

My heart thumps against my chest, and I back against the bathroom door and quietly lock it. Clicking across hardwood reaches my ears.

Whoever it is has come closer.

The TV goes silent.

They're in the bedroom. They've muted or turned off the TV. Which means they know someone is home. My chest squeezes so tight I can't breathe as a presence hovers on the other side of the door. This can't be happening.

I don't move or breathe, but ease a metal nail file from the vanity as a weapon. If it's not someone in Acelynn's social circle, I'm not taking any chances.

A light knock rattles my head, which rests against the door. "Ace? You home?" The knob turns back and forth. A woman's voice, but I can't say whose. Not a killer, but no relief comes because I can't pretend I'm not here anymore, and I can't be Charlotte Kane without Acelynn or questions will arise. Questions that will end in me going away and not of my own volition.

Pretending on a plane with strangers is one thing. Facing friends and family is a whole other animal, one that is feral, hungry and backed into a corner.

I'm going to wind up bitten if I'm not careful.

"Ace, what's going on?" The voice fills with concern, and if I don't open the door, it's going to be worse than if I do. She might break it down or call the police. No cops. Not a single one. No matter what. She might think I've been murdered by the Cupid guy who is leaving valentines on his victims. It's May, not February. Can't a killer change with the seasons?

"Yeah," I say, my voice cracking. "Hold on. I was taking a bath," I drawl in Acelynn's subtle, elegant tone, one I've rehearsed hundreds of times—but only because I was curious and it's so pretty.

"Why did you lock the door?"

"Hello, a killer on the loose. I'd prefer not to be found naked with a valentine splayed on my chest." That sounds like her snark, and any woman would fear a serial killer no matter how brave or brazen they might seem.

"Well, I'm not the killer. Unlock the door."

To whom? Who is on the other side? I unlock it and open it to a face I recognize.

Bianca Lambert is standing before me, her long, silky blond hair—a shade lighter than mine—hanging to her waist. She has some soft layers around her heart-shaped face, but her bangs are long and parted in the middle. Her icy blue eyes meet mine. "Why are you home a day early, taking a bath?"

She knows Acelynn left town and might be the friend who dropped her at the airport, but I don't know for certain. I have to tread lightly so no one finds me out or I'm a dead woman walking. This will 100 percent appear that I've killed my sister to assume her charmed life.

Which...I kind of did, but no one is going to believe my explanations. Not a single person.

I have no idea what Acelynn used as an excuse for her weekend trip, so I'm not sure how to respond to coming home a day early and have to improvise. "I think I might be getting sick and didn't want to be stuck in a hotel longer than necessary if I did."

Bianca presses the back of her hand to my brow, and her eyebrows rise. "You're a little warm, but it could be from the hot bathwater. Did you even meet with your potential client or enjoy Chicago?" She crosses her arms over her simple white V-neck T-shirt, and I can tell from the material it cost more than the $5.99 Walmart special.

Okay. I can work with a client in Chicago. "I met with her, but no enjoying the city. She hired me, so I'll be traveling some in the next few weeks." Any excuse for my absence and a great setup to me leaving for an extended period of time. Maybe I'll find a new client somewhere that can't be connected to me and that can be my final disappearing act, because I can't actually assume Acelynn's identity. People would eventually find out, wouldn't they?

My answer seems to make sense to Bianca, and she nods.

"Nice. You'll have to take me next time so we can paint the city pink." She winks and kisses my cheek. "You didn't miss all that much anyway."

I follow her into the bedroom, still wrapped in my towel. The TV is on mute. "Why are you here?" If she knows I'm out of town and not due back, then her arrival is odd.

"Because I needed my pink dress back for the barbecue this afternoon, and you said it would be Monday before you returned." She raises her keys. "Pink pact."

Acelynn never mentioned a pink pact, but I suppose every friend group has some kind of standards and rules. Do they answer phone calls on the first ring too?

All the keys are different shades of pink as Bianca jiggles them in my face. They must share house keys, and each friend is represented by their favorite shade of pink. Acelynn's is rose-gold, so I know that's her key—can't say I know the others, but I'll figure it out.

"Well, you scared me. I wasn't expecting anyone, and there's a serial killer running loose thinking he's some kind of bloody valentine, and it's not even February."

Bianca's freshly waxed eyebrow lifts. Can everyone do this except me? "Well, you're spicy today." She tromps past me in her white wedges and into the walk-in closet, thumbing through the dress section until she pulls out a little pink dress with an open back and plunging neckline. "You'll be at the barbecue since you're back now, right?"

What barbecue? Who will be there? I can't go to any event. "I'm not feeling well, remember?"

She pokes her head out of the closet. "You look fine other than you're a little paler than last I saw you. Schedule a spray tan." She shrugs, and a door slams downstairs. Our eyes meet, and she frowns. "You hiding someone?"

I can't tell if she's serious or teasing. Also, what part of sick doesn't she understand?

"B! B." A soprano voice carries up the stairs. "You rifling through Ace's clothing again? Me too." She laughs, and then a face appears in the doorway. Wide amber eyes meet mine, but it's her hair, moving in a liquid bob and the color of pink champagne, that catches my eye.

MacKenzie Newsom. The artsy friend, and one of the richest heiresses in Savannah. Her family has had a powerful presence in the real estate industry throughout the years and presently shares a partnership with Bianca's father. Most of the brothers work for Mr. Newsom and Mr. Lambert. But Acelynn's father is a neurosurgeon, and Drucilla's father is an attorney who brokers real estate deals.

I'm glad I paid attention to Acelynn and studied her social media accounts. This information will be handy.

"If I wanted to invite you to join the closet party, I'd have texted." Bianca rolls her eyes, and MacKenzie makes her irritation obvious in a glare, but Bianca completely ignores her and keeps talking. "And anyway, I'm here for one dress that's mine."

MacKenzie turns her attention to me now. "You told me last week I could borrow a dress for the barbecue." She sneers at Bianca and then turns back to me. "What are you doing here?"

"I live here." My voice is short, but I instinctively know Ace would not be happy about a secret closet raid that they do often when she's not around.

MacKenzie tucks her bangs behind her ears. "But you're home early. Did you lie to us about coming home on Monday so you could dodge the barbecue and a certain someone? What's actually going on? What's she got on you?"

Who is *she*? I'd like to know what's actually going on too or I'm done for before I've ever begun, and I have no game plan concocted. If I'm out, then I'm out with nothing but what's on my back. "Nothing. I came home early because I think I'm coming down with something."

MacKenzie studies me and squints. "Well, you don't mind if I borrow that little fuchsia number for the lunch, do you, then?"

"Borrow it, but don't get anything on it," I say as my mind spins. It's like I've been caught in a tornado, and pieces are flying by, but they're all hazy and undefined.

MacKenzie's nose twitches at my reprimand, but she says nothing and enters the closet to poke around.

"Is Cotton coming?" Bianca asks. Cotton is MacKenzie's younger brother. Does Bianca have a thing for Cotton?

"Now that he's living back at home, probably. You know the expectations." She groans and grabs the dress and a pair of matching shoes, then shrugs apologetically. "Forgive me?" she singsongs, and it's trite and annoying. A gesture—not remorse. If she's the richest of the group, then why doesn't she wear something of her own?

Why did Acelynn swipe lip balm and nail polish?

"Y'all see another woman's been murdered by that serial killer?" MacKenzie's more intrigued than frightened. "Allie Deardon—the latest—lives less than ten minutes from here. Gaw, Acelynn, good thing *you* weren't home. They're all blondes too, you know?" MacKenzie stares into the mirror and messes with her hair. "You think he's some lonely freak who never had a date or a girlfriend?" She grabs a tube of pink tinted gloss and applies it. Without asking. But friends share things, so I don't show my annoyance that this feels more like entitlement than borrowing. "Gaw, it could be you next."

"MacKenzie, sometimes you act like you don't have a brain. Like all that pink dye ate it away." Bianca puts her arm around me. "Don't listen to her. She's evil."

MacKenzie giggles. "Like the devil, baby—I wanna do bad, bad things."

Bianca laughs, and I join in, but I don't understand the underlying joke—and there is one.

MacKenzie pockets the lip gloss as if I don't notice and turns.

"For real, though, we need a night out. We'll plan it at the barbecue when we see Dru. What are you wearing, Ace?"

I can't go to a barbecue, and these women are messing with my head. Why do they steal things, and in front of me? What bad things have they done, and has Acelynn done them too?

Has she done bad things on the same level I've done bad things? No. No, I did things out of necessity. Acelynn has everything she could possibly want. So what gives? "Well, I wasn't attending in the first place because I'm supposed to be out of town. I'm home early because I'm not feeling well."

"You're not pregnant, are you?" MacKenzie asks as if it's not an unusual topic of conversation, and Acelynn did mention she wanted a brood of children.

"No."

Oh, I hope not. What am I going to do if Acelynn is pregnant and confided in one of the friends? Have I said the wrong answer? I search their faces but see nothing besides a mask of contouring, bronzer and mink lashes.

She looks at me, then Bianca. "Did you know she was out of town?"

"Of course I knew." She raises her chin. "But that's neither here nor there. You should go. You seem fine to me."

Does no one care that I might legit be sick? If I told Tillie I wasn't feeling well, she'd have a pot of soup on my doorstep within the hour. Why is it so important for Acelynn to be there? Big deal if she misses a barbecue of some kind. Unless there's something important about it. Something I don't know. Not to mention the *she* who might have something on me. My stomach turns like it did in elementary school when called on to read aloud. My palms are clammy, and I just want these women to leave.

"Yeah, although you need to schedule your spray tan again. That one wore off faster than usual. I'd demand a free one." MacKenzie holds Acelynn's shoes over her shoulder and sighs as if she's now bored because she found what she came for. Why do rich people always want something for free when they have the money to spend? I do not like MacKenzie Newsom. I'm still up in the air on Bianca Lambert.

Either way, I now have to go to this event that I am not prepared for. And if not this event, another one as long as I'm here, which is going to be a while now. I can't up and disappear or the Benedicts will launch a full investigation, including private detectives. Cops will discover that Acelynn went to Chicago and trace her credit card to discover she was indeed there and staying at the Ritz. Anyone could have seen her with a twin. Her parents will know her birth mother is from there and notify the police. Once they've turned over every rock and traced her every purchase and move in the city, they'll find me, and they cannot ever find me. My survival depends on it, and I will not lose my freedom. Whatever it takes. For however long it takes to form a plan that will never connect to me.

"Well, I'm out. See y'all at one." Three hours from now. Bianca waves and casts a long glare at MacKenzie before she leaves, her wedges clippity-clopping down the wooden stairs. But then they stop, pause and return. She pokes her head back into the bathroom. "Hey, where are the babies?"

Babies? What babies?

The dogs.

Acelynn's prized possessions.

"I've barely been home an hour, and yet again, I don't feel well, so I'll pick them up a little later."

Bianca studies me, and it raises a red flag through my system, an internal alarm ringing loud and clear. I've made my first mistake, and it might be fatal. I can't backpedal. Not on this one. All I can do is glare at her as if daring her to judge me or see beyond the superficial and hope it ends the conversation.

I know Acelynn's family and friends need to know she's dead

so they can grieve, bury...something. They'll never find her body, just like Tillie will never find Tommy's.

I'm not insensitive.

I'm scared and screwed.

Bianca tosses a long lock over her shoulder. "Okay. Guess you are really sick. I'm out for real this time."

Why would Acelynn lie about being sick? Does it have to do with the *she* at the barbecue? Has Acelynn cried wolf before, and if so, why? None of these answers will be found on a YouTube video, but I desperately need to know them before I walk blindly into the lion's den and am found out. Sunk.

Dead.

Now I'm alone with MacKenzie, hoping she'll leave too. She whispers, "Gaw, B can be total trash sometimes, you know? Why does she even care about your dogs, anyway? She hates them."

I have no clue how to respond to that, so I say nothing.

Awkward silence envelops us, and I'm about to ask a question that might help me gauge the afternoon and the mystery woman who will be there, but MacKenzie taps the door frame twice. "I should go too. Feel better and see you later." She kisses my cheek, leaving sticky gloss residue, and toddles off, but she's wearing designer tennis shoes that make no noise.

I am not ready for this on any level. I wipe off the gloss as my stomach churns.

Then it dawns on me. B's shoes clip-clopped. MacKenzie's made no noise.

And what I heard on the stairs earlier were boots and a heavy gait.

Too heavy and loud to be either of them.

A man has been, or still is, in this house.

Chapter Sixteen

No one's in this house that I can find, but it's almost six thousand square feet, so it's possible I missed something. I return the Mace to Acelynn's purse and the fireplace poker back to its holder, then collapse on the chair in the sitting room that faces the street. Joggers and dog walkers are going by as if a psycho isn't on the prowl for pretty blonde girls.

Dogs!

I have to get the "babies." Earlier I noticed a little closet in the laundry area full of dog clothing. Dogs dressed like humans—not a fan. I have Acelynn's phone and scan it for the info about the dog boarding and grooming shop. Then it's time to play the part after finding an allergy pill in the medicine cabinet over her bathroom sink.

I pull my hair into her signature bun. I don mink lashes and apply gloss. Her everyday wear is a floral designer sundress and strappy sandals to make it casual.

May heat in Savannah is suffocating and nothing at all like Chicago. Granted, we get summers and heat and humidity, but this is some kind of entity that haunts the city, ready to scorch it like dragon's breath.

After grabbing Acelynn's purse, I lock the door and go onto the app to secure an Uber. Acelynn has a car, but I'm not ready to drive in the city. Not yet. I thought rich people used private car services and stuff like that. Finally, my car arrives, driven by a woman who's a retiree and has gone overboard with cloying car scent spray. When she parks at the front door of the groomer's, I let her know I'll be a while and not to wait. Truth is, I don't want the small talk, and I don't want her to remember me. The more invisible I am, the better.

I enter Paw and Play, a fancy brick building that smells like dogs and flowers, which don't mix, in my opinion. Dogs are barking and howling. Workers in khaki pants and blue polos grin as they pass by with dogs on leashes and cats in carriers.

My nose twitches even with the allergy pill. That will be a dead giveaway.

I approach the counter, and the redhead glows with delight. "Miss Benedict! You're a day early. Miss your babies, did ya? They've been gold. They're having their massages, so it'll be fifteen, maybe twenty minutes."

"No problem." Dog massages? Seriously? My head will simply explode by then.

"Can I get you a latte or anything while you wait?"

A latte? That's when I notice other people waiting with drinks. "No, thanks." The last thing I need is caffeine. I'm already twitchy.

Instead I sit in a chair near the window. It's too warm and bright, but I don't feel like moving. Opening Acelynn's phone, I scroll through her photos. The ones she hasn't blasted on social media. Perusing them will hopefully help me put pieces together. I find photos of her, MacKenzie, Bianca and Drucilla in various places. Tons of photos of food and drinks.

Photos of the whole crew, the girls and their brothers. Do

pretty people gravitate to other pretty people? I can't find a single homely friend or ugly man.

A gaze rests on me, and my radar pings. To my left is a handsome man with coal-black hair and equally dark eyes, staring.

"What's your issue?" Then I remember I'm Acelynn, and she would never be so blunt. And he might know her, which is why he's gawking. Not to mention I'm in the South, and I'm fairly certain people are more polite here, but who knows?

His eyebrows twitch, and he smirks. "I'm sorry, but you look nervous. Your first time leaving your pet?"

I realize I'm bouncing my knee, and my thumbnail is in my mouth. "Yeah. I mean, no."

"Confused?"

"Nosy?" I need to stop blurting. Be Acelynn.

He laughs. "Job hazard."

"You a shrink?"

"Some days. Why? You need one?" He's getting a kick out of this. I am not.

"Everyone needs therapy." Fact. Not everyone can afford it, like myself. Also fact.

"Fair enough." He's wearing nice jeans and a maroon polo shirt with a sports jacket over it. He's not rich, but he's not living at the poverty level. The fact he's in a bougie dog resort is enough to know that. His fingernails are trimmed and clean. Not blue-collar. He reaches out his hand for me to shake it. "Christian Patrick. Nice—"

A huge commotion breaks out, and I stand along with the man beside me. What's back there, Bengal tigers?

"Grab him!" someone yells, and before I can register what's happening, a huge beast bursts into the waiting area and rushes me.

I shriek as I'm knocked off balance and topple backward.

The man next to me bolts into action. "Kitten! Down. Off. Now."

A massive slobbery fur creature obeys, and Christian's face turns bloodred. "I'm sorry. He's sweet, but he's a nightmare."

I've been violated by Cujo. Smoothing my dress, I frown. "This is your animal? He should be arrested for disorderly conduct." I'm not even kidding.

A tech holds his leash and wears an apologetic expression. "He got away."

"I noticed," Christian says. "I think we all noticed."

"I am so sorry."

"No worries."

Speak for yourself. Wait. "Your boy dog is named Kitten?" Not that I'm pro-gendered-names. But it's weird and grates on my nerves, or maybe I'm down to frayed wires and overly sensitive.

"I rescued him at the beginning of an ironic stage in my life." He hooks the leash on the animal and pets his enormous head. "He's a Saint Bernard."

He's something. "Did you ever think you'd come out of it and be stuck with a horrible name for a dog?"

"I'll let you know when I'm out." His eyes are playful and kind. He's not trying to be funny. He's naturally humorous, and I like it. In a different time and place, I might flirt. He's good-looking in a boy-next-door way, with a lopsided smirk that reveals a crooked eyetooth. The flaw makes him relatable.

But this isn't another time or place.

"Miss Benedict, your babies are ready."

Great. My stomach knots. I am so not good with animals. Before I walk to the counter, I look at this Christian guy. "That's mean, to name your dog something it isn't. It's labeling, and that can be destructive." I've had far too many labels slapped on me. I'm still working at scraping them away. *Troubled* is the one that stuck most.

He walks with me to the counter as if he's supposed to.

The redhead holds two balls of white fluff, one in each arm. "Tallulah and Rue are all clean and ready to go."

"And you're giving me fits over *my* dog's name?"

I agree the names are pretentious, but I didn't name them. If it were my choice, they'd be Cloud and Q-tip or something. I ignore him and reach for the dogs. The one on the right growls while the other one yaps.

"Guess they're mad at you."

No. They know I'm a fake. "Don't be mad, angels." It comes out stilted. "Mommy's back." That's what Acelynn calls herself concerning the dogs. Mommy.

Lady-behind-the-Counter puts them into a big, fancy purse and hands it over. I give her Acelynn's credit card, and we finalize the transaction. Christian is still lingering and follows me out. Between the dogs yipping in the purse carrier and my own purse, I'm having a hard time wielding Acelynn's phone to call for an Uber.

"You need a ride?"

"With a serial killer on the loose? No, thanks, pal."

He chuckles. "Fair. But I'm not a serial killer."

"Says every serial killer until you wake up in a dungeon chained to a wall or dead with a valentine on your chest."

He fishes into his sports coat, and I spot his sidearm. No. He doesn't even need to say it. I've figured it out and instantly quake. A cop. He's spoken to me. Heard me use Acelynn's name. His job is to remember, and the fact his massive, hairy dog nearly took me down for the count will ensure he will not forget my name or my face.

Things could not be worse. Is the universe holding a grudge against me for littering or something?

He shows me his badge. "I'm actually hunting that stupid guy."

"He's not that stupid if he's killed four people and gotten away with it. Seems like you're the stupid one." Why can't I stay in character and say less memorable things? Because it's a cop. Now I'm nervous, irked and nauseous.

Unoffended, he nods. "You're honest. That's refreshing."

No one thinks being called stupid is refreshing. He's delusional, a liar or something I can't pinpoint but that piques my curiosity, and I can't run down that rabbit trail. Not with a cop. However, I do feel the irony to my bones.

"The least I can do is give you a ride home after what Kit Kat here did."

"I'm good." I need him to walk away and forget me and this day. But he's not making it easy.

"I'm safe."

"These days cops aren't as safe as they once were."

"Not every apple in the barrel is bad." He points in the air to punctuate his truth. "Miss Benedict. Didn't get your first name."

I can't shrink into the background. He won't seem to let me, and now he's forcing me to admittedly impersonate someone, which is a felony. A felony I can't afford to be saddled with. "Acelynn." Did he see me use her credit card? Because that's another charge, meaning I'm double screwed.

"Acelynn, come on. I'll drop you at home. Or wherever you're headed."

He's not going to let it go. If I push too much, he'll get suspicious, and I definitely don't need that. I rub my sweaty palm on my dress. "Okay."

I walk with him to the unmarked car. He lets Kitten into the back seat, and I sit up front. The dogs are shaking and whining, but there's nothing I can do about that, and I pretty much feel the same way.

"Where we headed?"

I give him Acelynn's address.

"Nice area. You know, you actually look familiar to me, but I can't place you. What do you do for a living?" No. No. No. He cannot be familiar with me. This is the worst-case scenario.

"I'm an interior designer with expertise in historic homes." I bend and try to pet the pooches, but they shy away, then allow me to rub their cottony heads.

"Huh. I recently inherited an old historic home. My grandmother passed."

"I'm sorry."

"Yeah, it's a real run-down piece of work. Been passed down through the family since the late 1800s."

"I meant about your grandmother."

He grins. "I know. Thanks."

I dislike this man. He's too interesting and honest, and that's another red flag in my book. "You can work with bones. And I don't mean your grandmother's." I mimic his dark humor and he cackles, but I know men like this. They use easygoing banter and humor to soften up suspects, make them feel like everything is super-chill before they drill down and uncover the lies because you let your guard down. I'm not letting my guard down. I'm just playing his game. It can't be anything else. No one is this nice for no reason.

"My time is already stretched thin, and to be honest, I'm the furthest thing from a Property Brother." He's silent and then… "Maybe you could give me a consult at the very least?" He stops at the red light and looks at me. "I know where I've seen you."

My insides wilt, and heat washes through my chest, tightening it. "I have interior design videos, and if you're searching for *Property Brothers*, then you probably—"

"Nope. You date Philip Beaumont."

I was not expecting this. Not a chapter I want to discuss, because it's blank, and I nod my response.

His nostrils flare. Then he quickly gains composure, but I've already seen it. Christian Patrick doesn't like Philip Beaumont, and that's odd since they fight on the same side of the law. Why wouldn't he like the prosecutor? Who's the shady one? Christian or Philip? All I've managed to accomplish in the few hours since I've arrived is collect a stack of questions that, if not answered, have the potential to seal my fate.

He makes small talk until we reach Acelynn's home. "You got a card?" he asks.

"What kind of card?"

He squints as if to decipher if I'm joking or not. "Business."

"Why?"

"The consult? Help me with a paint color or give me a list of contractors."

He's not flirting, so this isn't some kind of shtick to lure me to his place, but showing up at his home does the opposite of making me invisible and forgettable. "I'm pretty booked."

He opens his mouth, but his phone rings. He answers, then listens.

"I'm on my way." He sighs. "Gotta go. Duty calls."

I hope his duty never brings him back to me.

Chapter Seventeen

The dogs trot around the house looking for Acelynn and peering up at me, confused. However, they're not growling or yipping at me anymore. I gave them each treats from the glass jar on the counter, and that seemed to show them I'm a friend, not a foe.

But I'm not sure that's true. I feel more like a foe.

I finish applying highlighter to my nose and cheeks, then stare in the mirror. Upon first glance or even a few, no one will suspect I'm anyone other than Acelynn. Except the Benedicts. Parents will know their daughter. Teddy will know his sister. They're close, and the photos on her social media accounts attest to that.

Can I avoid them? I have to at all costs or I'm going to be outed. That's not undeserved, but going down for a crime I didn't commit is off the table. Once they discover their beloved daughter is dead—missing, rather—with no one else but me to witness it, my coffin is nailed shut. Without question. A slam dunk. No one will believe I didn't murder her in order to assume her identity, to live the life of luxury. Not now that I'm here. My murky past will work against me.

Acelynn has zero gates up, and I don't see kennels. Looks like Tallulah and Rue have free rein. I let them outside to do their business. Then they return. Maybe owning dogs won't be so bad.

I found the Newsoms' address, and since Acelynn would never Uber to a weekly event, I have to take her car.

After snagging the keys and putting the address into Waze, I set off into an ocean full of sharks, and I'm the chum in the water. The diver without a cage. My throat is dry and tight, and every mile closer sends my pulse to dangerous levels. I have to pull this off, but how, when I've already raised a red flag with the white fluff balls and put a cop on my radar, all within less than twelve hours after arriving?

Acelynn's phone rings, and my nerves go off the rails. Just when I'm working to come to terms with this disaster, Philip Beaumont is calling.

Did he know Acelynn was out of town? Of course. He's probably checking in, but she's a busy woman, and blowing off one of his calls isn't a big deal. Except Acelynn ignored a few calls when she was with me. After I let the call go to voicemail, I check her phone. Three missed calls, all from Philip. Should I be concerned? Was she simply soaking up the time with me or is something else going on? I can't dodge him forever, especially since he's called three times before.

Wait. Did she end up talking to him? She was on the phone in her hotel room. I scroll back through the recent calls list. Unknown number. Huh. I click the blue circle with the *i* and see an incoming call that lasted fifteen minutes. Who was she talking to while I soaked in the hotel tub? Who else would she call *babe*?

What if Philip's supposed to be at this event? Does he think he's attending alone because Acelynn is out of town? Is this going to be one more thing that blocks my path to escaping without anything linking back to me?

I'm pretty sure I'm going to be sick until I arrive at my destination. And then I'm definitely sure I'm going to be sick. Tillie was right. I'm way out of my league this time. The Newsoms' mansion reminds me of a movie set in the Deep South, with pristine white columns that grace a long porch. Live oak trees flank the long drive up to the house, and curtains of Spanish moss drape the branches. Their tables are probably covered in white linen cloths, with crystal goblets and shrimp forks as everyday settings.

The drive is crowded with two rows of cars, meaning it's crowded inside, and that may be my saving grace.

My burner phone rings. Tillie. I need to answer because it gives me a reason to stay inside the car, where I'm cocooned and safe for the moment, and that's the rule. Always answer the phone, preferably on the first ring, but a roaring Harley-Davidson draws my attention as it pulls up beside me.

The rider removes his helmet, and I'm staring at Bianca's brother. Ford Lambert reminds me of rakes I've seen on covers of old romance novels one of my foster moms read. Big, wide blue eyes meet mine, and dimples crease like craters in his clean-shaven cheeks. He needs a haircut, but the unruly look fits his image. A brooding troublemaker who needs the right woman to tame his heart.

No, thanks.

I've now missed Tillie's call, which will send her over the edge, and Ford Lambert motions for me to roll down the window. Not ready to start the game, I raise my phone to signal I'm on it, and he laughs and touches his fingers to his thumb in rapid movement to signify I'm blabbering.

I roll my eyes. That's what Acelynn would do. He laughs again and points to the porch. I nod, and he struts to the house.

If this entire event could be mimed, I'd be gold. I file away that Ford and Acelynn pick and tease in good fun.

I return Tillie's call, and she immediately answers. "Everything okay? What's going on? I'm freaking out over here, Char. You know the rule." Tillie's mouth is on rapid-fire.

"Lying low didn't go as planned."

She pauses for a brief second. "What does that mean? What have you done, Charlotte?"

For once I wish she would think the best of me. I haven't given her much cause, though, so I refrain from voicing the thought. "Nothing. I did nothing. I hit a snag through no fault of my own." I share everything that has transpired since my arrival in Savannah, including the creepy serial killer at large.

"Who do you think was in her house?" Tillie asks. "Besides the women, that is."

"I don't know, but I'm adept at listening for footfalls." Too many entered my room at night over the years. "Someone who didn't want to reveal themselves." I can't be sure if that person thought he was alone or didn't care. Was he a stranger who was spooked by Bianca and MacKenzie, or was it someone Acelynn would have known? And if so, why sneak around in her house without her knowledge?

And what happens if he comes back?

"This is too dangerous. You have no idea what you've walked into, Char. People are never what they seem. We both know it, and the clients at my firm prove it on the daily. Have you ever thought she jumped so fast to meet you to escape something scary there?"

No, but my pride just took a hit. Tillie didn't mean to offend me, but here I am, offended. "I think she wanted to meet her sister as much as I did." Now I wish I hadn't mentioned the man in my house. But she has me wondering. What if that's true? What if Acelynn's trip was twofold? What if my email came at just the right time for her to run from something even as minor as a conflict with a friend or woman or mistress or… who knows what MacKenzie was referencing?

What if she'd been hearing footsteps in her house before I ever did?

"Just watch your back, Charlotte. We all know you're tough as nails, but you're not invincible, and I worry about you. Use the pretense of being sick to your advantage to lie low, and don't fall into this. Don't stay longer than you need to."

"What does that mean?"

"It means you and I both know you can pull this off better than Matt Damon in *The Talented Mr. Ripley*. You can't fool me. Stop pretending you're scared to try."

"I'm not pretending." Not really, and I wasn't scared until now—now that what I thought was straightforward might be all kinds of corkscrewed. I know what happens if this spins out of control—if *I* spin out of control. My life is over in so many ways. But she is right. I can…spiral on occasion. I'll be extra-cautious. I won't allow myself to be caught up in something I might not be able to escape.

Besides, I'm not fully sure I've stepped onto a stage that's been honest. I assumed I was walking into a happily-ever-after, but now…now I can't help but think I might have walked into a horror film. Instead of worrying about evading the truth and being caught and the dire consequences that brings to me, I have to worry about something darker, more sinister.

I'm in the middle of act two without a script, and there's a plot twist I haven't seen coming.

But I'm going to try. The alternative means I'll never have my life—any life—again.

If this fails, I might as well be dead.

Bianca steps outside and waves.

"I have to go, Till. I'll do my best and check in when I can. I promise." I end the call before she can protest or revisit my sins that can't ever be forgotten and absolutely will be held against me in a court of law.

"Where have you been?" Bianca asks as I reluctantly approach. MacKenzie marches out behind her with Ford and her brother, Cotton—his blond hair a clear indicator of his name—in tow. A flush creeps through my insides, and my cheeks grow hot. Could one of these men have been inside Acelynn's house earlier? I can't let my new ideas about Acelynn and the thoughts planted by Tillie throw me off-kilter.

I've spent hours studying my sister. I can do this. I have to do this. Inhaling deeply, I close my eyes, and when I open them, I am her. "I had to pick up the babies and change. Some moron's dog broke loose and mauled me. I should have sued."

Bianca shakes her head, and Cotton laughs. A few of my tight muscles relax. So far, so good. But I can't forget that I raised a red flag earlier with Bianca Lambert over the dogs, and I can't afford to raise another. I smooth my rose-gold strapless maxi dress and catch a delicious whiff of smoked meats as a cloudy plume rises over the massive home.

"Dru's not here yet." MacKenzie peers at me from under faux lashes. "Lucky for you."

Dru must be the "she." Okay, I can work with that. We're on the outs, or she's simply mad at me. Either way, it's not the end of the world.

"She never mentioned not coming," Bianca said. "She wouldn't miss it. That's the rule. And we must make our mommies happy."

MacKenzie snorts, and Cotton laughs but nods. "I called, but it went to voicemail."

Ford smirks at me but answers MacKenzie. "Not everybody is at your beck and call."

"Well, they should be," she says and frowns like a petulant child.

"You smother her," Bianca says, and MacKenzie ignores the barb like it's as normal as the sun rising and setting.

"Excuse me for caring about my friends."

"If that were true, we'd excuse you." Bianca winks at me, and I wink back. Then she frowns and cocks her head. Have I made another mistake? I've never seen Acelynn wink before, but how else would she have responded?

"I talked to her Thursday morning," Cotton offers. "At the office. She was hungover."

The unanimous eye rolling reveals a lot about Dru. "Gaw, that girl drinks too much," MacKenzie says. "She's going to turn out like her mother."

"Like all our mothers," Cotton adds. "Book club? More like wine club."

"For real," Bianca adds. "Speaking of wine, I could use a glass or five myself, and if any one of you hags or stags compares me to my mom, I'll stab you with the heel of my shoe."

Cotton winks. "Yes, ma'am." He motions for her to lead the way into the house. Into the lion's den, where the Benedicts will be, and maybe even Philip, who I can't avoid forever.

MacKenzie stops me in the foyer. "Where are the dogs? And you still don't look well." Without asking, she leans in and pinches both of my cheeks. "Add some color. If you aren't pretty, you aren't anything."

"Then your art is nothing," Cotton adds and breezes inside.

"The babies are home," I say.

"Gaw, you *are* sick," she adds, and Bianca squeezes between us, studying me.

"I've been telling you both this all morning. Why act surprised?" Then I make a bold move. "And stop staring at me like that." My words are an ice bath, and then Bianca grins.

"Well, you're not too sick to be hateful. There's hope for you yet." Bianca holds out her hand and takes mine, leading me toward the hubbub. "Let's get our drink on and try to eat ribs gracefully." The group rallies around me, and I recognize that I'm the nucleus of the group, even if Bianca is a step ahead, leading.

About a dozen men and women mill around the house as music wafts inside. Eighties hair bands. Marilyn always loved them too. Will I revert back to the music I grew up on when I'm in my mid- to late fifties?

Acelynn's phone buzzes in my pocket. I check it to see it's Philip calling again.

I decide on a text to appease him.

Can't talk right now. Call you later.

Maybe it's not Acelynn's parents who will out me as a fraud, but the man who worships her, whose job trains him to spot liars and fakes in a court of law.

Mrs. Newsom approaches. I'd know her from photos Acelynn has posted, but MacKenzie is her spitting image, aside from the pink hair. "Oh, there you are, darling. I wondered when you'd arrive. We all know it's not a party until Acelynn graces the room."

MacKenzie's nostrils flare, and her jaw tightens. "Yes, she's the light of the world."

"I'm pretty sure that's Jesus, sis." Cotton is met with a scowl, and MacKenzie finds a bottle of wine on the bar and pours a glass. Bianca follows suit, leaving me with Cotton, Ford and Mrs. Newsom.

"Renee, where's the meat platter?" calls a man who must be Mr. Newsom.

"Gavin, I swear you're blind. This is why I like caterers and servers. It's on the outdoor table by the grill." She huffs exactly like her daughter. "Is Philip attending?" she asks me.

"I—uh—I'm not sure." Is that why he keeps calling? He hasn't responded to the text I sent. "Technically I was supposed to be out of town on business, but I thought I might be coming down with something, so I cut my trip short. B and Mac dragged me out of the house."

"Nice try," Ford says. "No one drags you anywhere you don't want to be dragged."

Redirect. "I did want to come, but I hope I don't spread any germs."

"Well, go pour a drink and relax. I'm sure you'll be fine. Where are the babies?" The dogs. Who would have guessed the dogs would be my downfall? Mentally, I kick myself.

"I'm feeling so poorly, I left them at home."

She kisses my cheek like MacKenzie did, only without the sticky gloss residue. "Poor thing, you *are* sick. Well, take it easy. Maybe skip the hot tub."

Bianca brings me a glass of red wine, and I pretend to sip.

A man who reminds me of good bourbon and days in the sun approaches, and when he stands next to Ford, I see the resemblance. Hudson Lambert. "A detective with the Savannah PD is here with an FBI agent, and they'd like to talk to us individually."

"What about?" Ford asks.

Hudson's words don't register. I've lost my focus. My footing. And maybe my life.

Detective Christian Patrick, from the boarding and grooming shop, enters the kitchen with an almost silver fox. Must be the man with the alluring voice on the news earlier. The FBI agent for the Strange Crimes Unit. Asa Kodiak.

He doesn't worry me.

But Christian meets my gaze, and I know trouble is circling.

Then

"You are in big trouble." When Bubba's father arrives home, he's going to be punished. It's not like Bubs to act out this way. He would never do what he's been accused of doing—never hurt Mr. Whiskers in such a horrendous way.

However, Petal would.

Petal would plant matches in his room and steal his little Swiss Army knife to frame him. Then sit back and enjoy the show, which I don't understand. Petal protects Bubs. Or... maybe that's not what she's doing. She's controlling him and punishing him.

"Tell me the truth," I say. "Did you do it, or are you covering for your sister?" Again.

She's blamed him for all sorts of things, and he never denies it. Mother disciplines him, and that's about it. She says I spoil him and am too hard on Petal, and that's why Petal, on occasion, acts out. That's garbage. Petal has fooled the world.

Not me.

Bubba glances from the kitchen to the hallway that leads to

the living area. Petal stands there, her hair shiny and bright, but her eyes are simmering with cool rage. I'm not imagining it, and I'm sick of the gaslighting. I know I've done some sketchy things. Who hasn't? But Petal…

She's evil.

I've thought about taking her to a convent, where she might be kept at bay, or having a priest come in to anoint the place with oil or holy water or whatever. We're Baptists, so I'm not sure how all that works, but I'm willing to burn sage if it'll cast out what's in her.

Except I don't know that this kind of wicked can be cast out. I think it's just her. An embodiment of evil. Not like anyone will listen. Apparently, my thoughts are a sham.

So is my marriage. But it's cheaper to keep me than divorce me, and I'm no threat. These days I go nowhere. I used to play tennis and belong to a bridge club. I chaired committees and charities and had lunch every Thursday with sorority sisters from the University of Georgia.

I miss Thursdays with them. We've been fast friends since we rushed all those years ago. We met our men and all migrated to Savannah to work and raise our babies together. But college-girl dreams aren't reality.

Life isn't full of fairy tales, though every Thursday we pretended it was. No one's husband is a hound or withdrawn or cold. Our children are picture-perfect and gifted, as well as kind, sweet and polite. They'll be rushing too and following in their perfect mothers' footsteps. They aren't deviants or troublemakers or average.

I'm not sure why we lie to each other. Sisters should tell each other the truth. If you can't be honest with a sister, who can you be transparent with?

Strangers. Therapists. But you have to pay them to listen to your truths—and lies. Then they attempt to fix the problem, which is not the same as being supportive. I haven't spoken a single word to my friends about Petal. We pass off her behavior as being too gifted and bored. And, of course, her being in proximity to children who have accidents is all coincidence, which my own family believes.

I'm the only one who knows the truth. And maybe Bubba, but he'd never rat her out or admit to anything.

I believe it's fear. How does a fearful soul speak out if they know repercussions are inevitable and they will be worse than the initial suffering?

I was gone for three months, and upon returning home, things have changed. The woman in charge is no longer me. Maybe it never has been.

It's Petal. At ten years old, she runs this house and everyone in it. Whether by force with Bubba or flattery with her father or gentleness with my mother. She is the master manipulator.

I'm not saying children don't know how to manipulate at an early age. The crocodile tears and the pouty lips for one more cookie. But this manipulation is mature and refined. She's always been able to communicate well and concisely. I can't deny my child is gifted and bright. She is. And I'm not saying that as a doting parent. I do not dote on Petal.

I fear Petal.

I loathe Petal.

But I also won't deny she's light-years ahead in the brains department. Calculated and cunning. If something isn't in her, spawning and spurring her, then I don't know how else to describe it.

"Petal," I say now, "leave us. This doesn't concern you."

"Brother is my business, and I'm about my brother's business." Her smart-aleck remark comes from forcing her to go to Sunday school. We aren't regular churchgoers. We're from the South, so we know God by geography. But I'm desperate for help. Even God's. She hates church but plays the part when we attend. She's a little chameleon changing colors expertly, and on those Sundays, she's all white, down to her little New Testament. But she is not whiter than snow. I'm not sure God can wash her clean or if He'd even want to.

She's snowed everyone, including the pastor, who praised her one Easter Sunday for knowing scripture. She recited it for him, saccharin loaded in her animated words. And it wasn't John 3:16. No, the verse she knew was terrifying for a child, but she loved it, not due to the fact it forewarns of sin but that it's bloody and dark and speaks of her origin.

No one sees that but me.

And if thy hand offend thee, cut it off: it is better for thee to enter into life maimed than having two hands to go into hell, into the fire that never shall be quenched.
—Mark 9:43

"This is not your business." I've been hiding my meds under the mattress, and I'm feeling stronger in so many ways. I don't need them, but again no one listens. I have to hear that it's the meds that make me better, and I may think I don't need them because I feel good, but to come off them means I'll feel bad again and become confused, even hallucinate. "Upstairs now or I'll escort you up myself."

At first, her eyes widen. She's not accustomed to being spoken to harshly. But then they narrow to slits. "Yes, Mommy." The sweetness in her tone sours my stomach. She turns, leaving Bubba with one last withering look before she retreats.

"Bubba, did you hurt the Wilkersons' kitty?"

"Yes, ma'am," he says, and his eyes shine with moisture.

"You don't have to cover for your sister. Did she do it?"

He shakes his head.

"Did she make you hurt their kitty?" I ask.

He doesn't respond. Petal's influence to harm a cat will scar him for life. It's sick and disturbing. I wasn't even there, and I can't scrub the image from my head. And if she can do that to a cat, what will she do to a human being—to Bubs?

Rage boils my blood, and I march in my slippers and gown up the stairs and down the hall into Petal's lavish room. Soft pastels and everything girlie. I should paint the walls black like her heart.

Everything is nice and tidy and in its space. Petal has always been organized and neat.

"Stop playing games," I hiss and close the door behind me.

She sits on her bed, stroking a soft white stuffed kitty cat, and her head slowly tilts in innocence. "I'm not playing a game, Mommy."

"You made your brother hurt that cat." I pause and try to maintain eye contact, but it's hard. "I don't know what game you're up to, but you can't have him. He's not yours." My heart is thumping so hard and fast it hurts.

She stops stroking the cat, then slowly rises to her knees on the plush pink comforter. Holding my gaze, she squeezes the stuffed kitty's neck and begins to twist it around and around.

"Mommy, you're sick. Everyone knows you're sick. Everyone feels sorry for you. Your brain tells your heart things that aren't true. That's what Grandmother says."

She twists. Tighter. Tighter.

"Do you know what happens to sick people, Mommy?"

My throat dries out and forms a sandy, aching mountain that prevents me from breathing. Is this another worm-food reference?

"They die!" The head pops off the cat, and the foam inside springs out like entrails. She throws the cat's head, and it lands against my cheek. I shriek and bat it away. Then she strokes the headless animal and purrs. "No one will ever believe the things your brain tells your heart. But don't worry, Mommy. I believe you."

Then she rips out the stuffing and shoves her hand down the

cat's neck, bringing up a fistful. "I hold your heart. Your sick, sick heart. It'll all be okay now," she singsongs, and the blood drains from my face; my legs turn to iron.

My daughter has shown me her plan. My demise.

No. She isn't going to win this battle. I'm not fighting for only me. I'm fighting for Bubs.

But I cannot save my son.

Not without removing my daughter from our lives.

Now that I'm seeing more clearly, I know what I have to do. What needs to be done. I have to cut off the offending hand. Maim the mistress of evil.

After all, that's what the Bible says to do.

Chapter Eighteen

Detective Patrick's coal-black eyes meet mine and register surprise, but he masks it quickly. He's wearing the same thing I saw him in earlier at the groomer's. His back is made from titanium. He's not intimidating but confident and clearly comfortable in a room full of people. And this isn't just any people group, but some of the most influential and wealthy in all of Georgia. He's either comfortable around old money because he's from it himself, or he's an impostor playing a role as I am. He did inherit a historic home, so the former seems more believable.

"Why do you think he's here?" Cotton asks.

"I don't know, but I don't like it," I murmur and realize I've said it out loud. "I mean, cops mean something bad has happened."

"If the FBI guy is with him, then it's gotta be about the serial killer. Did any of you know the latest victim? Allie what's-her-name?" Bianca asks. "I didn't."

Everyone shakes their heads while keeping an eye on the detective and the burly FBI agent, whose badge I can now see.

"Ace, you live minutes from her. Surely you've seen her or bumped into her or know her." MacKenzie tucks a strand of her bob behind her ear, revealing several piercings.

I'm sure that as soon as MacKenzie has the chance to convey this to the law, she will. She has a point, though. Did Acelynn know the latest victim? I force myself to remain calm. "We have no clue why they're here. We don't know what we don't know."

"She's right," Ford says and tugs at a strand of long bangs framing my face.

A huge invisible shovel scoops out my middle, leaving a cold pit of dread. The detective and the FBI agent shake hands with the Newsoms and the Lamberts and come straight for us. I haven't seen Acelynn's parents.

"This is bad. I know it," MacKenzie says, and Cotton pulls her to his side in a gesture meant to protect and comfort.

"Well," Detective Patrick says to me, "we meet again. I'm sorry it's under these circumstances." He introduces the FBI agent, Special Agent in Charge Asa Kodiak, but all eyes drill into me, boring so deep I feel it in my bones.

I sense their questions but refuse to make eye contact with anyone except Detective Patrick. "What circumstances?"

He glances at the agent, who quickly inventories each of us, sizing us up. I don't like his stoicism and poker face or his calculating eyes that rest on mine, sending a massive shudder through my bones.

"I'm sorry," Detective Patrick says. "We assumed you'd been informed." His apologetic expression bats between us. "This morning, Drucilla Hilton was found murdered in her home."

MacKenzie gasps, and her hand goes to the hollow in her throat. Bianca's mouth opens, but no sound emerges, and Ford and Cotton squint as if Detective Patrick has spoken in a foreign language.

"It was the Cupid killer, wasn't it?" MacKenzie asks, but it's more of an assumption. "I mean, why else would you be here?" She looks to Agent Kodiak for an answer.

For the first time, the agent talks. "We can't directly speak to that at this time."

Why? Why can't he say she's the newest victim? If she's not, then why is he here? My mind is filled with possibilities, but I can't help them even if I wanted to. No matter my feelings for police.

MacKenzie freely sheds tears as Bianca's mouth tightens, except for the small tremor in her bottom lip. How am I to respond? Is Acelynn a crier? How would she mourn the loss of her friend? I never met Drucilla Hilton, and if she's anything like MacKenzie Newsom, I doubt I would have liked her at all.

Instead, I think of Tommy and how much I loved him. He wasn't perfect, and his last blunder has wrecked my life, but he would have given me the shirt from his back. My thoughts drift to Tillie. My world isn't right without her, even if she never lets me forget my transgressions. It's because she cares about me. The truth is, I need her to anchor me to reality sometimes.

Authentic tears blur my vision.

"I guess this explains why the Hiltons aren't here," Cotton says. "I assume they've been notified."

Detective Patrick nods. "I'd like to speak with each of you individually, and since I already have the honor of knowing you, Miss Benedict, how about we start with you? The rest of you can hang tight here with Agent Kodiak."

No. No. No. No. No.

He pulls a plastic pack of tissues from his suit coat pocket and hands me one. "I know this will be difficult for each of you, but it's important we talk now. Okay?"

Everyone nods, and he points to the sunroom.

"Can we talk in there? Would you be comfortable?"

"I'm not going to be comfortable anywhere." It's not a lie. I cast one glance back. Agent Kodiak watches us walk away.

Why do they need to be babysat by him? Something else is in play, and he doesn't want them conferring alone.

Are we being interviewed in order to piece together Dru's last days, or are we suspects? If so, how would that link to Cupid? Agent Kodiak has no other reason to be here.

Does he?

Inside the cheery sunroom, I perch on the wicker rocking chair, and Detective Patrick eases onto the sofa across from me. He unbuttons his blazer, and I catch a glimpse of his sidearm again and a tuft of fur from his dog, Kitten, on his belt.

"Again, I'm sorry that I had to break this news. It appears the parents planned to reveal the news later after they returned. They're with…they're with Drucilla."

At the morgue.

"I understand." Acelynn's parents aren't even here. They might be with Dru's parents.

"Can you tell me the last time you talked with Drucilla?" He pulls a notepad and pen from his inner suit coat pocket and places the point on the paper to note my response.

The last text I can offer, but as far as if they talked…I couldn't say. "We texted this past Wednesday."

"About?"

My heart is pounding, and my head aches. "She asked me to call her, and I told her I would when I got a chance." But I only checked Acelynn's recent calls from her time in Chicago, so I have no clue if they spoke or not or what about. It could be something bad since MacKenzie has made it clear there's some animosity at best between the two of us, but to reveal that might send him down a trail I don't want him tracking.

"And did you call her back?" he asks.

They're friends. Surely she did. "Yes."

"When?"

"I don't remember what day."

He scribbles on his notepad. "Can you check your phone for me?"

I pull out the phone and flip to the recent calls, but I can't find a recent call to Dru. Now I'm caught in another lie. He could obtain her phone records. "I guess I didn't call her back after all. It's not showing that I did. My days blur together when I'm busy working."

"I see. Did she have a boyfriend or anyone she was seeing?"

"Drucilla is casual in her romantic relationships. Sometimes it was hard to keep up. She often had one-night stands, but she never went into detail about them."

He writes my answers on the paper. "Did she mention feeling stalked by one of these casual flings? A man that was too handsy or pushy? Any arguments? Not necessarily the last time you spoke but in the past few months."

"Not that I recall." The lies are stacking up like a game of Jenga. Tall towers sloppily built topple. "Bianca or MacKenzie might know more. I've been pretty busy as of late, and—" I catch myself before I reveal that I—Acelynn—have been out of town. He'll ask me where, and Chicago cannot be on his radar. Not now or ever. "I've neglected my friends to some degree. It's no excuse, but it's the way things have been." I'm laying a little divide between Acelynn and the Pinks. He needs to focus on them. Not me.

"Understandable." He leans forward, his elbows on his knees. "Do you know a Jacob Moore?"

No, but his eyes reveal I should.

"Seems like her last long-term relationship. Can you tell me about him?"

Blood whooshes in my ear, but he's given me context, and I'm grateful. "Not really."

He cocks his head. "The Hiltons said that anything Dru was going through, the Pinks would know. And if you have a colorful name for your friend group, then I'd assume you'd know more than 'not really,' wouldn't you?"

I'm a frog in a water pot, but the difference is, I know the water is heating and won't be caught off guard when it boils. I need to jump out now. *Think. Think.* My mind flips through the catalog of information, but there is absolutely nothing about a Jacob Moore. Not their dating or breaking up. Not. One. Thing.

Wait! I do remember something that might help explain. "The truth is, Detective, Dru hired me to redecorate her house and believed it would be for free." Acelynn's words this past weekend echo in my ears. "I'm happy to help my friends. We chat at lunch, and I offer tips and advice, but the work I did for Drucilla was extensive, and I assumed she would pay for the services. Her presumptuous attitude made me feel taken advantage of and used. I do take responsibility for assuming she would pay and not nailing that down up front."

"Did you confront her about the payment due?"

"No. Our families are joined at the hip, and I didn't want to stir the pot. I let it go, but the situation created a rift, and we've not been as tight, so you see why I can't offer you more information."

He makes a note on his pad. "I appreciate your honesty."

Oh, the sick irony.

He folds the notepad and sits ramrod straight, his expression too kind for a cop. "That's all for now, but I may have follow-up questions." After standing, he sighs. "About the consult that we discussed on the ride to your house. I need to put a pin in that for now."

This is the best news I've heard today. Hopefully the others can fill in the gaps concerning Dru and this Jacob person, and I will be way behind in his rearview mirror. I could make it out of this unscathed.

"Thank you for your time, and again, I'm sorry for your loss."

We return to the kitchen and hearth room, where the FBI agent is still making small talk with the Pinks and Ford and Cotton. Their shoulders are relaxed, and the men are grinning. He's put them at ease, which is clever but dangerous. These men know how to feign camaraderie until they nail you dead to rights. These men are not allies. Their sole purpose is to catch my kind.

"Miss Lambert," Detective Patrick says. "Can we chat?"

Bianca nods and lays a hand on Agent Kodiak's forearm. "Try to enjoy Savannah while you're here, and congrats on becoming a new father. I don't foresee your little Owen getting away with a single thing."

His entire face lights up at the mention of his son.

Bianca follows Detective Patrick to the sunroom, and I'm stuck making small talk with the FBI agent, but I've discovered his weak spot—his kid. "How old is your son?"

"He's ten months."

"Show her his picture," MacKenzie offers. "He's adorable. You know, he looks a lot like you, Agent Kodiak."

I force my eyes not to roll at her lack of subtlety in hitting on a clearly happily married family man. His cell phone lock screen is a family photo of him, his wife and the little boy, who is actually quite adorable. His wife is striking, but MacKenzie is right. The child looks like his father in every way minus some curl to his brown hair.

"He's a cutie."

"Thanks."

Cotton asks him about the Memphis Grizzlies, and MacKenzie whispers, "What did he say?"

"Basic questions, but I'm not sure why the FBI agent is here unless they believe she might have been dating or had a fling with Cupid." That didn't sit right either. But they had their cards close to their chests.

"What does that mean?" She gulps her wine and licks a drop from her bottom lip.

I shrug. Nothing good. As I scan the crowd, Conrad Benedict strides into the room. He's an imposing character, who in his younger years would have resembled Chris Pine, but taller. His brown hair is slicked back with only a little gray at the temples. His blue eyes meet mine, triggering a chill through my body.

This is the real test. If he realizes I'm an impostor, he has the law right here to drag me out in cuffs. Lightheadedness overtakes me, and I grip the counter to keep from swaying.

He strides straight toward us, eyeing Agent Kodiak instead of me. If only he remains Conrad's focus.

"Dr. Benedict," he introduces himself and shakes the agent's hand.

"I'm sorry for your loss, Doctor."

"Thank you," he murmurs, then lays a hand on my shoulder. "I'm sorry about Dru, honey." The gesture is meant to be compassionate and sensitive, but the way his term of endearment rolls off his tongue sounds forced, and his hand on my shoulder is cold and stiff as if he's never done this before. But I've seen photos of the family. Seen his arms around Acelynn.

Is this a show for the agent, or is he grieving?

And if it's show, what's the issue between them?

Or worse…can he tell I'm not Acelynn? Does my shoulder feel foreign?

No words come, and Ford speaks. "Have you been with Dawna and Jack at the morgue?"

He clears his throat. "No, unfortunately. I had a consultation for a surgery, but I came as soon as I could. Lucille is not feeling well today." A dark flash crosses his eyes, but it's gone before I can pinpoint the emotion. "I've given her a sedative to help her sleep." He then turns to me. "Teddy says it's been a while since you've come by the house. You probably should."

This is news to me. According to Acelynn, she and Lucille lunch every Tuesday. But then, I haven't seen any of those meals documented on her Instagram, and Acelynn is a foodie.

Would she have lied to me about that? "Of course. I'll be by soon."

Conrad makes small talk with Ford and Cotton about real estate and then excuses himself.

"Am I free to go?" I ask Agent Kodiak.

He eyes me, and I force myself not to squirm. "No one is holding you against your will, Miss Benedict. Do you think that's the case?"

Yes. "Of course not. I just wanted to make sure I was available if anything else arose concerning Dru."

He's not buying it, and my intestines literally ache. "We have your number."

Figuratively, or my digits? I'm not sure, but panic is about to set in, and I need out of here. Stat.

I'm almost home free when Teddy Benedict blocks my escape through a side door. He's a younger version of Conrad Benedict and not as tall as he appears in his photos, but he's striking, and cockiness resides in his eyes.

"Why is an unmarked car out front?" he asks. He must not know about Dru yet. Before I can respond, he invades my personal space. "I need something from you," he whispers. "Can I come over later tonight?"

I don't like his tone. It's disturbing and reminds me of late nights when other men needed something from me. Or maybe I wind up too tight when a man enters my personal space without permission. "No, it's not a good time. Look, Drucilla was murdered."

He pulls back, his eyes wide. "What? By who? When?"

I tell him everything I know, concentrating on my accent. "They're still interviewing, and you'll be next."

Teddy swears. "Not a fan of cops."

Why isn't he a fan of cops? I know why I'm not. When has he bumped up against the law or been let down by them?

"Let's get out of here, and if I can't have it tonight, when? You know I don't like waiting too long. I'm too pent-up."

I don't know what Teddy wants, but I have a sick feeling it's not anything I want or can give to him.

Was he the man in Acelynn's house? When he heard Bianca's and MacKenzie's voices, did he sneak out?

What is going on in Acelynn's life?

Chapter Nineteen

After leaving the Newsoms' yesterday, I didn't have it in me to do a single thing. I ate a horrible vegan yogurt from Acelynn's fridge for dinner later that night because I needed to eat, not because I was hungry.

I ran from chaos to save my butt, and I've run right into more chaos trying to save myself—or Acelynn. Actually the both of us. Finally I was able to settle my mind enough to sleep, and I awoke this morning to several texts and emails for Acelynn. Clients and a few from Bianca and MacKenzie about Drucilla and why the police interviewed them.

I think it's fairly clear. They're all potential suspects in her murder.

I simply responded by echoing what the rest of them were saying. I don't know. I do now know, from their texts, that Drucilla dated Jacob Moore for about six months, and he was serious about her. Dru was never serious with anyone, and the fact she dated him for six months was a feat. They suspected she often cheated, which for Dru was business as usual.

MacKenzie said that Jacob has shown up uninvited to Dru's house, and once at the office where she worked part-time for her dad doing "Who knows what because Drucilla never did a day's worth of real work in her life."

I doubt any of them know about backbreaking work that comes in twelve-hour shifts or exhaustion that sends you to bed before eight o'clock with no time to recover before clocking in to do it all over again. No money for massages and spa days. I'm not saying I wish they didn't experience the good life. I just wish I had it too.

Not necessarily at this expense. Acelynn is under Detective Patrick's nose. I'm supposed to be forgettable, not in his stupid notepad with jotted scribbles. What was he scribbling about me? Did he not believe me?

Was my acknowledgment that Acelynn and Dru squabbled over work a reason to think Acelynn was involved in Dru's murder? What if I've made things worse?

What is in his notes? What's he said about the Pinks and the brothers? The parents?

This is all I've thought about today. Still in Acelynn's silky pajamas. I haven't showered or gone outside. The dogs are curious about me now but not overly friendly. I've had the decency to let them out to do their business and run around the backyard, but I can't even gather a game plan for the future thanks to what's happening presently. If I run off now with an investigation going, it will look unbelievably bad for Acelynn and ultimately me, Charlotte.

Acelynn's cell phone buzzes with a text.

Philip. Again. I never did call or get back to him after I texted from the Newsoms'. Can't evade him forever, though I wish I could, but he may be the one good thing going, and I can't afford more questions to arise from him.

But I'm not prepared for the cryptic message that feels ominous and certainly confusing.

Stop avoiding me if you know what's good for you.

What does that mean? Is this a threat? Why would the love of Acelynn's life threaten her? Has Acelynn been avoiding him? Tillie's words return that Acelynn may have taken my invitation to meet her as a way to flee something here. Or someone.

Was my sister running from her boyfriend? And if so, why?

One of the fluff balls paws at the back door. I open it, allowing them to run around the small fenced-in area.

The neighbor lady walks out of her house. Her hair reminds me of the dogs' white tufts. Her shoulders stoop as she hobbles out with a boy's bike. Behind her, a little boy bounds out with a basketball. She sees me and waves. Her bright pink lipstick bleeds above her slash of an upper lip. She reminds me of Mrs. Donlea, who I hope is being cared for and hasn't lost her hearing aids, but I'm certain she has.

"Sorry if Blake's loud. He has a lot of energy. I won't let him play near your courtyard, though," she says as if she's had run-ins with Acelynn before.

"Oh, no worries. Kids will be kids." I'm used to noisy kids bouncing balls down my hall with paper-thin walls. Living here will be like having soundproofing.

"Have you changed your mind, then?" she asks and fiddles with the little locket hanging at the crag in her throat.

Changed my mind? Acelynn doesn't like the kid playing ball near her house? I thought she loved children and wanted a whole brood. "I have. Again, no worries."

Blake dribbles up and down the sidewalk. "Thank you, Miss Benedict. If he's any trouble, you let me know. No need calling the authorities again."

She called the cops on a kid playing, but her dogs yap and bark all the time. What is going on? "I won't call the cops." For anything.

My phone dings again, and I'm almost too afraid to see if it's

Philip. But I have to. It could be a client, though I've let them all know I'm taking two weeks off due to a family tragedy. Dru is like family to Acelynn, and it makes sense while keeping me from having to do Acelynn's job, though I fully believe I could.

It's MacKenzie, and I relax as I peer at the photo she sent of her holding up a red dress.

On sale. Girl. You should get down here ASAP.

Who am I to judge how a person grieves? Retail therapy is a real thing. I reply that I have a lot of work and if she sees something I'd like, buy it and I'll reimburse her.

She responds with a sad face, but it seems I've appeased her. The dogs follow me up to Acelynn's home office. She has a formal office downtown but feels more creative at home. Was Acelynn and Dru's tiff solely about not paying for services? From the short time I spent with her and since I've been in Savannah, I'm finding there is far more than meets the eye when it comes to my sister. Acelynn Benedict's words do not match her behavior, from stealing polishes to making me believe her life is truly the dream she conveys on her social media channels.

I did not feel the love with her father—or her friends, at least not the way I feel the love from Tillie. I definitely am not feeling good vibes with Philip or her brother, who wants things from me late at night. My mind goes to all sorts of sick places with that one.

Now a murdered friend requiring an FBI agent?

I'm at the center of her disastrous life, which includes calling cops on elementary-aged boys who want to play basketball ten feet from the house.

Too many things aren't adding up. Fudging your life to appear a little nicer—like I've done from time to time—is one thing. We all wear harmless masks; it's no different from women who read to escape from reality, drowning out their problems and failed relationships.

Was Acelynn wearing a harmless mask in Chicago, or was she intentionally lying for darker reasons? If I'd been raised by two loving parents, never wanting for a dime and having the best education, I wouldn't see the reason to fudge or lie. What darkness might surround my sister? Certainly not the kind that enveloped my entire life.

Either way, I ran from one dumpster fire to another, and I have to find a way to put them out so I can survive. I have to see the full picture so I don't put the wrong puzzle piece in the hole and out myself. Researching people isn't terribly hard. I might have been a very good detective had my life gone that direction.

With social media and ample time to search her home and office, I'll be able to put the pieces together and discover who my sister was—or wasn't. Knowing proper information will give me weeks—maybe months—to hatch a plan that won't lead back to Charlotte Kane.

And that's all I want. To be free and clear.

Well, it's not all I want. But it's the only thing available at the moment. The best place to start is where she spends most of her time—her home office. I riffle through desk drawers and rummage through loose papers, envelopes and folders. Nothing incriminating or telling other than she has a soft spot for Reese's Peanut Butter Cups.

A manila folder holds a few sketches of Acelynn done by Teddy. He's better at shading than me. I assume they're his drawings. Maybe she lied about her artistic talents too. This is what Mrs. Thompson meant when talking about planks of trust that build a bridge. Every lie removes a stepping stone, creating space until it's a chasm. Acelynn's lies have removed planks, and she's not ever going to be able to rebuild them.

Without the trust, everything she's said is in question. Everyone is in question.

The dogs bark and run downstairs, their painted toenails clicking along the hardwood. Maybe this is why Acelynn hated the boy playing close to the house. His presence might have sent the dogs into a tailspin.

But no. It's not the grandson next door.

Heavy footfalls clunk along the old hardwood, and they're coming up the stairs.

Someone is in the house again.

Someone who thinks I'm away until later tonight, when Acelynn is set to return home? Or someone who doesn't know Acelynn is out of town and hopes to surprise her? Either way, I never heard them enter the house.

Cupid comes to mind. Some sick freak raping and murdering women. Or maybe it's someone much closer to home. Closer to Acelynn.

My heart jackrabbits into my throat. I can't leave the room. Whoever is slowly ascending the stairs will see or hear me.

I have nowhere to go. Nowhere to run.

Hide. Now. Move. Go.

My only choice is the closet. I close the laptop and scurry into the closet laden with fabric bolts, wallpaper samples and off-season clothing like fur coats. Does Savannah ever grow cold enough for that?

Quietly as I can, I close the door to the L-shaped closet and maneuver behind the long winter coats.

My breath is too ragged, and I concentrate on slow, even breaths, but my pulse spikes, and I can't stop trembling. My mind races to all the bad things that have happened to me before and what can happen again—or something new and vile.

Silence falls. He must be in Acelynn's bedroom, which is covered with a large custom rug. Can I make it out of here and downstairs while he's in there?

No. No time. I have to take my chances on the closet. Why is he here? Is he looking for Acelynn or something else? Shrinking to make myself as small as possible, I wait as footsteps sound again. They're coming down the hall. Closer. Closer.

I use a coat sleeve to cover my mouth to contain any scream or shriek I might involuntarily make. He's in the office now. Just a few feet away. I swallow hard and feel the aching lump pushing back.

He's silent. Is he listening or looking? Can he hear me breathing? Footsteps begin again and come straight for me.

The closet door opens, and I squeeze my eyes shut, willing myself to become invisible.

A whiff of men's cologne wafts inside, and it's not cheap. Its wearer is looking inside the closet, ruffling the clothing. He softly swears and leaves the closet, and the light dims. He's pulled the door closed, but it hasn't shut all the way, and a sliver of light drifts in.

Do I stay still or dare a peek? I have to know who is in Acelynn's house and assume it's the same person who was here yesterday and interrupted by Bianca and MacKenzie. Lying flat on my stomach, I slither like a serpent to the bend that forms the L and peek out from under a coat hem.

I see men's dress shoes.

But my view won't reveal a face. Slowly I rise up on my knees as drawers to the filing cabinet open and close. Each time he doesn't find what he wants, the drawer slams harder, and he curses again.

His fingers clack along her laptop keyboard.

He must know her password.

I inch up and closer, and when he shuts her laptop with a crack, I see him.

Philip Beaumont, the chief assistant district attorney.

He's dressed in a smart, tailor-made three-piece suit. He rakes a hand through his brown curls and cusses again, then checks his expensive watch for the time before glancing out the window and grimacing.

What *is* he looking for?

Was my sister avoiding him because she had something he wanted that she couldn't part with? Was it hers? His? Questions fire like bullets from a gun. I have no answers, only more questions to stack on the ones I'm already asking.

The dogs return, and he kneels and pets their fluffy heads. "Where's your mistress, little ones? Why aren't you on a walk with her?"

Philip doesn't seem to know that Acelynn went out of town and isn't due back until this evening—or maybe he's gotten wind she came home early and expects her to be on a walk. My mind shuffles through the Instagram photos, and yes, she walks the dogs three times a day, like clockwork almost.

Why didn't she tell her boyfriend of nearly two years that she went out of town to see a client like she told Bianca?

She must have been trying to escape him, if only for a while. But why? If she has something he wants, then wouldn't she hold power over him? Holding power over someone can do wild things like make them desperate. Desperate people make poor choices. They feel backed into a corner and become like scared animals. Scared animals attack, and the man is inside her home, in secret, hunting for something. And he's angry. Furious, even, that he hasn't found it.

He strides to the filing cabinet and rifles through each drawer once more, then kicks it and growls.

"Where is it?" He rakes his hand through his hair again, then eyes the desk and tilts his head. He drops to his knees, using his hands to feel under the desk. His last-ditch effort is fruitless, and he stomps from the office, but not the house.

For the next thirty minutes, I listen as he combs through each room, the dogs obediently following him, their nails clicking on the wood. My muscles are tight and my head pounds, and

I pray the dogs don't decide to come find me, giving my position away. What will I do then? How will I explain?

Finally the back door slams, but I wait another good fifteen minutes before I emerge. The dogs are sitting in front of the closet door now, clearly liking Philip more than me, and I'm not sad about it.

I search the rooms and find he's left no trace and is good at covering his tracks.

But what does he want, and why does he have to sneak around to find it?

Why would his girlfriend hide something from him? Or maybe she's not hiding something. Maybe he's after an item that belongs to her.

I know one thing. He didn't find it, and that means he's not done with his search.

I need to find it first.

Then

The day has been a blur, full of haze and fogginess. Darling Husband has had my meds changed after the *incident* last week. It was not an incident, no matter what my family or therapist insists. They blame my "fragile mental state" instead of where the blame clearly lies—with Petal. Mother throws my past in my face like the good mom she is. She's been a far better caregiver to my own children than she ever was to me.

I do not like these new meds, and I'm convinced they're unnecessary. They keep me off-kilter and too doped up to venture out. I'm being watched like a child, and Mother insists I stick out my tongue and lift it to prove I've swallowed them down like an obedient daughter. She's even gone so far as to swab my cheeks with her fingers after finding one in the toilet. I thought it had gone down.

Last Saturday, I entered Petal's room to wash the bedsheets, trying to be a decent mom and housekeeper and pull my life back to some sort of normalcy. When I threw back the comforter, doll heads with their eyes *X*-ed out with a black Sharpie had been piled underneath. Dozens of them.

Written across their brows was one word: *Mommy.*

I knew it had been another covert warning that she wanted me dead. I'm the only thing holding her back from unleashing her full capabilities in this house. Every single day, I fear for our safety. Bubba's become more withdrawn, rarely coming out of his room. He no longer visits me in my bedroom after school.

Petal won't let him. I know she's the reason. Her attachment to him disturbs me. The affection is real but abnormal. She must be in there lying about me to keep him from me. Brainwashing him.

I found the uncapped marker and had picked it up; some of the ink stained my fingers. At that moment, Petal had entered, and the level of anger came out in an ear-piercing shriek, a bloodcurdling cry that had brought her father into the room, and Mother had followed.

"Mommy hurt my dollies," she'd said and pointed to me with the marker in hand sitting dead center on her bed, looking as guilty as sin.

"I didn't do this. I found this."

My husband's mouth formed a grim line, and he huffed and glanced at Petal before he took her hands and showed them to me. Perfectly clean. Not a smidge of marker anywhere. I was the only one with stained hands. "I'm tired of this. I don't know how to manage this anymore."

"I didn't do it, Daddy. Don't be mad at me," she said through a syrupy-sweet voice that was nothing short of plastic. "Mommy's sick, isn't she?"

"I am not sick," I said. "I mean, I have a condition. But I did not do this. Why would I do this?" Why indeed?

"Why would you throw vases, put dead mice in the children's beds or cut up her clothes? Why would you run scalding bathwater for our son? You need… I think we might need to revisit a stay at Carewood."

"No!" I hollered. I didn't want to return to that place. Who would protect and watch over Bubs? "I didn't do any of those things. That—that monster did it! *She's* sick. She's wicked and vile and evil!"

His hangdog eyes met mine in utter disappointment, exhaustion and bitterness. He knew I had some problems with depression and other things when we met, but I had always been honest. All I saw was the look of betrayal and regret for choosing me.

"It might be for your own good."

No, for *his* own good. His life would have been much easier if I didn't exist, and out of sight meant out of mind. Then he'd be free to do all the things he didn't think I knew about.

My snake of a mother agreed. "Let's get you cleaned up, dear. Get you a nice, hot bath and fresh pajamas. You'll be right as rain. We can discuss this later when not in front of the children."

Yes, because a bath made everything better.

"No locking the door of the bathroom," he said before leaving the room, and I wondered if he was silently giving me the idea to do so. To lock the door, slit my wrists right this time and let myself bleed out in the bathtub.

Petal watched him go, then looked at me with narrowed eyes. Solid black like a monster from Abaddon. I've put Bibles in her drawers and hung the Lord's Prayer above her door. But a rotten stench clings to her like static.

Mother patted her head. "Go get you and Bubs a snack, darling. It's okay. Mommy doesn't mean it. She's confused," she whispered. "Like we talked about." She shooed Petal out and took the marker I'd been gripping in my hand. It had turned as black as Petal's eyes.

"I'll clean this up, dear. Come on. Let's get you a bath and some rest. Have you eaten today?"

"I don't think. I don't know."

No one has spoken of this incident since, and my mother has convinced her precious son-in-law to table the Carewood visit. For now. But he wants me gone. Away from him. I'm a glaring reminder that he didn't achieve the life he wanted. Well, neither did I.

Neither did I.

The room is dark, and I'm not even sure if it's night or day. I don't want to sleep. My dreams are fitful. Dreams of being locked away while Petal is unleashed to wreak havoc, to murder my family one by one until no one is left.

I doze off and wake, unsure of the time, but the room is cold. I shiver and reach for the duvet, but I can't find it. Patting the bed, I hunt for it, but it's nowhere. I open my eyes, but they're filmy and unfocused.

The sound of cotton rubbing cotton fills my ears, and I feel a slithering on the bed. Finally my eyes adjust to the pitch-black room that is mine alone. I haven't shared a bed with my husband in over a year. I can't even remember the last time he touched me with affection or at all.

As a sliver of moonlight spills through the window and shines on my duvet, it moves. It's slinking toward the foot of the bed. My scalp prickles, and fear paralyzes my muscles.

I watch in horror as the covers slide on their own farther and farther toward the end of the bed. The room's temperature seems to plummet. My eyes must be playing tricks on me. Covers don't move of their own accord.

I force myself to sit up. My hand trembles as I reach out to grip the duvet before it slips over the edge and falls to the floor. I'm too afraid to jump out of bed. I fear what's underneath.

As I lean toward the foot of the bed, a pale and ghoulish

face pops up, eyes boring into mine as a wicked beam spreads across its face.

"Hi, Mommy," Petal singsongs.

My heart arrests, and my mouth opens to scream, but nothing releases. Like a prowling nighttime creature stalking its prey, Petal springs onto the bed.

That's when I see the glint of the kitchen knife from the butcher block. She raises it so fast, I don't have time to snatch it. She brings it down on the pillow lying next to me, slicing into it with more force than a young child should have. Feathers spray across the bed, into my gasping mouth.

The overhead light switches on, and I squint as it blinds me. Petal is wailing and repeating she wanted to sleep with Mommy. See Mommy. Be with Mommy.

And somehow the knife is in *my* lap and a fistful of feathers in my hand.

This is it.

This is Petal's ticket to remove me from the house. Because I'm the only thing separating—protecting—my son from her. She's accomplished her dark mission.

This is going to send me back to Carewood.

Chapter Twenty

After spending the rest of Monday searching for what felt like a hopeless cause, I gave up and soaked in the tub, then perused some of Acelynn's design magazines and peeked into the room she was turning into a *Beauty and the Beast*–inspired library. Paint cans, tarps and tape littered the floor. She had begun the project before arriving in Chicago and had discussed finishing it up with reels to showcase her talent.

Maybe I'll finish it for her in her honor and to give me practice. Now it's Tuesday, and anyone who knew she was out of town knows she's back. I was supposed to take twenty-four hours to plan how to escape without anyone connecting Acelynn to Chicago and me, and to keep Tillie and me safe. That didn't happen. Now I'm trapped in my sister's life, and it's a train wreck, but I've dealt with wrecks before—most of them my own, if I'm being honest with myself.

Not that I'm happy about a woman's life being snuffed out, but Dru's death has given me at least two weeks to put off clients and some social events I'm not ready to brave. Hopefully by that time I'll make it look like Acelynn has a new client in a state I'd never visit. I'll book tickets and pack and do everything to appear gone and then...I simply won't return. They'll look in California or Montana or Oklahoma for her. They won't care about Chicago because she came home from there and was fine. Two weeks. I could do this for two weeks...if she's been forthright with me about her life.

Other than responding to the Pinks' texts about Dru and funeral arrangements—they cremated her and are awaiting out-of-town family before holding her service—I've been off the grid. Philip hasn't bothered to text or call, and I'm thankful, but I'm going to have to deal with him sooner rather than later. I don't like walking into scenarios blind, though most of my life has been exactly that. What I learned from those situations was how to read people and go with the flow regardless of how painful or disturbing it might be, and I'm confident Acelynn's life is all of the above.

Conrad mentioned I should stop by to visit Acelynn's mother. I might as well bite that bullet this evening, so I'm on my way to the Benedict family home and already anxious to the point of nauseated. Nothing is as it seems with Acelynn, and that means her mother too, I'm sure.

The Benedict home overlooks Forsyth Park, not far from Acelynn's house, and has vintage charm. The pale pink three-story home with a two-story carriage house is something out of a movie. Elegant and feminine.

Unsure of how Acelynn typically enters her home, I take the side staircase. The door is unlocked, which surprises me. Do all privileged people feel invincible in their facades of comfort and safety? A serial killer is on the prowl, and while Lucille Benedict might not be a target, she lives within the predator's hunting range.

I step inside to lingering hints of lemon and survey my surroundings while I have a chance. The updates are sleek and modern, and old floors gleam like still waters on a sunny day, but the atmosphere is ripe with unease. The house is eerily quiet.

I peek into the fridge. A fridge says a lot about a person. While the house is immaculate, is the refrigerator? If not, their cleanliness is surface-level, and they might care more about outward appearances, which may also translate into their persons. Or they're forgetful or lazy about meticulous tasks. People often don't see what's right in front of their faces. The Benedicts eat organic and the fridge is pristine.

I feel a presence and close the fridge door. Standing next to me is Acelynn's brother, Teddy. I was not expecting to see him here. He has a beach bungalow on Tybee Island that Acelynn renovated and updated last year.

"What are you doing?" he asks with a hint of mischief in his raspy tone, and his dark eyes meet mine in a scrutinizing gaze. His hair is full of product, and the ends appear a little crispy. Pretty people with pretty houses, pretty friends and pretty clothes and cars and lives.

"Just looking."

His thick, dark eyebrows rise. "For what—Mother? You won't find her in there unless there's wine."

Mother. The word feels impersonal and slightly condescending. "I was instructed to visit." That sounds like Acelynn's voice, and he buys it.

Teddy's shoulders relax, and he chuckles before taking down a white mug and filling it with rich brew. "You want? It's decaf."

"Yes."

"Well, you know how to pour it." He places the carafe onto the burner and moves around me to the fridge, his chest brushing my back. A wave of chill bumps prickles along my skin. Maybe the touch reminds me too much of foster brothers, but it's too close for my comfort, and I step away and open the same cabinet Teddy retrieved his mug from as if I've done this a million times. I pour my coffee and stare into it. I can't remember how Acelynn takes hers, though I've seen photos of her in coffee shops with decadent drinks. I add cream, and because I can't find the sugar bowl, I forgo it.

"Knocking out calories from your life again?" Teddy points to the cup of sugarless coffee, which is going to taste as bitter as this encounter.

"Since when did you become the calorie police?" I sip the hot coffee. The cream helps refine the bitterness. Sometimes you only need to mask a bad situation to make it palatable to endure.

He shrugs one shoulder. "Touché. Any more word on Dru's death? I ended up blindsided by the detective and an FBI agent at the office yesterday." He slides onto an oak bar stool and snags a banana from the bowl. I think it's more out of boredom than hunger. Or maybe he just really likes bananas. "Wanted to ask questions about Drucilla and her relationships. I told the detective he was running fast and loose with the word *relationship*."

"Except Jacob." I need more information in case I'm questioned again. Too much homework looms before me to be sitting here small-talking. Though to be honest, I dread seeing Lucille, but if she's on sedatives, then she may be groggy and in a haze, which will work to my advantage. "She was with him for a few months."

Teddy peels the banana and breaks off a piece. "Maybe so, but she wasn't monogamous, which is exactly what I told the detective and that agent. I got the feeling they weren't interviewing but interrogating, and they would never outright say it was a Cupid killing. The previous victims were splashed all over the news, but this is quieter, and I'm not sure if the Hiltons are keeping it quiet with money or it's simply not as attractive to the media as the Cupid's killings."

Teddy's smart and intuitive. Noted.

"I called Dad, but he said he didn't know anything," he tells me. "I figure Dru's parents would know details no one else does and would've told him, but I guess not."

Or Conrad is withholding information at their request.

"What did they ask you?"

I wrap my hands around the warm mug of terrible coffee. "Standard questions. If I knew anyone lingering around her that was new. You know, the same drill you'd watch on *Law & Order*."

He turns up his nose and finishes off his snack. "Since when do you watch crime shows?"

Acelynn loves them. Or so she told me. Why would she lie about entertainment? "Everyone has a guilty pleasure, Teddy. And everyone hides their guilt."

He chucks the banana peel in the trash and washes his hands. "Is that a dig at me?"

Should it be? What should Teddy feel guilty about?

"I wouldn't suggest aiming your shots at me," he says. "I have enough ammo in my pocket, sister dear, to fire away for decades at you."

I grip my cup tighter, hoping to keep my trembling hands still. He's thrown down a gauntlet. It's in his eyes, which are now shrewd and menacing. But then I think I see something behind his steely gaze, a chink in his armor, and I take a predatory step toward him to test my theory.

Teddy breaks eye contact and instinctively backs away.

I don't know if I should be startled or afraid, because this could mean something far more sinister. His whole "don't come for me" act is a failed attempt at false bravado.

Acelynn's brother fears her, and yet he still wants something from her.

Sister Dear has power over people, dark power. How diabolical was she, and have her wicked ways come full circle? If so, I'm in much more trouble than walking into a life of gossipy tidbits that stay quiet for petty favors. I've stepped into a hornet's nest, and any of them—maybe all of them—are circling and about to sting.

Chapter Twenty-One

After leaving Teddy alone in the kitchen, my mind reels as I climb the wooden staircase, one of the only things not redone or repainted in the house. At the top of the stairs is a long, winding hall with several small halls that branch out like a tree. I'm thankful Teddy isn't where he can watch my awkwardness. I have no idea which bedroom belongs to Lucille Benedict.

The doors are all open as I walk past, peeping inside. Guest bedrooms, bathrooms, a library and a sewing room. I wonder if it was Acelynn's bedroom when she was younger or if Lucille sews. At the end of the long hallway, a door is closed. By deduction, it's probably Lucille's.

I knock lightly and wait. Am I waiting for a sweet mom or the big bad wolf? The woman that is kind and on committees that give back and attends luncheons and spas and often has girls' nights out with Acelynn? Will this be the woman I meet, or will Acelynn have embellished here too?

I hear a groggy voice that cracks as if it hasn't spoken in days. "Come in."

The heavy cream drapes are drawn and the room is dark, but the white walls and trim and soft blues create some lightness. A huge king bed faces me, and I feel like I'm in the stepmother's room from *Cinderella*. I'm waiting for her voice to squawk my name. Cinder-ELLA!

Ace-LYNN!

But the woman in bed isn't a terrifying stepmother at all. Nor is she the bright and perky woman in her late fifties Acelynn has described. She's wan and pale, and it takes her effort to scoot up on her mound of white feather pillows.

"Hello, Mother. I saw…" Dad? Father? Conrad? "Dad," I go with. "He mentioned I hadn't been by in some time. I guess it sneaked away from me."

The room is filled with dark antiques, early 1900s, and the comforter is fluffy and white, dotted with powdery blue flowers. An array of pill bottles, half a glass of water and an empty wine goblet litter the night table.

She eyes me suspiciously and grips the covers at each side but remains silent.

"Would you like some light in here?" I would. Funny how we instinctively reach out for light to save us from what lurks in the darkness; a single sliver chases away shadows and breathes hope that whatever monster prowled beneath our bed or in our closet flees at the sign of light.

I don't wait for her to answer and switch on a lamp by her bedside table.

She squints as if she hasn't seen the light in ages. As I move toward her, she flinches. I'm not sure what to make of that reaction, but it reminds me of Teddy's earlier retreat. On closer inspection of Lucille—glassy-eyed, foggy expression and droopy mouth—my heart descends. In between the bed and night table rests an empty wine bottle. Tucking it into a crack might hide the container, but nothing can mask the fact she's doped up. Lucille Benedict isn't a woman medicated over grief.

I know an addict when I see one.

The question is, why would her surgeon husband contribute to her habit? He admitted on Sunday to prescribing her pills, and it's obvious Lucille Benedict loves her benzos. I suspect it started as self-medication for an earlier problem, as it most often does. The irony is not lost that our biological mom and Acelynn's adoptive mom are addicts.

But why didn't Acelynn confide once I clued her in about Marilyn? Why keep up the happy-life facade? If anyone would have understood the plight of an addict for a mother, it's me.

"Is that better?" I ask.

"Not particularly." Her words sound like someone is dragging her tongue through a river of syrup.

Her trembling fingers reach for the water glass and bump it to the floor, shattering it to shards. Instantly I move to clean it up, but she raises her jerky hand. "Leave it." She breathes out an exhausted sigh and rolls over, facing the wall.

This gives me a few seconds to pay attention to the pill bottles. Trazodone. Xanax. Percocet. Each bottle has been prescribed by Conrad Benedict. Does she not have her own doctors? Is this a way to conceal that his wife is a pillhead and hide his embarrassment? Why not send her to rehab? Maybe he has.

"When was the last time you were out of this bed?"

"I don't know."

How long has she gone without a shower and real clothing? I can't sit here and let this woman wither away. In some ways, she reminds me of Marilyn, and helping her feels pointless. In my experience, once an addict, always an addict.

But regardless of her mental state, her daughter is dead, and I'm responsible. When I leave, Acelynn will disappear, and she'll have to live with that uncertainty. For that I am truly sorry. All I can do is make up for it the best I can by not allowing her to rot in this bed. Perhaps the stories Acelynn told were from her days before the pills consumed her life. Happier times.

Even now I'm trying to see my lying sister in a better light.

I leave her and go to the spa-like bathroom and start the shower, then hang a clean bath towel on the heated rack before returning to Lucille. "Mother, you need to shower, wash your hair and brush your teeth. You'll feel better."

She doesn't respond, so I toss the covers from her frail body. She springs into action faster than someone as doped up as she is should, and it startles me.

"What do you want, Acelynn? Why are you here? When have you ever checked in unless you want something?"

That speaks volumes, and while addicts often have a distorted perception, based on what I'm learning, I tend to believe her about Acelynn. And her questions lead me to conclude she hasn't been told about the murder. If that's true, then Conrad's words were all lies to cover up the fact that Lucille couldn't get out of bed if she wanted to—and it appears she's in this condition at his own hands.

But don't they already know this about her? The Pinks have already made comments about all their mothers being lushes. Maybe some secrets are simply better kept.

Lucille doesn't wait for my response. She swings her bird-like legs out of the bed on the side the glass didn't shatter and stands on wobbly legs that remind me of Charlie's grandfather in *Willie Wonka*. Pretty sure we won't be dancing to the tune of a golden ticket.

She allows me to help her to the bathroom. But only because she realizes she has no choice. After leaving her to some privacy, I clean up the broken glass and use tissues to sop up spilled water.

Finally she emerges from the steamy bathroom in a fluffy white robe. Her dark hair is wet but brushed back and hanging to her collarbone. The hot water has given her cheeks a rosy glow, and she smells like coconut and vanilla. She was once a gorgeous woman; she's nothing but a shell now.

"Do you feel better?"

"A little." She slides back under the covers.

The side of her bed by the bathroom door is crisp and fresh. No hints of a male counterpart. Conrad Benedict doesn't sleep in this room. Has he sequestered her here to rot in her pills and wine? I have a million questions, but I've already deviated from Acelynn's norm, though it doesn't appear Lucille has noticed. Her lack of lucidity works in my favor.

My phone rings. It's Philip. What could he possibly say after sneaking in my house like a storybook villain and poking around for who knows what?

"How was the barbecue?" she asks. "Did your father attend?"

This confirms she has no idea about Drucilla. In fact, I don't even see a phone nearby indicating she has access to the world. "It was...smoked meats and wine, and he did."

"Did he tell everyone I was under the weather per usual?"

"You *are* in bed." I'm not judging, but would she rather he admit she's strung out?

"I am so sick," she slurs, "of keeping up appearances. I'm not sure we know how to do anything else." She sighs and pulls the covers up around her neck. "Renee talks up her daughter's art, and the only thing creative about Mac is her hair. Ford works for his dad not because it's the family business but because he can't grow up and failed college. And real estate is your brother's fall-back because he can't make a living at art even if he is good—which he actually is." Her words are slow and stretched, but I'm filing it all away.

"And don't even get me started on Christine Lambert. She's pretty much a prop." She bats her hand in the air. "None of it matters anyway."

It matters to me and my survival. I shouldn't have expected picture-perfect. This day and age, everyone lives a filtered life. But I was hoping Acelynn's life was genuine. I wanted that for her. And for me. Maybe I wanted to believe that somewhere out there, like Fievel, a family could be loving and kind and generous without underlying motives or secrets, like the Thompson family before their daughter blamed me for every rotten thing happening in the house, from stealing to setting a fire in the garage, and had me returned like a pair of too tight shoes or pants that simply didn't fit.

She's quite precious and we had high hopes, but she's too troubled, and it's starting to affect our daughter, Phoebe, in negative ways. We feel like utter failures and wish it could be different, but we're afraid we can't keep Charlotte. I know she'll find a good home, and we'll be praying for it daily.

They either forgot to pray or it fell on deaf ears, because after the Thompsons, things grew worse instead of better, until I cycled out and was turned loose at eighteen.

Easing into the chair across from Lucille's bed, I stare at the fireplace and ponder burned bridges. "Why didn't you divorce Dad?" I ask, surprised at my abrupt question.

At first I'm not sure she's heard me, but then she finally answers. "Because by the time I realized my dream was dead, I was a middle-aged woman with no skills and was too exhausted to fight it. Why are you asking me this? Was he at the barbecue with someone else?"

"No. It's just...you're unhappy, and he doesn't seem happy. He doesn't sleep in this room."

"He sleeps wherever and with whomever he wants. But we don't talk about that. As if I don't know Renee had the guesthouse redone so Gavin can sleep out there with his little trampy secretary— Sorry, that's not PC anymore. I meant admin assistant. They're all dogs."

I'm not sure how to respond or if she even expects me to.

Lucille runs a slender hand through her wet hair and tucks a lock behind her ear. "What really brings you by? And why are you pretending to care about me and your father's marriage? You never have before."

Yep, I've stepped in it. Doped or not, she knows I'm off, and she's looking through the haze at me. Really looking.

"Acelynn, answer me. What is going on? Why are you…?" She can't find the word. Because she subconsciously knows I'm not her daughter, but the pills and wine have fogged her brain.

I can do for Lucille what her daughter didn't do. Lucille's drugged-up state is clearly due to disappointment, and I can relate to that. It's hard when you dream up this amazing life and perfect world but then it comes crashing down around you, leaving you with broken pieces of dreams. Lucille longs for a redo, for a husband who loves her and a daughter who isn't self-absorbed.

What if I could be the daughter she always wanted?

What if I could give her a reason to flush the pills and live her life again? Make up for the pain I've inflicted that she isn't aware of in this moment? If I stick around, I can help her sober up and stay clean.

I have no choice but to tell her the truth.

"Mother, I'm thinking about life and relationships today. Dad didn't tell you, but…Drucilla was murdered over the weekend. They found her early Sunday morning."

I never said what truth I was going to share.

Chapter Twenty-Two

Last Saturday I spent the day with my sister. It's been a week since her murder. A week since I fled Chicago. Saturdays should be lazy days, but I have no time to be lazy. I have one more week before coming back to the real world as Acelynn. Her social media accounts are rife with comments from followers who miss her reels and tip videos.

I took a photo of me in the soon-to-be-redone library upstairs, letting them know I'll return, and when I do, this room will be conquered. I asked for book recommendations to fill the shelves. They've been eating that up, and my TBR pile is brimming. The warmth and support from so many people I don't even know—that Acelynn didn't even know—blows my mind, and for the first time in decades, I feel cared about and loved.

Of course, I'm not Acelynn, but my post was still me. My face. My words. Every few seconds I check to see more likes and new book recs. It's addictive. No wonder she stayed on there all the time. Adoring fans await her.

I've spent the past three days digging through her belongings and searching her laptop, but I'm not techy and haven't come across anything that appears incriminating. Other than having lunch with the Pinks on Thursday and drinks with them on Friday night, I've kept to myself. Philip has sent one text saying we need to talk, and I replied that I know and that I just need some time.

He seemed fine, as he liked the text and hasn't bothered me since. Whatever is going on, the fact I need time makes sense. It was another gamble, and I'm up right now. Teddy hasn't even reminded me there's something he wants.

The friends haven't seemed to notice I'm not Acelynn, but our conversation both times has revolved around Dru's death and what it all means. This Cupid is killing petite blondes, and MacKenzie is certain I could be in his sights. Bianca simply called her dramatic, and I tend to agree, but the thought hasn't slipped my mind. He's hunting too close to my home. MacKenzie said I should dye my hair brown. I think she wants me to look washed out. Every word out of her mouth has an underlying motive. No one seems to notice but me.

After I told Lucille about Dru, she cried and asked questions. I filled in all the blanks I could, and she mentioned she would call Dawna immediately. I left her fuming at Conrad for not sharing it first. That's their problem. Although it could come back to bite me.

I'm constantly looking over my shoulder for serial killers, Philip, Conrad Benedict, Teddy. And the scariest of all is Detective Patrick. I do not like the way our interview went, as if he could see right through my skin into my soul. Sharing that Dru and I—Acelynn and Dru—had a falling-out was a stupid mistake on my part, and who knows what MacKenzie told him. She walks a fine line between love and hate where I'm concerned. Are we friends or frenemies? Does she secretly hate me? She doesn't seem to have quite the spite for Bianca that she does for me.

I need to know more about Acelynn's life—the one she didn't share with me. Through the eyes of her friends, behind her back. If we were being secretly interrogated, they suspect one of us murdered her. Who?

This community of social butterflies is masquerading. Underneath they're yellow jackets, and I'm not safe until I know what is truly going on. But I can't leave Savannah until I tie up some of Acelynn's loose ends.

By finding out more about my sister, I might have a better idea what Philip wants and how to handle him. Intrusive thought: I might be able to use it for my benefit. But seeing him face-to-face isn't going to happen until we're on an even playing field. At the moment, he's at a dangerous advantage. My future, my survival, depends on me being one step ahead.

A new idea strikes. It's a gamble, but before I talk myself out of it, I'm in the car with my supply bag, laptop and notebook, heading for Christian Patrick's.

Detective Patrick's inherited home isn't far from Forsyth Park, near Acelynn's parents' home. It's supposed to be within walking distance from Acelynn's. I find a place to park across the street and grab my supply bag, which I wish held a dose of confidence and bravery, because they're starting to wane. After grabbing the laptop and notebook, I cross the street.

I climb the stairs to his home and ring the bell, waiting as my insides tweak like a meth-head. Kitten barks, and then a shadow appears. Christian is wearing trendy jeans, a button-down shirt and loafers. He shoots me a look of confusion and surprise.

"I know you said a consult for you was a conflict of interest, but I was in the neighborhood and thought I could leave you a no-strings-attached free workup for paint. Paint doesn't seem like much, but it's a lot if you have the right colors."

He's not buying it and can't be bought—and that makes him unlike any other cop I've encountered—which forces me to play to his compassion. "Besides, I need to keep my mind off the death of my friend." I'm thinking about Tommy, making the statement true. My gut tells me this man is only interested in truth. Me? I'm the villain playing on his good heart in order to slither into the house with hopes of garnering information pertaining to Dru's case. And to potentially manipulate him into coughing up his disdain for Philip. I don't want to be the snake, but I have gaps that need filling ASAP or all of Tillie's worries about me will come true.

And that will never happen again. Not if I can help it, which is why I'm operating in survival mode.

Christian opens his mouth, and he's going to say no. Can't blame him. But then he puffs a burst of air from his lungs and swings open the door. "Okay. I was about to heat up some left-over spaghetti. You hungry?"

The thought of food makes me sick. "No, but you go ahead, and I can talk while you eat." I follow him inside the old home, filled with furniture from the early 1900s. "Where's the big beast of a dog you call Kitten? I heard him barking."

He points to the back of the house. "I put him in the screened-in back porch when I heard someone at the door. He likes it out there."

Good. I study the place. Original wallpaper peels in places, and the musty smell lingering reminds me of Sobo's shop. But it's the winding staircase that's the real showstopper of this home. Original hand-carved wood. Deep brown mahogany. "It's lovely and has a lot of potential." Not a lie there.

"I feel like it's the setting to one of those cozy mysteries my mom watches on Hallmark. Do I look like a cozy-mystery kind of guy?"

"I mean, you *are* a detective." I shrug, and he laughs.

"Fair enough, Miss Benedict." He pauses and studies my face. I don't like the way his dark eyes sear through me as if he sees my sins lurking in the depths of my heart. "How are you doing? I'm asking as a man, not a detective."

A man. When has a man ever asked me how I'm doing, feeling? This only makes me feel worse than I already do about the false pretenses. "Call me Acelynn. *Miss Benedict* is a little too formal for me."

"Acelynn, then. How are you holding up?"

"Honestly, I'd be better if I knew the details of her death. Dawna and Jack haven't shared them yet, and probably won't until the funeral."

"I understand. It's hard."

"Yeah. My mind keeps spinning awful scenarios. Of what that Cupid did—or someone trying to be Cupid. Have you gotten any leads at all?"

He motions me to the kitchen, and I sit at the table while he takes a plate from the fridge and puts it in the microwave. "I suppose I can tell you what I told them. But that's all, okay? To give you some peace. There are some parts of the case I'm not at liberty to divulge. You understand."

I nod. "Thank you." I appreciate his kindness, but I'm not dropping my guard.

"Drucilla was found naked at the bottom of her stairs. A valentine was found on her chest, like the other victims. But there were enough differences, like her not being in her bed, for us to believe her death was staged to appear to be at the hands of Cupid."

"Maybe she got away and fell?"

"That was a consideration, but there were other inconsistencies I'm not at liberty to discuss."

The pieces start to fit together. "You believe someone else killed her, staging it. But because not all the details about Cupid's killings have made it to the public, they screwed it up. That's why you're interviewing us. Everyone is a suspect, including women."

His dark eyebrows rise as the microwave beeps.

"The question remains," I say. "Did she run and fall accidentally, and then someone freaked and staged it, or was it all premeditated based on what they thought they knew about Cupid?"

"You secretly a detective?" he asks.

"I watch *Forensic Files* sometimes."

He laughs, and it's a nice laugh.

He sits with his leftovers. "I know me eating and discussing this seems insensitive, but I promise you it's—"

"The job. Once you've repeatedly seen heinous things, it's still horrifying, but you become a little desensitized."

"Sounds like you know a thing or two about that, or you were a psychology major." He twirls the noodles onto the fork like a pro.

"I was never a psych major."

He holds my gaze as if trying to unlock what has desensitized me, and I manage not to fidget in his presence. The way he sees me scares and excites me. I can't pinpoint the emotion or why he makes me feel this way. It's unsettling, and yet I like being here. But I'm on a mission. A mission to survive the future, so I can't allow myself to like this guy.

"And speaking of professions, if you don't mind, I could take a quick tour while you eat and make some initial notes. Save us both some time." And help me into his office. No way he doesn't have one. "Would that be acceptable?"

He scrutinizes me again, as if he knows I'm lying, but then he points upstairs. "Feel free. You can have access to everything but the office—second door on the right once you're upstairs. That's off-limits."

"I hear you." But I never said I'd listen. If I'm right, everything that could help me put pieces together is in that off-limits room.

I hustle upstairs. A narrow hallway stretches out with open

doors except the one he's told me is his office. Every single nerve hums, and my stomach clenches. Pausing, I listen. How long does it take to eat a plate of spaghetti? How much time do I have?

Is this betrayal of trust worth yanking up a plank? If I'm caught, the repercussions could be devastating on so many levels. But not knowing is even worse. Knowing what the Pinks have said and/or what they may or may not think of Acelynn is crucial to my existence in this world. I need the level playing field or I'm done for, and I have no money and nowhere to go.

Returning to Chicago isn't an option. I'm already dead there, and going back would put Tillie in danger. I have to stay here, where I have food, shelter and money. I have to remain as Acelynn until enough time passes to disappear without consequence.

No going back. I turn the knob and the door creaks, freezing me in place. Blood undulates in my ears. Has the sound of the door reached Christian, alerting him to my disobedience?

When I don't detect movement, I swallow hard and dart inside the office, leaving the door semi-cracked. Dark earth tones meet my eyes, and the smells of peppermint and musk fill my senses. In the corner is a large table with a jigsaw puzzle of dogs in a meadow. I guess crime solving isn't enough for him, and he needs other kinds of puzzles to unwind.

My gaze lands on his massive antique desk, where his laptop is open. A pile of brown case files is stacked next to it. The notepad he used at the barbecue is lying open beside it. Looks like he's in the middle of transcribing the notes into a digital file.

I'm light on my feet in case the joists squawk and he can hear me. I don't have time to read anything. I pull out my cell phone and start taking photos of the notes in his notebook. Page after page of nearly illegible scribbles. I see Bianca's name, Cotton's, MacKenzie, Ford and even Conrad.

Click. Click. Click. Click.

I keep taking photos while my heart jackhammers in my chest and my fingers tremble. Is he wondering why he can't hear me walking above him?

One of the files is open on Cupid, and I snap more photos. What are the details not being exposed to the public? I wince at the victims and see what the police and FBI have been hiding from us.

Click. Click. Click.

Shoe soles thud on the stairs.

Just need a few…more.

"So, what do you think, Miss Benedict? Is my house salvageable?" Detective Patrick's voice is loaded with amusement. One more photo and I pocket my phone and race to the door, hoping I'm out before he reaches the landing or I'm caught dead to rights. He'll toss me out on my rump, and my invasion of privacy will pique further interest in me. *Why is she so curious? What is she looking for? She's either involved or protecting someone.* And those thoughts will force Christian Patrick to look longer and harder at me. I could be sealing my fate and not helping myself.

As I close the door and step into the hall, he reaches the landing. My cheeks might as well be molten lava. Does the flush expose my guilt?

"Anything is salvageable for a price. Depends on what you want to pay." Do I sound guilty? I need to appear chill, but inside I am wound up tight.

"Well said." He eyes his office door, which is now closed. Then he studies me, sending my pulse to a deadly level and resulting in lightheadedness. I can't prove he knows where I've been, but deep within me, I know he knows I've breached his trust and gone against his one wish.

My phone burns in my pocket. What if he asks to see it? Can I say no? Will I look any guiltier than I already am?

But he doesn't call me out.

Yet.

"Let's finish up downstairs." The closer to the front door, the better. "I'll leave you some paint sample cards. It's a good start." And the very least I can do for breaching his trust.

"Great," he says, but his eyes no longer sparkle. They're dulled by disappointment. I regret taking a peek and photos—the wicked images permeate my mind and I can't unsee them now.

But here I am.

"Great," I echo as a wall of tension goes up and another plank is torn from the bridge. "I'm thinking rich earth tones. Masculine but cozy. You know, for cozy mysteries."

"Nice." He motions for me to walk past him and downstairs.

At the kitchen counter, I mark *X*'s on the colors I like best and think would brighten the house. Once I've finished, I hand them over. "Okay, free consult. Done and done."

"I appreciate it." He tucks his hands in his pockets and walks me to the door. "I like the Summer Sandstone color."

I can't meet his eyes. "Solid choice. I guess I'll be going."

"Okay. Be safe."

I step onto the stoop, on pins and needles, and he says my name. I freeze and turn. Now he's going to call me out. Busted. My life is going to be over before it ever truly began.

"So you know, I'm exceptional at my job. Truth hidden in darkness always comes to light, and secrets with it. Sins always find you out."

I hope that's not true. "Good to know. I have full confidence you'll find whoever killed Dru."

"I will, and anything else that's buried under the same rock."

This visit was a mistake. Doesn't matter that I have what I

came for. He knows what I've done, and he's going to uncover all my other transgressions, which means I'm doomed.

Unless I ensure he never overturns the rock that would expose my greatest sin.

Chapter Twenty-Three

After Christian closes the door, I step into the sunshine, but I'm chilled to the bone. Nothing is going down the way I intended. My greatest threat might be a cop. But I have so many threats coming at me, and I feel trapped in a vortex. I'm spinning and about to be thrown.

Will what's in the files I photographed give me any clues into who killed Drucilla, what the Pinks and the families think about me, who they are behind the masks? Will it give me further insight into who Acelynn was and why Christian doesn't care for her boyfriend when they fight on the same side? These aren't questions I can ignore. They're like hunting traps laid out in a thick forest, and I'm walking aimlessly. Any moment, one of them will ensnare me.

Charlotte Kane was supposed to disappear. No longer a foster kid, punching bag or toy for sick people pretending to care about children. I was going to be a new Charlotte, like I've tried before and failed. But in a new city with a new sister, that was supposed to have been a success.

Instead, I'm trying to figure out how to prove I didn't commit Acelynn's murder when I'm found out, because it's going to happen if I don't figure out who my sister was and what she has on so many people—particularly Philip. I have a strong motive for killing Acelynn. What's to say I didn't hire someone to off her after I killed Tommy, blaming his death on Marchetti and then Acelynn's death on mistaken identity at his hands?

I'd believe it. I have access to criminals who would murder for drugs or sex.

An attorney could argue I obsessed over my sister's life and then became angry and bitter, even revengeful, because she was adopted into a privileged life and had a successful career. I wanted it. I took it by force. My past will be flung open wide, and it will bring down the axe, making for a thrilling Netflix limited series.

But I didn't do that, and there's no proof of that either. Just my worthless word.

I step off the curb and head across the street, my mind on overload, when a car engine gunning jerks me to attention. As I turn in the direction of the roaring, a black SUV with tinted windows barrels toward me.

My brain says run back to the sidewalk, but my body is frozen in place like a deer on a dark night with an oncoming car.

The impact slams my body onto the pavement. Searing pain radiates from my thigh to my head. Someone speaks to me, but the words are garbled, and my vision is blurred. Like I've been shoved underwater.

"Are you okay?" the voice repeats, and suddenly I'm up for breath. Detective Patrick looms over me, but the SUV has vanished. "Acelynn," he says with more force.

"I—I'm… A car hit me." I sit up and rub my head. My left leg has road rash.

"No. You were almost hit. You forgot your notebook. I hollered for you, but you didn't hear me, and then I saw the car."

He grazes the abrasion on my thigh. "I'm sorry I tackled you like a bear. I didn't have much time to show any finesse."

A few scrapes and throbbing pain are no big deal considering I could have died if he hadn't intervened. "No, I'm fine."

What if I hadn't left my notebook? What if he hadn't found it?

"Thank you. You—you saved me." Even though he knows I was in his office. Would I have done the same if someone I trusted betrayed me? I would say yes. That's the right answer. Only monsters would admit to watching a betrayer be mowed down. And I wonder…am I a monster?

Was my sister? Based on what I'm gathering, she would absolutely allow her betrayer to become roadkill. And if that's the case, how much alike are we? It must be in our DNA. We had separate upbringings.

The detective is nothing like me and has rescued me even though I'm undeserving. The magnitude of that burns behind my eyes.

His warm and gentle hand rests on my shoulder. "Did you see the driver or how many people were inside?" He helps me to my feet. "Do you need an ambulance?"

"No. Absolutely not." I soften my tone. "I hate hospitals." Not a lie, and I don't need hospital staff asking me medical questions I can't answer. "I'm okay, a little sore. And no, I didn't see inside. The windows were tinted."

Another wave of panic hits me. Could Marchetti have figured out the truth and found me? His reach is far. And if this is true, then Tillie might not be any safer in Chicago. I can't stop shaking.

"I only saw partial plates. Doubtful I can get a hit, but I'll try. It didn't look like a reckless driver, Acelynn. You were targeted. Do you know why? Any enemies?"

I have a ruthless enemy, and I'm not sure about Acelynn. Philip fits the bill with the threats and sneaking into my house.

But I can't reveal this to Detective Patrick.

"I don't think so." I can't catch a breath or a break.

"Then this might be about Philip. He has enemies. Everyone in the prosecutor's office does. Your relationship is public and easy to discover. Why don't you call him and have him meet us at the precinct? Or we can go to the DA's office. His choice."

No. No, I absolutely cannot meet up with Philip, and definitely not in front of Christian. Even if Philip keeps our interaction civil, Christian will pick up on the tension. He either has some kind of superpower at reading people, or he has facial expressions down to an art. His stares cause people to believe he knows their darkest secrets.

"I don't think Philip would discuss his enemies in front of me. Some of his dealings have to stay undisclosed to the public, and that would include me. But of course, feel free to reach out to him privately. It might be best."

Christian pokes out his lips, then strokes his clean-shaven chin. "Is there another reason you might want to be excluded from contact with Philip? Are you two in turmoil? A fight?"

I swallow hard. If we're in a fight, he goes on the suspect list. That might work in my favor. But if Acelynn has done something criminal that Philip knows about, he could retaliate. I've already burned a plank of trust with the detective, which makes Philip more credible than me. On the other hand, Detective Patrick didn't indicate he had a lot of love for Philip to begin with.

No scenario truly plays to my advantage, and my stomach is twisted like a braided rope.

"No turmoil, other than the normal relationship spats."

He eyes me a second more. "Then let's do this together. Once he sees you, he'll want to divulge. Someone attempted to murder you, Acelynn. This is serious."

It's even more serious than he knows. But is someone after Acelynn, or is someone after me?

He's already pulling out his cell phone. "We'll have him meet us at the station. I'll feel you're safer if we ride together."

Oddly, I will too. I do not want a repeat performance.

In about ten minutes, it's a done deal. He ends the call, and his eyebrows shoot north, but he says nothing as he escorts me to his unmarked car and opens the passenger door for me. I've never experienced this gesture before.

He presses the ignition button, and the car hums to life. After buckling his seat belt and pulling onto the road, he glances over. "You know, it's a funny thing. Philip never asked about your physical, mental or emotional condition."

This tells me there is no love lost between me and Philip.

It also tells Detective Patrick the same thing.

Then

The house is quiet and smells of oranges and lemons. Spring is in the air, and I love our city in spring. The windows are open, and a cool breeze freshens up the stale house.

Growling comes from the library, and I walk inside to find Bubs sitting on the floor with a card shredded and flowers smashed. Bubs is on his knees, small for a ten-year-old. But he's a striking image of his father and will grow up and fill out, and no woman would turn down a valentine from him. No one ever turns down his father now, never has, and that's part of our marital troubles, besides me being sent away to centers for mental health and the strain Petal puts on our family with each passing day.

"What's going on?" I ask.

Bubs looks up at me, frowning, and his neck and ears are flushed. He's just short of breathing fire, and only one person can cause this kind of anger.

Petal.

"I was going to give Shelly Barker flowers and a card, but—"

the sentence hangs for a moment as he clearly tries to find words "—now I'm not."

Shelly lives two houses down from us, and I've seen her a few times riding her bike when I'm out for a walk. I'm feeling so much better these days. I've even started having my Thursday lunches again and joined a book club, though I drink more wine than I read. I think we all do.

"We can buy a new card and flowers, Bubs." Forcing him to rat out his sister will do no good and bring repercussions as it always does, but red scratch marks trail down his neck into his shirt, and that I will not let go. "What happened?" I kneel and touch one of the angry claw marks.

"Nothing." He stands and kicks the remains of what was once a beautiful bouquet. It looks a lot like the ones in the vases downstairs. The new housekeeper puts fresh flowers out on Monday mornings. "The Wilsons' cat didn't want me to hold it."

The Wilsons' cat.

This reminds me of the last incident with a cat, the one Petal instigated or actually executed. I'll never know which one of them did it, but I know Bubs would never do something that heinous out of his own heart.

His heart is sweet and kind and good.

Pulling the collar of his little golf shirt down, I inspect the fresh bloody marks. "Did the Wilsons' cat do this for real?"

"It did." Petal's voice bounces against my ears like nails on a chalkboard. Each word that flows from her lying mouth is torture.

"But I smashed the flowers and card. Not to hurt him. He knows this. I was teaching him a lesson."

"And what lesson is that?" I ask through gritted teeth. I want to scratch her eyes out.

"Shelly Barker is nothing but trash. She doesn't deserve cards and flowers from anyone, let alone my brother. I will not stand for it." She crosses her arms over her chest and dares me to argue.

Shelly Barker is eleven years old, and she's not trash.

Bubs whispers, "She's not trash."

Petal marches into the study, picks up the mashed handful of the flowers and dumps them on his head. "She is, and you are not pursuing her. Besides, you're too young to love anyone but me." The last petal falls from her finger, and she slowly turns her head and tips it to the side, resulting in a wave of goose bumps on my arms. "And you of course, Mommy." She cocks her head and pokes out her bottom lip. "But you're sick, and who knows how long you'll live." She pats her brother's head and stands over him as if she owns him, and he humbly bows, allowing it.

Now he stares at the floor and kicks at the petals. I wonder if he's actually kicking Petal. One of these days he'll be strong enough to fight back, but he won't. The same reason I can't. Petal doesn't need physical strength to oppose an enemy. She's cunning and calculated. It's how I ended up in Carewood for six months and why I go to therapy on Friday mornings.

Even now, I hear the threat in her statement. She's tried to kill me before. One of these days, I fear she'll do it, and then Bubs will have no one on his side. She'll remove any obstacle between them. Including the neighbor child.

Petal kisses her brother's cheek, lingering as he squirms, and I ball my fists.

"I love you," she whispers, then walks away, bumping up against me as she strides past.

"I know what you did to him. You don't fool me." I can't reprimand her or retaliation will strike. Last time I overrode my own mother and sent Petal to her room, I woke up to a dead mouse in my wineglass sitting on my night table.

Other parents would judge me if they knew how terrified of

my daughter I am. But they don't know the evil I live with. The fear that always haunts me, forcing me to keep my mouth shut.

They don't have a child like mine.

Vindictive. Evil. A monster.

A child they fear.

I should have smothered her with a pillow years ago, but I couldn't bring myself to do it, which shows I'm not mentally unstable.

At the door, she pauses. "You don't know anything."

She's gone, and Bubba wipes her kiss from his cheek. His little nostrils flare.

"If you want to get new flowers and a card, we can do it. She won't hurt you." But she already has, and he knows as well as I what she's capable of.

A bloodcurdling cry sends a frigid tidal wave through my bones. I rush to the open window and Bubs follows. I look out and see Mrs. Barker fall to the ground, and her husband picks her up like dead weight as an officer speaks. His words are garbled, but his expression is filled with sorrow. Mrs. Barker howls while her husband clutches her, tears trickling down his scruffy cheeks. Something awful has happened to Shelly. Beyond an injury. That's a death wail.

"Where has your sister been?" My voice sounds rough and dry.

"Outside," he whispers. "She went for a walk a little while ago."

My blood runs cold. Whatever happened to Shelly Barker is Petal's fault. I rush into the kitchen, unsure of what to do. Do I go over there? What could I possibly say? How would I explain? I'd end up right back in Carewood.

I pour a glass of Malbec to calm my nerves instead of taking a trazodone, which would knock me clean out. And since they won't let me lock my bedroom door anymore, I need to stay as alert as I can.

I take a deep swig and gulp it down, but it's bitter and stringent, burning my throat. I drop the glass; it falls into a million shards, and I clutch my throat. I cough and the burn heightens.

What have I drunk? What is in my wine?

That's when I notice the big clear jug of distilled vinegar sitting on the counter, the cap next to it.

She's left it out on purpose as a warning, a threat. She can get to my food or drink at any time. Next time it might not be vinegar. Next time it could be deadly.

Later that night, as I slip into my bed, I turn on the TV. The ten o' clock news is on. They've discovered a little girl's body in the creek behind the playground. She apparently fell off her bike and hit her head on a rock, knocking her unconscious. She tragically drowned.

They've identified her as Shelly Barker.

Chapter Twenty-Four

"I'm not playing games," I say for the third time since being trapped in the car with Philip. Upon arrival at the precinct, he rushed in as if I was his shining princess, but it was nothing short of a facade. He smells good and he's attractive, but he gives me weird vibes. But I played the part, falling into his arms and asking him to be cooperative with Detective Patrick, who I thoroughly believe has both our numbers.

Though I don't know how. Maybe it's the trained eye. To anyone else, Philip and I sold it, and I'm definitely selling the fact I'm Acelynn. I suppose Philip is blinded to the little tells due to seeing me through the color red, which in some ways is a benefit, like the fact he avoids me.

Philip insisted he couldn't think of a single person who would attempt to kill me in an act of revenge, but he did promise to send a detailed list of anyone who had previously threatened him. My guess is that when he didn't find what he was searching for in my house, he sicced someone on me. Which just reveals the lengths he'll go to to obtain what he's after—something worth killing over.

Why not dump her? She might be using what's hidden to keep him from leaving her. Why not dump him? Who would want a man you can only keep through potential blackmail? Not me.

"Do you remember the first night we met? At that event to honor your father's work? You were vivacious and fun. We sneaked out and boarded your father's yacht. We joked about being *the* power couple, and we promised to help each other reach success. What happened to those two people, Acelynn?"

"I don't know," I murmur.

"We were in love once."

Past tense.

"Now it's nothing but games. No longer the power couple but power plays. Too much has happened. Been said and done. How long are you going to make me pay?"

I remain quiet because I'm not sure what to say. And I've found when you remain silent, it causes a wall of awkward tension that incites the other person to continue spilling in order to avoid the silence. But then, Philip would also know this fact as a prosecutor and remains quiet. But I don't cave either.

Finally he sighs. "What's the deal with the detective? The real deal? Leave it to you to take his questioning at the Newsoms' as a way to put him securely in your pocket. Be aware, he's a straight arrow. Not even you can seduce him into the palest of gray areas. He's known for his by-the-letter-of-the-law ways. It's pathetic."

"I find it refreshing."

He laughs. "I'd accuse you of sleeping with him, but he knows we're together, and when I say straight and narrow, I mean it. He'd never cross a line. I don't know. Maybe he's too good to be true. I can't find a single smudge on his career or in his personal life. But you'll at least attempt to sway him into your pocket, in case you need him."

Need him for what? I do need him, and I did sadly use him for photos. But what would Acelynn want him in her pocket for? The petty thefts? Doubtful. Does she use everyone?

"I'm not trying to sway anyone. He told you how we met and why I was at his home earlier today. If you know he's a man of integrity, then why are you questioning me?"

"Because you love a challenge, and you'd think it was worth a try." He slaps his blinker switch to signal a right turn. "Tell me who you've crossed a line with that would want you dead."

Besides him? "No one."

"I don't buy that." He glances over at me at the red light. "We're eyeball-deep in this thing. So don't even consider crossing a line with me."

I recognize the same look in his eyes that I saw in Teddy's.

Fear, but also fury—because somehow, I've trapped him, or rather she has.

I test the waters and hold his gaze with steel in my eyes. "Then stop hounding me and threatening me in texts."

His eyes widen, and the light changes. "You think I'm threatening you? I'm warning you. We have everything to lose. Everything we've ever wanted and dreamed for. Don't screw it up. I can only do so much to keep us above water. Stay away from the detective. I don't trust him."

What have they done? I can't ask questions or it'll raise suspicion. "You said he was honest to a fault."

"That's why I don't trust him. People want things, Acelynn. People like us. We're ambitious. We attain, and then we want more. We deserve our dreams and aspirations. He's content to solve crimes and live in obscurity. He won't even do press conferences. Christian Patrick could climb the ranks and become police chief, but he's satisfied to be a detective. I don't trust people who want for nothing. It's not normal."

For once, I agree with Philip and understand him. We're not too unalike. I want bigger and better things. The difference is I have yet to attain a single one. They're out of my reach. Is that at the crux of Philip and Acelynn's games—their climb to further success? "Maybe we're trying to fly too close to the sun." If I had what they did, I wouldn't want more. I would be content.

But deep down, I know it's not true.

Want is an open grave that needs to be constantly filled.

His eyes soften as he glances at me again, as if he's seeing the woman he went wild for two years ago. "Maybe," he murmurs. "Probably. But we're not Icarus, Ace."

I actually know some Greek mythology thanks to old books collecting dust at Sobo's. Icarus was too egotistical and cocky and sabotaged himself against Daedalus's warnings. He flew too close to the sun and his wings, made of beeswax, melted. Legend has it he drowned when he fell from the sky. "Maybe we're not Icarus. Maybe we're phoenixes and will rise from the ashes."

"You want to get burned and rise up, go on. Leave me out of it." He sighs. "I'm meeting your dad at the country club tomorrow, having lunch with some of his friends. Money that can help my campaign."

He's going to run for an elected position. District attorney. Mayor. Congress. Not sure, but it's going to be big and ambitious. The picture is now clearer. He wants Acelynn's father's influence and money—and friends' money. He knew Conrad before Acelynn. He might have had underlying motives for dating her from the start. What did Acelynn want from him? Did she peg him as an ambitious man from the get-go, or did she uncover it later? Did she feel betrayed and latch on to something to keep him under her thumb? What have they done together that no one can know about?

Why stay with him unless their shared ambition held them together? Power. Influence.

Was my sister vindictive? Ambitious? Or far darker than either of those things? What could Philip give her that her own father couldn't or wouldn't?

I think about Conrad's cold position toward me at the New-soms'. Conrad and Acelynn did not have the warm relationship she touted, but he liked Philip. Could Philip have been Ace-lynn's means to gain her father's approval or love?

"If you don't want to fly too close to the sun, Philip, stop sneaking into my house. Your last search was evident." Philip Beaumont is dangerous and possibly deadly, but Acelynn may be as well. This is how she would respond if she'd known he was searching her home.

Philip pulls up next to my car. "I wasn't in your house, Ace-lynn. Maybe don't give your house key to your so-called friends. I've said it before and I'll say it again. You'll never stay on top as long as you're dragging around dead weight, and that whole crew is nothing but."

He was in my house. Why is he lying? I can't confess I saw him. Acelynn isn't someone who would cower in the corner of a closet. If so, she'd never be so formidable, and two men wouldn't fear her.

"You're lying. We both know it." I step out of the car and toss him my most chilling glare, and he shivers. He physically shivers. "You won't find it. Stop looking."

"I'm not. I trust you won't do anything stupid—again, that is." He swallows hard and avoids eye contact. I hope he's more believable in a courtroom.

But his lies have presented me with new information. He's hiding his trespass to conceal the fact he wants out of this relationship—or arrangement—with Acelynn. Until he has possession of this item, or items, he can't sever ties. He fears what she might do if she discovers his intentions. Maybe he didn't put a hit out on her. Marchetti might have figured out the truth. But it's possible neither Philip nor Marchetti has it out for me, and it's about something else entirely.

Leaning inside the vehicle, I smirk. "You enjoy that lunch tomorrow. You won't make the climb to the top without the money. And stay out of my house without my permission."

If looks could kill... "Don't threaten me. I'm done with threats."

But he's not, or he'd admit to being in my house.

Without another word, I close the passenger door and collapse inside my car, setting the navigation system to home. Philip peels away, and I pinch the bridge of my nose as a stress headache hits the back of my neck and tightens my shoulders.

Fifteen minutes later, I arrive home and let the dogs out for their business. Then I put a kettle on and sit at the counter, waiting for the water to boil for tea. Time to look through the photos I took at Christian's. First I study the Cupid case.

The images sicken me. Lifeless bodies sprawled out on their beds, each wearing nothing but a gold necklace—none of them alike. Must be their personal jewelry, and I finger the gold necklace hanging at the base of my throat. I've become so used to it in this past week that I forget it's even there, dangling.

A valentine isn't simply laid out on their chests, as the public assumes. The cards have been stabbed into the flesh with a cupid's arrow. Each valentine has the same scripture verse about love being patient and kind. Never jealous.

I zoom in on the handwriting in the case files. The agent—Asa Kodiak—has written prelim findings.

UNSUB is likely a white male in his early thirties to late forties. Good-looking. Smart. But unable to connect emotionally with the opposite sex even if on the outside he appears comfortable with them. He might even be overly sexual in conversations and flirt notoriously but can't commit. Possibly due to a maternal heavy hand that demanded all his affection and attention or used this scripture reference. Women are all blondes and same pe-

tite frame. He's killing women who look like the woman
he wants or who left him. Heavy bruising on vics reveals
rage which is directed toward his initial target. *Note this
woman needs to be found or will be the final victim at
some point. He's working up to killing her, gaining confidence with each kill.

Each woman wears a gold necklace. Victims' families
identified the pieces of jewelry, so they didn't come from
the UNSUB, but he likes accessories and either forces
them to wear it during the assault or puts it on them
afterward.

I shudder at his working profile. What a sicko this killer is.

The UNSUB might be invited in, as there is no evidence of breaking and entering. Allie Deardon left her
bedroom window open, and that may be how he entered,
but unlikely, as no other victims left windows or doors
unlocked. He could be a deliveryman, repairman, anyone
who might have access to a home and be nonthreatening.

The teakettle clicks. I pour boiling water over a chamomile
tea bag and let it steep as I briefly scan interviews with neighbors, friends and family who were related to the earlier victims. After adding a heaping dose of honey, I turn to Drucilla's
case file.

Drucilla was beautiful. Hair like spun gold and worthy of a
shampoo commercial. She had a little dimple in her chin and
big blue eyes, but she could stand to eat a sandwich with white
bread. Her crime photo punches the air from my lungs. Her
hair is matted with blood that's almost black, and her body lies
crumpled in odd angles like something out of a horror movie.
She's naked but not wearing a necklace. A valentine has been

laid on her chest but no arrow. All details not revealed to the public.

So why was Agent Kodiak at the interview? To help Detective Patrick narrow down who might have killed Dru? Clearly we're all suspects.

Any of us could have done it. Why? The only animosity I'm aware of is the tiff between Acelynn and Dru. But that hardly seems a reason to kill her. I know the dollar amount in Acelynn's bank account, and she's not hurting for cash.

After a sip of tea, I hesitate to scan my own interview. But that's the main point for breaching the detective's office. I scroll to it and begin, bile rising in my throat.

I'm unable to move past the first two sentences Detective Patrick has penned.

I suspect Acelynn Benedict is withholding information and lying. Phone records show Benedict called Drucilla and they spoke for about eight minutes Friday, the day of her murder, but Benedict said she never returned the call.

Chapter Twenty-Five

Well, of course I'm lying! I'm not Acelynn, and I've made a grievous error. Acelynn must have deleted the recent call and I had to go with an assumption. This stupid slipup is going to lead to my epic demise. I think I'd rather die than be caught.

Not that I wasn't already on his radar, but the specific request not to enter his office now feels like a test to confirm his suspicions about being a liar. It's possible I could have forgotten about the call, but the fact I failed his test tells him otherwise. I'm now withholding information.

Except I'm not! This whole situation has gone from bad to worse. Detective Patrick needs to know that Acelynn didn't do it regardless of a phone call. But would Acelynn know who did? Who had motive among the friend group? Not that I suspect any of them, but the police do.

Acelynn's tongue has been nothing but forked, and she's spun a deceitful and sticky web of lies and deceit.

I turn to the next interview. Bianca Lambert.

Bianca has zero notes at the top of her interview. She was

at home watching a movie with her brother the night Drucilla died. *Die Hard*, to be specific. Ford spent the night, and they didn't hear from Dru. Dru's closest friend in the group was MacKenzie. She influenced Dru not to pay Acelynn for the work done. Bianca seems to stick up for Acelynn about the redecorating. She mentions Dru's serial dating as well, except for the longer relationship with Jacob, but she suspected Dru cheated on the man who owns and operates a gun range nearby.

Bianca said the cheating could have ended it, or she grew bored. Dru was the most private of the Pinks.

I'm not buying that. The Pinks don't let anyone stay private. They're literally pushing into every aspect of each other's lives. Is this statement true or not?

I flip to Ford's account—no notes on him either—and he tells a similar but more colorful story about Dru and her hookups. According to him, all the boys in their tight-knit group have made it into her bed at some point since she was sixteen. Was one of them in her bed recently? Could that be motive?

Next I read MacKenzie's interview.

★ Note MacKenzie Newsom is overly eager to give information. Personality or hiding something?

At least I'm not the only one being homed in on. MacKenzie seems to have more information on Jacob Moore. She states Dru revealed he was too controlling and narcissistic, forcing her to pull away from friends, which MacKenzie took the hardest. Acelynn didn't seem to care, as they'd already had a falling-out over Acelynn expecting a friend as close as a sister to pay for her services. Acelynn stormed from Dru's house and raged about it constantly with the other friends.

I zero in on an additional note at the bottom of the page.

★★★ Note They call themselves the Pinks. They have house keys to each other's homes.

Why are three asterisks before that? What does that mean, and why is MacKenzie throwing Acelynn under the bus? It's like she wants the investigative attention on Acelynn. Is she jealous of Acelynn's success or her sham of a relationship? Has something more sinister transpired between the two? Am I in danger from MacKenzie? If Acelynn is willing to hold something over a boyfriend, what might she be willing to do to a girlfriend?

I let my mind wander to my own past. My own superficial friendships.

I can't judge. I kept dark secrets from Tillie that ended up coming out. Maybe the detective is right. Sins find us out at some point. But even to this day, I hold secrets from Tillie. We all keep certain things about ourselves locked deep down. No one knows every single thing about us or our thoughts. I even try to hide truths from my own self. I can't be alone in that.

Cotton's interview reads similar to Ford's, but he confesses to seeing Dru at lunch the Tuesday before she died, which was common between them. He notes he saw a man's toiletry kit in her bathroom when he ran in to use it before driving home after lunch. He thinks Dru was seeing someone. One-night stands don't bring along toiletries. Cotton was asked if he inquired about it, and he responded no. He didn't care, and her business was hers.

★ Note This corresponds with the toiletry bag that was found on the sink in the primary bathroom. Follow up with Acelynn Benedict about the phone call.

But he didn't follow up. He didn't ask me anything about Dru other than how I was doing and then tested me with forbidden fruit, which I not only tasted but gorged on.

After I look over the rest of the interviews, none of them any more revealing, my tea is cold, and my thoughts return to Philip and the object he was searching for. I'm exhausted, but I know I'm not going to be able to settle enough to sleep, so I give the house another go.

If I was going to hide something, I'd want it nearby. The bedroom is the best choice, though I haven't found anything yet. But maybe what he's hunting is inconspicuous. After several minutes, I find nothing, or I've found it and it means nothing to me. The dogs follow me around the room, under the bed. I use my cell phone light to search under dressers and chests and behind drawers.

Nothing.

Nothing in the jewelry box either. From there I check the bathroom, unfolding towels and unzipping dozens of makeup bags and travel cases. Then I move into the walk-in closet, which is bigger than my own bedroom in Chicago. Dropping to my knees, I press around on the walls, which is over-the-top but always there in movies and books, so why not? Acelynn is clearly devious and sneaky. I might find a false wall full of nail polish and lip glosses.

As I push aside shoeboxes with high-end logos, a black box with no brand or logo comes into view. It's heavy, out of place and piques my interest. I snatch it up and lift the lid, unsure of what to expect. Stacks of cash. A bloody knife. Old love letters.

Not this.

Inside the box are dozens of folded paper targets. Excellent marks. Bull's-eyes every time. As I flip through them, toward the bottom of the stack, they become more amateur. It appears Acelynn had been taking shooting lessons and became quite the marksman. I assume they're hers, since there's no name on any of them. Who else would they belong to, and why does she have them hidden in a shoebox in her closet?

Underneath the paper targets is a handgun.

I remind myself it's the South and everyone has a gun, including women. It's probably no big deal. But why keep a gun in the back of a closet under paper targets? Why not put it in your bedside table drawer for protection, especially when some whack job is prowling and stabbing arrows into women's chests? No one would have time to race into the closet while being attacked.

What was my sister up to? Was there something more sinister to her need to learn to shoot? Was she afraid of someone? Her devious ways have someone angry enough to murder her. My hip throbs, proving it. A car tried to check me out of this life—her out of this life. As I stew on it more, I don't think it was Marchetti.

Will this person keep trying to kill me? I want to run away, but the cops will find me, and never seeing Tillie again breaks my heart. But if I stay, I may end up dead too.

I replace the papers and lid and don't touch the gun. I'm not stupid. My prints aren't identical to Acelynn's even if they might be similar. I return the box as I found it. Is this what Philip wanted? The gun? Would *his* prints be on it?

Did he murder someone, and Acelynn helped him cover it up to keep his reputation and their dreams intact, or...could he have tampered with evidence in a case and had her stash this gun? That's not just a movie trope; cops plant and hide evidence more often than we'd like to believe. But why try to retrieve it if they're in cahoots? My mind is an arsenal of ideas and questions thanks to my sweet lying sister.

And I thought I was the only liar in the family.

I exit the closet, which smells of her perfume, and pause. Wait a minute. Did I see what I think I saw? I rush back inside and snatch the box again, then open it and look at the right top corner.

A logo and business name.

Big Guns. A muscled arm holds a gun.

Same gun range mentioned in Christian Patrick's notes.
Owned and operated by Jacob Moore.
Drucilla's ex-boyfriend.

Chapter Twenty-Six

Monday I wake to the cotton balls playing tug with a rope and it's nearly 10:00 a.m. Yesterday they put Drucilla to rest. Dawna, her mother, asked each of us if we wanted a vial of ashes. None of us did. I stood with Conrad and Lucille—who was lucid—and Teddy. Afterward, a small meal was catered at the Newsoms' in place of the Sunday barbecue. It had been small and intimate and mostly quiet except for some reminiscing, which I did little of. I can't trust Acelynn's stories, but I remembered a few lunches and events posted on Instagram and kept it vague. I'm now looking at each person in a new light. A dark light.

None of these people tell the truth. Not to each other and maybe not to themselves.

I force myself out of bed and let the dogs out. The gun range was open yesterday, so I called about my last lesson or the next one booked—hoping to gather more information. But Acelynn Benedict isn't in the system, according to the guy who answered.

That could simply mean she had lessons off the books with Jacob Moore.

What if Drucilla and Acelynn had a fight over this man? I think about her dancing with the dark-haired man at the club. My sister might not have been the faithful and loyal girlfriend she claimed to be. She might have been hooking up as much as Dru, but hiding it better. Not that Dru hid her life from the Pinks. She was open about her escapades.

What terrifies me is if Detective Patrick talks to Jacob Moore again. What if Jacob tells him he's sleeping with Acelynn, or was, or that he simply knows her well because he was teaching her how to shoot guns? I'm in the dark, and any moment I'm about to be blindsided. How will I explain that without giving myself away? I can't. I'm in a constant state of anxiety over this.

Too much energy surges through me. I need an outlet. I decide to change into old jeans and a faded T-shirt and start working on that library with all the feels from *Beauty and the Beast*.

Was my sister beauty or beast?

A whisper floods my soul: *Am I beauty or beast?*

Maybe we're all coexisting, both sides fighting against each other. Sometimes the beauty wins, and sometimes it loses to the beast. But I don't want to think about dark sides or the fact I might have one. It's all too overwhelming.

The room has been prepped for painting, and the cans of paint sit next to the door. Might as well finish it. I can upload it to YouTube, do some tutorials. A week, and the funeral, has passed. Viewers will be ready to see me back on screen, working and doling out tips. Creatives have to give the people what they want, and I can't let my sister's legacy fall to the wayside.

Switching to reels, I choose camera and hold it up. Next time, I'll use the tripod, but this reel will be quick.

"Hey, y'all, Acelynn here. I'm in my *Beauty and the Beast* library-to-be and wanted you to take a peek at what I'm about to work on, which will be exactly what I need as I continue to grieve my dear friend's loss." Tommy. "I'll be back online with more routine reels and tips soon, though. But I miss you and wanted to check in. Stay tuned, and thank you for respecting my privacy."

I delete it and do it one more time, then post it. Immediately condolences bombard the comments, and prayers and good thoughts come my way.

Switching to the camera, I decide to film this. I can edit and splice it later for shorter reels. If I'm going to be my sister, then I have to be her in every way, which means thinking of myself as her. After pouring the paint into a pan, I start cutting in the edges. I've never actually painted walls, just canvases, but I find it cathartic. Did Acelynn? Did her eye for detail also give her a leg up in observing people? Seeing things others didn't, couldn't or wouldn't?

Between breaks and lunch and dinner, I get all the walls cut in and two of them painted. My upper back aches, and I'm tired, but it's a good sore. One that shows accomplishment. I step off the ladder and grab my phone, checking to see more comments on the short post I made earlier. Wow. The support is overwhelming.

Surprisingly, I've barely thought about the dark things happening or what might be hidden in this house. Now that I'm done for the night, they consume me.

I check Acelynn's contacts, searching for Jacob Moore. If Acelynn had off-the-books lessons with him, then his name would be in her phone. But I only find a Jacob Price.

A boom of thunder shakes the house, and I feel it clear into my chest. I gasp, startled, and check the weather app. Thunderstorms all night, which will lead into steady rain until after 9:00 a.m. tomorrow. Lightning flashes and brings another crack of thunder. I quickly put away the paint and carry the brushes to the downstairs mudroom, where I wash them as the bottom drops out and rain pounds the roof.

Another crack comes, but it's not thunder, and the power goes out, drenching me in darkness other than the few flashes that streak into the room with the bolts of lightning. Using my cell phone light, I see my way into the kitchen and open cabinets on my hunt for candles. The days have been muggy, and it won't take long for the house to warm up and become uncomfortable.

I hate the dark.

I know she has a candle in the upstairs primary bath. Several of them, actually. I can use those. But the sound of a joist creaking overhead catches my attention and steals my breath.

Are the dogs upstairs? Or is someone in the house again?

Would Philip return after I called him out earlier? I have no idea. Flashes of victim photos from Detective Patrick's case files carousel through my mind. Pulling a butcher knife from the block, I slowly make my way toward the staircase. The dogs are in the living room in their bed, their ears perked and heads cocked.

I should go right out the front door and drive out of here. That's the smart thing, but someone is disrupting my life, and I've had more than my fair share of disruptions. If it is Philip, now is the time to deal, and if it's anyone else, I'm a force to be reckoned with if I need to be. I'm not a victim anymore, and I will not behave like one.

The stairs creak, so I'm careful in my sock feet to avoid the squeaky joists. Other than the thunder and deafening rain pummeling my roof, the house is eerily silent. Gripping the knife, I reach the landing and cock an ear.

Nothing.

My throat is tight, and my palms are clammy.

Women brutalized. Bruised.

Assaulted.

Strangled. Stabbed.

My heart pounds, and my breath is ragged as I slink toward

the guest room on the right. No sounds. I'm hearing things. Spooking myself. Letting my fears overwhelm me. I creep into my bath to retrieve candles and the lighter.

The lights flicker, then peter out again.

I hear a thud. The dogs bark.

Do I call the police? Call Detective Patrick? No. That will lead to more questions that I can't or won't answer. Branches scrape along my bedroom window. I shudder, grab a candle and hurry down the hall and back downstairs.

I light the candle and set it on the kitchen island. The flame flickers and casts haunting shadows along the ceiling and walls.

Movement outside draws my attention and turns my lungs to concrete.

A dark shadow.

A form.

And I scream.

Then

"What are you looking for?" I enter my bedroom after my walk at the park. The doctor says the fresh air will do me good, and my sedatives have been lowered since I'm sleeping better.

I'm not.

I lied.

Sometimes one has to lie to find the truth. Strange things are happening in the house at night. I hear noises and scratching sounds in the hall. Darling Husband—a new name I've coined for him because he's neither of those things, and if I'm being honest, never was—says it's all in my head. I'm beginning to wonder if he says these things to make me believe it. To keep me medicated and out of his hair. Hair I used to love running my hands through.

A million years ago, I had an image in my mind of what a husband should be, what a marriage should be, and I set my sights on him. At the time, I thought he fit the bill.

He had everything going for him.

Old money. Athletic and handsome, charming. His fraternity

was the top-of-the-line, and it only made sense for us to be the *it* couple. After all, I was the cream of the crop in my sorority, though my dearest friend had her eye on him as well, but I won out. One can't fight a fair fight and be guaranteed the win.

Sometimes I think she actually won. I'm saddled with a man who doesn't love me.

Back then, though, I wanted tall, dark and handsome. White picket fences, big homes with pools and hot tubs. Friends who adored us and colleagues who respected us. I'd sit on charity committees and raise adorable children who had the same looks and physiques as us.

In order to attain those goals, to attain Darling Husband, I overlooked his dalliances with other girls—as long as they weren't from my own sorority. I had been a nobody my whole life, from a poor family. I faked it until I made it. And yet I never truly made it. Mother thought I'd landed a whale. Friends from my old hometown were green with envy at my climb to the top.

But to make it there, I had to pretend I never saw his arrogance and cruelty to others. In my feeble mind, I could change him. Like in romance novels when homely women tamed the gorgeous bad boy. I forgot those books were works of fiction, and in the real world, that rarely if ever happens.

Now he stands in front of my chest of drawers, his tie loose and the top two buttons of his shirt undone. I smell his last little number's cloying perfume from here, but I scrape it into the fog with all the other disappointments.

A frown forms a divot in his brow as he holds a glittering cuff link. "I can't find the other one. I have an important dinner tonight with colleagues. I thought I might have left it in your jewelry box."

"Do you need a plus-one?" I haven't been to a business dinner in ages. But, again, I'm feeling better than I have in a while. Although my thoughts toward Petal haven't changed in the past thirteen years. She's finally in a school where she's made friends outside of family friends. Tonight she's having a sleepover, and Mother will be here to keep an eye on them as if I can't. It's obvious I'm functioning just fine. But in their eyes, I'm a mental ticking time bomb.

"No, it'll be late, and no wives are attending. You know how these things go."

I want to ask her name and where he's taking her that he needs his fancy cuff links I bought him for our fourth anniversary. Back when I still had hopes of the life I'd dreamed about. Now I don't even have dreams.

I have nightmares, and their name is Petal.

"Of course," I say and approach him. Does he think I've lost my sniffer? He reeks of her cheap, gold-digging perfume. I touch his navy blue tie and undo it. He'll want to shower and change. "Well, I hope it goes well." At one time I could seduce him. I'm too tired to attempt it now.

I have bigger things to deal with. Like one of Petal's friends not dying and keeping my fears to myself so I'm not marched back to Carewood.

"I'm sure it will." He kisses my cheek. A peck. Zero affection.

"Petal's having a sleepover tonight." I slip my bangs behind both my ears and fold my arms over my chest. "I worry—"

"Have you taken your medication?" He cuts me off. He has no worries about the children.

"I don't take them again until bedtime."

"Make sure you do." He breezes by me to the shower. That's it. That's the crux of our relationship now. I head downstairs and open a bottle of Malbec and pour a glass full. The young me would look at almost middle-aged me and shake her head.

"Do you really think you should be drinking before my party?" Petal asks as she breezes into the kitchen. She's thirteen and developing faster than I remember doing as a child. I suppose everyone is different. Her hair is long and shiny with beautiful gold strands. She's striking, and I've noticed boys in eighth grade watching her as she exits the school building—at least on the days I pick the kids up.

She knows it too.

"I'm having a glass of wine, Petal. I'm a grown woman."

She waltzes to the refrigerator and opens it and takes out a seltzer water. What thirteen-year-old drinks seltzer? "A minute on the lips, a lifetime on the hips." She shrugs and pulls a protein bar from the cabinet.

"I can cancel this party in an instant," I snap. I'm sick of her taunts and belittling words.

"No, you can't. Because you and I both know what happens when I'm angry, Mommy." Her eyes meet mine with sinister amusement.

My blood curdles in my veins. I know exactly what happens when Petal is angry. People are hurt. Little girls have accidents and are drowned in creeks. I end up shipped off to mental institutions, though they're called care facilities now.

"What do you plan to do tonight?" Ignoring her remarks will hopefully come across as flippant, but I take all her threats to heart. She's capable of anything.

"Oh, you know, talk about boys and watch scary movies. Tell secrets."

"What secrets are you telling?"

She grins, and her pink lip gloss accents her perfect cupid's bow. She's the face of innocence with a heart of wickedness. My head feels fuzzy, and I realize I've gulped down this entire glass and poured a second in the few minutes we've been talking. Just one glass has become harder with each day. But it's more calming than my pills.

"None." She nibbles on her protein bar. "I want to know their secrets. Secrets are power. They can keep a group together or set it on fire."

She's perceptive, and I can't help but wonder if she's speaking in subtext to my friend group. What have the children over-heard and discussed? Affairs? Other sordid things? Adults as-sume children have no reason to eavesdrop, or if they did, the conversation might go over their heads, but not Petal. Petal is astute and hears everything, then collects those whispered words and saves them for a rainy day when she can use them to her advantage. She's done it before.

If Petal has her way, she's going to use these poor girls' secrets to burn them to the ground. "Secrets hurt people."

"Daddy's secrets don't seem to be hurting him." She carries her seltzer toward the theater room.

"What secrets?"

"Mommy, you don't want to know. You said it yourself. Se-crets hurt people, and in this case, that person is you." She saun-ters from the room, then pops her head back into the kitchen. "But her name is Candi with an *i*."

My hands tremble. How would Petal know anything about this woman? Does she have some otherworldly knowledge? Or has her father been sloppy?

My own mother must know and be keeping it from me. For fear of losing her own fattened calf. Living here is a dream come true for her. Her every need is met. She's pathetic, and in some ways living my own dream. My husband dotes on her, and the children adore her—although Petal's kindness and flattery are for the sole purpose of manipulation.

Like this stupid party. Tonight is nothing more than a power play for Petal.

I carry my last dregs of the Malbec, along with the bottle, upstairs and into my room. By the time I'm finished with the entirety, the room spins, and my mouth is dried out. I look at the clock, and it's almost 8:00 p.m. Have I lost time again or dozed from the wine? I can't remember, but a soft rap draws my attention to the door, and I stumble to it. A girl stands before me, but I don't recall her name, even though I do recognize her. She's Hollywood material even through her tearstained cheeks.

"Darling, what's wrong?"

"I would like to go home, please." Her voice is shaky as she peers down the hallway.

"Come inside." I point to the sitting area near the windows, and she tiptoes into the bedroom. As she passes me, I gasp and clutch my chest.

My vision might be blurry from the bottle of wine, but there is no mistaking that the back of her hair has been sheared into choppy sections while the front has been left long. "What happened? Who did this?"

But I already know.

"I just want to go home." She covers her face with her delicate hands, perfectly manicured and painted a soft pink. She wears a dainty opal ring on her right ring finger.

My heart aches for her. "Sweetie, your mom is going to want to know what happened to your hair. It's okay to tell me. I'll believe you."

She feels the back of her head, and new tears fill her eyes. She knows there's no hope, nothing to be salvaged. All her hair will have to be buzzed to the scalp in order to match what's been sheared already. What will her parents say? Do? They might sue us.

Petal bursts through the door, fury burning in her eyes. "There you are, Tabs." She thrusts her hands in the air. "I didn't think she'd actually do it. She had a choice. We were playing truth or dare. She chose dare." Petal cocks her head and shoots Tabs a glare. "Tell her the truth."

"I—I…"

Petal stomps over to the velvet chair and yanks her up. "Come on. I'll fix it. You'll look even better with short hair. Not everyone can pull it off. But you will. And don't worry," she says as she guides the child from my room. "If your hair is Robbie's favorite thing about you, then he's not worth it." She almost shoves her out of my view, flipping her own long blond hair behind her shoulder. "Robbie can find someone else."

I stand gaping, unsure of what to do. By morning, Tabs's story will be organized and without tears. The cut will have been her doing, and Petal will get off scot-free. If I dare repeat anything other than their story, I'm the lunatic.

Tabs might have cut her own hair on a dare. Petal might have done it herself. No one but them will ever know the truth. What I do know with certainty is that Petal had an agenda in which no one would outshine her, and with the toss of her own sheen of hair, she's just declared victory.

And that victory is Robbie.

God help Robbie if he rejects her.

Chapter Twenty-Seven

Lightning reveals the shadowy figure. It's Tillie. Tillie has come to Savannah, and she's standing outside the kitchen door with a rolling suitcase and rain matting her hair to her face.

I'm still terrified, but I'm probably hearing things, as the darkness and storm have triggered old, frightening memories for me.

I rush to the door and throw it open. "Tillie!" I wish relief would flood my system at seeing her, but she's just flown into a brand-new nightmare. I've shared only a few details over the course of the week and few days I've been gone.

Tillie enters the kitchen, the dogs going berserk. She drips on the tile floor and swipes a mass of wet hair from her face. "I was worried."

"Let me make some tea. The power went out with the storm, but the stove is gas."

"I wondered why the house was so dark. It's awful out there." She shivers from the cool air, though it's warming up by the second to me. "Why'd you scream?"

"You know, the whole dark-and-stormy-night thing. Creature outside the house lurking." I'm not that far off base, and I'd rather not share I'm still afraid of the night and all that goes bump in it.

"I'm not a creature." She grins and squeezes her hair out over the sink. "I need to change."

"Of course." I light the candle and hand it to her. "The half bath is right there." Better to keep her close unless I'm wrong, but I hear nothing at this point and convince myself that it's all childhood trauma. My house is empty besides us and the dogs.

I pull mugs from the cabinet and the tea bags from the pantry. Tillie is still standing in the doorway leading to the half bath.

"What is it?" I ask.

"Nothing. Just that you were always a quick study when it came to new places. I was constantly turned around, but you had layouts figured in seconds. I would never have guessed this wasn't your home, that you hadn't lived here for years."

I read between the lines, and my new concerns aren't fabricated in my rampant imagination. She's worried. Not about me. *For* me. "I was always a quick learner in life. Books were your thing."

Tillie's eyebrows rise. "I'll change and be right out." She closes the door behind her, and I put the kettle on.

It's still silent in the house other than Tillie digging through her luggage and changing and the soft hiss of the gas heating up the kettle. By the time I pour boiling water in mugs, Tillie returns in dry clothes, a hand towel around her hair. "Smells good."

"It'll warm you up." I scoot the hot tea toward her as she sits on a bar stool at the island. The candle flickers, and the dogs jump on her ankles with wagging tails. She bends and pets them. "So you came all the way here out of worry? Has something happened in Chicago? Marchetti?"

"No. It's like the world has…" She drops the rest of her sentence, but I know the final words. The world has gone on like Tommy and I never existed, because we were nobodies.

"I had two weeks of vacation, so I took it." She shrugs. "It wasn't hard to find Acelynn's address or hop a plane and call an Uber." The lights flicker, then stay on, and the hums of the fridge and air-conditioning return. Tillie undoes her hair and lays the towel on the island, then adds sugar to her tea and takes in the large kitchen. "This place doesn't suit you, though."

"I wouldn't say that. I love the pink hues and soft blues. It's elegant." Why can't I be elegant and soft? I want to be. I simply haven't been given the opportunity.

"It's frilly."

I grimace. She's not intentionally insulting me, but indirectly it's rude. "Maybe the real me is frilly. I just haven't been given an opportunity in life to show it." I love this house.

Tillie eyes me over the cup of tea but says nothing. I hate when she does that. Silently judges. Finally she says, "What's all over you?"

I look down at my painting attire. "Oh, I'm remodeling one of the rooms upstairs into a library and reading room, although there's already one down here."

I glance up, and she's standing now, one eyebrow raised. "You're remodeling?"

"To pass time. I'm too anxious to do nothing, and Acelynn was already beginning it. I might as well finish what she started for the time being. I have no clue how long I have to stay now that they made me."

"Have to or want to? You said you were going to lie low a few days. Two, tops. Charlotte, this is feeling a lot like—"

I thrust a finger toward her. "If you say it, I'll scream. I will. I was caught on day one. I can't help that. I never planned to take over her life. It's not like I went out and purchased thousands of dollars of supplies. I haven't paid for anything but Ubers to drive me around and boarding for the dogs, which she would have done anyway."

Why can't bygones be bygones? Because I'm still replacing the planks on our bridge. This is why she's shown up unannounced too. She doesn't trust what I've been telling her, which isn't much, but I can't push her to leave now without revealing the whole truth or she will take it all wrong.

"Okay," she murmurs. "Then tell me how it really is."

So I do. From the beginning, even Acelynn shoplifting and playing games with me, like to see if I would dine and dash. Her face pales with each new scenario, and her mouth drops open when I tell her I was almost flattened by a car at the detective's house.

"Why were you at his house?"

She's not going to like this part at all, but I don't lie or fudge.

"You photographed his reports and notes. That's illegal!"

"What other choice did I have, Till? I can't stay here and be in the dark or I'm the weak gazelle about to be picked off." In some ways, it's worse than being in the grips of Marchetti. At least with him, I know where I stand and what his plan is.

"Well, at least you weren't caught. If you get caught, Char..." She covers her face with her hands, and I feel her anxiety. I carry it daily times ten, so I refrain from revealing I think he does know and was testing me, because that's a thought, not fact. I don't lie about facts.

"I know." Nobody knows better than me.

"And the family?" she asks. "They haven't suspected?"

"They're not the tight-knit family she made them out to be either, and that works for me."

Tillie pushes her mug to the side. "Okay, then we start one person at a time and figure this out."

"No. The whole point of me leaving was to keep you safe."

Her quick raise of her eyebrows says she doesn't fully buy that.

"You aren't safe here either. You have to go."

"No." Her set jaw and steely eyes let me know she's not budg-ing, and even though I want her to leave and be safe, I am glad she's here. I was alone, and it's nice to not be.

"We're going to figure it all out. But then what?"

That's why she's staying, for the *then what*. To make sure a *then what* does happen. "Because you cannot stay here and pre-tend you're Acelynn Benedict the rest of your life. You—you know that, right?"

Yes. But if I could be a better daughter than Acelynn ever was and make new friends or try to help the friends Acelynn already has, staying wouldn't be in vain. Would it? "Right," I murmur. "For now, I have to stay or it will be too suspect."

"Then we have to determine if the car that tried to hit you was targeting you or Acelynn. Marchetti got his girl, as far as he's concerned, and Tommy too." Her voice cracks, but she pulls it together. "Acelynn was probably in trouble from more than one person. If she would hold something over a man as powerful as Philip Beaumont, she might have found someone equally as powerful—or someone more dangerous."

She's right. "Maybe she has a lot of somethings."

"Give me her laptop and I'll search it. Worst-case scenario, I can ask one of the tech-savvy guys we use in our firm to hack into it. But I'm not bad myself. Maybe there's something on it you haven't found that might indicate what she's hiding or where or if there's anyone else who might want to run her down in a car." Tallulah jumps off her lap and curls up next to Rue on their pink bed. They have one in every room.

"We have another issue."

"What's that?" she asks.

I splay my hands. "Everyone has a key. They show up un-announced whenever the mood strikes. They'll know all my friends, so if they barge in and you're here, what do I tell them?"

Till toys with the tea bag string hanging from her mug. "If Acelynn keeps secrets, then I can be one too. An old friend who was in design school with you. We reconnected, and I moved to the area or am moving to the area and staying here while I look at property."

"Nope. Won't work. Bianca Lambert's father owns a massive real estate company, and pretty much all the kids work for him in some capacity. Including Teddy. But you could be here on vacation. More truth makes for a more believable lie."

Tillie nods. "Tillie Smith. Smith is an easy name to get lost in a search. I live in Chicago. No one will go looking me up, will they?"

"Not Chicago. I don't want that word coming from either of our mouths. Michigan. Grand Rapids. Detroit. But nothing in Illinois."

"Got it."

"I'll ready your room upstairs. The one at the end of the hall has a private bath and overlooks the courtyard. You'll like it."

She throws me another skeptical glance. "What I'd like is for us to squeak out of this mess, but I agree if Acelynn disappears and an investigation is launched—and it will be—it will lead back to you, and you won't be able to be found. Foul play will be the focus, and you'll be the prime suspect in her death."

She's on my side—at least outwardly. I'm still not convinced she doesn't think I had something to do with Acelynn's death.

"But this is not your life, Charlotte. You are not her."

I don't need a nag. I need a friend. "I know. Let me show you to your room."

After taking her upstairs and helping her settle in, I give her Acelynn's laptop.

As I return to my bedroom and pad across the floor to close the blinds, a streak of lightning hits the sky, and I see a figure running from my yard.

It wasn't childhood fears messing with my mind. I haven't been alone in the house. *We* haven't been alone.

Someone has been in here, hiding. And I can't be sure if they heard our conversation or not.

A presence hovers above a dark, watery surface and scratches against it.

Scratch. Scratch. Scratch.

A foreign scent wafts into my nostrils that doesn't belong in my room or my house, but it's intoxicating, and my eyes flutter open.

Before me is my wall of windows. The old-school alarm clocks tells me it's 1:54 a.m. I must have been having a weird dream, which makes sense with all I've been butting up against. But the noise, the scratching or swiping, from my dream continues. The hovering presence is also still with me, and my heart stutters as my body stiffens. Cupid victims' photos flash in my mind.

Get up. Run. Do something.

I can't. I'm cemented in place as the scratching continues. I listen, trying not to breathe or reveal I'm awake. The noise is familiar, but I can't place it. Then it stops, and I hear rustling and the hiss of a cushion release as someone rises from the chair.

I have nothing. The gun is in a box in the back of the closet, and I can't grab my phone without being seen.

The empty side of the bed dips, and a gentle hand slides into my hair.

My breathing hitches.

"Shh…you're having a bad dream. It's okay now."

Teddy's in my room.

On my bed.

I slowly roll over, and he's peering down at me. On the nightstand is a sketch pad and pencil—the scratching. The sound of an artist sketching and shading. He's…he's been drawing me while I sleep.

I don't think this is the first time.

"Why are you here?" I whisper, my body on high alert and ready for fight or flight. Was he who I saw running across the yard earlier tonight?

"I couldn't sleep." He shrugs and fishes in his pocket. "And I needed this, which you wouldn't give me last week when I asked." He holds up a hot-pink key that belongs to one of the Pinks. I don't know whose or why he wants it, but it's clear I'd be okay with it. His questions to me at the barbecue make sense now. He's been wanting to draw me—he has pent-up energy, and drawing is his release.

I sit up, pulling the covers over me. I spot his sketch of me sleeping and the likeness is uncanny, the vulnerability while I sleep terrifying.

He holds up the sketch pad and shows me the drawing. "You like this one?"

No. I want him to leave my house immediately. Why does he want to draw me sleeping? Why is Acelynn giving Teddy keys to the Pinks' houses? Is that a common occurrence?

A cold chill creates an involuntary shudder through my body. Did he take Drucilla's key?

"Yeah. It's good," I say through a mouth that feels like sawdust.

Teddy pockets the key again and grins. "You want to see the last one?"

No. I don't. Then it hits me he's been slinking through the house, which means he might have seen Tillie. But if he has, he hasn't asked any questions. I nod.

He flips the pad back three pages and holds it up.

"It's not the best one I've done, but she wasn't sleeping sound, and furrows marred her flawless skin." He leans in. "But she's my favorite."

I slowly turn to the sketch, illuminated by the moonlight

filtering into the room. The date catches my eye. Two Fridays ago.

My insides go black and cold as I stare at a sleeping, naked Drucilla Hilton.

Chapter Twenty-Eight

After I pushed Teddy from the house, I never went back to bed. Drucilla slept in the buff, which is why she's Teddy's favorite. But is that all?

Did she wake up and catch Teddy secretly drawing her? Did he try to make her death appear to be at the Cupid killer's hands? If so, would he have left her dead, bought a valentine and returned to the scene in the middle of the night? Doubtful.

I never should have let him walk out with that key, but what was I supposed to do to stop him?

Why would Acelynn allow him to invade the privacy of her friends, to sit in a dark bedroom and draw them while they slept? How long has he been doing this? Why does he do this? What does Acelynn get out of it besides playing a game no one knows about, like shoplifting?

It's creepy, and I don't want to imagine what else he might be doing.

Tillie enters the kitchen, yawning. At least he didn't find her or he never let on, but someone was in the house last night and could have heard everything. Was it Teddy? Why leave and return later? No, I don't think it was him. Could have been Philip again, though. But if he heard our conversation, and knew I wasn't Acelynn, he'd have called me out, wouldn't he?

Now that I know Teddy comes at night, Tillie's exposed, and I have to figure out what to do. If I change the locks, he'll suspect.

"What's up with you?"

"You don't want to know, but you have to." I unload about Teddy drawing me in my bedroom in the middle of the night. "Keep your bedroom door locked at night. I don't need him to find you."

She curls her nose. "That's sick. Why does he do it? Does it feel like he's drawing a dead person? Is he into dead people?"

I wince. "I don't know. I feel like Dorothy after the tornado dropped her into the land of Oz. But I can't go back to Kansas."

"What are you going to do?"

"I don't know. That seems to be my default answer."

"I'm gonna shower. We'll unriddle it. We have to." She leaves me with my many thoughts and jittery nerves.

Around ten thirty, the doorbell rings as I stand in the kitchen making two pieces of toast. With a butter knife in hand, I walk into the living room, my heart skipping several beats, causing an ache in my chest. Christian Patrick stands in front of me, his face a mask of unreadability. Perhaps he's here to check on me or bring me news from the near hit-and-run. Possibly call me out on snooping in his office and stealing photos of the files.

Or it's something else, and I try not to panic.

"Detective, hello. Come in. Everything okay? I was just making some toast. You hungry?"

"No, thank you," he says as he follows me to the kitchen, scanning my home. The dogs must be closed in upstairs with Tillie or they'd be down here barking and carrying on. "You feeling okay after the incident? Anything else happen I should know about?"

Why? Is he testing me again because something did happen? Has Jacob Moore revealed something about me? The toast pops, and I jump. "Toasters are like jack-in-the-boxes for adults, am I right?"

He smirks but says nothing, and it freaks me out even more. Sometimes what people don't say is far more important and telling than what they do.

"I'm doing okay, maybe a little jumpy." I point to the toaster since the joke fell flat. "Have a seat. Can I pour you a cup of coffee?"

"Thanks," he says and sits. "No coffee. I've had my three-cup limit already." He doesn't say anything else, so I slather butter on the sourdough toast, though I've lost my appetite—not that I had much of one to begin with.

"What brings you here? You get an ID on that partial license plate number?"

"No. Not yet. I wanted to share some information on Drucilla Hilton's case."

I wrap my hands around my mug of coffee to keep them from trembling. "Oh. Okay." Why would he want to divulge more information—more than what I already discovered in the files? And why with me? Has he discovered Teddy has used my key to enter Dru's home? Am I an accessory to murder?

"Two empty wineglasses were in the dish drainer. They'd been washed—maybe by Drucilla. Maybe the killer, washing away DNA evidence before they left. We also found a man's dress shirt crumpled in the back of her closet on our second visit. It's at the lab now."

That is new information, but it's irrelevant to me. Unless... Was it Philip's shirt? Teddy's? "Well, we told you she had a boyfriend up until recently and that she has many casual affairs. A crumpled shirt and wineglasses aren't out of the ordinary for Dru."

"True. We did talk to Jacob a second time as well."

My stomach plummets, and I try not to sway, but my head is fuzzy. "Oh. Okay. Good." But it can't be. Or he wouldn't be here. I'm on a sinking ship and drowning. This can't be happening.

He pauses as if he wants me to squirm. "According to him, he wasn't exactly a boyfriend but a hookup. The hookups fizzled, and end of story."

From what I read in the reports, Dru and Jacob were a real thing for six months. Why would Jacob lie unless he too had something to hide? I have to stick to what the Pinks have said. "I don't know why he's lying."

"Maybe he's not lying. Things aren't adding up, you know? And that bugs me. I'm a puzzle man."

I've seen the massive jigsaw puzzle in his office.

The sound of the dogs' nails on the wooden floor clip, and then Tillie emerges with them. I didn't have an opportunity to tell her to stay put, and now she's here. For him to see.

"Oh, hey," she says, and her cheeks redden.

"I didn't realize you had a roommate," Christian says.

"I don't. This is Tillie. She's an old friend from college visiting a few days, maybe a week."

He shakes her hand and introduces himself.

Tillie is the worst actress on the planet, and fear nearly radiates visibly from her person. She's going to inadvertently out us. Christian Patrick is bright and intuitive. A quick glance at him reveals he's interested in her bizarre reaction. I hope he passes it off as surprise.

"He's here about my friend I told you about." I'm the Hail Mary here. "The tragic death of Drucilla Hilton."

"Right. That's just awful. I'll leave you two to talk, then." She scurries out of the kitchen, and he watches her with fascination and those uncanny eyes that make you feel as if he has already read your thoughts before you even think them.

Once she's out of sight, he turns his attention to me. "I have this gut feeling—you ever get those?"

Do I ever. "Sometimes."

"Well, my gut says that information is being swept under the rug. Oh, one other thing the lab found. Wild. Dog hairs. Short and white and curly." He eyes the cotton balls playing in the living room. "Lot like your dogs."

A blazing heat sweeps into my bones, and my hands turn clammy. "Not surprising. I take my babies everywhere, including my friends' homes and work. I did do a lot of work for her."

He nods. "You take them everywhere."

"They're my children."

"I didn't notice them at the barbecue."

I have zero answer for this. I always have answers. "Are you saying without saying I'm a suspect?"

"I'm saying truth always reveals itself. In time. I simply keep working the puzzle pieces. Eventually, they fit and paint a picture of reality. I thought you'd want to know that we're doing everything to find her killer." He stands. "Oh, the dog hairs. Also wild. They were on the man's dress shirt. Do you wear men's shirts when you work?"

I can think of only two men dog hairs might end up on. Philip because we're dating. And Teddy because he's a freaky night lurker. "I don't. I probably should. They're comfortable and roomy."

He laughs. "For your little frame, I'd say yes. For me? They're nothing like a T-shirt."

He begins walking to the living room. He came over to tell me my dogs' hairs were on a men's shirt and to shake me into confessing something I don't know about. I think back to his note about me. Withholding information. Lying.

"You know what else my gut says?" he asks.

"You really are hungry?"

His smirk is sweet, and I hate that even though he's my enemy, he's likable and frightening at the same time. Like a thunderstorm. You want to take cover, but you want to draw closer in fascination too. I clutch my necklace, adopting Acelynn's habit. Detective Patrick notices it. "Faith?"

"Heirloom."

"Ah." He says it like it tells him everything he needs to know. "Back to my gut. I think all these bizarre things happening to you and the death of Drucilla might be connected."

He thinks Philip and Dru had an affair and I found out, which is why Philip hired someone to run me down. I could ruin him. And I would. Acelynn would, that is. I would never think to do such a thing. Well, I might think it. I'd never actually do it. But Detective Patrick must believe this. It makes sense. Is he trying to goad me into admitting Philip and Dru slept together? So not out of the realm of possibility considering Dru. Why bring up Jacob unless he's withholding and testing me, or he's trying to shake us all down again for the truth? See if a story changes.

"I'm not sure how, Detective. My best guess—and I'm not good at puzzles—is my dogs napped on a crumpled shirt in her closet when I was working. As for the shirt, I can't say whose it is, and to be honest, Dru might not have been able to either. She was a bed hound." I sound exactly like MacKenzie and Bianca. Like Acelynn.

"It's possible." He doesn't buy it, and I'm not ratting out Philip because I'm not sure it's his shirt or that he cheated with Dru. Also, he's warned me to steer clear of Christian Patrick, and he has ammo on me that he can fight back with. Ammo I'm unaware of but trying to find. I hope Tillie found something— anything—on that laptop.

"One last thing before I go." He steps onto my porch, then turns, and his dark eyes are dancing again. "I really like that paint you picked for me. Got a guy coming out this weekend to strip the old wallpaper off. Thanks."

He doesn't trust me. He knows I've been in his office, and he thinks I'm lying in regard to this case, yet his compliment is genuine. His eyes, sincere. I have no idea what to make of this man. Why didn't he throw out the samples? Why show up on my doorstep like this? Other than to shake me up. I know what he thinks about me. Liar. And he's not wrong. I am a liar. A deceiver. And many other things.

I feel guilty simply by being in his presence, and I haven't done anything sinister in regard to Dru. Okay, the snooping was wrong, and I'm genuinely remorseful for that.

I'm not who he thinks I am, except part of me wonders if he knows I am an impostor. He's just doing his job, but his job happens to threaten me and my future.

"You did? You do? You know you can paint over wallpaper. Saves time."

"I could." He eyes me in that weird way again. "But when you paint over another layer like that, it eventually peels, and what's underneath is revealed. A real eyesore that you wanted covered up in the first place. I find stripping away the old, even if it appears pretty, is the right way to go about it. It's so much easier to work with a completely bare source. It's fresh and clean and ready for color. I don't mind the time it takes. I'll be happier with the results." He shrugs one shoulder.

My heart pinches. "Are you actually talking about paint?"

He rubs his chin. "Do you think I'm talking about paint?"

Always a question with a question. "I don't know."

He reaches out and takes my necklace in his hand. I don't flinch at his move into my personal space—not like I would with any other man, which is disconcerting. As quickly as he holds it, he drops it and steps back. "Or maybe you do."

I stand there staring as he leaves, my mind all over the place. Tillie enters the living room as I close the front door.

"If I'd known a cop was in the house, I'd have lain low. But, man, if he ain't easy on the eyes. You think he's early forties? Maybe late thirties."

"I don't know." I don't care. This man terrifies me because I think he sees me more clearly than I see myself, and yet I feel drawn to him. He's a mystery—a puzzle of his own. But I have too many mysteries and puzzles to add on another one.

"What did he want?"

The truth. The one thing I can't give him.

"Follow-up on Drucilla. They found a man's shirt with white dog hairs, implicating my dogs."

"He thinks you killed her?"

"No." I tell her what I suspect about Philip's philandering ways, though I have no proof to indicate he's a cheater. "What I need to know is if Jacob mentioned Acelynn being at the gun range off the books. That gun is stashed, hidden." Acelynn has been keeping secrets for people, and some of her own. What secret is she keeping for Drucilla? "What if that gun isn't mine?"

"Acelynn's."

I wave off the faux pas. "Right. Same thing."

"No. Not the same thing."

I huff and continue because I know I'm not her; I'm not delusional. "What if the gun isn't Acelynn's? What if it's Dru's? What if she used it or was planning to, and Acelynn knew about it? Was holding it for her or took it from her, using it against her?" She was holding things over Philip. It fit.

"I can go to the gun range," Tillie says. "I won't be recognized. Maybe I can find out if Acelynn was there and with whom. That might tell us if it's her gun or not."

I shake my head. "It's too dangerous. I may be smack-dab in the middle of a nightmare, but you don't have to be."

Tillie frowns. "Charlotte, I know you're always trying to protect me, but I understand what I'm up against. Going to the gun range to shoot a few rounds and drop some names isn't going to kill me."

That's where sweet Tillie is wrong.

"It absolutely could kill you."

Chapter Twenty-Nine

"I might have something, Charlotte," Tillie says as we sit in Acelynn's office downtown, which has large glass windows overlooking the Savannah River.

Tillie is on the couch, her feet up, and I'm on the floor going through a rug catalog, hunting for colors similar to the stained-glass windows in *Beauty and the Beast*. I keep going back to the animated movie's image. This is what Acelynn wanted, and I can give her that. My deepest form of regret and love.

I drop the catalog and give Till my undivided attention, noticing the dogs love her and are cozied up next to her. I don't mind because they make my nose itch, but not as bad as some dogs. The allergy pills help tremendously. "What is it?" We searched the office earlier and found nothing.

"I found a hidden file. It's photos. Look." She hands me the laptop. The photos are from a gala, but I'm not sure when it was held. Philip is at a bar with a woman, and they appear intimate but not obscene. In the next photo, his arm is draped around her as they exit the event. Following this photo, he's kissing her by a car before they leave together. It's a deeply passionate kiss.

"Are these from a cell phone?" They look a little grainy, like when you zoom in too much on a cell phone camera.

"I think so."

If Acelynn took them, did she AirDrop them to her Mac and delete the photos from her phone? Or did someone else email or text them?

I notice a banner in the first photo. "The gala was for Savannah's historic preservation, so it's local. Can we research the events and see if they're held in the same place? If not, maybe we can figure out where this was held and when. Could this be what Philip is looking for?"

The pictures could be icing on the cake for something else. He and Acelynn aren't married, so if he did cheat, it's not a career breaker.

Unless this woman is seedy somehow. An upscale call girl?

I study the young woman. Late twenties, maybe early thirties. It's hard to tell age anymore. She's wearing a classy but revealing black dress and has her platinum hair pulled into a pretty updo. Hanging on her neck is a gorgeous locket.

A text comes through.

MacKenzie.

Don't be late tonight. My parents' home. Eight o'clock. Bring Philip. Cocktails and drinks to celebrate Dru's life. See you then, Pink!

I groan and hold up my phone. "Big party to celebrate Dru. We just went through this." I wonder if they selected that name from the Pink Ladies in *Grease*. If so, I'm pretty sure Acelynn is Rizzo, and MacKenzie is Marty with Frenchy's hair. "She said bring Philip. Do you think Acelynn has hidden the truth of her relationship from everyone?"

Lucille's words return to me, but I don't need them to know that people keep secrets and skew their lives through a filter. We all paint pictures.

What I'm finding is it's as real for people with money as it is for people without. No one is immune. We're all on an equal playing field when it comes to the heart and what we wish for versus what is.

"Probably. Sometimes when you're eyeball-deep into a lie, you hide it from everyone." When she meets my eyes, I know she's referring to me. I did hide dark things from even Tillie.

Now an awkward silence fills the room, and I wish I'd never asked the question.

"You know I don't hold any of that against you, right? When I ask what's going on, it's not because I'm judging. It's because I care and don't want to see you fall down another rabbit hole."

She's right, even if it does often feel like judgment. "It's part of why I love you."

"I don't condone either," she says firmly.

"I know that too." It's why I hid things in the first place.

"You have to call Philip. Or don't. But if you don't and you make excuses, these people are going to sense something, and they'll look harder than they are now. Your only saving grace is they're so self-absorbed they don't see the subtle differences between you and Acelynn."

Tillie always said I should go into acting. I could have won dozens of Oscar awards by now. Now when she says it, it's not a compliment but a warning.

What do I have to lose? "Okay." My stomach feels like it's been punched by Rocky Balboa, but I press Philip's name, and he answers on the second ring.

"Hey," he says softly. Maybe they did once love each other, or Philip is in the wrong business too.

"Hey. How was the country club with my dad?"

"I'm an Ace in the hole, pardon the pun." He chuckles, and

it's nice. Like he's not even mad at me. "I'll be receiving sizable donations for the campaign fund. Senator Beaumont has a nice ring, doesn't it?"

"President sounds even better." He's ambitious. He wants more than to be senator.

"You'll make the White House so pretty," he says in a condescending tone, and finally the piece of the puzzle fits. Acelynn wanted power and hitched her cart to Philip's star, but his star needed fuel, and she helped him with that through her father's powerful and sickeningly rich friends. But somehow they flew too close to the sun, and the sun is the puzzle piece that's still missing.

"The Newsoms are having an event tonight to celebrate Dru. We're invited. Will you be able to make it?"

"Do I have a choice?"

"Important people will be there. People with fat wallets." People who want favors returned. People who will crawl out of the woodwork when the time comes and ask him to do something for them in return. Philip will never make senator or president on his own merits but on the backs of those who will stab him in his if he doesn't do their bidding. That's how the world works. You scratch an itch, and your itch is scratched later. Eventually you're scratching out eyes.

"What time?"

"Eight." I decide to throw him an olive branch, because I need him on my side or at the very least believing I'm not going to turn on him. "Detective Patrick came by this morning. They found a crumpled men's shirt in Dru's closet and my dogs' hairs on it—or hairs consistent with my dogs." If it's his shirt, I'm giving him a heads-up to explain it when the DNA comes back.

"Your dogs have been in that place a dozen times."

"I'm not worried about me and my dogs."

"You think it's my shirt?" His voice rises. "If it's my shirt, you put it there, and I'll testify to that."

"I didn't." Now he's angered me. I was trying to help him. "But you can't prove it if I did, and I'll testify to that." These are the games they play. I can play them too.

"Well, I didn't sleep with that tramp. I'm just sleeping with one tramp, and we're not even doing that right now."

My blood boils on behalf of my sister. "Be my ally or be my foe, Philip. Can't be both."

"I hear you loud and clear. See you at eight," he says in a seething tone, then ends the call.

He heard me, but he didn't respond to which side he wants to be on.

"Well?" Tillie asks. "Didn't sound good."

"Backfire. He says he didn't sleep with Dru. I don't believe him, and Christian Patrick doesn't either or he wouldn't have dropped the shirt-and-dog-hairs bit when he came over."

The only person who understands men like Philip in Acelynn's world is Lucille Benedict. She might have some insight, and I owe it to Acelynn to take care of her, to be a better daughter. I know Acelynn would have regrets. We all have regrets at the end of our time. "I need to go see my mom."

Tillie pauses and tilts her head. "Whose mom?"

"Acelynn's. I know who I am." Except I don't. I never have. "I can't slip up, so I'm staying in character. Ever heard of method acting?"

"Ever heard of crazy talk?" She sighs. "I notice you're trying to figure out everything except our escape plan. You can't live here forever as Acelynn Benedict, Charlotte. You do know that, right?"

"Of course I know that," I snarl, then apologize. "One day at a time. Priorities." Once I'm home, I'll dig around in *my* closet until I find a little black dress that's modest but complementary, then do *my* hair in *my* signature style. Because for now, this is *my* office and house, *my* clothing, *my* family and *my* life.

Déjà vu. I park behind Bianca's convertible, and my nerves hum. Showtime. Philip will be here soon, and inside the home I'll rub elbows with people I'm supposed to know, but only my inner sanctum has appeared in my social media. My palms are damp, and my legs feel like gelatin. I keep my oversized sunglasses on my face and enter the front door to the sounds of glasses clinking and chatter. The house no longer smells of lingering smoked meats but lemon and Murphy's Oil Soap. The windows are so clear I imagine many a bird smacking into them and falling to the ground, discombobulated. Much like I feel at the moment.

The people are my parents' age, and I wonder if they'll be here. Or at least my dad. I haven't seen MacKenzie, Cotton, Bianca or Ford.

Nor have I seen Teddy, and I hope I don't. His freaky behavior still has my teeth set on edge. A few men and women acknowledge me, and I nod in return and move throughout the house, unsure of where I should go and who I should be chatting with. My mouth is dry and my chest is tight, but on the exterior, I'm glowing and killing the role.

After a few rounds of chitchat with friends of my family, I need a breather. Since I haven't seen a single Pink or brother, I slip upstairs.

I stride along the balcony that overlooks the living area below and pick the first door I see, hoping it's a bathroom where I can splash water on my face and not be disturbed. But as I open it, I hear that the room is occupied by not one but two people.

A woman is on the bed, her long blond hair spilling down her bare back, and I gasp. "I'm so sorry. Excuse me," I say, thoroughly embarrassed.

Bianca swivels her head at me and grins. "No worries, but

lock the door from the inside out on your way elsewhere." Her tone is light but carries a threat behind it, and I can't tell who she's with, but a man's white dress shirt and black dress pants are sprawled on the floor. I don't want to stick around to find out. I quickly press the lock inward and close the door.

I suppose everyone handles grief differently.

Rushing to the next room, I knock, and when no one answers, I open the door to a spa-like bathroom. Inside I turn on the water and splash my face, now even redder from having witnessed Bianca and some mystery man. Half the people downstairs are in white dress shirts and black pants. It could be anyone.

Why hadn't they locked the door? Was this one of those games where they hope they're caught? At this point it wouldn't surprise me. But who did she—or they—hope would catch them? Me? Everyone? Anyone? Did it simply heighten their fun knowing they could be walked in on? I pat my face dry and stare into the mirror.

What world am I living in?

A banging on the door startles me. I gasp, then pull myself together and open it. MacKenzie enters, her hair pulled into two tiny knots on her head like Princess Leia, and all I can think is, she's not twelve anymore. She wears a tight-fitting black dress that dares her not to bend over and tall spike heels. She points to her dangling earrings that are gold and silver. "What do you think?"

I couldn't care less what hangs from her lobes. This isn't a fashion show but a celebration of life—for the second time—and none of these friends seem too torn up about the fact they've lost a woman who was practically their sister. I wish we could have had a celebration of life for Tommy. I've barely had time to even grieve him, though I feel the dull ache every single day. He had his problems, but he always had my back in a crunch.

"You hesitated," she hisses. "It's part of my new jewelry

line, but clearly you won't help promote them on your reels and videos." She rips them from her ears and slings them into the toilet, then flushes it. "Dru saw right through you, and you really are a heinous—"

"Hey!" Ford enters and glares down at MacKenzie. "Out."

She tosses me a fiery look, then storms from the bathroom, slamming the door behind her. Ford sighs. "You okay, Ace?"

"Uh, yeah. That was…" I can't even begin to find the words. An outburst steeped in grief? I don't know, and I don't want to know. Those eyes held more contempt and venom than any snake in the grass I've witnessed before.

"That was MacKenzie being the brat she's always been. We put up with her because our moms are sorority sisters, and apparently that means life without parole for us." He smirks and glances in the mirror, finger-combing his hair. His looks are classic. He leans on the vanity. "How you holding up, kid?" he asks, and it makes me laugh, putting me at ease. I suspect it's what he intended.

"Not well. She's dead, and it's like no one cares."

"Dru wasn't easy. Well…she was in the sack." He chuckles. "But personality-wise, she was a real monster at times. I guess we all are."

He's not wrong. I think about Acelynn and myself. Did money make her deceitful? Did the privilege push her to play games because she never thought she'd get caught? What about me? Survival. I'm a survivor, and that means doing what has to be done when there's no alternative. My sis and I are not alike, even if we are. "But we loved her." Didn't they?

"We did. It's why we're here for the second time. MacKenzie's just lashing out because she knows she's the new 'last one.' You and B were always the bestest of the best. Then MacKenzie came into the trio, and Dru was always the last one. Probably because y'all didn't trust her with your men."

Where's the loyalty? The devotion? But if Dru had no boundaries, then that shirt could have been Philip's. Could he have killed Dru? No, my prime suspect is still my creepy brother who has keys, and the reports said that there was no forced entry. That could be why.

Ford pulls me to him and I let him, inhaling his fresh-showered scent with a hint of aftershave that suits him.

"It all just feels too close to home," I tell him. What if Dru's death and my near death are connected, just like the detective said?

His hand massages my back, and it's clear he knows what he's doing. I instantly relax and lean into him. His arms are powerful and strong. He gently raises my chin to peer into my eyes. "It's all going to be okay. They'll find who killed Dru. Our families won't let them rest until they do. Don't let Mac get in your head about living close to this killer's hunting ground."

"I don't think I am okay, Ford." And I tell him about the hit-and-run. "I haven't told anyone else except for Philip."

Ford studies me for a long time. "I've never made how I feel about that moneygrubbing man a secret. He's after your dad's friends' money. Why can't you see that? You deserve to be with a man who will spend his life loving you and spoiling you rotten."

Is he talking about himself? "Yeah?"

"Yeah. A man who gets you." He rubs his thumb over my cheek. Why aren't we together? It's clear how he feels about me. Power. Acelynn wants to be the wife of a senator and a president.

"Do you think Philip cheated on me with Dru?" What's his take? I need someone who will tell me straight.

"I don't know. Definitely wouldn't put it past her. Why? Do you think he killed her? That she threatened to tell you, and he couldn't afford for you to break things off before he cinched donations? And don't deny it. It's right in front of your face."

I know. Acelynn knew it too and didn't care. "I hope not,

but they found a man's dress shirt at her house with dog hairs from what could be my dogs."

"If he did and he knows about the dog hairs, he'll use that to make sure you go down for a crime he committed. He's slimy, Ace. If you have anything on him, you better use it to keep him in line." Ford holds my gaze, and there's a tenderness there hovering behind the shrewd suggestion. "You have a little fleck of yellow in your eyes I hadn't noticed before." He runs his thumb over my cheekbone again. "I like it."

"Maybe you haven't been this close to see it," I mumble through a dry mouth and realize I may have unintentionally invited something.

He leans in even closer until his lips barely hover over mine. I smell the mint on his breath. "We both know that's not true. I guess maybe I wasn't paying as much attention as I should have been."

What does this mean? Are we…a thing? Have they been? Did Philip come between them? Did Ford miss his chance to make his feelings known? Or was Philip right in his accusation earlier about Acelynn?

The bathroom door opens, and we pull apart from each other. Bianca enters. Her hair's disheveled, and the buttons of her top are uneven. She halts and bats her gaze from Ford to me and back to him. "Have I interrupted something?"

"No, of course not." I clear my throat. "We were discussing who might have killed Drucilla."

Bianca's eyes narrow. "If I had to guess, I'd say a jilted lover, of which she had many. Including Philip, so…"

"That's harsh," Ford says. Was he sparing me the truth earlier, or did he not know about Philip cheating with Dru? Maybe it was Philip and not Teddy. But that doesn't explain what he's looking for in my house.

"That's fact, brother dear, and it's not like Acelynn is un-aware."

And she might not have let it slide with Dru or the woman in the gala photos.

"She has standards, and you're just angry you didn't meet them." Bianca realizes her buttons are off and rebuttons her shirt while Ford looks at me with an apologetic expression.

I shoot him one in return. I am sorry because it didn't take but two seconds to see Ford Lambert is in love with me, and while his sister's barb didn't cut me, because I am not in love with Philip, it's left a gaping slash that Ford feels.

Once her appearance is smoothed out, she sashays to the door and turns, batting her lashes. "By the way, Acie hon, Philip's here."

Maybe he's been here much longer than I have.

Chapter Thirty

I find Philip downstairs conversing with influential people and drinking a beer as if he's comfortable with the crowd. And why shouldn't he be? I also note he's dressed in a white shirt and black dress pants. But so are Cotton, and Teddy, who is standing in the breakfast nook with MacKenzie, and even Ford, but Ford wears a silky red tie, unlike the others.

I have to play this to the hilt and force myself to enter Philip's presence without interrupting his conversation, which includes Jack Hilton—Dru's father—and my father, who is also in a white shirt and black dress pants. Do these men not have any personal style? Are they carbon copies of one another? For all of MacKenzie's faults and weirdness, at least she adds some pizzazz to her hair.

"There she is," Philip says in the most adoring tone I've ever heard, and I want to puke. Instead, I beam as he puts his arm around me and hugs me tight to his side. Too tight for my liking. "I was beginning to wonder if you were going to show. I know how hard this has been on you." He kisses my cheek as

I catch Ford's eye, and he raises a glass in condolence. Philip the cheater.

Tillie has never believed once a cheater always a cheater. But people most often, like leopards, do not change their spots.

I nod at Ford and steal a glance at my father. "Is Mother here?"

"She is. I last saw her with Dawna and the girls." I assume that means the other sorority sisters besides Dru's mother.

"I think I'll go find her. You don't mind me dashing off, do you, Philip?" I bat my lashes, returning the facade.

"Of course not, darling. But don't stay away too long. I miss you when you're gone." He kisses me again, this time on my lips, and his feel cool and unkind.

I slink through the crowd until I see Teddy hovering over MacKenzie again, and she's running her yap. Likely about me. I have no time to deal with entitled, spoiled brats and find Lucille Benedict sitting with Dawna Hilton, Renee Newsom and Christine Lambert. The original Pinks, if I had to guess.

They're high-society and would fit right into a *Stepford Wives* movie. Perfectly put together with cloth handkerchiefs to blot their eyes. Lucille is glassy-eyed and the only one not wearing her wedding ring, but a huge sapphire perches on her right-hand ring finger.

They're all out of sorts, and I'm not sure it's from death. Beneath the surface, I see more than sisters. I see rivals, and the apples don't fall far from the trees. Bianca's mother, Christine, catches my eye and stands. "Oh, honey." She comes toward me a little wobbly, and merlot swishes to the rim of her glass. "How are you holding up?" She echoes Ford's words and hugs me.

"Best any of us can," I say, hoping it will suffice.

Lucille is now on her shaky feet, walking my way. I'm not sure how to respond to her, but I let her embrace me as Ford approaches and wraps an arm around his mother, mostly to keep her upright. She's imbibed too much, as they all have. Can't say if it's drinking to cope with grief or routine. He leads her back to her seat, then returns.

"I'm so glad you came," Lucille slurs. "This is all too much to take."

Ford takes Lucille by the forearm. "Mrs. Benedict, I'm so sorry. How about I pour you another glass of wine, and you can rest by Mom."

She nods but leans into my ear, and I smell the fermentation on her breath. "Stay away from that snake Philip. I don't trust him. He's just like your father." Then Ford gives me a wide-eyed look that says *I told you so* and guides her back to her seat next to Christine.

Now that she's nice and drunk and chatty, she might spill more tea that I desperately need and not even remember me questioning her like the stranger I am.

"How about I help you to the bathroom to freshen up?"

Ford leans in, and I catch his spicy cologne. "We'll pick up where we left off later," he whispers, and an odd sensation passes through me. I don't think our moment in the bathroom upstairs was our first moment. But whatever is going on between us is a secret. Bianca mentioned Philip's cheating, but not mine. MacKenzie easily could have thrown it in my face during her rampage, but she didn't use specifics as to why I'm so heinous.

"You can be sweet when you want to," Lucille slurs. "Why do you want to?" She continues her incoherent rambling as I escort her to a guest bath. After turning on the faucet, I hunt for a washcloth and run it under cool water. Lucille's cheeks are flushed, a mix of wine and pills. She sits on the commode lid, and I dab her face with the cool rag, hoping to ease the flush of her skin. Nothing I can do about the glassy eyes.

"Have you talked to your father?" she says through a slow, thick tongue.

"Briefly. Did he bring you?"

"Ha! Of course not. He'd rather keep me locked up and

out of the public eye. Heaven forbid I embarrass him. Teddy brought me. He's such a darling."

Teddy. A darling ghoul. "Does Teddy show you his drawings?" Does she know he creeps around like a shadow stalker sketching sleeping women, then acts as if he's done nothing wrong?

"Not recently, no." She puts her hand over the washcloth and stares into my eyes. "Your eyes."

Has she seen the small yellow flecks that Ford has? Is this the defining moment that outs me? "What about them?" I ask nonchalantly.

"Something's different. Off. Not in a bad way, just… I don't know. I've had more wine than I should have. But it helps, you know?"

"Helps you how?" I continue patting her cheeks and neck, noticing her confusion at my kindness. Maybe that's what she's seeing. A lesser monster staring back than before. Because I am a monster. I won't deny that. Ford was right.

"I was the belle of the ball once upon a time." She raises a hand haphazardly. "I know you've heard this before, but it's true. I had everything going for me, from looks to a keen mind. And your father. We were going to be the power couple among power couples. I don't know where it went wrong. Before you even came into our lives, things weren't as I envisioned them. Wine got me through tough nights. Still does."

Wine was ruining this woman. And the pills.

"We're all liars," she says through a laugh. "Dawna hadn't talked to Dru in three months, including at the weekly barbecues." She presses the corner of her eye. "Do you think I should get an eye lift? Renee looks ten years younger since hers."

I think she needs to focus on sobriety more than cosmetic changes.

She breathes out a long, dramatic sigh. "They say do what makes you happy, but they forget to add long-term happiness, because everything I've ever done to make me happy faded away over time. Some stretches were longer than others. And sometimes what I've done to be happy didn't make me happy at all. It made things worse. You, for example." Though I'm not her daughter, I'm struck by the salty words. Has she said this before? To Acelynn?

"Sorry for not being the perfect daughter." The sarcasm comes at my sister's defense.

She laughs and pushes my hand away. "Why are you even doing this? Do you think this will make your father love you? It won't. It never does. And this whole thing with Philip. You're following in my footsteps, and you're going to trip. Because that's what he is—an open grave. You'll die in him. Just like I did."

Is that what Acelynn is doing? She'd rather have power and influence than love? Over someone like Ford? Or Detective Patrick?

Detective Patrick? Where did that thought come from?

"You can't buy love, and influence and money aren't enough to sustain you. I've tried to tell you this before. I don't know why I keep attempting. You're going to do whatever you like and with whomever you like, no matter the cost or pain it might inflict."

"I don't think my relationship with Philip is hurting anyone."

"It'll hurt you in the end, if you have any feelings within you at all. I suppose on some level you do or you wouldn't bend over backward to seek your father's love and approval. Or maybe you just can't stand the fact you can't win them all over." She shoves the cloth from her face, and it hits me in the mouth, but it doesn't sting like the words about my sister.

I've been here before. With Marilyn. Addicts say heinous things that aren't true, and in ten hours she will likely not remember any of them. But I will. I still remember Marilyn's vitriol. The blame for all her problems. The bane of her existence. How life would have been much better without me in it, and yet every time she sobered up, she attempted to regain custody of me.

Lucille stands on wobbly feet and toddles to the door.

"Has it ever crossed your mind that I'm trying to help? That the problem might be with you? Has it ever once registered that you're killing yourself and your mind is suffering from all the sickness you bring to it? I'm not the problem. You are." I know I'm not talking to Marilyn. But the words still fit.

"Selfish as ever." She stumbles from the room unscathed by my remarks. Lucille Benedict is a woman who didn't attain the Burger King life and is now nothing but bitter and resentful. I can't fix that. No one can fix that but her, and maybe not even her.

I leave the rag on the sink and decide I'm done here. I walk right out of the Newsoms' home, head for my car and spot Conrad Benedict on the phone.

Teddy's SUV is right next to mine, and I duck down beside it.

"No, it's not an imposition. I'm on my way now. Give me about thirty minutes." He pockets his phone and kicks a tire before cursing. "Acelynn, what have you done now?"

I can feel the wave of cool fury from here. Where is he going? Why does it involve me? He gets in his car and speeds from the circle drive. I stand, shaking, and glance in Teddy's back seat. His leather-bound sketchbook is lying right there.

After making sure no one is nearby or watching, I try the handle to the back passenger door, and it's unlocked. Rich people feel so untouchable. Quickly I snatch the book and quietly close the door. They aren't untouchable. I've taken his prized possession, and it's his fault for leaving the door unlocked.

I have to see what's inside besides drawings of me sleeping. Painting reveals the heart. That's part of being a creative—

emptying your feelings onto a page. When I search this book with an artist's eyes, I'm going to see Teddy's heart.

And I'm already terrified.

Chapter Thirty-One

I sit at my kitchen table, my head thumping. Tillie sent a text that she's taking the dogs for a walk and that the gun range was closed due to some plumbing problems, so her visiting was a no-go. I don't love it being so late at night. But she's not the one in danger of being run over, and the park is always full of late-night joggers, mostly women.

A cup of coffee steams beside me, and I open up Teddy's sketch pad, trying not to think about the fact that a car missed me thanks to Christian Patrick. Will someone try again? When? I can't leave the house without looking over my shoulder and believing I'm being followed. And I can't help but wonder who was in my home that rainy night Tillie showed up. If someone heard us, why haven't they confronted me? Maybe they're waiting for the right moment when it will benefit them. I know that's what Acelynn would do. And quite frankly, it's what I would do. When they do come out of the woodwork to expose me, what will they want from me? How will I explain I'm innocent? Will they even care?

The first drawing is me sleeping at the Benedicts' house on the couch. And by me, I mean Acelynn. Most of them are of Acelynn. At the Benedicts', at this house, Teddy's beach house on Tybee Island. But I also see drawings of MacKenzie and Dru. Different nights. Different poses. Dru is always nude. Lucille's sketch pops up, and it's the most peaceful I've seen her. She almost looks dead.

Is that what Teddy is doing? Drawing women who look dead?

A smattering of sketches feature women unfamiliar to me. Are these women Teddy knows, and are they aware they've been sketched? Have they given permission? I tend to think not, after giving him my key to one of the Pinks' houses.

Teddy's a real estate agent, which gives him access to all sorts of homes. He has ways into them without consent. What would he do if one of these women woke and caught him? How would he respond to that? He could go to prison. Someone would have to be in a deep sleep not to feel an alien presence in the home. His sitting by my bed brought him into my dreams. I can't believe no one has ever woken and called the cops.

He could also easily have kept keys from homes sold. Not all homeowners change locks on houses once they purchase them, though they should for reasons just like this.

Not a single photo out of hundreds is of a woman awake. My skin crawls, and I shudder as the door opens. I jump up and shove the sketchbook under the sink, behind the trash can and cleaning supplies, then move toward the butcher block in case I need a weapon.

The dogs come running, and I release a relieved breath. It's Tillie.

"You look like you've seen a ghost." She sniffs. "Coffee sounds good." She makes her way to the Keurig, takes my pod out and replaces it with a new one. "What's going on?"

"I stole something."

She sighs. "What now? And how much trouble will it land you in if you're caught?"

"It's not the same, and no trouble at all, because if anyone ends up in hot water, it'll be Teddy. I took his sketchbook from his SUV. You need to see this." I open the cabinet and retrieve it. When I look up, she's frowning, her arms folded over her chest. She wears a simple gray V-neck T-shirt and black running shorts, and her dark hair is up in a high ponytail. "I wasn't sure who was coming into the house. Pinks have keys and no personal space boundaries."

The Keurig squirts the last of the coffee into her mug. She adds sugar and cream and sits beside me. The dogs are lapping water from their bowls and sloshing it onto the dog mat beneath. I scoot the sketchbook to her and motion for her to browse the disturbing drawings.

"What in the world is this?" she asks. "It's like he's obsessed—"

"With death, right?" All of these women, including myself, look as if we're being laid to rest. "And he's not asking them to pose. He's sneaking into unsuspecting women's homes and drawing them while they sleep."

"What a freak show, Char. Things just become more bizarre by the second."

"Tell me about it!" I fill her in on everything that transpired at the Newsoms', from Bianca in the bedroom, to MacKenzie's murderous outburst, to Ford's displays of affection for me. "I can't trust any of these people. There's no loyalty, and it traces back to the mothers. They're in some kind of competition for the better life."

Tillie slowly glances up at me.

"What?"

"Nothing."

My hackles rise. "You can't possibly be comparing me to them. I would…" My words trail off, because I have taken things that don't belong to me. Things I coveted and wanted but couldn't afford. And dark things transpired with a particular person who used to visit a restaurant I worked in. She was glamorous and well-liked. Rich.

She had everything I wanted. She was the person I wanted to be…and when you dream every moment of being someone else and living another life, escaping your own for a million reasons, those thoughts become your reality. You enter it, slipping over the edge until you don't even know what you've done or how far you've fallen until it's too late. All you can do is try to clean up the mess but in turn make it messier until people are hurt.

But I'm not that woman anymore.

Am I?

What constitutes change? Actions. Behavior.

Maybe I am still the old me. I can't think about that right now. I have too many other things piling up on my plate. It's just that now my plates are china and not paper.

Tillie flips through page after page. "Do you think Teddy might have killed Drucilla? What if she woke up and found him in her room in the middle of the night?" She points to the last sketch of Dru with the date of the day she died.

"I've thought that already. It's possible. She might have threatened him, or she might have woken up to him doing something besides drawing her. She ran. He followed, and it turned into a homicide."

"What are you going to do with this?" she asks and stops on the sketch of me from the other night. "This was… Charlotte, you need to change the locks in this house. Too many people have a way in, and someone has attempted to murder you. No one would think it strange."

"True."

"I know I'd feel safer. This guy is sick." She closes the book and scoots it to me. "Take it to the detective. If Teddy is sneaking into homes, it's a crime on women."

"I've thought of that, but Teddy will know someone took

his sketchbook from the Newsoms', and I'm the likely culprit. Plus, bringing the detective to Teddy brings him back to me, and I need him out of my life or I can't live it. Every lie I tell him is another strike against me." Not to mention Teddy says he has ammo on me for decades, and I believe him; he can't turn against me. And if I end up hauled to prison because they find out the truth, they'll charge me with Acelynn's murder.

Tillie sips the coffee. She always could handle caffeine and sleep like a baby. I'll be up all night. "What will you do, then?"

"I'm going to hide it for now." I pick up the sketch pad, finish the last lukewarm swallow of coffee. But Philip has been in the house, and I don't want him to find it either. At least, I think only Philip has been in the house. I never actually saw anyone the first morning I arrived, and I didn't see the face of the figure darting across my yard in a thunderstorm. I assume it was all Philip. But I also know what they say about assumptions.

I head upstairs and stash the book under the shoebox with the paper targets and gun in the closet, then set a large beach bag in front of it. Tillie is standing in the doorway, her face ashen.

"That detective…he's here again," she whispers. "Won't tell me anything, just that he'd like to talk to you." She licks her lips and wrings her hands. "I'm scared, Charlotte. It's very late for a detective to be knocking on doors."

"Acelynn. You call me Acelynn. And don't be scared. Cops work all hours." Detective Patrick likes showing up when least expected. Keeps people on their toes, especially persons of interest. He's like a thief in the night. I'm not ready for him. "Stay up here and I'll handle it." I have no other choice, and my insides squeeze tight with each stair I descend.

Christian Patrick sits at the table, scrolling on his phone. He's super chill, but when he makes eye contact, steel is in his black eyes.

"Please tell me no one else has been murdered and that you've figured out who tried to mow me down."

"Nothing on the near hit-and-run yet, and no one else is dead, but I have a few more questions, Miss Benedict. My gut said you're a night owl, and it was right. Told you." His manner is light, but I'm not buying it. If he's here, it's something big. I've been in the hot seat before and raise my chin, giving no indication I'm sweating in places women shouldn't.

"It's come to our attention that Drucilla was seeing a much older man. Would you know anything about that?" He taps his pen on his notebook, the only sound in the house at the moment.

"I wouldn't."

"We pulled her phone records and found quite a few calls and texts to a particular number over the past few months. We matched that number to a name in her phone. Big B. Any guesses who that is?"

I shake my head.

"That's odd. From what we know, your friends call your father Big B. Big Benedict. How would you not know that?"

I mentally kick myself and try to process what I'm hearing. Conrad? Drucilla was sleeping with Acelynn's father? Nothing should surprise me with these people, but I am shocked. Not that Conrad cheats. Lucille all but said he does, but with girls my age? Girls who grew up in and out of his home. That's just icky on so many levels. "It's been a long day, Detective, and I'm not thinking straight. Of course they call him that. I can't imagine him and her, so it didn't process right."

"You really didn't know?" He lays the pen down.

"I didn't." He believes me, but I'm not out of the woods yet. Then it dawns on me that Conrad was on the phone earlier, leaving the celebration. He must have been going to the precinct, and he probably suspected that I said something to tip off the cops. Why would I do that? Because Acelynn must have known about the affair. What else would he have meant when he asked what I'd done now?

"The lab hasn't confirmed DNA, but your father has admitted the shirt was his. We showed him a photo, and the toiletries in the bathroom he copped to. He says he was with her the night she died. They had wine and an intimate evening. Then he left around ten."

I wince. The thought of him cheating on Lucille and betraying Acelynn. That was her friend. But was she? Would a best friend sleep with your father when he's married, or at all? "You think my father killed Drucilla?"

Was this a pattern, sleeping with his daughter's friends? He was wearing a white shirt at the party, and someone was in that room with Bianca. Even if she implied it was Philip, that didn't mean it was. Could he have slept with all of Acelynn's friends?

"She never mentioned the affair?" He glosses right over my question.

"No." If she had, would Acelynn have cared? Yes. Lucille noted she wanted Conrad's approval and love. If I thought my father didn't love me but was sleeping with one of my best friends, I'd care. I can't believe Dru would have told her.

"See, that's interesting to me."

My heart sinks. He's caught me in a lie. An indirect lie, but a lie nonetheless.

"In my interview with your father, he noted an argument between the two of you because you discovered the affair, and he said it was heated. You were inconsolable and irrational." He holds up the notebook. "I'm reading verbatim here. He thought you came to me with this information, which I assured him you did not."

My tongue sticks to the roof of my mouth. How do I backpedal out of this? I'm burning with guilt and shame. But I'm trapped in my own web of lies and Acelynn's, and the only way to free myself is with more lies. I open my mouth, and he halts me as if he knows I'm going to give him more garbage.

"I have the impression you're going to tell me that you didn't want to throw your dad under the bus because he isn't guilty of murder, and knowing he was having an affair with Dru would implicate him. I'll spare you the words. I don't buy it anyway."

I remain silent. That's exactly what I was going to say.

"But if you want to tell me the truth," he murmurs, "I'll take that. I can help you. I want to help you make whatever you did wrong right. Something is going on with you, Philip, Conrad and this case with Drucilla. Maybe they connect, maybe not, but you've gotten yourself in over your head, and I'm not your enemy."

Is this man a fly on the wall of my mind? Tears burn and threaten to release, but I keep them contained. He can't see me cry, can't know that he's dead right. I am in so over my head, and even if he did believe the truth, once he did a little research on me, he'd change his mind.

He waits a beat in case I want to come clean with my sin, but my sins can't be his burdens to carry. Disappointment pulses in his eyes, and he sighs. "I'm going to drill down to the truth, Acelynn. I always do. Better to come clean now than wait for me to come for you later. Lying doesn't become you. It's ugly, and you are anything but unattractive. Don't let it mar you."

He walks out the side door and closes it behind him.

As the room slants and slides, the edges of my vision grow black, and I use the wall for support to keep me upright.

I've just become a prime suspect in a murder investigation, and based on what I know about Acelynn Benedict, I might be guilty.

Conrad could have killed Drucilla, but he has no motive I can think of off the top of my head. If people found out, it wouldn't be that big of a deal.

Teddy had access to her house. Teddy watched her sleep. What if Teddy saw her with our dad? Saw him leaving. She was his favorite object to draw, and maybe he wanted more. Maybe he'd slept with her too. Ford implied she'd been around.

I retrieve the hidden sketchbook and flip pages again, searching for something, anything, to reveal Teddy as more than a stalker, but nothing pops.

Wait. I flip back a page. I didn't notice her at first, but now I recognize the woman. I've seen her photo flashed on the news.

Allie Deardon. The most recent victim of Cupid.

Chapter Thirty-Two

"Charlotte, you have to run. The detective believes you might have had a hand in this murder, and you can't afford the cops to be poking around. What if they charge you and fingerprint you! They may not tag you for Drucilla Hilton's murder, but once they find out who you really are, they absolutely will try to get you for Acelynn's."

Flashbacks of Andi Delaney, the woman who frequented the restaurant, hit me hard.

I didn't intend for it to go as far as it did.

Curiosity got the better of me. That's all. She twisted all my words and took my actions out of context. Things skyrocketed out of hand. I close the door on the memory, but it always hovers, especially now. Because of now.

"I'm going upstairs." The dogs stay with Tillie, and I stomp upstairs angry. At the past. My lot in life. My own rotten decisions and impulsive moves. I never meant to hurt anyone. I wanted a taste of the life I never had the opportunity to live. It might seem whiny and pathetic but it's how I felt—feel.

Inside my room, I lie on the bed, facing the ceiling fan, and watch it spin. My phone buzzes. It's a text from Teddy.

Did you take my sketch pad from my SUV?

My insides flush fever-hot, but I reply.

Why would I do that?

I don't know. That's why I'm asking. Half the time I never know why you do what you do. Someone took it. Who would have?

Maybe you misplaced it. Did you hear about Dad?

What about him?

Great. Another can of worms I get to spill. I don't want to be the one to share it, but he might give me insight into Conrad. Did my father throw me under the bus to cover up his murder? Did we truly fight about Drucilla? How did Acelynn find out about them?
Keys. They have keys and use them without asking.
I text back.

Detective questioned him and then came to see me. He was the one having an affair with Drucilla.

No more bubbles surface. He's processing or collecting his thoughts. I can't lie here waiting. I have more anxious energy than I know what to do with. I pace the floor, then sniff the perfumes on the vanity. Comb through the jewelry box, which is brimming with more jewelry than I've ever seen, and yet she only wore this one necklace I'm wearing now.
She had it all. Excess! Everything I ever wanted and never

had. It all just hangs in this wooden trophy case showing off her lavish life. She doesn't wear it because she doesn't have to; she can afford it but she steals. Not out of necessity but because she can.

I'm literally seeing red as my blood turns hot. I pluck the wooden box from the vanity and hurl it to the floor, releasing some of the dark anger coursing through my veins. Jewelry scatters, and the mirror under the lid splinters into tiny shards on the thick rug.

What have I done?

I can't be mad at someone for what they have and I don't. That's unfair. I kneel and begin cleaning up the mess I've made. All I do is make messes and leave a trail of misery. It's stupid and ridiculous, but I don't know how to stop. Like trying to stop an avalanche instead of the snowball.

I set the jewelry box on the vanity and notice a piece of wood protrudes now. Great, I've broken an antique jewelry box. But on a closer inspection, I notice it's not broken; it's a false back.

A little tug releases it, revealing a small plastic sandwich bag. Inside is a necklace with a heart-shaped locket and little rose-gold flowers etched along the front with three diamonds. Why is this in a plastic bag like police evidence? Why does Acelynn have a false back to a jewelry box, anyway?

I open the locket, using the plastic as a glove. I don't need my prints on it. On the left heart is a woman with shimmery red hair, and the opposite side holds an older couple who I assume to be her parents. The older woman also has red hair.

The young woman is familiar, but I can't place where I've seen her.

What is Acelynn doing with this? I have no doubt it's here for nefarious purposes—hidden and encased in plastic as if she's preserving fingerprints or attempting to keep it free from her own. How did I not see my sister's darkness and how deep it ran? Because I only saw what I was looking for. And you will always find what you want to see. I wanted a sweet, endearing, loyal sister who loved me. I wanted a sister with a special family who would always accept me. I ignored or justified the red flags that pointed to someone superficial, diabolical and flat-out deceptive.

I wasn't fooled by her. I fooled myself about her.

I catch my reflection in the mirror—her reflection. Perhaps we are the spitting image of each other. Outside and inside.

I've lied. Deceived. Manipulated and pretended.

But I had legit reasons and no other choices. That made my deception less icky and hurtful. What else was I supposed to do when backed in a corner? When my life was on a thin line? What were my other options?

I want to believe that someone gave this locket to Acelynn for safekeeping, but it's not true. Why would it be in a plastic bag and hidden? Is this what Philip was searching for?

Wait. I know why this woman is familiar. I clutch the bag and race downstairs to find Tillie on Acelynn's laptop, a cup of chamomile tea in hand and the dogs sleeping beside her on the couch. "Pull up those pictures you found in the hidden files on Acelynn's laptop."

"Why?" Tillie sets her cup on a coaster on the end table beside her.

"I found this in Acelynn's jewelry box."

"Why did you put it in a Ziploc bag?"

"I didn't."

Tillie's eyes widen, and she clicks a few times, then shows me the woman Philip was with at the gala. They're one and the same. Why does Acelynn have this locket and the photos?

"We need to identify this woman and her connection to Philip and Acelynn. This locket has to be what he was searching for. Why?"

A piece isn't clicking into place.

Tillie lays the laptop at the foot of the couch. "Based on

what I experience at the attorney's office, if it's in plastic, it's preserving DNA or fingerprints or both. You didn't touch it, did you? To open it?"

"No. I know better."

"Cheating on someone you aren't married to isn't something that's a big deal in the sense of blackmail. You might have been on to something when you suspected a high-end call girl."

"To keep him, she might be holding this necklace like a noose around his neck. If he tries to leave her, destroy her dream of being a politician's wife, she'll blast the fact he's sleeping with a sex worker everywhere."

Tillie grabs the laptop. "I have an idea."

"What's that?"

"Reverse image search on Google. I can copy and paste this into the Google search bar under the photo icon. It'll bring up related images or searches and possibly the search site if this photo was posted elsewhere."

Hope blooms in my chest. We need to discover who this woman is in order to secure a name and information. No one else can help me, not even Detective Patrick, who all but begged me to come clean and let him help.

I'm not your enemy.

I want to believe that. But my past is too muddy and my experiences with the law too sharp.

"Well, that blows. Nothing. Okay, let me look on the gala site on Facebook and see if they have any other photos of her. Maybe she was tagged, and I can follow the trail to her own social media site."

"You should be a private investigator."

"I'm not doing anything the average person can't do. Do you know how many people end up dead from stalkers because they put everything on their social media pages? They check into gyms, smoothie shops, restaurants, clubs. All one needs to do is show up. We make it way too easy to end up on a true crime podcast or *Dateline*."

I laugh, but it's not funny. It's simply Tillie's delivery that cracks me up. She clicks through photos while I pace. This could be what Philip is hunting for. If he swipes the evidence of…a crime? A call girl?…he's free of Acelynn. But she would never make it that easy for him. There has to be more to this story. To them.

To Drucilla. To Cupid, who I strongly believe might be my brother. And I can't help the police, unless I send information anonymously. That's risky. If Teddy suspected me, he has dirt on me, and he'd make sure to sweep it right into Detective Patrick's path.

Could Philip have killed Dru?

If so, he would have known the details about Cupid that were not released to the public and executed a more believable crime scene. Wait. No. Not necessarily. Philip would only need the details of the investigation if they charged someone with the crime and it was time for him to build a case. Why kill Dru at all? If he had an affair with her, would Philip care if Acelynn discovered it? Maybe. Acelynn has a trump card, and it might be to keep him in line, no more cheating. I'm sure more is in play here than the little I've pieced together, and most of that is conjecture.

"Booyah!" Tillie does a victory fist pump. "I got her. I know who the pretty redhead is. Tamera Hunt."

"Till, you are brilliant! We need to meet her."

Tillie's face falls. "Not gonna happen, Charlotte. She's dead."

Chapter Thirty-Three

"Dead? When? How?" I can't believe we almost had a lead, a big, fat piece to fit into place for the big picture.

"She died over two years ago. Murdered in her apartment. Strangulation. She worked for the historical society and was involved in various charities."

An invisible heavy force slams into me, and I collapse in the armchair across from the couch. "Philip killed her."

"No. He didn't. But he did try the case and won." She turns the laptop around, and a news article is on the screen. "She was strangled by a man named Travis Walker, who also killed two other women before her. RayEllen Mosby and Trisha Landsbury."

"This necklace must be about that case. What else could it be?"

"I work for a criminal defense attorney, so I tend to agree. But we need more facts." Her fingers race across the keyboard. "I'm looking for more articles about the case, the trial. The victims."

"The lead detective could have been Christian Patrick. He

doesn't like Philip. I could tell when I met him and he realized we were dating—or whatever it is we do. This case could be a reason." I run my hand over my face, frustrated that I'm back to square one. "I need to talk to Travis Walker."

Tillie almost chokes on her tea. "What? Are you insane?"

Maybe. I feel like I'm losing my mind, like I'm being pulled into a haunted house and with each floor I enter, new frightening scenarios pop out. Someone is trying to kill me, and I can't tuck tail and run. I'm locked in. And I do not do well in locked places.

"This guy murdered three women," Tillie says. "I don't see him being forthright, and he's clearly dangerous."

"A prosecutor who has an intimate connection to a victim shouldn't be trying the case. Tell me that's not true."

Tillie's lips pull tight.

"Exactly. Admit something here reeks."

"I admit it. But it could be that he tried a case with a conflict of interest because it was high-profile and a great boost to running for senator. He hid his relationship, or whatever it was with this woman, and Acelynn holds it over his head. The defense could appeal the conviction if this comes to light."

"What if it's something else entirely? I need to talk to this guy, and then we'll go from there. You search what you can online."

Tillie puffs a breath of air. "Be careful, Charlotte. You're not dealing with crackheads or even Frank Marchetti. You're dealing with people who wear masks of justice and goodness, and they're far scarier than those who do not pretend to be anything other than what they are—evil."

She's nailed it. I'm not sure I've met a single person in Acelynn's life who isn't pretending to be someone they aren't.

And that includes me.

I've been sitting on pins and needles for two days, waiting to speak to Travis Walker. And for two days, Tillie has tried to talk me out of it, but I've come too far. And while I'm not a fan of prisons—is anyone?—I need to be here today.

Travis's mug shots from the newspaper articles had shown a gaunt man with hollowed cheeks and pale blue eyes hiding behind dark circles of fatigue. No one said life as a criminal was easy.

I ought to know.

My crimes are piling up like a garbage dump.

Will visiting this inmate stir up more than I bargained for? Tillie wanted to go back to the gun range, but I talked her out of it. Jacob Moore could have killed Dru, and if he reads Tillie, it could put her in danger. Best to let sleeping dogs lie. The cops are on his tail, so that's enough, and I'm not sure him knowing Acelynn is relevant at this point.

After signing in and going through security checks, I bob my knees at a table in a large room that smells like dirty mop water and catfish.

Men in the standard prison gear enter the room. Hugs and tears are shed. Children bounce up and down yelling, "Daddy!"

Is my daddy somewhere in a correctional facility right now? Is anyone visiting him? Is he even alive? A man with a shaved head and arms the size of helium balloons enters the area and scans the crowd. Huge tattoos cover his arms, his eyes narrow, and then his gaze shifts to a waif of a woman with roots darker than syrup growing on top of bleach blond, burned-out hair. "Baby!"

I relax and focus on the open doorway, where more inmates trickle in. Guards are stationed in the corners of the room, watching with wariness. Is Travis Walker going to show? If for no other reason than curiosity, I'm banking that he does. He could be my only shot at answers, solutions and securing my future. Whatever that may look like.

I wait, and the clock ticks. We only have an hour, and it's wasting away. When I finally push back my chair to leave, calling it a bust, a man resembling a toothpick with tennis shoes enters the room. Pale blue eyes scan the tables and spot me, the only person alone at a table. I notice he limps, favoring his left leg, and I imagine him being shanked in a fight.

His copper-colored scruffy jaw is set hard as he approaches with shifty eyes. "You Acelynn Benedict?"

I nod and try not to fidget as he sits across from me, his arms folded over his chest. He's not much older than me, but his eyes put him light-years ahead.

Every question and thought evaporates.

Every syllable lodged deep within my throat melts.

"Visiting hours won't last too much longer. You a lawyer or something?" he asks.

Pull it together.

"'Cause I've been trying to get one to look at my case. No luck so far." A glimmer of hope fills his eyes.

"Why are you looking for a lawyer?" He either wants a way out or he's legit not guilty.

"So you're not a lawyer? You from the media or something? Want an interview? Because like I told those others, no. I got nothing to say. To nobody. Except a lawyer." He lets out a breath, and his shoulders sag as he assumes I'm no hope to him. I'm probably not, but he's potentially hope for me.

"I'm not from the media, and I'm not a lawyer, but I am interested in your story."

He sizes me up, then nods for me to continue.

I lick my lips. "I'd like to hear your personal side of the story, not what I've read online."

His brows knit together. "Why, if you ain't no media person or lawyer?"

This man isn't someone I plan to confide in. "I don't think you murdered those girls, Travis." At least, not Tamera Hunt. "But I want to know why they think you did. How did they convict you?" I lean forward. "If you tell me your story and I believe it, I might be able to help you out of here, but you'll have to trust me." I mean every word too. No innocent person belongs here, and Tillie can help me find someone who can exonerate him. Maybe her boss, LB, knows a Georgia lawyer willing to take the case.

He laughs and pounds a fist on the tiny round table. "I been told that before. Trust? You cain't trust nobody. Not out there—" he points toward the exit "—and you sure can't trust nobody up in this joint."

We have far more in common than I do with the Pinks or anyone in Acelynn's world. I don't need to be Acelynn right now. I need to be Charlotte Kane, the woman bruised and beaten and scarred by the world. A woman who never had anyone on her side to protect, defend or watch out for her. "I know. But we have to trust someone—or try to. I'm going to try and trust you. To believe you. I can promise you, I understand what it's like to be thrust into the system only to watch it fail and fail hard. Look at me. Look in my eyes, Travis. I'm telling you the honest truth."

"What other kind of truth is there?"

"Half-truths. Twisted truth. People who call their reality truth, but it's not absolute." I'm not sure what is truth anymore. But there has to be one—that's solid and unshakable. I stroke my necklace. A truth that stands the test of time. A truth people are willing to die for, even if no one else believes them. "I know all about those. But we can fix it. We can help each other and turn the tables on the system. We can make it, Travis. If you'll trust me. Will you trust me? It's just your side of the story. It won't hurt you."

"Might not help me either."

"What do you have to lose?" Me? I have everything.

I know when I have him. It's in the thawing of his eyes. "I don't see any better offers." He nods. "Guess I'll give you a shot."

"What led to your arrest? And listen, you're already convicted. You aren't going anywhere, so lying makes no sense."

I know I need more common ground. Travis is clearly not
educated and hasn't read dictionaries like me to learn how to
use more sophisticated words, which is as fake as anything else
I've ever done. He's a survivor, and I speak that language. "Tell
me about the first two women you were accused of strangling."

"I didn't even know them. But I hung out at the same bars.
Don't mean a thing, ya know? Cops said being at both bars
where they was drinking wasn't coincidence. One bar, maybe.
But not both."

I can't have an ink pen in here, so I listen hard. "How do
they know you were at those two bars?"

"Cameras. Seen me in the background."

The police had watched footage and could put Travis and the
women together in the same place on the same night of each
murder. Convenient. I have to agree with the cops, as much
as it pains me. This might be a dead end. "And you never met
either one? Never bought them a drink? Hit on them, even a
little bit?"

"I might have bought that second one a drink. Trisha. Trisha
Landsbury. But it didn't go where I wanted it to." He shrugged.
He didn't know her, but he did attempt to approach her for
something sexual. Nope, this isn't looking favorable for me.

"Did that make you mad?"

"You sure you ain't no cop? You sound like one."

I make an X over my chest. "I promise."

"Nah, it didn't make me mad, but the cops said it did. They
kept saying it made me mad until it did. So I said yeah, it made
me mad."

He's an easy mark, easy to confuse and trip up, and he has a
short fuse. Making someone angry enough to blow can move
things into your court. You just have to know the right buttons to push.

"Did you by any chance have a lawyer present when they questioned you?" I shift in the plastic chair and roll my shoulders, trying to remove some of the tension.

"They said I didn't need one, so I did that thing where you don't get a lawyer." He runs his tongue across his crooked teeth and looks up at the clock. Time is running out. Possibly for the both of us.

"You waived your rights..." I coax him to continue.

"I told that detective I didn't do it, but he was mean and in my face for a long time. I remember getting so tired. I just wanted to go home, ya know?"

I nod. "So they had you on tape both nights of the murders. Did you see those tapes?"

He nods again.

"Could anyone prove you didn't do it? Do you have any friends? Did you go to the bars alone?"

"My pal Walt. He knew I didn't kill those girls. We left that bar before Trisha and was gonna go gamble, but we was broke." He chuckled.

"Where did you go, then?"

"My house. Drank some beer and watched TV." He shrugs. "But I don't know 'bout RayEllen. I saw me on the tape, but I go to that bar all the time too. Never bought her a drink."

I bite my lip and try to make sense of everything. "You don't know where you went after you left on the night the first woman was murdered, correct?"

"RayEllen Mosby. You don't forget the names of the women you're accused of killing."

No, I wouldn't think you would. "But you remember the night of the second girl, Trisha, because you bought her a drink. You paid attention to her."

"Right."

"And Tamera Hunt. I want to know about her." Please let him have something to help me.

"I knew Tamera. From the YMCA. I took some GED prep classes, and she volunteered there for crafts for seniors and taught water aerobics. She was real nice."

Another connection. "So you knew her work hours. Did you know anything personal about her?"

He runs his hand over his head, his buzzed hair never moving. "I know she had a sister that stole her shoes all the time, and she went to church nearby. You mean things like that?"

How does he know this information? Had he been stalking her, or had she offered these details in conversations with him? "Have you ever been arrested or charged for a crime prior to being accused of this one?"

He hangs his head. "I got me a record. Robbed me a few gas stations for booze."

"Armed robbery?"

"Yep. But I never would have hurt nobody. I just wanted the beer and the money." He looks up at the clock again. "And some peanuts."

"What about the man who tried your case? Philip Beaumont. You remember him?" *Please let Travis know something.*

"Tall guy with a chip on his shoulder?"

Definitely him. "Yes."

"You asked me 'bout my friend. Walt. Walt was gonna tell the jury I didn't do it. We was together the night of Trisha's murder. But he was killed before he could be questioned."

"What do you mean, killed?"

"Someone hit him with their car, but they never found the driver. I think it's because they didn't look. Wasn't no accident. He was murdered. But no one believes that but me."

My insides harden like blocks of ice, and a shudder runs through me.

A hit-and-run.

Like my own near death.

"What evidence convicted you?" Something that would

make sure there was no reasonable doubt. A solid alibi had been taken out. What was left?

"Found my DNA in Tamera's house, which they said gave them permission to search my place, where they found a button from RayEllen's coat in one of my drawers with her blood on it. But I was never in RayEllen's house and never took a button. I don't know how it got in my place other than they put it there. And they found a necklace that belonged to Trisha, which I never took." He slams his fist down and the guards take a step toward him.

"I'm fine. I'm fine," he says and inhales a few cleansing breaths.

"Do you get real mad often?" Blind rage is a real thing. It's possible he was in the house and killed her and doesn't remember.

"They said I got mad when they rejected me and I done killed 'em. Raped 'em and strangled 'em. My hands were big enough to fit the marks. But I don't need to rape no girl."

I hold up my hands, trying to hush him. If the guards take him away, I won't acquire the info I need. Might not anyway, but I have to try. Travis has a record and a short fuse and was seen at the bars before the first two victims died. That's all circumstantial evidence. The necklace and button sealed the deal without Walt there to alibi him out. "Are you saying someone planted evidence in your house when they secured a search warrant?"

"That's exactly what I'm saying."

Now more than ever, I believe my near hit-and-run was from the same person who hit Walt before he could testify. Philip has connections to Tamera and to this case. Possibly to RayEllen and Trisha. Too much is stacking up to be coincidence.

I have Tamera's necklace. Why?

"Who defended you?"

"One of those public defenders."

"A name?" I might need to talk to him or her about reopening the case.

"Matthew Martinson. But since I been in here, he ain't seen me one time, and when I called about my case, he said just do my time. So I'm screwed and don't nobody care!"

I glance at the guard who's watching with serious interest. "How did they find DNA at Tamera's?"

He drops his head. "I been there. I cut my hand cleaning out her gutters and used her scarf to wrap it with because I couldn't find anything else, and she was on the phone. Felt bad but she said keep it, so that did legit end up in my place. And I did have prints in Tamera's house too, and I guess some of my blood on her sink or counter…somewhere. I needed the money. She invited me to have a cup of hot chocolate. That was it."

My heart sinks. "How many days after you cleaned out her gutters before she died?"

"That night. She was going to some dance or something."

The gala.

The evidence is stacked against him. An easy win, especially with Walt out of the way. No wonder the public defender said do the time. Unless there is some major evidence to overturn the conviction, Travis Walker is here for the duration.

Tamera wore that locket to the gala. It was on her in the photo. Acelynn must have gotten a hold of it that night. Philip was seen leaving with Tamera. He either spent some time with her and left, and Travis returned and killed her, or Travis is telling the truth about her.

"Now what do I do?"

I'm asking the same question. "Hang tight. I'm going to look into it."

The buzzer sounds. Chairs scoot across the floor, kids whine and women cry.

He stands. "I'll do my best. You smell good. Hadn't smelled anything that good in a while. Days feel like years in here."

"I hear ya." Especially if he is innocent.

I stop short before leaving. "Oh, wait. One more question. Who was the detective on the case? The one who would testify for the prosecution? Was it Detective Patrick?" Tillie hadn't come across that information yet.

"Don't remember his name."

"Was he late thirties, early forties, with jet-black hair and eyes?"

"Nah, he was bald and midfifties, maybe. But don't matter. He disappeared two days before my trial."

Chapter Thirty-Four

I return home and enter through the back door. The dogs run to me, barking, and stop once they see me. I bend and pet their heads, knowing it'll make me sneeze, but we're growing on each other even though they prefer Tillie. Speaking of Tillie. "Till, I'm back. And I have news. Also some theories, but things are so nuts, who knows?" I drop my purse on the counter and frown.

Where is Till?

I try upstairs in case she's napping or in the tub or shower, but she's not there, and she hasn't texted. My chest tightens as I return downstairs and search all the rooms. She's nowhere to be found. After shooting her a text to call me, I notice a thick yellow envelope on the counter with no return address or postal stamps.

Where did this come from and what's inside? Across the front in black marker is my name. Acelynn Benedict.

Trembling, I open it. Inside are black-and-white glossy photos. Me checking the mail. Walking the dogs. Sitting in my car.

And Tillie. Tillie playing with the dogs. Walking in the park.

Each photo of us has red *X*'s drawn over our eyes and mouths.

I can't breathe. We're being watched, and this is a warning to prove it. Does that mean someone knows I visited Travis Walker in prison? If I'm on to something big—and I believe I am—then what will the consequences be for talking to Travis? As I reach the back door, my phone rings.

Tillie.

Relief floods my system.

"Girl, you scared me half to death. Where are you, and has anyone been in the house?"

"Charlotte..." Her voice is wan and cracking.

"What's wrong? Where are you?"

"Someone...hit me. I think? I'm at Acelynn's office downtown."

Hit her? "I'm coming. Do you need an ambulance?" While I want her to have all the medical attention she needs, I kinda hope we don't have to call someone. I freeze. How could I possibly think that about my best friend? What is wrong with me? Am I becoming like the Pinks, who don't seem to sincerely care for each other? Not the way Tillie and I do.

"No. I don't think so."

"I'm on my way. Lock the doors, and if there's ice in the kitchenette, use it." I lock the back door and fumble with the keys, jump into Acelynn's car and press the ignition button, praying that Tillie isn't too broken and grateful she's not dead. I don't think I'd survive her death. Did the attacker think she was dead? The memory of the red *X* over her eyes and mouth in that black-and-white glossy photo activates my gag reflex, and I fear I'll have to pull over and puke. But I make it, hitting green lights all the way.

Once I arrive, I fly inside. I come to a skidding halt when I see the place. Unlike my house after Philip searching it, it's a disaster. Filing cabinets are open, and the contents are littered on the floor. Pictures that hung on the wall now lie in glass shards, mixing with papers and files and fabric samples. It looks like the desk vomited. Chairs are overturned, and stuffing spills out of the couches, exposed like guts.

Blood drops trail the floor, and my stomach turns.

I rush to the back, where there's a bathroom and kitchenette. Tillie is sitting on the floor, the freezer door open and a bag of ice against the back of her head. Her hand and the side of her face are bloody, but she's alive.

Dropping down beside her, I pull her into my arms and rock her. "I'm so sorry." This is all my fault. Instead of making things better, I'm making them worse. "Can you tell me what happened?" I move the ice pack to inspect the wound. I don't think it needs stitches, but she has a goose egg, and blood mats her hair.

"I was thinking about that heart locket and wondering if Acelynn might have anything hidden here, so I came to look. But when I got here, I walked in on a man already ransacking the place. I didn't see him at first. I just saw the mess, and then I heard him behind me and started to turn, but...crack! I went down."

"So you don't know if it was a man."

"I caught a glimpse from my peripheral. It was a man's arm and build, but I didn't see his face." She winces and leans against me. "I wasn't knocked out, but I saw spots and stars dancing like on a cartoon."

Hugging her closer, I thank God she's safe. "Let me find you some pain relievers." I hunt through the cabinets until I find a bottle of ibuprofen, then hand her three and a bottle of water from the fridge. "Did you check the mail this morning?"

She winces and takes the pills. "No. Why?"

"Someone's been inside the house—again." Five billion people have keys. Could be anyone. I tell her about the photos and the X-ed out eyes and mouths. Whoever was in the house the night Tillie arrived is my best guess. And I don't know of anyone who might want to threaten me or her except Philip, and yet he hasn't mentioned her or even asked about who Tillie might be.

"Help me up."

I do and follow her to the bathroom, where she uses a rag to clean up the blood and dab at the head wound as I tell her about my conversation with Travis Walker.

"Has to be Philip, Char. And I found the name of the lead detective on that case. It was Sam Honeycutt. He had a long career with Savannah PD, but now that he's missing, I'll dig up what I can on that."

The dots connect. Philip is the common denominator between all of these people, including Travis, the missing detective, Sam, and the dead alibi, Walt.

"It sounds like Philip wanted to put Travis away for a crime *he* committed, and the detective helped him plant evidence, then vanished. He's either dead or ran in fear of his life."

"He disappeared before he could testify, which would hurt Philip's case, not help, so maybe Walt's death made him fear for his own life and he ran," she says. "He likely knew after his testimony in court, he was a loose thread Philip would clip. So he bolted beforehand."

"And after Philip couldn't find that necklace, a car tried to take me out. I'm a loose thread too, but why now? Over two years after Tamera's death." I returned the necklace to the jewelry box after fixing the false back. If he hasn't found it so far, he won't find it now. It was well hidden and it might be the only leverage I have to keep me and Tillie safe.

"Maybe he's sick of being with Acelynn and wants out."

Perhaps. "If Acelynn has something big on Philip—like that locket as some kind of proof, plus the photos of him with Tamera Hunt—then why would he rattle her cage by sending photos of us with *X*'s on our eyes and mouths? Philip isn't stupid. He hunted quietly for the necklace, didn't find it and potentially put out a hit. I buy that. But this feels different. For one, the way the office is ransacked. Philip didn't want Acelynn to know he'd been inside the house. Whoever did this didn't care."

"Acelynn played a lot of games and held a lot of secrets. It's possible more than one person is trying to kill her." Tillie splashes cold water on her face and dries it with a hand towel. She's a little green around the gills, and I worry she might have a concussion. "We should just pack it up and leave. If they make it to Chicago based on her airline tickets and connect her to you, you'll be long gone. On a beach sipping a drink somewhere safe. You can start over for real this time. The longer you stay here, the more danger you put yourself in. Is this life really worth that?"

"No, but a guy is in prison who might be innocent." If I walk away, he might suffer forever in there. Lucille needs an advocate for sobriety and to get to the bottom of why Conrad keeps pushing her pills instead of sending her to rehab. "Would you come?"

Tillie's mouth turns down, and she slowly shakes her head. "I don't know, Charlotte. My home is in Chicago, and I'm content there with my job."

I remember Philip's words that people who are content aren't normal and can't be trusted, but I wonder… Maybe it's people who are discontented with everyone and everything that might be the issue, not the other way around.

"Would you at least consider it?"

She nods emphatically. "I would. For you. Definitely. But you'd have to promise a real fresh start. No more of your *curiosity*. It lands you in trouble."

I would promise her anything. I don't want to be out there alone. "We have a chance to really help people. I want to try."

Tillie's eyebrows shoot north. "Do you mean that, or is that what you want me to hear? To justify darker thoughts. You can say all the right things and think you even mean them, but do you? Do you, Charlotte?"

Yes is on the tip of my tongue. I do want to help someone, or several someones. But do I have underlying motives and self-ish ambition? I want to tell myself I don't. I might. I hate that I might. Is it so wrong to want to stay if I can do some good? But is the most good also benefiting me? I pinch the bridge of my nose. "I want to," I whisper.

"That's a start."

"You've been hurt. It's probably time you go. I don't want anything else to happen to you."

"Neither do I, but I'm staying. You've always put yourself in harm's way to keep me safe. I know you originally came here to protect me. But for once, Charlotte, please let me stick my neck out for you. I can't in good conscience leave you know-ing that your life is literally at stake. If you won't run, then I don't want to either." Her tone is firm, and her face is resolute. No point arguing.

I don't like it, but I appreciate her bravery, and I can't force her to leave. "Okay. Then who else might be ransacking this office and sending me photos to warn me to give up something, back off of something or keep quiet?"

Tillie lays the ice pack on her head again and winces. "You did take Teddy's sketchbook."

Chapter Thirty-Five

It's late and my head hurts. I'm exhausted and can't sleep, but I need to. I've stared at Teddy's sketchbook, Tillie's words echoing in my head.

I fire up the laptop and search for the other victims of the Cupid killer over the past six months. I don't find their sleeping faces in Teddy's sketchbook, but this is not his only book. He's an artist, and artists draw often.

I don't think Teddy had me almost hit by a car, and I don't think the strangulation of Tamera Hunt, Trisha Landsbury and RayEllen Mosby were at his hands. Philip may not have killed them either, but he has direct ties to Tamera.

With Allie's sketch, Teddy ties to the serial murders or at least the most recent victim. Could it be coincidence? The victims have all lived within a ten-mile radius of me. Teddy visits often and he doesn't live that far away from the victims either. He has two dead women in his sketchbook. He was pretty ticked it was gone and he assumed I took it, though I'm not sure why other than it's his private property. The ransacking of my office could have been him.

The only way to know for sure if he's who I think he might be is to search his house for other sketchbooks and see if I can identify the other victims. If he's drawn them sleeping, then I need to know if they purchased their homes within a decent timeline of their deaths. Teddy might have been their agent, or they used his company. Either would give him access to keys.

What are the odds Acelynn is sandwiched between two different murderers? That seems far-fetched, unlikely and straight-up insane. I've seen it before, though. On true crime shows and documentaries. People's real lives are so twisty and shocking that no one would believe it in fiction.

Acelynn mentioned she and Teddy often watched late-night movies of the horror genre, which is Teddy's favorite, and Acelynn always had a hard time telling Teddy no. Or so she said. Is anything she relayed true? Is what I'm about to do going to sell me out or help me out? Because I need inside Teddy's home. I need to see those sketches. And if I'm right, Detective Patrick needs to know regardless of whether it brings heat onto me. Before it was a theory, but if I discover concrete evidence, I have no choice, and I'll deal with whatever sins Teddy has of mine tucked into his pocket. It can't be worse than serial murders.

Tillie is cuddled with the dogs on the couch, sleeping. I shake her awake to let her know I'm leaving and tell her if she has a concussion, she can't sleep. At first she's dazed, but then she focuses in on me.

"I have to leave. I need to see Teddy's other sketchbooks, see if he's drawn more of Cupid's victims."

"I don't like this."

"He's my brother. It'll be fine." I hope her head injury fogs her brain, as this is far from fine.

"I can't stop you. How are you going to sneak past him to steal another sketchbook, or even to look at them?"

I'd rather not tell her that I have sleeping pills from Acelynn's cabinet in my pocket or that I plan to crush one up in his drink. "I'll figure it out. I'm quick."

"*Adept* is what you mean." No judgment. Just fact in her voice. "Be safe and be smart."

"I will."

I drive to Teddy's bungalow on Tybee Island. It's on the water, and the smell of salt reaches my nose. It's almost midnight. His car isn't here, and I'm relieved. I don't want to drug him, but I need a peek at his drawings.

Just in case he's home and his car is gone for some weird reason, I ring the bell. These days everyone has affordable cameras on their porch, and I nonchalantly search for evidence of one but see nothing. So far, so good.

No one answers, and I start trying keys on my key ring. The fourth key slides into the lock and does the trick. Inside, I'm hit with cool air and a hint of lemon and something I can't put my finger on, but it's not a bad smell. The bungalow is a remodeled open concept, done by Acelynn. Her style is all throughout the nautical designs. She often stages homes for L&N Realty, the Lamberts' and Newsoms' company. A surface light left on under the microwave lets me know Teddy plans to return home at some point before daylight.

The downstairs consists of a study, a gaming room, bathroom, kitchen, living room and a laundry room. I suspect the primary bedroom is upstairs and head up, praying and hoping he is not watching me from his phone right now. That there are no cameras inside this house.

If so, I'm in serious trouble.

The house's silence has my teeth on edge, and every pop and crack sends me into a new wave of panic and dread. Using my cell phone flashlight, I enter Teddy's bedroom. It's neat and tidy, and the bed is made. Where is Teddy at midnight?

Probably sneaking in windows and drawing unsuspecting

women as they sleep. Gah, that's vile but likely. I drop to my knees and shine the light under his bed. Where all monsterish things creep and lurk along with socks and dust bunnies, but there's nothing except cords and dust.

He has a leather-bound journal by his bed. I snag it, opening it up to more drawings of women sleeping. Many of them are me, a few of Mother, more of Dru and two more of Allie Deardon. He's been to her house multiple times since she's wearing different pajamas in each drawing.

MacKenzie is crashed on a couch in one, and the rest are of women I can't identify. None of Bianca in this journal. Why?

I realize that many of the women are in *his* bed, but none of them are Cupid's victims—or Trisha Landsbury, RayEllen Mosby or Tamera Hunt—though I haven't combed through all of his sketch pads.

On the next page, my breath catches.

It's Drucilla Hilton, but she's not alone.

She's sleeping next to Conrad Benedict.

Teddy's known all along about the affair. Why pretend not to? Unless he has something to hide…like murder.

A car pulls up, and the squawk of a car door locking sends my pulse through the roof.

Teddy Benedict knows I'm in his house.

Chapter Thirty-Six

"What are you doing here in the middle of the night?" Teddy asks as I make it to the bottom of the stairs. In the dark.

"Where have you been?" I fold my arms over my chest. "Drawing late-night models going night-night?" I am not anxious Charlotte. I am confident and commanding Acelynn Benedict. I have a key to this home. He's given me the right to be here.

Reading his body language and tone, I decide he's not mad, but he's wary, and has been since our first encounter. Not sure if he suspects something isn't right about me, or if this centers around Acelynn.

He tosses his keys on the counter and opens the fridge, takes out a Miller Lite and offers me one, but I decline. "I don't remember me having to report on every move I make with you." Teddy takes a long pull of his drink, and it gives me a second to size him up—dark jeans, black T-shirt and black tennis shoes. Something a night creeper would wear to slink around homes and peep in windows—or sketch unsuspecting women.

"Why are you here for real?" he asks, ignoring my question and swaggering to the living room. He switches on a lamp, then returns, towering over me like an oak tree.

I notice a dark duffel bag by the door that wasn't there when I entered. I itch to look inside but can't right now. "Been at the gym?"

"Sure," he murmurs and leans on the counter, becoming eye level with me, boring his gaze into mine. I swallow but keep my composure. He twirls a strand of my hair around his finger. I'm wearing it down, which isn't exactly like Acelynn, but she can't wear it in a bun 24/7.

"Did you take my sketchbook?"

"You already asked me that. You have so many, you probably misplaced it. You'll find it when you least expect it."

He bares perfectly straight white teeth. "If I find it, it's because you just now brought it back. You're not fooling me, sissy." His breath is hot and minty with a hint of barley and hops. "Why'd you take it? You jealous they're not all of you?"

What? Ew. "Give me a break." Time to redirect and make this meeting work for me. Teddy has known about Conrad and Dru's affair. I want to know why he's been pretending not to. "I'm here for two reasons."

"There it is," he says as loud as his grin is wide.

"One, you and I both know Dad was sleeping with Dru. When I broached the subject, you acted like you had no idea. Why?"

He runs his tongue along the inside of his cheek, and it bulges like he's chewing a wad of tobacco. "If you know I know, then you've seen the drawing. What are you planning to do with this?"

I was hoping he wasn't this smart and wouldn't put two and two together. "Nothing if you answer my questions. Because right now, the detective thinks I'm involved. Dad told him I knew about Dru and we fought. Why would he do that unless he was trying to bounce the heat off of him and burn me?"

Teddy's eyes widen. "He said that?"

"Yes. The detective visited me a second time. Does Dad know that you sketched them? That you know?"

He tsks and swigs his beer. "Does he know? No way. But you gotta admit, the drawings are pretty good."

"You want to talk about shading and lines in the sketch you drew of our father in bed with our friend?" I'm not faking my disgust.

He chuckles. "I'm not gonna lie. I was surprised to see the old man there. Not surprised he's plowing in other fields. He's been doing that our whole lives. I didn't tell you because you were already mad at Dru for not paying you for all that work, and you've been mad at Dad for half your life. The two together would have been a dumpster fire, and let's be honest—you're vindictive. Not to mention you fixate on things and can spiral."

"I am not and I do not."

"You are, and you do." He rolls his eyes and finishes off his beer in a long gulp. After a raucous burp, he tosses it in the trash. "And don't snipe over the fact I don't recycle."

My mind spins and the room slants. Acelynn and I have a thing in common. Not fixation but curiosity. It sometimes steals the best of us. How far has Acelynn gone?

I know how far I have.

"Why would our father implicate me? That's what he did. Agree?" I'm raging on behalf of Acelynn, on behalf of daughters everywhere. Dads protect; they don't throw children to the wolves. And I have no idea if that fight actually took place between us, or if he's lying and hoping I'm charged and tried and found guilty. Maybe he wants me out of his life. He never wanted children and certainly not adopted ones.

"I agree."

"I never approached him about the affair." She might have,

though. "He must have assumed I'd be angry based on my and Dru's relationship."

Teddy laughs. "What relationship? Don't act like you care about that skeezer. We got saddled with her because of our parents."

"Sounds like a bitter lover," I snap back.

"Bitter? No. We've all had our sloppy seconds. She means nothing. But…I like it when she sleeps. I like them all sleeping. You know that. Why can't they all just sleep?" he murmurs, and a chill stabs into my bones. "They're at the most peace sleeping."

Sleeping or dead?

"I didn't kill Dru, Teddy."

"I didn't kill her either." He shrugs.

We're dancing now. Because I don't believe him. And he doesn't believe me. Which means Teddy and Acelynn might be capable of murder, and they know it. I've never murdered anyone, but I know I'm capable of it. I've…thought about it. I'm believing more than ever that maybe it's not our upbringing or financial status or even education that shapes us, but our hearts. And our hearts seem to all be dark and wicked at the core.

I came here to incapacitate a human being in order to achieve what I want. The sketches. Teddy violates women's privacy to morbidly sketch them—and maybe even murder some of them. What has my sister's dark heart led her to do? And what will mine keep leading me to do? How far will I go?

I don't know. And that scares me too.

"Now that we've declared innocence, what's the second reason you're here if not to bring back my sketch pad?"

Two. What is my other reason? "Did you ransack my downtown office looking for it?"

He frowns. "No. I want it back, but not enough to put that kind of effort into finding it. Why did you take it?"

"I don't know. It was there. You know how I like to take things." Nail polish. Lip gloss. Dining and dashing.

He clips my chin lightly. "Ah, the thrill of taking what we want against the ticking clock of being caught. Remember when you stole the answer key to the history test from Mrs. Patel in eleventh grade? Right behind her back while she was grading papers."

He expects me to reminisce, and I grin.

"How much did you make off that before you stuck it in MacKenzie's locker and sent an anonymous tip that she stole it?"

"I don't know," I murmur.

"MacKenzie was so freaking mad. But that's what she gets for stealing a guy you were interested in. At least Drucilla had enough fear to never mess with your boyfriends."

Except Bianca said she slept with Philip and then implied she herself might have been with him that afternoon I caught her. What is true and false?

"MacKenzie never did it again." It's an educated guess.

"No, but her daddy saved her from being expelled. She never did rat you out."

Her hatred of me now makes sense. "She knew better."

"Bet." He stretches and yawns. "Those aren't very good reasons to be here. What's really going on?"

"I couldn't sleep."

"Then you should be at Philip's. Not here. I can't help you with that." His grin is wily, and goose bumps break out along my arms, my neck hairs rising. "Kidding. Yes, I can."

Ew.

He pushes off the counter and grabs the black duffel bag. After unzipping it, he pulls out a plastic baggie. Inside are several white pills. He takes one out and dangles it between his fingers, swinging it like a pendulum. "Pay the toll," he says, "and you can sleep like a sweet little baby girl."

I don't know what the toll is. But Teddy has a lot of money

in those pills. Does he slip them in drinks so he can later slide into homes unnoticed and sketch women for hours? I'm almost certain of it. He eyes my purse and makes a *gimme* motion with his fingers.

Keys.

He wants one of the Pinks' keys. But he never gave me back the one he already snagged. Dru is dead. He already has one, so it's either Bianca or Mac.

"I'm going to give B another shot. Maybe I can stop by and slip her a pill, keep her asleep. Except she never drinks with me."

Maybe Bianca Lambert knows what he does, who he is, and is too smart to fall for it.

If I give him her key, he might end up killing her. If I don't, he'll be suspicious. He knows Acelynn wants pills, and they've made these exchanges before.

"Look, Dru is dead, and they think it's one of us. If Bianca wakes and sees you, she might link you to Dru's murder and call the cops. And if she has insomnia and sleeps for several hours after you've been there, she will know you've drugged her. You don't need any heat on you right now, on any of us."

He grimaces.

"If cops keep sniffing, they'll find your drawings. Find your drawings of Allie, Mr. Real Estate Agent."

Teddy's brow furrows. "I didn't break real estate agent code. I met her at a bar near her house…"

Near my house.

"…and dropped a pill in her drink. She needed a ride home, and I gave it to her. While she slept, I did a little artwork. Big deal. I didn't rape her. And I didn't kill her. In fact, she invited me over a few more times after that. It was all on the up-and-up."

None of what Teddy does is on the up-and-up.

Frustration grinds my muscles, tightening them. I can't tell if he's lying or not. "Well, lie low for a while."

He hands me the pill anyway. "For looking out for your little bro."

"If that detective swings by, I expect you to inform me immediately."

"And I expect to find my sketchbook back in my house before the week's out if you didn't bring it tonight. Fair?"

"Whatever, Teddy."

I stride out the door and clamber into my car, leaning my head on the seat.

Teddy looks guilty, but his cover story is good, maybe even true.

Now I have more insight into my sister. She kept tight tabs on her friends and family and wasn't above cutting their throats for betrayal. So which one of them might be tired of it and seeking revenge? Even Conrad Benedict seems to be taking a swing at me.

What if they're all taking swings, and she knew it and ran to me? I've survived a lot.

But can I survive this many secrets and knives plunging into my back?

Chapter Thirty-Seven

Friday morning, I wake up at nearly nine o' clock to a text from Bianca.

See you tonight. I'll bring the wine. Just us Pinks celebrating Dru.

Great. Tillie needs to be scarce.

I shower and dress for the day, pull my hair into a perfect bun and pad downstairs to the smell of coffee and bacon. Tillie's cooking breakfast. Color has returned to her cheeks, but shadowy half-moons rest under her eyes. I want her to leave for her own protection, but she'd only argue again, so I tell her about my jaunt last night at Teddy's as I pour coffee and snatch a piece of bacon.

"I worry about you and how far you might go to…protect yourself." Those last two words feel like cover words for what she actually wants to say.

"You think I set all this up on purpose to steal my sister's life?

How could I have known about Tommy and Frank Marchetti? I did what I had to do in the moment."

"No. But I think if things hadn't played out like this…you'd decide to keep up the ruse. It never goes the way you plan, Char. The way you dream things up in your mind. And when it all falls to pieces, you…you spiral."

"Well, I guess I have that in common with my sister," I bark. "Spiraling is in our DNA. Even Marilyn was delusional…" My words trail off. I've hurt the one person who cares about me. Me—Charlotte Kane. The poor white trash from Chicago who cycled through foster care with a black trash bag of hand-me-downs.

Am I a victim or am I playing victim? I don't want to ruminate on it. I don't want to see or explore the ugly parts of my soul.

I don't think I can bear it.

"Till, I'm sorry. I could give you a litany of excuses, but I'm not going to." I stand and hug her.

"I just worry about you," she whispers.

"I know. I worry about you too."

Tillie breaks the hug. "Have some more bacon. Bacon makes everything better."

I don't argue and put three slices on a paper towel, then take a bite of a piece of toast she's laid on a little dessert plate.

"Oh, here's one thing I learned this morning. That case involving those three women, Trisha, RayEllen and Tamera? Tamera was the daughter of a judge, which made it a high-profile case that Philip would want to propel his career, and being on the right side of an important judge wouldn't hurt him."

"So if he put away the wrong man, then his career is toast." If he withheld the locket from evidence in order to seal an innocent man's fate, Acelynn might have known. Then she stole and hid it for leverage to keep them together as some kind of power couple, or to advance herself somehow. Love wasn't a factor to Acelynn. Not in any relationship she was involved in.

She only looked out for herself.

Is that what I'm doing? Deep down? Am I using Tillie's safety as a justification to... No. No. "Have you found out anything on Detective Sam Honeycutt?"

She shoves a whole strip of wobbly bacon in her mouth. "We have a PI back home. I could ask him to look into cases to see if Sam was crooked, if you want him snooping. Philip might catch wind, and then what? I mean, if Philip's even guilty. We only have our speculations. We could be way off base."

Good point. "Okay, hold off on your PI and see what you can dig up on your own."

She slathers honey and butter on her toast. "We should go into an investigative services business together."

I snort. "Hard limit."

She shrugs and licks butter from her lip.

"I'm heading to the office to clean. Be back in a few hours." I tell her she can't be here for the girls' night, or she has to lock herself away quietly upstairs. The Pinks can't find out she's in town or in this house. But whoever ran across my yard in the storm the night Tillie arrived likely knows the truth—not only about Tillie but me. And if they know, why are they keeping it quiet? What are they going to do with the information? My bacon churns in my gut at the thought.

But I'm not sure how to find who it was on my lawn. I have no choice but to look over my shoulder, stay on guard and be prepared to do whatever it takes to keep us safe.

And I will do whatever it takes.

I arrive at Acelynn's office and groan at the mess, but the windows are large, and I can't have someone seeing it and calling the police. After turning on a playlist with some upbeat pop music, I start working. A new thought hits me. I didn't suspect Philip of ransacking my office based on his careful searching of my home. But that doesn't mean he didn't hire someone to search the office in a desperate attempt—someone who wasn't as cautious.

An hour later, I wipe my brow with the back of my hand and wonder if the person who did this found what they were looking for. I slide two drawers into their slots in the antique desk, but the bottom drawer sticks. Something is wedged in the back. Growling, I kneel and reach into the crevice to remove the blockage.

Leather meets my fingertips, and I dislodge a thick book with cracks like spiderwebs along the spine and cover.

An old diary. Too old to be Acelynn's.

It must have been taped to the back of the desk and fallen in the search. Why is she hiding an old leather diary? Is this what someone was looking for here? I skim the first page. Oh. Ooooh. As I skim a few more pages, words like *manipulative*, *deceitful*, *wicked* pop off the page.

Younger brother… Petal…

This could be Lucille Benedict's diary. She hasn't called me Petal, but to be fair, she hasn't called me anything the two times we've been together. I continue to read the pages written by—at first glance—a mentally unstable woman who uses words like *dark* and *evil* to describe her baby. She wanted to kill her, to smother her with a pillow. If this is Lucille's, no wonder Acelynn has hidden it. She'd never want a soul to find it. But why not simply burn it? Is this another game? Another way to control and manipulate someone?

This woman hasn't been out of the house but in spurts for years other than to a mental health facility, but upon further reading, she believes she's being drugged by her husband, and I know Conrad prescribes Lucille's pills. I've seen Acelynn at work, manipulating even me, which is hard to do. She's toyed with minds and played vindictive games, like almost having MacKenzie expelled over a boy. According to this book, she cut a girl's hair, and if Lucille isn't wrong and delusional…Acelynn has murdered a little girl over the fact that Teddy liked her.

My blood runs cold.

Could my sister be even more wicked than I imagined? We share the same DNA. We've played some of the same games. Most of what I did was to simply survive, wasn't it? Can I be this dark? This deceptive? I simply haven't embraced it like my sister?

Is this why Teddy draws women asleep—like they're dead? Did he see Acelynn kill this little neighbor girl, and it fueled his sick need to see it over and over again, drawing it to fantasize or make sense of what happened when he was just a boy?

I am physically ill, my heart pounding with earth-shattering force, but I'm compelled to keep reading.

Checking the dates, I notice long stretches between some of the entries, and I imagine she wasn't lucid enough to write every day. But these are the writings of a madwoman who reminds me of Marilyn at times when she was high and delusional. Accusing me of incredible things that never happened. A woman fueled by paranoia.

They have to be. They have to be written from delusions and paranoia, because if they aren't, then my sister is truly, without doubt, evil.

A bad seed.

And I can't deny that some of the darkness that lived in Acelynn also lives in me.

Then

Halloween is the most atrocious holiday ever celebrated, in my opinion. I live with a ghoul and the ghosts of my past. The hauntings of my family that was never what I'd hoped or believed it would be. These past nearly two decades with children have been lived in a gloomy fog that hovers over my soul, and with each devastating disappointment, a new wave of horror has penetrated into it. I no longer try to fight it. I can't fight through the barrage of pills.

Petal has overtaken this home, and she has won the war. Without Mother here and with her father absent, whether physically present or not, she is stronger than I, because I can't fight evil with evil. It's not who I am.

She has no mercy, and I am merciful.

She has no regard for any living thing, and I am sad when flowers fade in the hot summer heat. And that is what I feel like. The petal. The flower withering under the scorching heat of her devious mind.

I finally caved and told my therapist my thoughts, but she

only wanted to diagnose me, not listen. I even called the pastor of our church, which we haven't attended since the children were small. To be honest, it was all part of the American family facade we've been living our entire lives, going but not believing. Not really.

I wish I'd never met Marilyn Kane on our trip to Chicago. Sitting outside a bar with a beer and a cigarette hanging from her thin red lips and her belly swollen with child. I'd wanted a baby for so long and been denied by my husband and then by my own womb. All I could think about was a baby, and I saw her and knew she could be bought.

I bought a baby girl.

Of course, it was a harder sell than I anticipated with Darling Husband, but in the end, he gave me what I wanted. Looking back, I think he hoped it would occupy my time and distract me from his wandering ways, his string of mistresses.

I suppose it did, only in the most awful way. I regretted her from the start. No, it wasn't postpartum depression, because I never carried her. When Bubs came along, naturally I was stunned. Shocked. We all were, and he came out the most joyous child.

But she's tainted him. From fear, then through comfort. Like a victim of Stockholm syndrome. I should have protected him better. Harder.

Between the meds and her threats of poison, leaving her shoe for me to trip down the stairs and having me sent away…it kept me leashed and quiet. Even now she holds the power to send me away for good or kill me. I expect it daily.

My sweet Bubs has changed from that special boy. Her vile darkness permeates his soul in a way that terrifies me. She's nurtured him in wicked ways. No longer does light flicker in his eyes, but her evil pulses behind them. He's trapped.

I often wonder about the other child. Does she too have the darkness in her? Can two of them be born this evil? Does destruction surge through both their DNA? I might never know, but I do know that it crosses bloodlines. It's living in my son. Now sixteen, he's moody, distant and sullen. Sneaky and conniving.

Muffled voices and music flow from his room. Angry and scratchy. Depression has overwhelmed me and held me hostage inside my room. Dark curtains pulled. My son doesn't even visit me here anymore. She forbids him.

You'd think a strapping young man would stand up to her. He has the physical prowess and yet…he never does. She holds all the power.

But maybe I can get the upper hand. Somehow. I creep from my room and push my ear up against the door.

I hear a slap. Biting and cracking. She's hit him. Again.

"How dare you," she says as the grungy music plays. I hate this music. "You can't keep them. You can never keep them. Don't you know you can't have two masters? You'll be slave to one and hate the other, and you will never hate me. I love you. And you love me, and we will always belong to one another."

What is she talking about?

"What are you going to do to her? Are you going to hurl a rock against her head and drown her in the creek like you did Shelly Barker or set her on fire like Abby?" he asks with a tremor in his voice.

"That was so long ago, and child's play. Puh-lease. I've handled it more maturely," she quips. "She's not pretty anymore. Definitely never as pretty as me, but you thought she was. You won't now."

"What do you mean?"

"I mean your loyalty and your love belong to me. Who protects you? I do. When Ben Masters beat you out for quarterback, I fixed it. And you played. When I saw you liked to do things to animals, I covered for you. I take care of you. I let you be you. No one understands you like me."

"You did?"

"Of course. We all need an outlet. Who was your first? I was. And I will be your last. Your forever."

My jaw hits the floor, and I press my hand to my throbbing chest. I'm sick. Vomit hits the back of my throat.

I'm not hearing this right. It's the meds. It has to be. He did not intentionally hurt those cats or enjoy it. My children are not... They can't...

My mind races, and I scroll mentally. Valentine's Day. Abby Morlowe. He'd been sweet on her and taken her to the dance. He'd bought her a card and roses and chocolates. And Petal had seethed. I knew she was territorial. She had a fit over cards and flowers before. She'd killed before, though I couldn't prove it, until now. But...I didn't realize...

Abby had almost died in a fire in the school locker room that night of the dance. Now she was a burned husk of the lovely blonde girl who'd caught my son's eye. And my daughter's.

"Now, put on your costume I bought you. Seems fitting."

My hands and legs tremble. I don't know what to do.

"Where'd you find this?" he asks.

"Vintage costume shop by the river. Don't worry—I'm not going to make you go shirtless or in tights, Cupid. Just the mask and whatever you want to wear. Oh, and check out the quiver of arrows. Nice touch. Speaking of touch..."

"I don't want to."

"You don't want to be my Cupid? Brother, don't act like you don't want me. You prove every time that you do. But if you want to pretend, wear the mask. Be anyone you want."

Only music fills the room until she laughs, and I know what transgressions are happening. No, I will protect him. I stagger back down the hall and into my room. We have a camcorder we barely use, but it works. I can prove she's a spawn of the devil. I'll finally be believed.

Rummaging through the closet, I find it. It's small. Hand-held. I shove it in the pocket of my robe and return to his room, but I don't want to go in. I can't stomach what I'm about to see. I'll never be able to unsee it.

She's holding my son's heart hostage and seducing him to her ways, and while they aren't blood kin, it's still sick. And furthermore, neither of them knows she's adopted. I chose not to tell her for fear she'd use it against me. Blame all my cries for help on the fact I just don't love my daughter because she's not from my own DNA.

For once, I have to be brave—for him. Opening the door, I hold up the recorder, but the image I see is so filthy and disturbing, so shocking and appalling, I shriek.

And she sees me.

I run from the room, unsure of what she'll do. Throw me down the stairs? Poison me? Set me on fire?

I stand with one clammy hand on the railing and the other pressed on the pain that constricts my chest. Am I having a heart attack? This must be what a heart attack feels like. Tight and heavy with shocks that ripple like electricity along my left arm, leaving me stunned and my pulse out of rhythm.

My hand slides along the cool wrought iron, my knees languid. One push is all it would take to send me to my death.

I know she's thinking about it.

Her calculated gaze swings from me to my hand to the stairs and then to the cold marble flooring below.

"Whatever you think you saw—you didn't," she says with a narrowed glint. "You shouldn't even be awake. Have you taken your pills? The doctor said you can't skip them. If you do, you could hallucinate."

"I—I didn't hallucinate what I witnessed just now." But I haven't taken my pills tonight, and I can't remember if I took them last night. My days have run together lately. However, my eyes didn't conjure up the atrocity I walked into five minutes ago.

She creeps into my personal space, predatory like a lioness. She's hungry to pounce, but she's careful, strategic. I am her prey, and I don't understand how we've gotten here.

That's a lie.

I do know.

I know exactly how we've gotten here.

"You're sick," she says in a gentle but mocking tone. "You've been sick a long time. You know this." Her lips turn down as if she feels sorry for me. She doesn't. She has no pity or compassion because she feels nothing. Her heart is a black abyss.

"Let me help you back to bed. Give you your meds and some water. You'll feel better in the morning."

I don't want to take my pills. I'm fine without them. I've been having more good days than bad. Besides, they make me tired and foggy. She eyes me, holding my gaze. She's not going to back down.

But I know what I saw.

The horror was real, and the terror that races cold through my blood proves I saw it with my own two eyes.

And I have no idea what to do but allow her to gently but firmly guide me to my bedroom like a naive child. I've tried a million different things. Interruptions. Distractions. I thought distance would solve it.

It didn't. Things actually grew worse.

"Okay. You're right. I—I'm not thinking clearly. What would I do without you?" I fake a smile, and she returns it in an equally saccharine measure as she helps me into bed. After I slide into the soft sheets, she picks up the brown pill bottle and empties two trazodone into her palm, then holds them out to me.

I willingly accept them, and she hands me the water, the glass cool against my fingers. I drink and swallow.

"Good." She pats my head like I'm a petulant child. "You'll feel much better now. You'll see more clearly in the morning."

No, I won't.

"Good night, Mother."

"Good night," I murmur. After she leaves the room, I spit out the pills. I'm seeing more clearly now than I ever did on these things. I've been on and off meds, switched meds, new meds, old meds for decades. I'm over it.

And I know what I saw.

I slip my diary out from between the mattress and box springs and grab my pen from the nightstand. I've been chronicling her behavior for years. No one has believed me. According to her, it's nothing but a diatribe from a broken woman.

But I know the truth.

I fear this will be my last entry. But I fear every entry might be my last.

She's tried to kill me before.

Chapter Thirty-Eight

I close the diary as I sit at the kitchen island, shoveling Doritos from a family-sized bag in my mouth, not out of hunger or enjoyment of the disturbing show, but it's how I work through my feelings. And right now, I'm sickened and numb. My fingers have stained the pages orange from the cheese.

Teddy's sketches... She lets him have these women, but he can't keep them because he's only supposed to have eyes for her. He can't have a real relationship. She won't allow it. So he takes them by force wearing his Cupid mask, and leaves them pretty in death for fear she'll mar them in unimaginable ways and make them live. The Doritos turn in my gut. I have experienced deviancy and darkness. But this is unbelievable.

Lucille wondered about me. What I'm like. I'm nothing like my sister. And...I am everything like my sister. I just haven't slipped over the edge into complete depravity. But I've done things that are secretive, deceitful, unkind. I've obsessed my whole life, dreaming of something better, more. Tillie is right. I brush the cross on my neck, the one Acelynn wore but that held no meaning for her. An heirloom, the cross a symbol of hope and goodness. But she was rotten inside.

Maybe we're all rotten inside and capable of more than we want to consider. I don't want to admit it, but I know that same darkness lurks in me.

What else is in there lurking?

This world that Acelynn lives in, the world I wanted... I can't continue deceiving myself. I wanted to be Acelynn 2.0. The daughter, the friend, the woman she never was. I justified my own dark thoughts in order to make this situation feel right and even honorable. If I did enough good deeds as Acelynn, it would make my own deception palatable.

All I taste is the sour truth.

Now what do I do?

I have to take this to Christian Patrick. He has to know who Teddy is and what he's done. Who Acelynn was... I know what it means for me—coming squeaky-clean, and for once taking responsibility for my actions instead of glossing over them with a myriad of excuses and blaming it on my past, my circumstances, the unfairness of it all.

But still, knowing the truth, my heart rebels.

I don't want to lose this life. I just want the bad parts to go away, and I'm still working through how to make that happen.

"Hey, girl, hey!" Bianca calls. She's used her key. Panic hits me, and I shove the diary in the bag of Doritos, then fold it up and tuck it next to the coffeepot. "I'm early, but I come bearing gifts." She enters the kitchen in cute athletic gear and a high ponytail. In each hand is a bottle of wine. "But also bad news."

I cannot take more bad news and grab my phone, pretending to be excited at her arrival. "Yay, wine." I text Tillie that Bianca is here. She'd intended to visit a coffee café with Acelynn's laptop for more research. Too late now.

"What's the bad news?"

"MacKenzie can't make it." She cocks her head. "That's actually good news." She laughs. "I think she's still mad you hesitated to tell her that her earrings were spectacular. You know how she is. She's probably plotting your demise." She doesn't laugh now, and neither do I, because we both know there's a kernel of truth to that statement. "But we can popcorn-and-movie-night it all by ourselves. Dru's favorite was *Legally Blonde*, and though I hate it, it feels right, you know?"

"Yeah. Yeah, that's fine." I couldn't care less about movie night. My muscles are bunched up like concrete, and a dull ache palpitates behind my eyes. Detective Patrick needs to be called ASAP. Out of this whole crazy mess, the man I thought I could trust least, I trust most. However, he doesn't trust me. But he saved me in spite of my failures and flaws, and has kept the door open for confession and truth.

Bianca grabs two wineglasses and pops a bottle of red, letting it breathe. "What's got your panties in a bunch? It's all over your face." She digs into my pantry, snatches a one-hundred-calorie bag of popcorn and tosses it in the microwave.

Acelynn and Bianca seem to be the closest of the Pinks. Does that also make Bianca as sadistic or afraid to cross my sister? I decide to test the waters.

"My father implicated me in Drucilla's murder because the detective discovered they were having an affair."

She pauses and slowly turns, her mouth hanging open. "Shut. Up."

"It's true. And…I'm worried about Teddy. You know." I leave it hanging for her interpretation. Does she know about his fetish? Is her insomnia faked to deter him, or does she know other sinister things I haven't discovered yet?

"I don't, and why would Conrad implicate you? *Did* you do it? Tell me you didn't, Acelynn. Tell me that you didn't find out Drucilla was sleeping with Big B and go into one of your tirades."

"No. I didn't." She didn't bite on my Teddy bait. Tirades?

According to the diary, they're more than tirades. They're homicidal rampages. "But…"

The microwave beeps. Bianca pinches the edge of the hot popcorn bag, removing it but leaving it unopened. She picks up her wine and spies my orange-stained fingers, which results in a raised eyebrow. "But what?"

Am I taking the biggest risk yet? I need help from someone who knows what the actual freak is going on, and she might. I go with my gut. "I—"

"You're confused by these things you've just discovered, and you're frustrated. Makes sense."

"I am."

Her sympathetic gaze comforts me. "I think we need to have us a genuine heart-to-heart. Tonight isn't a celebration of Dru's life. I lied. Let's be honest—there's not a lot to celebrate about her." She waves off her lie like it's nothing. Maybe I can't trust her.

"Why the lie?"

"MacKenzie was never invited—though my theory that she wants to kill you still stands." She blows a heavy breath. "I'll just be direct, as we both need the truth."

After her lie? After mine? "I agree."

"Good." She seems satisfied. "Where's Acelynn? Because I know two things. She went to Chicago, and you came back in her place."

Chapter Thirty-Nine

My head spins and my knees melt as Bianca holds my gaze. The dogs. I knew those things would out me. Can I backpedal? No. I'm sick of covering lies with more lies, and I'm going to Detective Patrick after this anyway.

"Before you try to deny it," Bianca says, "I've known since that first day. Something was off, and then you didn't bring the dogs to the barbecue. We all talked about that, but no one else suspected you weren't Acelynn, just chalked it up to grief. But not me. Acelynn is self-absorbed, but she'd take a bullet for those fur balls."

She sips her wine and pushes the glass toward me.

"I tested you. About the client. You went right along with it because that's what Acelynn said she told everyone here. But she confided in me. She was going to meet her identical twin sister."

My soul plummets.

"And I tested you with Philip. He never slept with Drucilla. Acelynn knows this, but you didn't defend him."

Bianca has known this entire time but said nothing. Why?

"So, you're made. It's over. Besides, if I didn't know then, I would know now." She points to my cheese-stained fingers. "Ace would never eat Doritos for this very reason. I can keep going."

I shake my head, knowing my time is up. "No. It's true."

"Why did you two swap? Is this another one of her annoying and petulant games? She exhausts me with those, but I figured I'd let it play out until now. You're cracking."

I am. "She's played them with you."

"Games? Hardly," she says with utter confidence. "But it seems she's played you. The question is why."

I can't allow Bianca to believe we swapped. Though it would be the easy way to keep what I want, even if not permanently, I have to be done with this kind of behavior.

"I...I don't know what to say." I can't tell if she's mad or amused or indifferent.

"How about, 'Nice to meet you, Bianca. I'm Charlotte Kane.' For starters."

"She told you I emailed her?"

Bianca nods. "But she already knew about you, Charlotte."

"What?" No. That can't be right. But the diary was in her desk, which meant she read it, and Lucille mentioned the other child...me. She did know. I hadn't connected those dots yet, due to the traumatizing entries. If Acelynn hadn't died in Chicago, what would she have tried to pull with me? Would she ever have let me come to Savannah? Why did she meet me at all?

She played a wicked game, and I was nothing but another pawn.

"Acelynn has her problems, but we are friends, though I'm not sure why she never called to tell me she was swapping places with you. It's a weird friendship, and one has to be careful around her at times, but when she's in a good place, she's the best friend to have." She places the wineglass on the table with a soft click.

I seriously doubt that.

"She never intended to reach out to you, even though she figured out she was adopted and a twin at sixteen."

She knew before reading the diary, then, depending on how long she'd had it hidden away. Not like Lucille would know it was gone with being doped on pills.

"Acelynn never wanted a sister and definitely not a twin. That would make her less special and unique."

Then what was her agenda in coming to meet me?

"But then you reached out, and she said she'd changed her mind. She was going to meet you. But I didn't buy that. Acelynn doesn't change her mind after it's made up."

Was she coming to end me? Like Abby? Like the girl on that bike in the neighborhood park? Had her intentions been sinister until Marchetti mistook her for me? I grip the counter as the information hits me from every angle. "I don't know what she was up to."

"How long have you known about her?" she asks.

"Our birth mother died two weeks before I emailed her. She...she overdosed. Battled addiction her whole life."

"I'm sorry." Bianca takes my hand. "Were you close?"

I snort a laugh. "No. Never. I always wanted a family, though, and when I saw the letter from Lucille, learned that I had a twin, I thought maybe I was finally going to have everything I dreamed about."

Bianca hugs me. "It's uncanny how identical you are. But you're not her. You have rough edges but a soft middle. I see that. How did she rope you into doing a *Freaky Friday*? Where is she, and when is she coming back?"

"I, um..." How do I say this and not look guilty? "My friend landed in some trouble." And I unload it all on her. "And they killed her. They shot her and dumped her in the trunk, thinking it was me. Me and Tommy, just...gone. Like trash."

Bianca's mouth drops open. "She's dead?" She sets her wine on the counter. "I—I wasn't expecting that."

"I came here to figure out what to do next. I had nowhere to go. I didn't plan on anyone seeing me, but you showed up. Like two hours after I arrived. I couldn't hide." And deep down, I wasn't sad about it. "I couldn't up and run. I'd look guilty of her murder myself, and my track record isn't all that stellar, to be honest. The police would never have believed me."

Bianca sits on the bar stool, quiet. I can see her mind racing as she tries to decide if I'm lying or telling the truth, and I keep going.

"Everything she told me is a lie. She had this great life and all these great friends and close relationships with family and her brother." My stomach roils at the *Flowers in the Attic* relationship she's got going with Teddy. "I think Philip tampered with evidence, and she knows it."

She snaps to attention. "What do you know about Philip?"

I tell her everything I've found out and my theory. I only keep Tillie a secret because if Bianca doesn't trust me and calls the cops, I don't want her involved in this. This is all on me.

"Acelynn didn't keep concealed evidence, Charlotte. Philip killed Tamera Hunt. He killed her, and his print is on that locket. A locket Acelynn took from the murder scene. After I sent her photos of Philip with Tamera. Cheating. Philip's just like Conrad—wandering eye and a loose zipper. Tamera could have given him what he really wanted, but things got out of hand in the bedroom, and his fetish got the better of him and he strangled her to death."

Acelynn used the locket as leverage to keep them together so she could gain more power and influence. But Philip was tired of dragging her along. No evidence as leverage meant his freedom.

"He's tried to kill me."

"What?" Bianca's voice reaches eardrum-blowing pitch.

I tell her about him searching my house and that I suspect the hit-and-run was at his request, but Detective Patrick saved me and is running the partial plate, though it could take some time. "We have to go to him. Tell him all of this."

She shakes her head like a dog with a chew toy. "No way. I can't."

"Why? You know Philip killed those three women."

"No, he only killed Tamera. I have no idea who killed the other two—maybe that guy who's in prison for it."

I don't believe Travis Walker killed anyone, but she's right. If Philip didn't murder all three of them, then at least one more murderer is still out there.

"He knows I sent Acelynn the photos. He saw me there that night. He could do us both a lot of harm. You'll go to prison. I might too. There are other things...I'm not proud of. Things she roped me into. She made you love her, worship her and then held things over you like fire. When she found Tamera dead and called me, I came. She had me put the locket in the plastic bag. My prints and Philip's are on it. I'm an accessory to murder, and he will use that to make it look like I killed her. Acelynn isn't here to tie him to the murder, and I never saw him go in or out."

I rub my temples. "I can leave you out of it."

She glances away and then looks me right in the soul. "Or you can let me help you," she says in a calm and collected manner. "I can help you be Acelynn. We can all be free from her. Would you want that?"

Chapter Forty

Would I want that? The temptation tastes like honey to my mouth. To remain here and live a life I've always wanted. Without the murders. Without Philip. Teddy behind bars. I'm torn like a woman being sawed in two. Between what I've desperately sought my whole life and what is right.

"I don't know."

"Yes, you do. You could give that locket to Philip and be done. That's all he wants. Freedom from her. I can help you acclimate. Keep you out of prison. I don't think you killed Acelynn. Can't say the court will see it that way."

They won't. Bianca doesn't know what I've done.

"She got what she deserved, as bad as it is to say. Karma's a witch. But mark my words—if you tell the truth, you will go away, and you don't deserve that. You were handed a bad set of cards, Charlotte. Is there no one you love that needs you?"

Tillie. What will become of her if I go away...? She won't be able to handle it. I can't bear the thought of her coming to see me in prison with those sad blue eyes. Lost. Alone.

"Why would you do that for me?"

"I like you, and maybe helping you be a better version of her will redeem myself." Her eyes shine with tears.

Would being a better version of my sister redeem me too? Can we redeem ourselves, or will every good deed continue to make me feel just out of reach of righteousness? Will I still live in guilt and shame? Always waiting for the hammer of judgment to drop. A judgment I deserve.

"Even if I said yes and we took care of the Philip problem, we have a Teddy problem."

Her eyes narrow. "Does he know who you are?"

"I know who *he* is. Cupid."

She cocks her head. "Why would you think that?"

I crook my finger at her. She follows me to the window seat, and I lift the lid and retrieve his sketch pad and hand it to her. "He has a lot more. Including the latest victim, Allie Deardon. Look. Acelynn's been giving him the keys to the Pinks' homes to do this."

She flips through each one, and her eyes bulge. "Did she give him my key?"

"Yes. But you have insomnia."

Bianca snorts. "So my sleep disorder spared me being showcased in his book of horrors." She studies the sketchbook. "Okay. We go to the police. I will go to the police about this book and any other information you have on Teddy the Twisted. But we deal with Philip on our own."

"What about a man who's in prison for a crime he didn't commit? The detective that vanished. The alibi witness who was hit by a car and died. How do we fix that?"

Her eyes brighten. "You leave all that to me. You can't be Acelynn's BFF and not learn a few tricks of the trade. We can make this work."

I want to believe her. I also want to run. She's making it

easier by the second to say yes when the right thing is to say no. Tillie would say no.

"You want to stay and be Acelynn?" she asks with a slightly irritated tone.

"No. I don't want to be her. I want to be a better version." Again, I have no choice. Nowhere to go. No money. What other option is there? 'Cause I don't see a sea parting for me if I say no. My phone rings, and it's none other than Christian Patrick, like he senses I'm about to fall into a hungry grave and once it swallows me up, there's no returning.

I can help you. I want to help you make whatever you did wrong right.

I hover over the green button, then send him to voicemail. Because I can't go back.

I can't go back to prison. I may not try to kill myself there again, but I've only been out six months. I've only had a taste of freedom, and I'm right back to doing what landed me there in the first place.

I can't do that to Tillie. To me.

"Okay. Okay," I say impulsively.

Bianca beams like sunshine and hugs me in a boa-like manner before releasing me. "I just need one thing. She stole something that would destroy my family's good reputation. I suspect it's how she leveraged Teddy's job with my dad. He should have been fired months ago."

"What'd she steal?"

Bianca takes my hand in hers, and it's cool and dry.

"A diary."

Chapter Forty-One

My brain sputters. Did I hear that right? "What's it look like?"
"Old. Cracked leather."

The room spins, closes in on me. The diary isn't Lucille Benedict's but Christine Lambert's. Bile rises in my throat. I haven't been reading about my sister. I've been reading about Bianca...and Ford. Maybe Teddy isn't Cupid. Maybe it's Ford.

I've just relayed every ounce of information to the real enemy—except that I possess and have read most of the diary. She's boring a hole through me now, and I fear my face has given me away.

Has she played me too? Is anything she said about my sister and their relationship true? I don't know who or what to believe, and panic is tearing through my veins.

Philip wasn't in my house that first day. Bianca and Ford were. Acelynn wasn't supposed to be home, but the TV was on. I was in the bathroom, so she covered for him to slip out. They've been searching for the diary. Ford ransacked the office and hurt Tillie. He hadn't expected her to be there.

That means they know about Tillie.

Sweat slicks my neck, and my body turns hot.

Ford was also wearing a white dress shirt at the Newsoms' party. He came into the bathroom and fixed his tousled hair after I caught him and Bianca in the bedroom.

I really am going to be sick.

Bianca Lambert is far more formidable than Acelynn—not that she's innocent. Not that she wasn't up to something in Chicago, but Bianca Lambert is a psychopath if that diary is even halfway true.

"Charlotte, what's wrong?" Bianca tips her head to the side, eyeing me like a lioness stalking her prey. She inches toward me. "You can tell me. Have you found it already?"

I quickly move to recover and shake my head. "No. Just the locket. This is a lot to take in. To process." My mind reels, and I can't connect the dots fast enough.

"Of course it is." Bianca's tone is sickeningly sweet. "You don't need to worry, though. I'm going to take care of everything. You just have to trust me. Do you trust me?"

The only person I've ever trusted is Tillie, but my gut says to acquiesce. Play the part. "Yes," I whisper. "We'll search for the diary, but I have no idea where she'd keep it. Do you?"

She pauses. Her guard is up, and she's on high alert. Bianca Lambert and I share the same gift—reading people—though I've been slacking as of late. I fear she's read my mind and knows everything within the pages of my brain. Or at the very least, she senses fear. Like a shark detects blood in the water. I use all the force within me not to glance at the Doritos bag.

"No, I'd have already recovered it. I admit that I wasn't really here that day to pick up my dress. I'm fast on my feet."

She's on her phone now. "Who are you texting?"

"My brother. Let him know everything's going to work out and our family's reputation will stay intact. You know how important and powerful my father is. Or...I assume you do now." She flashes a shrewd grin. "You know, I think you and I can

have a relationship that Acelynn and I never could. We're...
more alike."

I'd rather be struck by a semi going a hundred miles an hour
than be anything like Bianca Lambert. I believe every word
from poor Christine Lambert.

Wait... My mind rewinds the words in the diary, and I start
to shiver uncontrollably. Lucille was worried about the other
child, which I assumed was me, but it wasn't Lucille's diary. It
belongs to Christine. So the other child she wondered about...
was Acelynn.

"Oh, you're shaking like a baby leaf. Poor thing. I'm going
to take care of you." She smooths my hair and lays my head on
her shoulder. "That's what big sisters do."

Chapter Forty-Two

Sisters.

I have yet another sister. I can't quit trembling.

"I don't understand."

Bianca pulls away and puts her finger to my mouth. "Ssshhhh…"
She leans into my ear. Her lips are on my lobe. "You don't have to
be afraid of me. I can tell that you are." She leans back enough for
me to look into her eyes. And I see what Christine saw in Petal,
her pet name for Bianca. The hollow, empty eyes. Like Abaddon.
Waiting to swallow up anything and everything she desires.

She softly kisses the corner of my mouth, letting her lips
linger.

And I don't think I've ever been more afraid.

"My mother took me from Marilyn Kane for twenty grand.
Two years later, when that junkie got pregnant again, she reached
out to my mother to see if she wanted two more. My dad didn't
even want me or Ford—no way he was taking twins—and from
day one, she called me evil."

If the shoe fits.

"I'm sure that was a crazy train he didn't want to board again, but Lucille was having trouble conceiving, and my mother connected Marilyn and Lucille."

"Did Acelynn know you were sisters?"

"Not until she stole my mom's diary, which records that and the rantings of a mentally ill woman. I can't let that get out, you know? I'm protecting her, my whole family."

No, she's protecting herself and Ford.

"I didn't know my mom even kept a diary until Acelynn decided to play yet another game with me about a month before you emailed her. She did a refreshing in my mom's bedroom for her and found it under the mattress and snooped and stole like she always did. I'm not real sorry she's dead."

She has no feelings at all but twisted ones.

"Lucille and Conrad flew to Chicago, but Conrad only wanted one baby. I think he wanted no babies, to be honest. You were bawling and squalling, but Acelynn was being all quiet and sweet and still. Lucille chose her." She shrugs. "That's what you get for being vocal, Charlotte. Shut out."

I saw no evidence of another, older daughter. No letter. No blanket. Nothing. No photos. I guess Christine didn't want the contact. But Lucille didn't feel that way about Acelynn. It wasn't her diary. Lucille was a sad woman who used pills to cope with her dead dreams and cheating husband. She loved her daughter and became depressed that Acelynn didn't return that unconditional love.

"You're…you're…?" I still can't make my brain process, but I see it in the skin tone, bone structure and shape of our eyes, though hers are ice blue.

"Yes, I'm your other sister. And I'm trying to be a good one. I tried with Acelynn. I did. She repaid me with attempted blackmail after thieving the diary. As if she thought I'd allow that to ever take place, to be at her beck and call and under her thumb."

Another chilling thought hits me. Did Acelynn plan on swapping with me—enticing me here with a promise of the good life because she knew what Bianca was capable of? Did she realize she'd bitten off way more than she could chew? Was she going to set me up to fall at Bianca's hands in her stead? What sick irony that *she* fell in *my* stead.

A loud knock startles me.

"Hold up. I'll get it." Bianca strides to the front door and opens it.

Ford walks in, and I'm waiting to see his quiver of arrows and the plastic vintage Cupid mask from the diary—the one Christine saw. "What are you doing here?"

"Just gonna help you two hunt for that diary." Arrogance radiates in waves from him, and I'm irritated that I teetered on trusting him. Never judge a book and all that.

"Oh—" I throw my hands up like I'm happy "—the more the merrier." This is the one thing I have going for me. They don't know I've found it, read it and see through their lies.

"How about you and Ford go upstairs," Bianca says, "and I'll look down here." She and Ford hold a private conversation with their eyes. My skin feels like bugs are crawling underneath it. Bianca stalks to me and circles me like that lioness. Or a boa about to suffocate its prey. Her sweet perfume is cloying and gags me. "Charlotte, you look afraid."

Tillie is upstairs!

I throw a glance to Ford, and he grins. Was he toying with me in the bathroom, or did he have a real thing for Acelynn?

Victims within ten miles.

Blonde. Pretty. Naked but wearing necklaces.

I touch my cross. The one Acelynn wears religiously but with no religion backing it up.

These women he's raping and killing…they're Acelynn. Over and over again.

He can't keep them. Can't have her. He picks replicas that look like her.

I have to go upstairs with him, and no one looks more like Acelynn Benedict than me.

Chapter Forty-Three

Ford stares at me, and I see the hunger. He's starved for me. "Let's take it upstairs."

I know what he wants to take upstairs. If it will keep Tillie safe, I'll do whatever he wants. I've done this before to protect Till, to keep her innocent.

"Find that diary," Bianca says. "Then we'll make all this go away, Charlotte."

Or make *me* go away, like six feet under.

Ford grips my arm and leads me upstairs. He smells enticing, but it sours my stomach. "Did you kill Acelynn?" he asks as we enter her office.

"No. Someone who thought she was me killed her."

"Who would want to kill you?" he asks as he rifles through the filing cabinet. I search too, though we won't find anything.

I tell him as we tear apart the room, finding nothing as I knew we would.

"Let's go to your bedroom."

I swallow hard. "Okay."

We go into the bedroom. Ford picks up Acelynn's pillow, holding it to his face and inhaling. "Acelynn's always been my favorite. She was funny, always made me laugh. Bianca doesn't like that."

"Why not?" Will he tell me about his twisted fling with his sister?

"She just doesn't," he snaps and points to the bed. My heart lurches in my throat.

"What?"

"Get under the bed. I'm too big. She might have tucked it under the felt in the box springs."

I sigh, relieved he's not asking me for something else. Yet. I drop to my knees and lie flat on my back, looking up into that gorgeous but haunting face. Was Christine right? Was he a good boy who was stained by Bianca's twisted ways? Could he feel remorse? Compassion? Two things his sister—my sister—cannot.

"Were you and Acelynn a thing?" I ask. "Because in that bathroom...I felt something. And I don't know if you were toying with me because you knew I was Charlotte or what."

He's taken aback. Not expecting this. "Uh...no. I didn't know you weren't Acelynn for sure until after the bathroom. Bianca told me after we left, but I suspected. The flecks in your eyes, and I noticed a faint scar on your left wrist."

The scar from the second night in prison, when I tried to take my life. The reason that I have to answer my phone at all times, even in the shower. The rule Tillie put in place for all three of us.

"I wanted Acelynn, but I couldn't."

"Why? Because of Philip?"

He laughs. "No. Philip was a means to Acelynn's end. She liked being his arm candy and mingling with powerful people, and it did increase her business quite a lot. I told her it was trouble and a bad idea, but she was good at what she did. She redecorated my parents' home, and that's when she stole the diary, on a follow-up visit, we think. My mom accused B of stealing it to hide her wicked deeds so no one would find out, including the police. She always accuses B of things. That's when Bianca figured out that Acelynn stole it. Acelynn didn't blackmail her like she told you, but she would have tried, I think. Eventually."

"Did Bianca do any of the things you say your mom has accused her of in that diary?"

"We haven't read it, but probably," he says quietly. "Or...I don't know. Bianca could be lying and have known about it all along, allowing Mother to write in it while Bianca bided time until she wanted to take it away and use it against her somehow. Bianca likes control, power...and lying."

Has anything she's said to me been true, then? Is Ford being truthful? For once, I'm having trouble reading the room, but I'm going to ask more questions anyway. "Is it true that Acelynn held secrets over people? Blackmailed them?"

He nods.

His hangdog eyes slay me. It's a look I see in my own reflection every day. Regret and the look of a person imprisoned in a life they can't escape.

"Okay." I ease up off the floor and sit on the bed, patting it for him to sit next to me. My nerves are frayed, and my adrenaline pumps so hard I can barely breathe, but I need the upper hand. He sits beside me, and I lay my hand on his. "I know I'm not her, but—"

"I knew you felt a connection." He cuts me off. "In the bathroom. I've always wanted to have Acelynn. But you're different. There's a tender spot about you. I recognized it and it was confusing. I think that's why Bianca spilled the truth."

"So that was real?" I blow out a breath, hoping to tamp down my nausea. This man has raped and murdered at least four women, according to the news articles.

"Yes." He brushes my cheek, and I refrain from flinching

outwardly. Inside, I'm shrinking into a dark crevice. "But I can't keep you. She won't let me, and if I try... It's best if I don't."

I frown. "Why can't you keep me? You can do whatever you want, Ford. She doesn't hold power over you. You can be your own man."

"You don't understand." He drops his hand, but it rests on my thigh, and the door bursts open. He jumps up off the bed as Bianca stands at the threshold, her eyes burning with fury, nearly knocking me back.

"Well. If this isn't something," she says. "Looks like you play games too, Charlotte. I guess it's in the family blood." She focuses on Ford. "Whatever she's told you is a lie. She's been lying all along."

"I haven't been. I've told you everything." My heart pumps so hard it hurts.

She holds up the diary. "Nacho cheese flavor."

Checkmate. I've lost my only upper hand.

"And don't think we don't know about Little Miss Tillie. But she seems to be gone. I've looked. She go back to Chicago? Don't answer that. I won't believe you."

Tillie. She must have left or hidden somewhere Bianca hasn't found her. But now I know for certain that someone was in my house that night it stormed—and it was Ford.

If Tillie is in the house and they find her...she's as dead as I'm about to be.

Bianca's lips sour in disappointment. "Charlotte, I meant what I said. I wanted to protect you. Look out for you. This is how you repay me? With lies?"

Pot meet kettle, but I keep my mouth shut. I can't say I haven't read it. My fingers were orange, and the diary was in the half-eaten bag.

Bianca sneers. "I'd tell you none of it is true, but it's clear you believe the ramblings of a mentally unstable woman over your own sister. Your own flesh and blood. I was willing to lie for you. Give you everything you ever imagined. You only had to bow to me. Pledge your loyalty to me. Let Teddy go down in flames. Acelynn would have done that, I think. Conrad loves Teddy. And Acelynn loved Conrad."

"But Conrad didn't love her," I say. "She's not really his in his eyes, and he never wanted a baby in the first place, until he had a son."

Bianca raises her hand and taps the air. "Ding. Ding. Ding. You earn a gold star. And it's Ford's lucky day." She turns to him. "You can have a pretty face, but you can't keep her. You handle it or I will. I'll give you an hour."

Ford's face crumples, but a flare of excitement in his eyes nauseates me. "But I don't have— I mean, I don't—"

"You don't," Bianca says in a mocking tone. "You can't. Oh, give me a break. I never should have purchased that mask. It's a crutch in your life, Ford. It makes you weak. Be glad. You can finally do what you've always wanted to do, what I wouldn't allow. But no ritual. We can't bring the cops any closer than they already are."

Killing me in Cupid fashion absolutely will.

She draws a knife from her pocket and hands it to him. "Pretend it's an arrow. Quit acting like a weak little boy, or I'll take this opportunity away, and you'll never have it again." She slams the door behind her, leaving me alone with Cupid.

Chapter Forty-Four

"You don't want to do this." I shudder and search for ways to flee. Anything I can use as a weapon. Where is Bianca? What if she finds Tillie? They know about her. Maybe they think she's gone.

"I do. I've wanted you since I was fourteen."

"You wanted Acelynn. Not me."

"I love you," he whispers. "Not like the others. I wanted them and took them, but they couldn't ever compare to you. I did them a favor, actually, making their end quick, or B would have done much worse."

My abdomen tightens, and my mouth fills with saliva. The girl set on fire in the locker room at a Valentine's dance.

"Abby."

He's surprised at this. "Was she in the diary?" He steps toward me, and I retreat and nod.

"Then you know. And all that talk before. You were just lying. Manipulating."

"No. That's what Bianca's doing." I'm trying to escape unscathed. "The truth is, we are the same. I know what it's like to be imprisoned. She scares you, and she makes you think you love her, but that's not love. That's not freedom. I know what it's like to think you have to pretend to be someone you're not. You wear a mask. To hide the real you. Because she won't let you be the real you. You're never going to be free from her. You'll never keep anyone. She just keeps you."

He pauses. I'm making sense. I'm getting through. And I need him to turn on her.

"You're right." He puts the knife on the end table by the bed. I've got him.

As I peer into his eyes, I see me. I'm in all their eyes. Greed. Jealousy. Lust. Resentment and bitterness. Lies.

I sicken myself. Telling myself I didn't have choices, but I did. They just wouldn't all benefit me.

I have hurt people and still am. I'm lying. Lucille loved her daughter. I can't make up for that. I'm not that little girl who felt loved and safe in the church that day. I don't know what happened to her.

Except I do.

Life and pain invaded her world. Her innocence was stolen. And stolen. And stolen again. Ten times. Until she vanished. A tear wells in my eye. Ford moves into my space and wipes it away. He lifts my chin. "Don't cry," he whispers. "It'll be gentle."

His hand wraps around my throat, and his grip tightens as he pushes me onto the bed. "You don't have to do this."

"I know." He lowers himself onto me, his weight suffocating me. He kisses me. "But I want to."

He's not imprisoned or simply lost. He's voluntarily jumped and remained in an irredeemable pit. This isn't a forced way to have a twisted relationship with someone who isn't his sister. It's a thrill. He likes it. And Bianca knows it. She's always known it—the cats.

I'm done being a victim and playing a victim. I knee him in the groin, and he howls. I roll out from under him and jump off the bed, grasping for the knife, but he's too quick. He blocks me. I race for the door and scream, praying Tillie hears me and can help me if Bianca hasn't already found her. He wrenches me back inside the room and throws me three feet onto the bed. I bounce, and my head snaps back, causing me to bite my tongue. The metallic taste fills my mouth and gags me.

"I love you," he says again. "Be my valentine?"

I want to tell him to take his valentine with him straight to hell, but my brain is foggy, and I can't push a word out. As he climbs on top of me, his hand wraps around my throat, and his other hand gropes me as the door opens.

"Get off her right now."

Tillie stands inside the door, pointing a gun. Where did she get— The closet. She must have been hiding in Acelynn's closet, heard me scream and took the gun.

"I know you. You were in the office when I was there. I should have killed you."

"You should have." Her words come out braver than she is. Her hand is trembling, and her face is pale like snow. "Get off her this instant."

Ford waits a beat, then eases off my body and the bed, his hands raised. I jump off the bed and race to her. "Toss the knife. Over there." I point to the other side of the bed. "Till, give me the gun." I easily take it from her and push her behind me. "Where's Bianca?"

"I don't know. She was downstairs with the TV on."

She expected screams and turned on the TV so neighbors couldn't hear. "On your knees. Tillie, call the police." I know she hasn't done that. And I know why.

"We can't. You'll be arrested, and you can't go back there, Charlotte. I can't let you do time again. We're gonna have to kill them and run. They'll think Acelynn murdered them and

344 *The Other Sister*

fled. It wouldn't be out of the realm of possibility, and the fact Dru is dead and she's linked… This is our out. We don't have another choice."

Except we do.

Tillie doesn't want to kill anyone, but my influence has spilled into her life like Bianca's into Ford's. "Yes, we do. We always have another choice. We just don't want to make it because we don't like the consequences. Call them. I mean it."

She pulls out her phone as Bianca strides into the room with a gun trained on Tillie. "You shoot him and I shoot her, and I can do it before you swing that onto me."

She's right. I can't turn the gun on Bianca before she fires it and kills the only true sister I've ever had. A sister by choice who has loved me completely and at my very worst. I've been terrible to her in many ways, and yet she's never given up on me or walked away from our friendship. I can't lose the one person in this world who has loved me unconditionally.

The cross at my neck feels heavy, and I touch it with my free hand. Maybe Till isn't the only one who's loved me unconditionally. Maybe I can cry mercy and it won't fall on deaf ears. 'Cause I need it. Though I don't deserve it.

"You know you owe me. I did you a solid, and I thought we could be real sisters," Bianca says as if she's crushed by my actions.

"You did me no favors."

She tosses me a *take that* expression. "Yes, I did. You just don't know it, because the cause of death was overdose."

Marilyn.

Chapter Forty-Five

Bianca glances at Ford, who is standing like a statue with his hands up. Tillie does the same as Bianca continues to hold her gun on her.

"I needed you to know about Acelynn. Who wouldn't reach out to their sister?" She grins. "Except Acelynn. She didn't like the idea. She didn't want to compete for the prettiest. Although we all know it's me." She actually has the nerve to appear humble. "But I wanted us to be together. Sisters. A family. She didn't, so I took a little trip to Chicago. Met Mother Dear. She was as pathetic as Christine. Worse, maybe, because Christine has a legit mental illness. She gets a pass. Marilyn's just a junkie. She had the audacity to ask me for money because you wouldn't answer her calls. I did you a favor."

"Are you saying you set this up to bring me here to be in some kind of warped family with you? You could have just shown up on my doorstep."

She shakes her head. "Acelynn had the diary and wanted nothing to do with you. If I'd have brought you here myself, then it jeopardized me and Ford. But if you reached out on your own…"

"She wasn't obligated to respond."

"No. She wasn't. But I told her if she didn't, you'd show up. I was right too. I did my homework on you. I know what you did to Andi Delaney," she singsongs. "Ace did too. Charlotte Thompson. Hiding your past so she couldn't google you and see the truth. That you went to prison for four years for stalking, breaking and entering, identity theft. All to *be* Andi Delaney."

"It wasn't like that." But it was. It was exactly like that. I saw her life and I coveted it, from her filtered life online to her day-to-day activities. I did stalk her, insert myself into her life and break into her house. Multiple times. I stole her credit cards. I stole…a lot of things, and by the time Tillie found out and shook me to my senses, it was too late.

"You've only been out a few months. No job. Looking for that new life. I handed it to you, and you wrecked it."

I can't think straight.

"You overdosed Marilyn? She didn't do it herself?"

She sighs as if she's getting bored, and I have no way out of this thing. I could yell *duck* and hope Tillie does it in time to miss a bullet, but I still have Ford to contend with, and I've never fired a gun. No wonder Christine Lambert has mental issues. She bought Rosemary's baby and no one believed her.

"How else was I supposed to bring you here? Marilyn said you hadn't answered her calls or seen her even before you went to prison. I paid the landlord to make sure you received that box of baby goodies Marilyn showed me after I introduced myself as her first daughter. Either by delivering it to you or giving it to you if you went by to collect anything you might find worthy of taking. Nothing in that box is mine, though. Christine didn't want to speak with Marilyn, but you know what? She was happy enough to send Lucille to her. Maybe she thought she'd end up with a wicked child too. Misery loves company."

She did end up with a rotten apple. I'm starting to believe all of humanity is, just not to the degree that Bianca is. Yet.

"I'm done waiting around." Bianca's finger twitches. Then she howls in pain. But I see no one. She drops the gun. Ford starts to sprint, but I halt him. I think I hear knocking on the door, but too much is happening to worry about that. Whoever it is will be far better off anywhere but here.

Tillie rushes to the gun, and next to her is Rue. Little sweet Rue—the ankle biter has taken a hunk out of Bianca. Tillie holds the gun over her, and then a sound like a tree splintering echoes through the house.

"Acelynn Benedict. It's the Savannah police. We have a warrant to search your premises and for your arrest for the murder of Drucilla Hilton."

Bianca's high-pitched, hysterical laugh sends dark chills down my spine.

Footsteps pound the stairs, and uniformed officers appear with their guns aimed. Detective Patrick enters the room. At first, he's confused, and then saddened. Uniformed officers order us to drop weapons and hit the floor, and I'm flipped on my stomach. I know how this goes down. They'll read me my rights next as they cuff me. Fingerprint me. And my world is over, but Tillie's safe.

"He's the Cupid killer," Tillie says as she is placed on her knees. "He attacked her."

It's complete chaos, and we're all going to prison. Only, I'm the one charged for a murder I didn't commit, but they'll know that soon enough. I don't resist arrest or admit to anything. Neither does Tillie.

Ford and Bianca demand a lawyer.

"Take the diary," I say as a uniformed officer leads me out of the bedroom. "And search Ford's house. You'll find what you need."

Detective Patrick nods, and I see disappointment in his eyes.

★ ★ ★

I sit alone in an interrogation room for what feels like hours. Finally Detective Patrick enters and sits across from me. "Well, would you like to properly introduce yourself?" He slides my fingerprint card across the table. He knows I'm Charlotte Kane. "And tell me what in the world is going on and where Acelynn Benedict is. Are you harboring her so she can flee the country?"

"No," I softly say. "No, she didn't flee the country. She's dead."

"You killed her?"

"No."

"You sure? Her life was a nice opportunity for you."

"You read my report."

"I did," he says softly. "I know you stalked Andi Delaney for months. She had a restraining order on you. You broke into her home, stole clothing and credit cards, then pretended to be her and maxed those cards out. You were caught in a department store trying to use one of them. That's the short version, I'm sure."

The shame is overwhelming. "I was curious about her life. And I hated mine. I regret what I did, but I served my full sentence."

"I know. Model inmate, according to the warden."

This is why Tillie was afraid. My past is stacked against me. She fears if I am sent back, I'll accomplish taking my life where I failed last time. "I didn't kill Acelynn. But she is dead."

"Would you like to tell me the truth now, Charlotte? That's a nice name, by the way."

His kindness and the endearing way my name rolls from his lips crack a hardened dam within me, and hot tears spring forth. He offers me a box of tissues and waits patiently for me to gather myself. Then I spend the next hour telling him every single detail, withholding nothing.

I'm ready to face the music. Do my time, which will be a big one.

"Charlotte," he says.

I've looked at the table while I've been talking, unable to hold my head up for the shame.

"Charlotte, look at me, please."

I manage to peer into his coal-black eyes filled with compassion that I don't deserve.

"I believe you. I'm sorry about the things that happened to you in your childhood. I'm sorry you made bad decisions. But thank you for telling the truth now."

"You believe me?" Police have never believed me. Not once. I don't know what to do with this, but cry again.

"I do. I do." He leaves me for what feels like hours.

Finally he returns and brings me a bottle of water and a deli sandwich, but I'm not hungry. I drink the water, though. I'm exhausted, and I can see he is too.

He rubs his hand over his face and sighs, then sits. "We found the evidence in Ford Lambert's home. We've read the diary and talked with Christine Lambert."

"And?"

"We found the murder weapon that killed Drucilla Hilton. It was in Conrad Benedict's study, but Acelynn's prints were on it. From what we gather, she found out about the affair from Dru, who called her, we think to tell her. She went over there and got into a heated argument, we assume. She hit her with a brass bookend, and Dru fell down the stairs. Then Acelynn attempted to frame her father by putting it in his office. Then she went to Chicago. I don't have any idea what she planned to do from there or how you factored into her schemes. But I don't think it was anything that would have benefited you."

She never wanted a sister. Me or Bianca.

"What about Travis Walker and Philip?"

"Philip Beaumont is already being looked into."

That's why Detective Patrick frowned when he realized Ace-lynn was dating Philip. He knew he was dirty.

"The locket has his prints, and the photos on the laptop will help. Bianca Lambert will tell the tale for a lesser sentence, I imagine. We believe Philip hired someone to run down Walt Witemeyer and that he used the same man to try and kill you too. My guess is he left those photos in your house as well."

Why didn't he call me and ask about Tillie? He clearly knew she was staying with me and important to me. He's a lawyer. My guess is he was looking into who she might be, thinking I was at one of Acelynn's games, and if he dug hard enough, he'd have discovered the truth. I wonder what he would have done with that information? Now it won't matter.

"Bianca and Ford Lambert knew you weren't Acelynn, so trying to scare you into coughing up something you never knew about makes no sense."

"Travis?"

"He'll likely be exonerated, and we may never find who killed Trisha or RayEllen, but it wasn't Travis or Philip. Philip just used the conviction to his advantage to climb the ladder. As far as Sam Honeycutt, I don't know if he's dead somewhere or took money and ran. We've looked into that, and it's a cold trail."

I'm relieved Travis will be exonerated, and I close my eyes, glad that it's finally over for him. But it's just beginning for me.

"What about me?"

"Well, you have two choices."

I've never been good at making the right ones.

"Neither of them will be easy."

"My sin found me out. That's what you said. You're right."

Detective Patrick leans across the table, and his eyes hold mine. They're black as night but radiating light. And mercy. And hope. My fingers wrap around the cross still hanging around my neck.

"You know that's not just a symbol you wear. It's a choice you make." His smile is soft and sweet and hopeful. And I want to cry all over again. Because I know he's right.

"I'm ready. To make new choices, even hard ones."

Chapter Forty-Six

Six months later

I smooth my black pencil skirt and tuck my hair behind my ear. I'm back to wearing it in long waves past my shoulders. The hard wooden chair is uncomfortable, and I shift and glance at the scales of justice. The trial is today, and my stomach is knottier than an oak tree.

My two choices that were equally hard were, first, to wear a wire and secure Philip's confession, since he had no idea I wasn't Acelynn, and testify against Marchetti for immunity. The other choice was to do time. Again.

I made the harder choice and accepted the mercy that was extended to me. That I didn't and don't deserve. I wore the wire and used the necklace as bait to set Travis free. Philip sang like a bird. Wasn't hard to make him confess. So long, Senator. So long, White House.

Ford and Bianca didn't receive bail and will be going away for a long time.

The night Tommy died, when I set off the alarm, the cops came. For once, good cops were in charge. I suppose not everyone can be bought, and it's refreshing for this cynical woman to see.

Today, I'm putting Marchetti behind bars for Tommy's murder, although I'm just icing on the cake in the case that is stacked against him. But because I didn't actually see who murdered my sister, he's not being charged with that. But they promise they'll keep investigating, and for once I believe them.

Peering into the crowd, and not at Frank Marchetti, I answer honestly and not just because I'm under oath.

Tillie's out there. My sister of heart and choice. If she hadn't shown up in Savannah because she cared about me, this story might have a different outcome. Sitting beside her is Lucille Benedict, who is sober and clean, for three months. She's forgiven me for impersonating her daughter and for giving the sketch pad to the police, which has put Teddy in a prison of his own. I can't and don't want to replace Acelynn, but Lucille and I are friends-ish. She left Conrad after rehab. Their marriage had been over for years with Conrad's infidelity. He kept her supplied with pills to prevent her from begging friends and causing their family further embarrassment. And according to her, he also supplied Hudson Lambert with pills that kept Christine Lambert overmedicated, though she truly does have some mental health problems. But the extra meds made it worse, kept her confined and foggy. Lucille did another good thing and gave permission for Tillie to keep Tallulah and Rue, as she is allergic and didn't want to take them to a rescue.

On the other side of Tillie are Glenda and Sobo, who I worked for before he retired—and I confessed that I had stolen a mixer, several wooden bowls and spoons, and a few antiques; his daughter, Janice, wasn't out to get me. He forgave me. She did not.

Can't win 'em all.

My eyes fill. I never realized before that I was loved. I couldn't see it for focusing on everything I didn't have. All my trauma, abuse and hurt factored into my view of myself and the world around me. I thought being anyone but me would make all that go away, but it never did. It snowballed into an avalanche that overtook me. I chose a filtered life, but there's no such thing. No one's life is filtered on the inside. We're all a bunch of messy, broken people pretending.

Except for those who are free.

And even then, it's easy to slip into a facade when you don't feel peace and contentment. I didn't. I didn't know where to find those things before. Too much out there distracting me, telling me I could have it all, and I fell into that trap. Life should be easy. Says who? I can have it all. Can I? What *is* all? Because in my quest to have it, find it, accumulate it, live it, I only found prison. Metaphorically and literally.

I've been living with Tillie again. Mrs. Donlea was moved to a home since she couldn't care for herself and no one looked out for her. She was found roaming Navy Pier half-dressed, no hearing aids and shoeless. I've visited her a few times. She doesn't recognize me. But that's okay.

I finish testifying and scan the small crowd again, and this time another familiar face comes into view. One I didn't expect to see, and my heart hiccups.

Detective Christian Patrick is on the end of the back row, shooting me that lopsided grin that says *well done.*

I leave the stand and sit next to Tillie while a guilty verdict is passed, and I sigh with relief and hug her. The courtroom files out, and Christian stands by the doors, waiting for me to finish talking to the people who have come to support me.

I walk over. "Hi."

"Hi." He smirks. "You did good, Charlotte. I'm proud of you for telling the truth. I hear you passed on WITSEC."

"I did." I know Marchetti has a far reach. "I've spent my whole life with this name. But I don't know who Charlotte

Kane is, and I don't want to pretend to be anyone else ever again. I'm going to trust that I'll be okay." I stroke my cross necklace that belonged to my sister. The only possession of Acelynn's I kept, with Lucille's blessing.

"Not so much a symbol anymore?" His dark eyebrow rises.

"No. A choice. Reality in my life." My peace. My freedom. My contentment.

His dimples crease his clean-shaven face as his grin spreads wide. "Good. So, what's next for you?"

"Tillie and I leave this afternoon. She's got a job at a law office in Hilton Head, South Carolina, and I'm gonna work in an art gallery down there. I'm signed up for some classes. I like the beach."

He nods. "That's less than an hour from me."

"Yeah. I needed to get out of Chicago but didn't feel right about returning to Savannah. The Lamberts and Newsoms are there, and it's just..." I trail off because I'm nervous. "Why are you here?"

"You did a hard thing today, and I wanted to be here to champion you." He graces me with his signature shrug.

I've thought about him over the past few months, but I never dreamed he might be thinking about me. I'm forgettable. But maybe...maybe I'm not. "It's turning out better than it should. You finish painting your house?"

He laughs. "Yeah. You're kinda all over my home." He shoves his hands in his pockets. "Take care of yourself. And if I'm ever in Hilton Head, I'll pop in. Maybe we can have lunch."

Is he serious? He would want to take a liar and deceiver, a convicted felon, to lunch as if I never did anything wrong and vile? "Um...I don't know." Shame sends heat into my cheeks. "I've been guilty of so—"

"You were given immunity. You're free. And you're on a new path, right?"

I nod.

"Then I'm not holding your past against you. And it's just lunch. You gotta eat." But I see a sparkle in his eye, and warmth and light that draws me. A man of justice, fairness and goodness, who should condemn me and walk away, doesn't. Instead he's inviting me to a meal with him. In public.

"You're not afraid of ruining your reputation by being seen with a woman who's served time?"

"No. Are you afraid?"

I'm terrified. "Yep."

He laughs. "Fear not," he says and winks. "I'll see you soon."

And he walks away. My heart flutters. I don't deserve a meal with this man, let alone what seems to hint at something special. Who am I?

An arm wraps around my shoulders, and it's Glenda. "He's handsome."

"He's too good for me."

She holds me closer. "Then he's a gift. Never turn down a good gift, Charlotte."

I touch my cross again. "I won't." I know I'll go to lunch. Because I know deep within me that Christian isn't going to forget. He's not going to lose my number. He's going to come for me.

And I'm going to say yes.

Epilogue

One year later

I stretch out on the chaise and let the salty breeze off the ocean tickle my sun-kissed skin as I sip the fruity drink that's almost gone. I love the beach. I love the salty air and the way my hair looks because of it. Going south was the perfect plan.

"Is this seat taken?"

I grin into dark eyes. "It's reserved for whoever will lather my back up with sun lotion."

"I can handle that."

"Just be sure to warm it up with your hands first this time, babe." I close my eyes and enjoy the massaging and the feel of heat on my skin. From the sun and his skilled hands. "How long can you stay?"

"Just the weekend." My cheek is met with an apologetic kiss.

"Why can't you just move here?"

Laughter tickles my neck. "You know why." He collapses on the chaise next to mine, and the ocean pounds the shore. Squawking seagulls skitter along the sand.

He stretches out, and I admire his strong physique, but the bartender catches my eye. He's new, and my gut turns every time he looks at me. But then, I'm always looking over my shoulder. I have to.

"Question," he says.

"Shoot."

"Back in Savannah, that detective interviewed me, and something he said has stuck with me ever since. He said that your sin will always find you out. What do you think that means?"

I hear the same discomfort in his voice that I feel in my chest. I dart glances around the beach.

"I'm not sure." Now I'm paranoid, but I've been on edge since we staged my death and he tossed me in his trunk. "Relax, Jacob. I've covered all my bases." I have a fake identity and have been using mostly cash. It's not easy to deplete a bank account without it appearing suspicious, but I've had money in offshore accounts for years. One never knows.

"What if she realizes you faked your death? That I didn't actually shoot you and that the blood was fake?"

"Jacob. My sister is a scavenger. It was obvious she wanted my life. I gave it to her. What she did or does with it is none of my concern. She believed what she wanted to believe, and it was believable, babe. I had bruises from you chucking me in that trunk."

He shifts on his side. "What if she hadn't gone to Savannah?"

"Nothing. The point was, I was gone. Philip could take the fall. I couldn't care less. And you shouldn't either. I just needed her to see me die. That's it."

"You're so chill. I love that about you."

I'm not as chill as I appear. His question about the sin finding you out has me anything but chill. However, I can't fall apart or even hint that I'm unsettled. Jacob appears like a big bad wolf, but he's a kitten. A follower, and after Dru dumped him, I knew I could put him in my pocket for a rainy day. Women wield all the power because men typically don't think with their brains. After I pushed Dru, which was an accident, I called Philip. He owed me, and I had Tamera's necklace. Philip helped me set the stage by bringing me a valentine, and he actually planted the evidence in Conrad's office. I failed to wipe it completely clean and we missed a few details apparently, but I was long gone and didn't care. Our deal was once the investigation was over, I'd give Philip back the necklace. Not that I ever intended to do that. That would make me vulnerable and give Philip all the power. Charlotte's email couldn't have come at a better time for me.

But I also needed Jacob. I needed him to help me fake my death, and we'd been lovers awhile, ever since I used target practice to seduce him. He's been my eyes and ears in Savannah this entire time.

He can't run away or it will be suspicious. And quite frankly, he's fun for a weekend or two, but I don't need the same man tagging along all my life, especially if he can't benefit me. Jacob Moore can't benefit me in the way Philip could have.

"But do you think it's true? That your sins will find you out? It was so ominous sounding."

I need to keep him appeased and calm. And clearly he's not letting this go. Not that I like that statement the detective made. I don't. "It's a scare tactic, is all. No one can know all your sins."

"Are you sure, Acelynn?"

"Don't call me that in public. I go by Lynn now. You can't keep slipping up."

"Sorry. So, you really think that's just a scare tactic? Not true?"

I want to answer yes, that I'm sure it's nothing but a way to press people to confess their transgressions, but the stoic dark-haired bartender heads my way.

And he's not carrying a drink.

★ ★ ★ ★ ★

Acknowledgments

MacKenzie Gregory, thank you for your input in my reader group for naming Acelynn's Bolognese Rue. I hope you enjoy seeing your name in one of the characters!

My dear friend and first eyes on every draft, Susan L. Tuttle. I'm glad that elevator opened with me on it.

My editor, Shana Asaro, for pushing me to the limits with this one. I'm glad you did!

My agent, Rachel Kent, for always giving me solid advice and being such a good friend and champion of my books.

The team at Harlequin for their superb work and all they do to bring a book into the world.

Mr. Anonymous (FBI agent) for his help back in 2012 when I first noodled the idea.

My sister, Celeste, and brother-in-law, Rob, for taking me all over St. Louis for research. I changed the setting, so it was fruitless, but we had fun, especially listening to Celeste yell at honking drivers when we drove too slow.

Luke Williamson for giving me information pertaining to the law. Anything I stretched a bit is on me.

My husband, TP, for always believing in me. I don't dream about killing you nearly as often as you think I do (wink, wink).